health agent

Jeffrey Thomas

RAW DOG
SCREAMING
PRESS

Published by Raw Dog Screaming Press,
Hyattsville, MD

First Hardcover Edition

Cover image: Jeffrey Thomas
Book design: Jennifer Barnes

Printed in the United States of America

ISBN 978-1-933293-44-8

Library of Congress Control Number: 2008935997

www.rawdogscreaming.com

health agent

Other books by Jeffrey Thomas

Punktown
AAAIIIEEE!!!
Monstrocity
Letters from Hades
Everybody Scream!
A Nightmare on Elm Street: The Dream Dealers
Deadstock
Blue War

Acknowledgment:

With deepest gratitude to my sister-in-law Nancy, who typeset this novel from a manuscript handwritten between February 1987-February 1989.

INTRODUCTION

DANGEROUS PLAYTHINGS

There have been recurrent themes through much of my Punktown fiction, but maybe a few words of introduction to Punktown itself are needed first, should this be your first outing there. Punktown is my milieu of choice, my favorite haunt, a vast megalopolis established by Earth colonists on a far-flung world, its streets rife with criminals and lost souls, aliens and mutants, and the occasional hero, however reluctant or troubled. And then there are the villains...

Health Agent revolves around biotechnology put to trivial, dubious, even dangerous uses—science unfettered by moral responsibility, become a kind of plaything—and I suppose it's an obsession with me, judging from other Punktown-based fiction of mine. There is my 2003 novel *Monstrocity*, in which a company that produces grotesque edible life-forms also grows an even more grotesque secret army of monsters. The novel *Deadstock*, 2007, concerns a biotech company that creates little bio-engineered pets to sell to children—one of these living dolls, concocted from mysterious cell samples, turning out to be the larval kin of H. P. Lovecraft's god-like Old Ones. And then there's *Deadstock*'s 2008 follow up, *Blue War*, wherein an organic building material becomes infected with a virus, and instead of forming an apartment village begins replicating Punktown—to disastrous effect—on another colony world. Add to this short stories like *The Reflections of Ghosts* in the collection *Punktown*, 2000, about a man who makes distorted clones of himself as an artistic statement, and I think you can see what I mean by obsession.

THE FUTURE VIA THE PAST

The Reflections of Ghosts—probably my favorite of my Punktown short stories, and the most reprinted—also intersects with another favorite subject of mine, that being the artist and his work. But before *The Reflections of Ghosts*, art and science collided in *Health Agent*, which also predates all the other novels I've just listed. *Health Agent* took form as a handwritten manuscript, begun in February of 1987. (Over twenty years ago, yes, but I'd already been writing stories set in Punktown for seven years by then, though the first Punktown short story wasn't to appear in print until 1992.) Between February of 1987 and February of 1989, when I completed it, I broke off from *Health Agent* to write the novel *Everybody Scream!*, which takes place at an annual carnival outside Punktown, as I had recently been to the Spencer Fair in Massachusetts and was full of impressions and inspirations. It amazes me now that I took such a long break in the middle of *Health Agent*'s action, because I still consider it one of my most intricately plotted stories, with a lot of driving force. I don't think this break between Parts One and Two would have been apparent to a reader had I not made this confession, nor would I think it apparent even after I've confessed it. But I almost made what could very well have been a grave mistake at this halfway point, when I returned to it. I had just become involved with my first wife, Rose, a gentle young deaf woman, and I came *this* close to making her the novel's love interest, and chronicling in a fictitious way our romantic relationship within the remaining plot. Thank God, good sense won out (as it doesn't always do), and I resisted going this route, sticking instead to the tight police-type thriller I had fashioned to that point. There exists somewhere in my house, however, a page or maybe several pages that started down that road, and I might have suggested the material appear here as a kind of DVD extra if I were ambitious enough to hunt for it.

It was my desire to leave *Health Agent* as close to its original form, here, as possible. I did give the story a slight polish after it had been typeset from its handwritten manuscript by my sister-in-law Nancy, several years ago, but I stuck with my style from that time because, well, that's who I was back then, and that's what Punktown was like back then, and though the years may have evolved both myself and Punktown, I very much want *Health Agent* to remain true to all that. I wouldn't go back now and add references to the Blue War, for instance, or other places, events or characters from the later stories, to tie them all together, though it's okay for the later stories to make references to those that have gone before—and before the Blue War of my 2008 novel there was a Red War, as you will see. But I did make a few alterations during my polish, one of these being to change the name of the character Pink Cowrie to Opal Cowrie. When I did this, I guess I worried people might think too much of the pop star Pink (though a few years later, maybe not), but also I felt having the health agents named Black and Pink might be too contrived. (Even if I did drink coffee from matching, marble-patterned black and pink mugs during the writing of the book.) So I'm still going with the altered Opal. And as for Black; as I was writing the novel, I realized I was referring to the character Montgomery Black primarily as Black in the first half of the book, and Monty in the second half. I think this had less to do with the long break in my work on *Health Agent* than it did some changes in Monty's character. He starts out as a more morally ambiguous protagonist, committing a pretty shocking act in the first chapter, but as the story progresses and some major events befall him, I think Monty becomes more fully engaged morally, less an agent and more an individual, and this is reflected in the switch from the hard-sounding Black to the softer Monty. So when I did my polish, I made sure to make this switch from Black in Part One to Monty in the remainder of the book fully consistent.

I have to give my friend Thomas Hughes some credit for the creation of my villain, Toll Loveland. Like my brother Scott, at my invitation Tom has written a number of stories set in the Punktown universe (well, mostly set in the neighboring city of Miniosis), one of these—*Domino Diamond*—appearing in an anthology I edited called *Punktown: Third Eye*, which consists of Punktown stories by other writers as well. One of Tom's follow-up stories about the beguiling "gender bender" Domino Diamond features a mad artist as its antagonist, and I sort of, uh, stole that basic idea for *Health Agent*. Thanks, Tom, and I hope to help you get your other two Domino Diamond stories into print to return the favor.

COVERING ART

A little background on the cover art might be of interest, it being rendered by the author himself for a novel about an artist. I created the cover for an earlier publisher that was to have released *Health Agent*, before they dropped all their forthcoming projects (thankfully, returning later to publish some other of my books instead). It's primarily a collage. The lower portion, the city, is from a photo of Hong Kong, which I distorted by flipping it in mirror image and elongating it. I then cut up the resultant photocopies and shuffled the pieces around, and did a little touch up by hand. (Since making the collage I have flown over—and switched planes in—Hong Kong numerous times and it is indeed a sight to behold from the air.) The cells floating down from the sky represent both a biological threat and a strange black blizzard from the novel. I photocopied the cells from a book, pasted them in and touched them up (giving them cilia, etc.) by hand.

When I scanned this composition into my computer, I originally gave it a maroon sort of tint to meld it all together more uniformly. But experimenting further, I inverted the colors and came up with an effect I loved: a sort of luminous green, negative look that put me in mind of gargantuan fleas and horny skin cells and such, as photographed through an electron microscope. So to further this scientific effect, I added my name and the title in green glowing letters to resemble readouts on some kind of medical monitor, maybe. For the book you hold in your hands, the publisher made some tweaks, reproducing my type with type of their own, sticking to the same look but moving things around just a bit and adding another line of type.

Now you have more on *Health Agent*'s origins than perhaps you require, or my humble novel warrants, but I hope you found it of at least some degree of interest. I turn you over to health agent Montgomery Black, who two decades ago—before private eye Jeremy Stake roamed the streets of Punktown in *Deadstock* and *Blue War*—was unraveling mysteries, bringing enemies to justice, and learning about the mysteries of his own heart along the way.

—Jeffrey Thomas, January 5th, 2008

Part One:

Cupid of Death

One

The Serdab Memorial was no single obelisk or monument, but every tile of Red Station, a subway stop in Paxton, known better as Punktown. The walls, the sides of descending/ascending escalator banks or wide staircases, were set with red tiles as glossy as porcelain, and set back inside these somewhat murky translucent tiles were apparently three-dimensional faces, each one different from the next, the visages of soldiers killed in the Red War. They were holographic reproductions taken from information stored in the dog tags of the soldiers represented, the resulting death-mask tiles called serdabs, after the ancient Egyptian word referring to a hidden cell in the masonry of a tomb into which were placed images of the dead. The rows of faces, male and female, human and otherwise, were more or less distinct depending on the quality of light which reached them, and on how much grime or graffiti obscured them. Some tiles had been pried out and stolen, maybe to decorate the dashboard of a car or mantel of an errant art-lover's apartment.

Bum Junket stepped off one of the trains of the Red Line into the echoy strumming of a guitar further down the tunnel and a man singing about knock-knock-knocking on heaven's door in a twangy nasal voice. Almost instantly Bum was lighting a cigarette, jostled and bumped by the flow from the phallic silvery train. He felt a bit watery in the legs, having had to stand on the train, but he couldn't give up smoking. Anyway, why should he? It was a cool, soothing brand that didn't make him wheeze any much more than he already did. Bum took his time in strolling along the tunnel toward some benches against a long unbroken stretch of tiled wall, although he couldn't wait to sit again, feeling weak and tired as though hungry but not in the slightest bit hungry. Bum was twenty-four, black, and very thin, resembling closely a child emaciated by starvation, his dry skin taut over the hard definition of eye sockets and high cheekbones, his cheeks sunken and teeth distended, whites of his eyes a foggy yellow-brown and large squiggly veins rooted at either temple. He looked most like an unwrapped, animated mummy. His hair, however, was neatly close-cropped, he wore an outsized black and white checkered jacket with a caricature of sharp-edged padded broad shoulders, a silken silver shirt, baggy white pants with a narrow belt riding high above his hips, and silver slippers that revealed his bone-spurred ankles. Over a shoulder hung a black and silver checkered giant's handbag in proportion to his jacket. Bum was ever highly concerned with his look.

"At last," he groaned aloud, reaching the benches like a shipwrecked sailor having swum to shore. He lowered himself carefully as if setting down a box of rare china.

"Scum," said a Choom to him on the next bench over. Bum was alone on his bench but the Choom shared his with an old man curled in sleep, wearing a faded bathrobe over his graying street clothes. The Choom—native to this planet, Oasis, and human in form but for the great mouth rambling back to his ears—wore black lipstick and his red-dyed hair was draped with shiny glamour to hide one eye.

"Oh, fuck you," groaned Bum, looking away, then he looked back briefly to ask, "Who is that with you, Blo, your new boyfriend?"

"I know about you, Junk-it, Rump told me everything," sneered the Choom. "Look at you. Who do you think you are coming back here? You don't care who you kill, do you? Don't you care about anyone but yourself? You selfish pus-bag scum."

"How do I know I didn't get it from you, oh high and mighty?"

"I doubt it sincerely. I take care of myself, I take herbs and vitamins and every kind of immunity pill I can get my hands on."

"Oh that doesn't help; there's no cure…"

"*Preventative* medicine, fudger… a stronger house is less likely to be blown down in a storm."

"Blow down on this." Bum made an open fist at his crotch.

"Oh, you mean it hasn't fallen off yet?"

"You know the risks—go get married if you're so fucking afraid."

"Why should I have to give up my lifestyle because of you?"

"Ah-hah!" Bum lifted his chin at Blo. "And why should I? God , we're all going to get it anyway, aren't we? Should I give up eating and smoking and reading, too?"

"You won't infect anyone else by reading, you ass. You had better go, Bum, I mean it…some of us will get together and throw you out if we have to, I promise."

"Do that. And I'll go down to the Blue Line station and make friends there, and those friends will come through here, and they'll be your friends. So what's the fucking difference?"

"Get off the streets altogether, you selfish bastard! My God, what do you need the money for—a fur-lined coffin?"

"What are you so afraid for, Blo? Your herbs and vitamins will save you."

"We have to keep our world as clean and safe as possible! Can't you make a little sacrifice instead of doing a lot of damage?"

"My God, you sound like the Health Agency! My *life* is not a little sacrifice."

"Your life is *over!*"

"Not yet. Leave me alone. You could have caught it as easily as me if you haven't already, and you'd feel different if it were you."

"I'd take myself into an experimental program."

"Oh mutant-shit," Bum dismissed, looking away to blow out smoke.

"Look at you! Who would want you anyway?"

"I'm not a fat pig like you. No one and nothing will suppress me…I don't give in to life."

"Such pride from a selfish skeleton that guzzles sperm in bathrooms." Bum was a john-head, as the local slang went, while Blo would get picked up by the commuters passing through, go off with them to their apartment or his, a hotel or a car. He serviced less individuals but made more money for his efforts. These two types of male prostitutes in the Red Station had never happily coexisted even before this new, super-resistant mutant STD.

"I'll hold on long enough until they find a cure," Bum said, more quietly.

"You're already dead." Blo rose from his bench. "I'm going to find some others who feel my way, Bum, I mean it. You'd better leave before I come back. We'll even make a call to the Health Agency, if we have to."

Tremulous anger flashed out through the foggy glaze over Bum's eyes. "Go ahead! You're the selfish one, trying to control *my* life! Call whoever you want! I'll just get myself a lawyer like that girl on VT!"

"How will you afford a lawyer?"

"By guzzling sperm in bathrooms." Bum smiled hatefully.

"Oh, fine." Blo nodded. "Fine, alright. I'll be back, Bum."

"Fine, too." Bum stubbed out his cigarette against the side of the red marble bench, cried out after the red-haired Choom, "I'm still alive, you bastard…I have rent and bills to pay!" His slim mechanically-boned hands trembled as they pinched a fresh cigarette from their package. Bum muttered, "Unsympathetic fudger."

Three well-dressed women clicked by in their hard heels, laughing, laden with colorful shopping bags, two with large bags featuring a painting by a Choom artist whose work was being spotlighted this month at a nearby museum. The painting, his most famous, was of a starved dead dog lying on the street which the artist had encountered and painted on the spot. The laughter and clicking ascended to the open upper-world where it was gray, cold late winter. The guitar music and singing had ended, too. Bum swivelled his attention to the right; tensed inside. Two teenage boys and a girl vaulted up onto the subway platform from down in the train trench. The Trogs, a gang numbering in the hundreds. All three were dressed entirely in black, with long black raincoats and black fedoras, black goggles with a dot of red light in the center of each lens, skull-like on their impassive pale faces. All three carried a hooked black cane. People near the mouth of the tunnel from which they'd emerged drifted off like leaves before a wind. A nearby solitary forcer, also garbed in black—but with a full-head helmet and, hanging from a strap, a machine-gun which fired short individual ray bolts—turned his inhuman head ever-so-slightly to follow them. One pair of goggles swept Bum's way and he quickly averted his gaze. One time a passing Trog had idly hooked his neck, slender even then, with his cane and jerked him off his feet.

The Trogs strolled off down the tunnel; Bum's stomach unknotted. Two good-looking short-haired boys of about seventeen came to sit where Blo had been. One had a white polo shirt, tight white pants ending just below his knees, white slippers, and the other a white wool sweater, tight fading blue jeans, black slippers. College boys. Into Bum's third cigarette a tall man in an utterly unrumpled ash gray business suit just off a train approached the boys and opened a conversation but didn't sit. The sweater-wearing boy left the bench to accompany the commuter to the escalators. Bum sniffed in distaste. Fucking punks, most likely were even straight, just working their way through school or picking up a bit of weekend fun-money. To Bum their ilk were exploitative invaders. Of course, a few genuines dressed like the pretty college boys to attract those who were drawn to that flavor.

Red Station was conservative, for conservative tastes. There were seldom if ever surgical hermaphrodites, strangely-endowed mutants, smoothly muscular naked men posing about with glamorous hair cascading down their backs, or obese naked men with studded leather masks over their heads, as you could find elsewhere in Punktown. And no little boys, as in that part of town called the Meat Rack…this was too public a place, and the police and vigilante groups kept the fauna from getting too exotic. Still, in his time Bum had given head to a few men seated right here on these benches, late in the night, and once to a man on a train itself, in a mostly empty car. Here he had met several of his life's major loves, Max and Philly and Ream and a few others. Poor Philly had recently died of this very same STD in Miniosis, having moved there a few years ago; they had kept in touch. There hadn't been time for Bum to go see him, since Philly was into snakebite again, one of the sources of their break-up, and the drug had chewed up all his body's defenses. They would work this station together nearly every afternoon and evening, Bum and Philly, mostly to buy Philly his drugs, but that had been a happy six months. Bum was more lonely for those six months than for the year he had lived in Max's cute apartment, with Max supporting him, keeping him off the streets…but ultimately stifling him, dominating him, denigrating him and the past he had "saved" Bum from. Fuck you, Mom, Bum thought at the memory. He ached now for Philly to be seated beside him, breaking up sandwich bread for the few city birds that found their way down here out of the rain or cold, joking with their friends, drinking coffee on Christmas Eve while they waited for the train that would take them across town to Philly's mother's house, while a street musician played carols on a beat-up old keyboard. A tear slipped like a single raindrop from the clouds of Bum's eyes. Yes, Red Station was his place…he *had* to do his dying here. And he thought that his face, more appropriately than any of these soldiers, should become immortalized as part of these walls.

Maybe I'll do that, damn it, Bum considered, triumphant pride swelling to choke in his throat. Philly's mother had a holographic portrait of Philly, in full natural colors, visible from every angle like an eerie decapitated head in a box, and it moved and talked when you hit a button, played back a recorded message. A valentine present— Philly had loved his mother so. Could somebody make use of that in replicating the style of these tiles, and create one of him as well? Then Bum would pry away two tiles and replace them, and he and Philly would be together again.

"You're so fucking sentimental, Bummy," he chuckled/blubbered to himself, more tears coming, as if it were Philly saying it to him. Bum thought it couldn't hurt to at least make some inquiries around. It would have to be soon, though.

Familiar squeal; men's room door opening down the tunnel a bit, by the base of a huge red marble support column, so bulbously thicker than it was tall ("I've seen them like that," Philly had joked). Out floated something like a black jellyfish with an oil-slick iridescence, trailing long blue translucent tentacles just brushing the ground, from their looks hardly capable of supporting it but stronger than a man's arm. Three smooth black balls like marbles floated several inches above the body. An extra-dimensional, Bum decided, never having seen this type of being before but not alarmed. Just another example of the magic of Red Station; it was so fun to simply sit and watch the people.

He wondered if Blo really would come back with some reinforcements. He knew they wouldn't kill him, so he didn't regret not having a gun in his bag like the one Philly had carried. Still, he was a bit anxious. Maybe it would be best to change his hours to times he knew Blo wouldn't be here. Too bad—he loved his specific hours; it was his time, with specific kinds of people coming through, and this was *his life*…

Wiping his eyes, blowing his nose, Bum stubbed out his third cigarette and pushed himself off the bench with a wheezing strained groan. He swayed as a fuzzy ball of light rolled around in his skull a few times. His first few steps were a trudge until he got his bearings; he turned to watch the black jellyfish being float down onto the train bed and disappear into the tunnel from which the Trogs had come, the blue tentacles luminous for a second, then gone. Bum walked to the men's room. Once Philly had stolen its sign and they had put it on the door to their apartment and laughed and laughed. Funny how Bum missed him so much now, when there were days and days in the past when he wouldn't even think of him. Bum squealed open the men's room door, entered.

The smell nearly gagged him, filling his paper bag lungs like rotting garbage which threatened to tear through the bottoms. Smaller red tiles like snake scales on the walls, no portraits locked in them like ghost reflections—just his one moving portrait, temporary. Trash, graffiti, broken tiles and handles and faucets. Every stall was unoccupied, no one at the rank of red porcelain urinals, only one man at the counter of red sinks, sitting against it, picking at a fingernail moodily.

A man in a business suit walked toward the men's room. A small young blond woman who had been leaning against the squat marble pillar reading a magazine while waiting for a train pushed off from the pillar and caught the man by the elbow before he reached the men's room door. "Excuse me..." she said.

"Pardon me," said Bum to the man at the sinks, whose eyes were on him. The smile Bum's face made was like a nylon stocking being stretched across a yellow skull. "Contemplating the nature of the universe?"

"Maybe."

"This is as good a place as any, I guess."

The man smiled, an abrupt change in expression that made Bum fall back a step internally and then captivated him. The man was tall, with dark blond hair swept back from a high broad forehead, his eyes heavy-lidded, deep in dark sockets and set far apart, a cold gray. A new blond mustache and goatee gave him an artistic, sensitive air, and before he had smiled he had looked icily solemn, disquietingly so...his small mouth still, light glowing on his forehead and high cheekbones and nose, the rest shadowed. But the smile, grin actually, cracked the face open into crinkles, the icy eyes warmed into glints. The man wore a V-necked navy blue pullover, baggy black pants and black slippers without socks, a large black leather pocketbook over a shoulder.

"Good a place as any for a smoke, too," Bum continued. He deftly plucked a cigarette, his hands remembering how to act now when he needed them. "You?"

"Another brand." The handsome man reached in his bag, produced a pack, tapped out a black herb cigarette. "Need a light?"

"Thanks—yes." Bum smiled anew. The tall stranger straightened up casually to extend a lighter, lit Bum's cigarette and his own. The man held the lighter up to his eye to look at something on it.

"Needs more fuel," he mumbled softly, looking serious again.

"I like your goatee. Don't let it get too long, though...it looks more arty while it's still fresh."

"I won't." The lighter made a bleep.

Bum's smile took on a narrower aspect. "Is that a camera?"

"Mm—almost." The blond man dropped the lighter into his pocketbook. "Are you Bum Junket?"

"No...no, that isn't my name...why? Who are you?"

"The lighter is a scan for mutstav six-seventy, which you were also diagnosed as having at the Forma Street Clinic three days ago..."

"That's not true, you have the wrong person!"

"Look at you." The tall man nodded toward the mirrors without taking his blank eyes from Bum.

"Who are you?"

"I'm a health agent with a warrant for your arrest as a carrier of a lethal communicable disease."

"Show me your warrant, or your badge!" Bum felt that fuzzy ball of light rocking into movement again, the bones liquefying in his legs, which were really just bones only.

"I'm not required to." Instead of a warrant, the man's dipping hand brought a pistol up from the handbag, aimed it from his waist calmly.

"Jesus, don't!" Bum screeched.

"Please step outside, Mr. Junket."

"Alright, don't shoot!" sobbed Bum. He wobbled coltishly to the door. "My tests at the clinic were confidential," he moaned over his shoulder.

"The Health Agency has access to any and all Paxton medical information, sir."

Outside the men's room, the small blond woman waited with a drawn snub-nosed revolver, the helmeted forcer keeping back a crowd, his fists clenching his ray blaster. Bum's eyes found Blo in the growing throng—had he betrayed him, the traitor? No, they had his records, he remembered.

"Back off, back off!" the woman growled huskily at the crowd. The forcer shoved a man's chest with the length of his machine-gun.

"Stop here, Mr. Junket," said the goateed agent. "Could you go to your knees, please?"

"Why?"

"Go to your knees. I won't ask you again."

Bum sank to his knees, shaking, laced his fingers on his head without having been asked, expecting his wrists to be cuffed. The half-circle of faces familiar and alien above him was too much; he clamped his streaming eyes shut, skull grimace bared. They would experiment on him now, his last weeks or months spent as a lamentable lab animal…

The handsome health agent closed the distance between the back of Bum's skull and his pistol barrel to six inches and fired one shot.

The audience cried out in unison as though a trapeze artist had fallen to his death. Some recoiled, hid their faces; a teenage boy widened his eyes and said, "Jeez!"

Though the handgun was a tarnished silvery revolver with a four-inch barrel, slim black rubber grip with a ring through the butt, and sounded like a lead-firing weapon, the bullet was a powerful plasma capsule. The plasma spread over Bum's entire form before he could even pitch forward onto his face, a vividly glowing green, a pulsing form-fitting blanket. Bum's brief writhing was languorous, probably painless. Then the arms shortened away to stumps, to nothing, the head diminished, and there was only an unmoving blob of torso until that too dwindled and vanished. No trace was left of body or plasma, no blood or char or stain.

Less than ten seconds. Just a smell like burning plastic. The health agent returned his gun to the handbag and this time he did produce a badge and a warrant, holding both aloft and pivoting for all to see.

"I am a health agent with a warrant to destroy and dispose of Bum Junket as being a wanton carrier of the lethal STD mutstav six-seventy. Mr. Junket is a previously arrested male prostitute and meant to continue these activities with full knowledge of his condition and its properties. He did not contact the Health Agency as required for a mutstav victim, despite the warnings of the Forma Street Clinic where he was diagnosed."

"You executed him!" hissed someone in the audience.

"Those were my orders." The agent lowered badge and paper. "It is the Health Agency's hope that any other mutstav victims will pay heed to the consequences of Mr. Junket's selfish and reckless conduct."

"He would've died soon anyway," the woman added. "Slow and painful."

"That was for him to decide," hissed that same someone.

"Not under the circumstances," replied the man. "The hazardous nature of Mr. Junket's disease and actions superseded his rights as an individual…"

Down the escalator came two men in baggy black rubbery suits, black hoods with face plates, orange tanks on their backs connected to orange spray guns. They charged into the men's room to disinfect it. Out here you could hear the hissing sprays and smell the pleasantly-perfumed disinfectant. Only outside of a living host could the virus be killed…most easily by killing the organic matter it was nesting in; in effect, starving it to death. Nevertheless, the men's room would be secured for a full two days, the period necessary for the virus to die on inorganic surfaces.

"Sorry to alarm you, and thank you for your attention," concluded the health agent. His female companion had holstered her snub revolver; together they walked to the escalators.

"Murderer!" cried Blo. Despite his dislike of Bum and his own threats, he had never expected this. A public execution, without a trial even, meant to threaten the prostitutes of Red Station! "How do you know he was going to sell himself again?" Blo shouted at the impassive backs moving up the escalators. "Did he suck your sausage? Next you'll be rounding us all up!"

"Maybe we'll have to," said the woman, but only to the blond man.

Bum had died in his beloved Red Station, at least…though there would be no tile bearing the epitaph of his face.

TWO

The headquarters for HAP—the Health Agency of Paxton—was a thirty-story structure off Route Forty, outside the compacted nucleus of Punktown in case of mishap, patterned exactly after the Health Agency of Miniosis—HAM—except that older building was gray stone and this one was shiny turquoise plastic, right down to the flowery scroll-work and crouched gargoyles around the multi-tiered beehive cupola that topped it. It was a bleak area of highway; rife with vehicle dealerships, new or used (mostly rented, either way—one could scarcely afford to fully own one, and to go through a bank meant only buying the illusion of ownership). There were distant woods within view, but they seemed as remote as clouds. From the windows of the Health Agency building one could see more of the woods below like a sea from an airplane, and small roads branching off Route Forty like tributaries from a river, lined with ominously blank-looking, lifelessly interchangeable plant structures. One of these plants, not far from HAP, set off a bit from the others and larger but still blankly inscrutable, was the waste processing plant for the town—an independent corporation commissioned by the Health Agency with a renewable five-year contract. The town's water supply was purified from this building, and waste materials relayed by truck, teleporter and pipeline to be thoroughly disintegrated.

Also in view, but more isolated in the forest sea like some oil refinery of old, was the "air factory" or atmosphere recycling center for this township, fully government-run by HAP, dominated by two tall conjoined cylinders of sky blue enamel, with a separate feature like a set of gigantic blue-enameled organ pipes. Like HAP and the waste plant, the air factory was gated, with guard shacks, and patrolled, security hovercraft ready on the roofs of all three establishments as though ranked on aircraft carriers in the battle to keep the environment from invasion. It was a war never won; just fought day by day.

HAP's gargoyles were actually cannons, with angry bulbous eyes that could move and blaze deadly rays below or at threatening aircraft. HAP's security hovercraft hid like bees in the beehive, apparently so as not to conflict with the architect's sense of aesthetics. Montgomery Black believed that this was the reason for the cannons in the gargoyles also, more so than simply for camouflage.

Black and his partner, Opal Cowrie, entered their twenty-ninth floor squad room. It was mostly one great room portioned into individual cubicles like a noisy mall at Christmas time; a bustling little microcosm town. They had undergone a half-dozen security scans to get this far, the last outside the squad room door. Instantly their comrades greeted them.

"Monty," grinned a man with rolled-up white shirt sleeves falling in beside him, "how was it going undercover in Red Station? Do you feel that you penetrated the bowels of Punktown's dark underside?"

"I saw your name on the bathroom wall, Catch…you should at least charge for it."

"Did you probe the inside of Punktown's deepest recesses?"

"Get a job, Catch." Catch fell behind, Black paused to add over his shoulder, "Anyway, no, I didn't meet your wife down there."

Catch's grin collapsed into a gape. "Hey, man, that's not funny!"

Black cracked his charming grin. He and Opal Cowrie continued on to their chief's office. Opal rapped on frosted glass and a voice invited them in.

"Good job, kids," greeted their chief, Nemo Nedland, field captain of Organic Control division. Captain Nedland was thin, wan, pale, dark-haired and black-suited, like a caricature of a funeral director. Soft-spoken, sad, as if every conversation were the consoling of the bereaved. "It went well. But then I didn't really expect Red's boy prosties to be stupid enough to gang up on a health agent."

"A few were pretty riled," Opal grumbled.

"The condom dispenser in the men's room was smashed," Black said absently.

"We'll replace it, and put an antibiotic dispenser in there too, for whatever that's worth. Immediately. It won't look good if we're killing people in Red Station without even making sure the condom dispensers work. Idiots down there. Maybe a photo of Bum Junket on the men's room wall would do more good. What was it with him?"

"A drowning man loves company."

"I guess." Nedland paced in the constricted cubicle office; he hadn't asked his agents to sit, but he never seemed to sit much himself. Just drifted broodingly about. "I have a revelation, kids—hope you aren't mad."

"Uh-oh, what?" said Opal.

Sad apologetic smile. "The boss has told me from on high to run Junket's elimination on VT."

"Who shot it?" Black purred, somewhat wary.

"Red Station security cameras."

"Big deal," said Opal, "so we're celebrities for a night. I'm not afraid. I'll just disguise up a bit if I go undercover in the near future."

"I'm not concerned," agreed Black. "Run it." Though secretly he was afraid he might have to shave his mustache and goatee for a while, also to alter his appearance.

"I suppose a few gay groups will make some noise, but not for long if we can get Auretta Here," said Captain Nedland. "If we can eliminate her they'll see we aren't prejudiced. And I want her."

"Unbelievable selfish bitch," fumed Opal.

Auretta Here had been on VT already. An attractive young female human prostitute, Miss Here had been diagnosed as having M-670 at a street clinic, which reported her to the officials when she didn't admit herself to the Health Agency's control and study program. She believed that victims of M-670 were actually being disintegrated in the HAP building by the scores, which was in fact not true. Only a hundred or so victims were interred at HAP itself, and their deaths were by M-670 with its one hundred percent death rate. Yes, *then* they were either disintegrated or dissected and preserved. Other victims were patients of hospitals cooperating with HAP, while many more victims were free to return to the streets after checking in with the HAP program... where they received drug treatments to fully negate their sex drives. Only if the plague worsened beyond program containment would diagnosed M-670 victims be forcefully rounded up for mass detainment—and possible mass disintegration, probably at the waste plant. HAP hoped not to have to resort to this, however...as it could mean full-fledged war in the streets of Punktown. Seldom had the Paxton Health Agency had to deal with an organic threat of such potential proportions.

Auretta Here was in hiding, and on VT her lawyer was defending her civil rights as a free individual. He had been truth scanned and honestly didn't know her whereabouts, so he was not harboring a fugitive. Auretta's vids which had appeared on VT had been shot by friends, apparently, and mailed.

She seemed to relish this publicity, felt Black.

"Do you want us on it?" asked Opal.

"Not yet—four's enough for now. Two would be plenty except that she's shoving her vids up our arses."

"Arrogant whore," Opal raved. "She must resent everyone who isn't infected and want them to die if she has to die, like a guy who kills his wife and kids before he commits suicide. She can't bear to have the world go on without her so she's gonna tear down as much of it as she can and take it with her."

"Whatever makes you a star," mumbled Black.

"I don't want her to be a star, or hero, or rebel or martyr," said Nedland. "Damn irresponsible VT...they won't stop running her vids. And when she's dead in six months or a year they'll make a VT movie about her, I'll bet you a year's salary."

"No bet," said Black.

"Just go back on your regular assignments until further notice, kids. Soon we'll be drafting people as health agents to keep up with just our M-670 problem! As if we don't have enough to do." Nedland watched his agents move to the door, teased, "And change your faces if you're itchy about that tape."

"No way," said Black over his shoulder, only in a half-joking way. He would be adamant about not changing his natural features. This was *his* face, even though he had been born with it, with no more influence over it than over his having been born, hadn't created or altered it to match his individual personality and identity as many people did. It wasn't out of loyalty to his parents, who were somewhat reflected in his flesh, since he wasn't particularly close to them—having been primarily raised by their computer—otherwise he wouldn't have altered his name. It was simply that he was pleased with, and rather vain about, his given appearance.

The halls of the third floor labs were quite empty at the moment, but much of the work down here was performed by robots anyway. Narrow halls with white-tiled walls, many doors, some open to reveal bright laboratories glittering with metal and glass, studious figures in white smocks intensely peering through microscopic goggles. Many looked like pre-med students. Some were. The target-like yellow/black symbol for radioactivity affixed to many doors; a door with the warning BIOHAZARD was left carelessly open. Agents Black and Cowrie parted to allow a young man in an open smock, flowered shirt, faded blue jeans and dirty sneakers to run between them. He jumped up and slapped a NO SMOKING sign over a door before skipping through, singing aloud.

A robot admitted them into a room. It was a hovering box with probes and cameras and insectoid arms, and someone had attached to its top a blankly smiling department store mannequin head with foolish hair like a toupee. Sometimes they put a surgical mask on the head.

A small Asian woman swivelled on her metal stool. "All set for you."

Opal bent her eye to the scope of an instrument. "Hmph. The chromes look like Tikkihotto hieroglyphics."

"There's a whole pack of a half-dozen that've been reported. They could breed. Their blood is poison. Pests had fed on this one." A nod at a tacked-up, blown-up photo of—supposedly—a dog carcass. "I'd say a pretty good hazard."

"Now we're dog catchers," smiled Black.

"I'd hate to have to kill a dog," Opal moaned, smiling apologetically as she straightened. "Any kind of dog."

"You didn't mind helping me melt Bum Junket down today and you're whining about a mutant dog," Black chuckled.

"Everybody's got their soft spot. Really, I don't want it—let's give it to somebody else, huh?"

"Certainly."

"Even exterminating pests makes me guilty," Opal said. "Their poor little shiny eyes." She pouted.

"Yeah—once I saw a rat with five poor little shiny eyes. Maybe Bum would've fared better if he'd been gnawing on some celery, huh?"

"A carrot would be more appropriate." The three laughed, the robot's head smiling blandly. "What else has come in here?" Opal asked the tech.

"A human body was brought into Path-4, Rena told me…they don't know what the hell happened to it. A high degree of noncongenital mutation. Lethal progression. It was in a lot, pretty purulent; they have the site sealed off for investigation and sanitation."

"Ha," said Black. "Who's on it?"

"Ahh, Beak and Woodmere."

"Maybe I'll see if they need a hand, if I have time."

"We're going to a show tonight," said Opal.

"Oh?"

"Some kind of actor-artist is performing tonight at the old shut-down Greenberg Products plant on Pigeon Street. He's licensed—the owner is letting him—but we're gonna make sure everything's secure."

"I used to love their Greenbread. I can't believe one chem spill would put them out of business."

"Well, Mr. Greenberg passed away, too, and his wife took over. She should sell what's left so they can make something out of it while there's still something to sell."

Black eyed a wall clock. "Better be off, if you want to catch us on the news," he told Opal. "We've gotta change into our tux and gown for tonight, too."

"I'm in the tux," Opal told the tech.

They left, though in no actual hurry, since Black had phoned home and ordered his VT to tape the news on the channel he had found out would be playing the story. He confided to his small companion, "Greenberg Greenbread always made me gag." He chuckled…

Ground floor was all security, aside from reception. Joking, Black and Opal entered the standard decontamination unit. It was large; no one left the building without at least this much decontamination. In a glistening white changing room they stripped, alone but for the sounds of two men distant in the labyrinth of lockers, echoed laughter, slamming metal compartments. Bare-chested, Black waited for Opal to meet his eyes and he wiggled his brows. She gave him a blank look but he knew humor was behind it. Most of her expressions seemed a bit cold, blank, intimidating on the outside, her eyes the same mysterious impenetrable gray as his own. She was pretty, not beautiful— not very pretty, even—but there was a natural unforced sensuality. Her mouth was a pouty sneer, small, twisty as if from being compacted, unevenly bee-stung, her smile haughty and tough when she did smile. She could be cute, with her diminutive body, pale skin, wavy dirty blond hair cut short of her shoulders, unkempt and falling across one eye, but her pouty profile was rather flattened-looking, the lower jaw subtly thrust. She turned away from him as if to hide but also probably to tease him with her moving back and the bisected sphere of her bottom as she stepped out of her panties, her bare feet making sticky slapping noises on the tiles.

"Yum." Naked, Black stepped over, held her shoulders, nuzzled her hair-curtained ear; his hardening but still downward-pointing arrow nuzzling in the cleavage of her bottom. "Can I show you some tricks Bum Junket taught me?"

"Not until you been through the shower, scum."

"You're so romantic."

"Come on, don't get me going." Opal slipped out of his hands and walked towards the showers. "It's getting late."

Black sighed, trying not to get irritable. He knew it was late but she didn't have to turn so cool and make him feel stupid. He gathered up his clothes, pushed them into a numbered compartment in a honeycomb of sealed compartments outside the showers, tapped keys on a small panel. While he showered, his belongings, gun and all, would be disinfected. It was just as well...too many times they had punched in late because he had instigated sex with Opal when he knew there wasn't really enough time. Just a little, he told himself, nice and quick, but they ended up having to scramble to work with uncombed hair, unshowered (though he soaped and rinsed off his genitals—otherwise he couldn't bear it). When it came to sex he was undisciplined, he recognized, too impulsive. But wasn't that spontaneity, that crazy abandon, where the fun came from?

Still, in the showers he chose a nozzle a good four nozzles away from her, barely looked at her pink body misty in the hissing spray of chemicals. This was why they couldn't love each other in a romantic way, he mused...she was so hard and cynical. A woman didn't have to be vulnerable to be soft and inviting, he believed, but she had to at least—or rather, most importantly—be capable of sweetness, gentleness, sensitivity. Opal could, if in the mood, manage gentle...sensitive...but sweetness was a coat that fit her uncomfortably; she squirmed in it. Opal had a terrible temper, had stormed out of their apartment, left him—once for a full month—had struck him, though he had never struck her...not so much out of respect but out of fear of letting loose his own temper. They both bedded other people occasionally, with little or no lasting jealous conflict. Mostly they were partners, friends, who conveniently shared a rent and enjoyed a nearly compatible sexual relationship.

Black and Opal had tried to fall in love but it had been a grating attempt, two gears in a machine that didn't mesh, and they had given up. Black supposed he had been in love a few times in his life and Opal said she had once (she was more than ten years younger), but neither of them were going out of their way to look for it or even wait for it now. To Black, love was like the lottery, and you couldn't count on winning the jackpot, just a lesser prize (an extra free ticket) here and there.

More sober than before but still speaking, they moved on to a rank of individual clear plastic cylinders which they entered and in which they were blow-dried while invisible rays cleaned them further but didn't penetrate outside the special plastic tubes. By the time they stepped out their clothes were ready, still warm to the touch, as were their guns.

Opal dropped her disposable foam slippers into a trash unit to be disintegrated. As she turned, a peripheral movement caught her eye; it was a frantic scurrying black beetle near the foot of the trash zapper. She caught it in her hands, rose, cooed to it, "Poor thing," and then dropped it into the zapper.

THREE

The parking lot to Greenberg Products lay adjacent to the Beds, a sort of train yard, ill-lighted now that it was also no longer used since the chemical spill, of indeterminable extent in the void of night. Mostly just the fringe of the Beds bordering the parking lot was lit, the tran tracks stretching off into the black like snake skeletons—or, more properly analogous, the spinal columns of dinosaurs. A few of the old trans squatted about in the yard, a couple of them disused for a decade even before the spill. They resembled old-Earth locomotive steam engines but weren't intended to pull cars…they were trans, after all, not trains.

Rising from Opal's stilled hovercar, Black lit a cigarette as some measure against the cold and squinted out across the Beds. Beyond them somewhere two cats were howling a challenge at each other. Opal took in Greenberg. "Anybody die in that spill?" Black asked her.

"No, it was handled pretty well. The place is salvageable, too. I guess Mrs. Greenberg's waiting for a buyer instead of reopening. She's probably afraid the spill will discredit the reputation of the products."

"Nobody would remember it." Black glanced over his shoulder. "Place is lit up pretty good. This is more of an event than I thought—I figured a dozen people." There were maybe forty vehicles in the lot so far. "Half of 'em are probably critics. I've never heard of Toll Loveland, have you?"

"Not before today. For his last one-man show, he called himself Vicelord Godfucker."

"I like a reserved, humble kind of guy like that."

"For his last show he cut off his left hand's little finger on stage and swallowed it."

"Really?"

"Yes."

"Brilliant."

"He had mixed reviews. It was a one-night show only, like this."

"He probably used all his proceeds on hospital bills."

Opal had run a search on Toll Loveland through their home computer while Black had dressed. "He cloned it back as the climax of the show, the whole finger, in just three minutes."

"A magic trick."

"No. He majored in bioengineering at Paxton Polytech and then got his masters in Liberal Arts from P.U.—a weird combo, eh?"

"A man with a vision. What's he gonna do tonight, decapitate himself and tap dance while he clones his head back?"

"A 'Mixed Media Presentation', is all I know. Brrr, let's go in."

"Lemme finish my cigarette."

They had a few minutes. Opal produced a small pink-enameled pipe, thumbed the "on" switch and puffed. Black strolled toward the Beds and after a moment his partner trailed him. Tall yellowed weeds, a rumpled guard-rail which he stepped over. He stopped to stare down at a few objects of debris like shells washed on a lonely shore. A child's ski boot. In Punktown one might seriously stop and pick up such a thing to see if a foot were inside it. He nudged it and it seemed empty. A flattened cat, like a skinned hide, was camouflaged with the dead grass, but the tail was still roundish and he could feel it run through the hand of his mind, silky and alive. One tooth bared and unflattened in tiny defiance; a cat to the end. Maybe it was the ghost of this cat challenging another spirit that he had heard, Black fancied in self-amusement. As he had expected, Opal said, "Awww."

"Give me a break."

"Shut up. Poor thing. Maybe it was somebody's pet. Or if it wasn't, it should have been."

"Street cats are like bugs; they live and they die by the millions. Fast lives, like bugs. A six-month to one-year span, I read."

"In a home they can live twenty years; decades more if you don't mind paying for it. And you're just a bug compared to some species—even to a tree. Stop pushing me about animals, Monty. You just don't like to see yourself in them."

"I had a cat as a boy. I loved it. Happy? I just hope you have an 'awww' left for me when I die, after all your 'awwws' for these millions of stray animals."

"What an ignorant and pointless thing to say. You're the only guy I know who gets jealous over a cat mummy."

"You're the only woman I know who has more compassion for a dead cat than a live man."

"Maybe some dead cats are more deserving of it than some live men."

"Me?"

Opal glared through the mist of her breath. "No, not you. How did this ever get to be about you, anyway?"

Black didn't know. This gear sometimes still moved mindlessly of its own accord even though hers didn't try to turn and mesh with it. She was right; he was talking stupid. He walked toward the nearest of the hulking black metal trans, one of those decommissioned and set off the tracks for a decade or more. When he had climbed up inside, Opal could see his flashlight in the few windows, sighed and followed, glancing at her watch.

By the time Opal had hauled herself up and joined him, he had dropped his light back into his coat. There was just enough soft, eerie illumination from two crystal globes set into the control console, filled with a glowing, translucent milky liquid—Navigator fluid. Moving shadows inside; a beautiful metallic blue fish swam close to the glass in one globe and lazily vanished again—purely a decorative touch, the only life left to this forgotten machine. Black expected Opal to comment on their abandonment, suggest they take them home for their aquarium or free one fish and join it with the other for company, but she said nothing—maybe out of embarrassment, he considered guiltily.

Below the globes were six silver rings, in two rows of three, like miniature steering wheels which in a fashion they were. Trans had been ridden by the Bedbugs, as they were nicknamed; bipedal giant black beetles with six whip-like arms ending in pincers. Sometimes they would have mechanical arms implanted in addition to or in place of these feeler appendages, better suited to this hominid-dominated society. They were extra-dimensionals who used the trans to enter this material plane or return to their own. The acceleration of the tran along its pattern of tracks sent the device and its occupants beyond. But they used another bed of tracks these days. For whatever reason that a particular group becomes feared, scorned, abhorred, many people hated the so-called Bedbugs. Black was sure it didn't help that one of Punktown's most notorious street gangs, the Dimensionals, was composed entirely of Bedbugs.

"What do you say we drive this baby home after the show?" he joked, trying to restore camaraderie.

"I say we get to the show before we miss it."

A tall dark being stepped up into the tran with them. "Freeze!" it snarled.

"Shit!" Opal and Black slapped their hands to their guns.

"Hold it, hold it, hey—it's me, Beak!" the newcomer babble-laughed.

Opal had gotten her snub-nose out first and seemed reluctant to put it away, in her anger. "You freakin' demento."

Beak came forward, still laughing. "You're no fun, Opal." He had the look of a weasel in clothes; long-bodied, short-limbed, with short brown fur, coarse and sleek, but with a hard little black bird's beak. He had on a black windbreaker over a purple wool sweater, and a purple ski hat over his tiny pointed ears.

"What are you doing here?" Black asked him, restraining his own temper.

"Woodsy's here too. I wouldn't miss Toll Loveland for the world!"

"Come on."

"The body of a guy named Tate Hurrea was found today in a lot on Block Ave.—a noncon mutant, real sludge."

"Yeah, I heard—so?"

"In his wallet we found a ticket stub to Toll Loveland's last show, *The Godfucker.* A little funny. Woodsy thought we should come down here and double-date."

"That is funny, huh? It's not like Toll Loveland is a household word."

"After the show Woods wants to ask this clown if he knew our boy in better days. Shall we go?"

A young woman at the plant's reception desk took their money and traded them ticket stubs. Black read the show's title from the stub—*Pandora's Box*. The ticket girl was dressed all in black with a pretty face but waxy-milky skin and no expression and her choppy black hair falling over one eye like a shielding visor.

They trailed after a wall-dressed couple who strolled and conversed, chuckling. Red stick-on arrows and bare hanging light bulbs led the way through narrow halls and then out into the dark, open plant itself. The path narrowed again to a tight squeeze behind a giant oven the size of a house. Voices ahead, and more light. When they emerged from behind the oven, health agent Vern Woodmere was there around the corner smoking a cigarette.

"Shit," breathed Opal, "I wish you guys would knock off the jack-in-the-box stuff."

Woodmere stubbed out his cigarette on the oven and slipped the remainder in a breast pocket of his scuffed, brown leather flight jacket. He had been a young, long-haired pilot during the Red War, now had permanent shadows clinging to his worn face like moss to stone, rust to metal, the lines of his mouth a hard dragged-down scowl, eyes like metal—maybe rusted, maybe not—in deep sockets, and short silvered slicked-back hair. He was in need of a shave. Hard to get along with. Black had joked to Opal once that Vern looked like an axe murderer.

"You two can punch out, we got this one now," he drawled.

"And miss my idol?" said Black.

"Hey, I'm not stealing your glory, pretty boy, I'm doing you a favor. We'll keep an eye out for ya, and we have some questions for Loveland, too."

"I appreciate the offer but we might as well stay. Big place—some idiot might stray off and make trouble. Anyway, Beak's got me curious. This guy might have accidentally got some poor theater-goer killed with his tricks."

Woodmere glared at his partner. "You tell everybody our business, dung-dong?"

"Hey, they're agents too, Vern!"

"Moron." Woodmere left them.

"Nice to feel wanted," Black muttered.

"That's Vern," said Beak. "Come on."

Ahead was an open area, high-ceilinged and vastly black in all directions around an oasis of light. Ten rows of ten folding chairs were ranked and being filled before a stage made from a large sheet of plastic supported on either side by a fork-lift. Inside these little vehicles were complete skeletons (fake? wondered Black) wearing old-style goggled fallout masks. There was a three-sided black curtain behind the elevated platform. The only other prop was a seven-foot-high monolithic replica of a box of *Screaming Pink Nazis* cereal, very well painted, obviously by Toll Loveland. *Screaming Pink Nazis* cereal came with a holograph chip which, when slipped into your home computer or VT, released ten miniature pink holographic soldiers to run about the house, ghost-like in that they were not solid, though they looked solid and disappeared when they passed behind material barriers. You would then hunt them down and kill them with your SPANK (Screaming Pink Automatic Nazi Killer) gun (which you had to send away for).

Beak said, "You'd think the guy would be more original than that—everybody's spoofed *Pink Nazis* by now."

"It's become mythic by now," Black said. "This guy's obviously into symbolism."

"I'm bored already."

Vern had fallen back a bit so the others turned to him. He said, "Let's not sit together. We might spook him. He knows you two are coming but not Beak and me. Anyway, we can see more if we spread out."

"Whatever," said Opal. "Where you do you want?"

"Second to last row, far left."

They split up and stepped into the light. Black and Opal seated themselves in the fifth row, far right. Black strained his eyes into the murk around them. Here and there light was snagged, as if on barbed wire, on the metal of a conveyor belt, glinted dully on a machine or lonely fork-lift.

The lights dimmed away but for those illuminating the stage, which were soft. The eighty or so people in the audience grew quiet, and then gasped as the front of the giant cereal box opened out like a door with a sound effects haunted house creak. Standing in the box was a figure, but difficult to see at first through the bluish luminous cloud of smoke billowing out.

Before Black could say anything Opal was analyzing the smoke with the portable toxin scan from her purse, now held in her lap. She leaned to Black. "It doesn't rate poisonous."

He settled back, but was aware now of the weight of his holstered gun like a parasite affixed to his ribs. The spreading fog thinly wafted over him, had the powdery perfumed smell of concert smoke bombs. Now he could see strange fluttering shadows in the billowing clouds, darting and zig-zagging. He realized they were moths of all sizes, mostly large white ones he could see when they spun out of the reach of the smoke, which was clearing. Both moths and smoke dispersed; Black ducked and batted one insect away from his hair. He hated moths; they gave him the creeps. Butterflies too, even. Weird, erratic things. He had punched a wall and hurt his hand once trying to kill a moth as it ricocheted in his bathroom. Opal caught bugs in cups and put them outside.

Visible in the box was a man dressed in a white jumpsuit, with gloves and high gray boots. Over his head he wore a rectangular box three feet wide and two feet high, which was a VT monitor. On the screen were the words:

PANDORA'S BOX
BY
TOLL LOVELAND

The audience applauded. The title cleared and the man stepped down out of the cereal box. At the edge of the stage he stopped, and a film opened on the screen that was his head. Black could feel the leaning attentiveness of the audience along with his own.

It was a traveling shot apparently filmed out the window of a car down a street in Punktown; Black recognized the street. The car came to a stop at an angle in a parking space. Across the street were two banks side-by-side. There was street noise, but no noise from the cinematographer. There was a cut. It was later—twenty-five minutes, by the clock in front of one bank. Superimposed at the bottom of the screen was the title:

CUPID OF DEATH

Then gone. A woman stepped out of a sporty red hovercar that had just arrived in front of the banks, walked to a black hovercar with windows tinted black on the outside and leaned into the open driver's window. Other cars passed. The woman's cold breath rose. She had blond hair and big dark glasses, a short coat of silvery-blue fur and tight faded jeans, clinging to the rear which proudly and slyly projected toward the street like a moving beacon, a second face scanning for attention. As she shifted her weight it would sway and seem to follow a passing car. It might be winking its asshole at the cars under the tight jeans, for all its studied animation. Black wished the camera would zoom in on it.

It did, a moment later, though not in the manner he would expect. The camera floated out of the car window lazily as the film wound down abruptly to slow motion. No sound. Slow, slow, smooth and languid. The camera was out of the car and into the street. It was floating toward the young woman. A number changed finally on the digital bank clock. Black noticed now that this film had been shot only two days ago, by the date shown in smaller numbers over the time. Odd, since this performance had been scheduled for several weeks at least...

The camera was out in the middle of the street. Had to be a remote hover camera, operated from inside the car. Black began to realize that the camera was zooming in as well as moving closer, and that it did seem to be focusing in on the blue-jeaned rear of that blond. Was it only zooming and still inside the car? But it felt so like the camera was actually in motion itself…

The blue-jeaned bottom now a blue-jeaned planet, subtly bisected under those dull woven oceans. Sound was welling up, a whooshing of air. The zoom abruptly jumped up and the weave of the jeans was of great ropes, great tree trunks criss-crossing, and then a great fizzing-ripping sound as the camera plunged into darkness. My God, thought Black, as did the audience, judging from some of the mumbles and soft exclamations.

"Did that go *in* her?" Opal hissed.

"I think so."

A light came on in the movie. The camera was plummeting through a strange red ocean, sinking, and finally coming to a rest. Stillness. The zoom increased, however. There were *things,* alive, swimming in and out of the light like moths. The camera was now a microscope.

"Some kind of dart or arrow," said Black.

"Is it fake?"

"I don't know. The film might have spliced in the dark part."

A hissing, roaring, rushing, gurgling—and rising up from it in slow motion came a demon's wail, growing to a near-deafening, shrill but also bass-thick rumble. Black scrunched his face. It was meant to be, or actually was, the woman's scream from inside her body.

The screen went black. The scream echoed away throughout the great dark chamber of the factory. The audience murmured and hissed with whispers, shaken…there was a scattering of meek, obligatory applause, and a few people applauded enthusiastically.

"A bullet?" said Opal.

"It would spin or tumble. A stabilized dart of some kind. Some kind of homing probe."

"Should we call the forcers down?"

"Maybe. It could be fake. Let's wait until after, talk to Vern."

"Do you remember hearing about a woman sniped in the ass in front of those banks two days ago?"

"No, but this is Punktown." Enough said. One would have to watch the all-news VT stations all day, and even then some days they couldn't list every major crime and killing. Mostly, one just got an assorted sampling.

The man on stage remained unmoving, robot-like, hands flat to the outsides of his legs, but the screen flashed to a new image. It was the head of Toll Loveland in proportion to the body, but the background was of swirling luminous blue vapor filled with darting moths. A white moth had alighted on his hair. He was smiling faintly.

He was a handsome man, in his mid-twenties, with a high smooth forehead and his brown hair slicked back to further emphasize its highlighted surface with its low, dark brow. From under this bony brow his blue eyes stared, deep and dramatic. His lips were thick and sensuous, compressed in the smile which seemed to indicate that he knew how charismatic his attractiveness was. It was a face both intelligent and primal, sensitive and brutal, twinkling with humor but sullenly dissolute.

The head seemed truly to be seeing them, the eyes flicking. Black felt sure they would flick onto his. Perhaps it *was* seeing them, or perhaps just a recording. The lips moved.

"I broke the lock—of Pandora's Box
I pried open her chastity belt
It smelt
Of the decay of repression
I sought her depression
Then—wagon before horse
I became dragon
Of our intercourse
She was the cart—I was the ox
With a new-found freedom
I built a kingdom
From tumbled disordered blocks
I tore castles down
Built them inverted in ground
Turned backward the hands
Of clocks
I spread my new vision
Borne on glassy veined wings
My song was transported
In the buzz the bees sing
My art they inscribed
With their ink-dipped bee stings
I became God
You are my flowers
Your colors my whim
To be cultivated
Or plucked
To be rejected or fucked
Such is my power
Shapes you ape hapless
The Void opens mapless
This box was inside me
No longer you ride me

You won't make me hide me

Now I am inside thee

Inside me you'll see"

Throughout this the face had gradually enlarged until now the mouth alone filled the screen, the pores over the lip like craters, the lips hideously seamed and split. The mouth opened, wide, wider, the image still enlarging, the blackness inside the mouth becoming a cavern…starless space. Black empty screen.

More spotty applause.

"This guy's kind of baroque," mumbled Black.

"Kind of sick," opined Opal.

"Ow—shit." Black slapped at the back of his neck, twisted in his chair. A small brown moth bobbed as if on a string—an indigenous blood-drinking variety. He swatted at it and lost sight of it. "Fucking guy. I hate three-dimensional art."

"Is it over or what?" said Opal, as though cheated.

Black saw that the jumpsuited man was bowing to a polite, half-convinced applause. Hesitant, sharing Opal's confusion and surprise. The figure turned and walked to the curtain, slipped through it; gone. The empty cereal box remained open.

The lights came up. "That's it," Black marveled. "Ha. What a genius, huh? I've never been so moved."

"I've never seen such a bowel movement. There's Vern." Opal and then Black rose from their seats to catch up with Woodmere and Beak, who were already walking up front to the stage, while the rest of the small crowd milled about chatting or trickled back reluctantly the way they had come—these people no doubt convincing themselves and their companions that they had appreciated and understood the brilliance of Toll Loveland, and hadn't really wasted their money or time on something they hadn't enjoyed or comprehended in the slightest. There was almost a lost, disoriented dejection to their solemn filing out. Two security guards who worked for Mrs. Greenberg appeared to make certain that no one decided to do some exploring beyond the lit path. Another guard stepped in front of the stage to block the health agents.

Woodmere flipped his badge out. "Step aside, gramps."

Opal trotted up beside him. He was replacing his badge and slipping out a big semi-automatic pistol. Opal asked, "You hear anything about a woman shot in the ass with a dart in front of those banks?"

"Witness said she was pulled inside the black car and driven off."

"God."

"A guy in the row behind us recognized it, too," said Beak, his own handgun emerging. "I heard him tell his girl he was gonna call the force down here."

"Want me to call them, too?"

"We got it under control," growled Woodmere, flashing his eyes onto Black. "You and the girl go around the other side."

Woodmere and Beak stole around to the left of the curtain behind the makeshift stage, Opal and Black trotting softly around to the right, their guns sliding out. Those remaining in the audience stood staring as though this were a part of the performance.

After allowing a moment for agents Black and Cowrie to reach their side, Woodmere swung around the corner of the curtain with gun extended in both fists. Opposite him, Black appeared in a mirrored pose. Their eyes briefly touched. Nothing behind the curtain. "Fuck," snarled Vern, whirling to Beak. "He must be in the plant somewhere—get those security clowns to bring the lights up. Tell 'em to escort out the rest of the audience and secure all doors they can."

"I'll call the police now," Opal intoned grimly, lowering her snub.

"Yeah yeah," grumbled Vern. "But first go grab that ticket girl—cuff her."

Opal darted off. Black came beside Vern to look off into the impenetrable blackness as though standing on a wharf's edge gazing out at a night sea. Vern was unfolding a pair of sunglasses from his pocket, put them on, flicked a tiny switch and a red dot of light appeared in the center of each lens.

"I'm going to look around before the fucking troops come in and treat us like meat inspectors." And with that, Vern plummeted into the darkness and disappeared.

Black was left with little to do. He had a flashlight, but what was the use? Loveland had planned this all out, mapped it, designed it. Vern would become lost and Loveland would already be out of the building. Rather than follow Vern, Black trotted down the lighted path past the last of the filing out audience, past Opal hand-cuffing the unresisting, pale and gaping ticket girl (Opal nodded to him that everything was under control) and out into the parking lot. Starting cars. Black bolted for his, long legs pumping, dodged out of the way of one departing hovercar.

Black knew the password for Opal's car, keyed it in, wished they'd brought his helicar with its capacity for greater elevation, its spotlight beacon. He wheeled the car around, drove toward the plant. He activated the magnetic, rotating health agent lamp and placed it on the roof to keep the security guards from opposing him. In a vehicle he could more quickly cover the area around the plant and its various doors and loading docks.

Ahead, a side door of blank metal, no insignia. Black paused the car, stepped out, pistol drawn, scanned around him, swept the flashlight. A high chain-link fence, barbed wire atop it—and the fence hummed softly, giving off the faint bluish glow of a mild current. Beyond this, dead yellow grass stretching off to a patch of black woods, a gray marshy stream cutting through the grass, sulphurous yellow mist curling up from the stream in ectoplasmic exhalations. Not a likely escape route. Black moved to try the door. Rattled the knob—locked. As he began to turn the door flung open behind him and a voice hissed, "Freeze!"

Arms raised above his head, pistol dangling by its trigger guard, Black swallowed a baseball of saliva. "Who are you?" he asked, expecting a bullet to plow into his nape at any moment.

"Oops," said the voice. "Sorry—you're one of those health agents, aren't you?"

Black faced the teenaged security guard with a drawn-out sigh. "Yes. Stay on that door; no one gets out. Be careful what you shoot—one of our people is running around in there."

"Right. I only have a tranq gun anyway."

"Thank God."

Black stopped the car next at a small loading dock in the rear of the plant; not the primary loading dock. This one had a large, powerful waste disintegrator backed up to one of the dock openings. Again, the docks faced toward those bent-down tall yellow weeds and the black patch of forest, partitioned off by the charged fence. Out there in the weeds was an abandoned empty husk of a helicar, its plastic shell not corroding but tangled in brown vines, as if they were tentacles that had reached up to pluck it out of the air and had spider-like sucked out its juices, leaving only an exoskeleton. Unlikely and illogical, but Black imagined that something was crouching inside that husk, peeking out at him. Well, unlikely it was Loveland, at least—maybe a dog, or a mutant. Black briefly passed his beacon over it but saw only skull socket windows.

He mounted the dock platform—the two accessible doors were locked.

Black continued skirting the plant in his car. One door was open and a security guard stood in the threshold. Black paused, the police lamp swinging green light around over his head like helicopter blades, out across the weeds, briefly restoring them to life, but barely touching the black trees—a solid wall of barbed branches. Leaning out, he asked, "Was that door open when you found it?"

"No sir—I opened it. It was locked."

Finally there was only the main loading dock. Two gigantic tanks on elevated scaffolding towered above him, the dock like a multiple vagina between the skeletal legs, the four openings locked like a chastity belt, he discovered a moment later. What kind of liberties had Mrs. Greenberg allowed Loveland—a full set of keys? Impossible—the security guards must have supervised his comings and goings. How had he escaped? *Had* he escaped?

Black heard distant police sirens. Then he heard a gun blast, loud but muffled and distant, from inside the plant. Black charged to his car.

Opal was still with her captive. "Did you hear a gun?"

"Yes." Black walked up to her. "Where's Beak?"

"I don't know. Stay here, Monty, the police are coming. This has gotten too weird. It's murder, it's out of our hands."

Reluctantly Black obeyed her, glanced at the seated ticket girl, her hands clasped together on her knees. She avoided looking at him.

"You. Does Loveland have a gun?" he asked her.

"I don't know."

"Do you know anything about that woman he killed?"

"No, nothing…I'm not his friend, I don't know him, I just *wanted* to know him… I'm a fan of his art."

"Some art."

"Her name's Ivory Ebon. She's nineteen," Opal informed him. The girl's right eye was hidden under her jagged black hair; she seemed to want to pull all of her being under that projecting curtain to hide.

"Black," called a voice. He looked up. It was Vern approaching, his night glasses off, his pistol hanging loosely by his leg.

"Are you alright, did you hear a gun?"

"It was me." Vern stood before him. Black felt instinctive dread at what he saw in the older agent's face. It was doughy white, more agonizingly haggard and worn and bruised with perpetual shadow than usual. The eyes silently screamed, blinked hard as if swatting away the nearing bugs of tears. "I shot one of the guards, some stupid kid. Dead."

"Oh my God—Vern!" Black breathed.

Defensive anger leaped into Woodmere, his face becoming a nexus of angry lines converging at snarling mouth, flared nostrils and especially between eyes blazing with a fury which almost caused Black to step back from him. It was an inhuman anger, tremulous, too much for a man to contain. The Red War had struck him like lightning and still crackled inside him. Black found himself remembering the story of how Vern had cudgeled to death a trail guide who turned out to be an enemy spy—with a crowbar.

"The fucking kid popped out from behind a tank and he wasn't wearing his fucking hat! He should've been wearing his damn fucking clown hat!"

"Alright, man, ease it…ease it. Give me your gun, Vern."

"My *gun*? My *gun*? Do you think I'm sick or something, boy? You think I've lost it? You think I'm gonna go on some fucking psycho-vet berserk shooting spree and kill you and your little slice?"

Spit had hit Black in the face. His face remained cool but twitched inside. He held out his palm. "No, Vern, but the forcers might think that. Don't make them take it from you—you don't want that."

Woodmere cocked his head; the sirens were near. The taut lines loosened, his eyes brimmed again, looked ashamed. The heavy semi-automatic was handed over. "I'm sorry, man," he croaked. "Shit—that's it for me."

"It'll be alright," Black sighed.

The lights in the plant finally came on, a glaring flood that stimulated several moths from the show. They danced excitedly, frenzied, electrified in the air.

FOUR

From a machine in a small cafeteria Opal bought a coffee for herself and a hot mustard—a drink favored by the indigenous Choom—for Black. At a table sat their boss Captain Nedland, already with a coffee, Beak smoking, and Detective Churchill Jones, the investigator assigned to head the case, a drab and tired-looking man who was making no effort to halt the thinning of his hair. This was the police station of Precinct 4, nearest to the Greenberg plant, and it was the early hours of the morning.

"There is no sign of Loveland's escape, no prints on restricted door knobs, no indication of his still being in hiding inside, according to our scans," said Jones. "The girl Ivory Ebon submitted to truth scan and she isn't lying; she isn't an accomplice, never even slept with the suspect. She's been released for the time being."

"Does she know where Loveland lives?" asked Nedland.

"No, and he isn't on current census. His last residence on file has been rented by someone else. The identity of the woman in the film your agents watched, who was seen being dragged into a black hoverlimo, has also not been determined...but the forensics lab at Precinct 34 has sent us an interesting development. Especially interesting to you people."

"What's that?"

"Blood on the scene has been found to contain the mutstav six-seventy STD."

"Ha," said Nedland.

"What about Vern?" Beak grumbled unpleasantly.

"We'll probably release him tomorrow pending trial, which shouldn't go too badly for him, but of course you are required to take his badge."

"It's done," said Nedland gloomily. He and Vern had collided on numerous occasions, and Vern had showed Nedland his fury face more than once, but Vern had been one of his best agents. That was over now, for good, as Woodmere himself had predicted.

"We'll be working closely with P-34 on this and we'll keep you people informed, particularly about that blood, but for now we should be all set," Jones told them.

"Shouldn't we be in on questioning Mrs. Greenberg?"

"We'll keep you informed if there appears to be a need."

Captain Nedland nodded. The Health Agency and Punktown's police force often had a conflict of interest, or at least a competition—the forcers resentful, the agency felt, of their authority to investigate and arrest, and sometimes exterminate.

"Now, could one of your agents submit to a memory imaging session so we can review and copy Loveland's *Cupid* film?"

Black was tired and reluctant, though interested in the outcome, and if Opal stayed he would have to stay. Fortunately Beak volunteered. His memory of the Loveland show would be located in his mind, extracted, projected and recorded via computer hook-up. The film could then be slow-framed, frozen, blown up, etcetera. The entire Loveland presentation could be minutely examined, scrutinized for clues as to how he had executed his magic escape.

"Well," sighed Detective Jones, "I guess the rest of you can go home." Jones nodded at Black, who had given him Agent Woodmere's pistol. Like all health agents' firearms, Vern's gun took a photo of its target every time the weapon was discharged, the photo transmitted instantly to Health Agency headquarters—this to insure that the agent did not misuse his authority to kill, owing to the consideration that the gun's plasma rounds could leave no body and thus no evidence and an agent might otherwise kill anyone he/she desired. Anyone found overriding the photo insurance mechanism was subject to immediate termination, by law, though it was still done and Vern had been caught once and merely quietly suspended by Nedland for several weeks. His gun had sent an alarm to headquarters with his tampering; he'd been drinking at the time. When he had shot the teenaged guard his gun had been loaded with lead bullets, however, not plasma. Vern liked lead. Lead freed blood. He'd laughed this once with a teasing menace to agents Black and Cowrie.

Crushing out his cigarette, Beak mumbled, "Let's get this brain drain over with, huh man?"

"See you all later," Opal drawled, rising. "Good luck, inspector."

"Thank you all for your help and patience with this."

Black and Nedland exchanged parting glances; Nedland gave Black a sigh and a shrug.

They lived on the third floor of a huge tenement house, on a short street on a hill lined on both sides with tenement houses of similar character. Old, but pretty well kept. There were actually large trees on this short road, thick-trunked, leafy and shady in the warm seasons, copper and brass in fall, though the street was only a few minutes away from the town's deep core, far from being in the suburbs. One man owned five of the big houses, three of these being sectioned into low-income housing apartments. He was allowed certain tax write-offs for providing this service to the town. Black and Opal lived in one of his two high-rent buildings. The situation was the same with the rest of the street, and so the inhabitants of this pretty, tree-punctuated oasis were an odd yin/yang mixture of quiet, well-paid, work-oriented office types and loud, poor, jobless types. But their landlords were very strict and the outsides as well as the insides of the houses remained surprisingly clean, so that it was hard to tell from the street which types lived in which houses.

Outside the door, Opal drew her snub-nose. Black looked at her.

"We were VT stars tonight, remember?" she explained curtly.

"Oh yeah—I want to look at that before we go to bed."

"You look at it—I'm exhausted." Opal tapped out their code on the panel by the door. The hall beyond was black, seemed empty. She led the way in.

At each of the three landings there was a huge, long open window which made the landings more like porches. Black and Opal had to pass through one and two to reach their porch, but no one ever had cause to come up to theirs. It was dark, but out through the breezy window the Earth-founded colony-city of Punktown loomed up its thousands of thousand-eyed heads to eavesdrop on them, filling the sky. Even now lights burned. There were people out there working, watching VT, having sex, laughing, crying, dying…so distant. The town never slept, just rested various limbs, laid down assorted parts of its immense body at different times.

On the broad sill were potted plants, a few more hanging from the top frame. Opal. The rules against pets were firm, but often a certain stray cat sunned itself sphinx-like on the sill; Opal put out food and water every day. Feral, Opal had named him, though he was becoming ever less so. He hadn't come around for a week now at least. His water was ice. His food untouched. Someone took him in, Black kept assuring Opal. Yeah—to eat, she'd said.

In the summer they sat out here in lawn chairs, in bathing suits, drank beer, cooked on a grill, watched a small VT, fucked on the mattress from the small guest bed that Black slept on when they fought. In the summer on weekends they spent whole lazy days out here, fucking again and again until they sweated and filled the porch with their smell, and then they would sleep naked on the mattress until day. Have coffee, smoke. Listen to their trees rustle. This porch was Black's favorite place in all of the world that he knew.

But it was cold now, lawn chairs and VT put away, the mattress back on the guest bed. Opal let them into their apartment and put a few lights on. She moved directly into the bedroom to change for sleep.

Black played back the recorded vid of tonight's news, scan-forwarded to the story on the extermination of Bum Junket.

The tube station's security cameras showed a good, clean picture, and the tapes were replayed at a higher magnification, one zooming in on Bum's disintegration. Opal was hardly noticed, but Black's face filled the screen. He groaned, wagged his head. He'd have to shave the new mustache and goatee. And he liked himself with them.

Angered male prostitutes from Red Station were interviewed. Then an outraged spokesperson from a gay community organization. Then a cool, rational someone from the Health Agency—a public relations person. Black heard Opal pad up behind him.

"A lot of attention, huh?"

"M-670 is great for ratings," said Black. "The news people probably creamed their panties when they heard about this."

"Did they mention our names?"

"No, but I got enough close-up time to make a movie star drool."

"Yeah, but they've got you cast as the villain. Let's see how monstrous they think we are when this thing spreads up to their doorsteps. It's a flood, and we're trying to save them from getting washed away. We plug up one hole in the dam and they act like…"

Black leaned backwards on the ottoman he sat on and smiled at Opal upside-down. "You're so romantic when you start getting poetic."

"Fuck you."

"Oh—you *are* in a romantic mood, aren't you?"

"I'm wiped. I'm going to bed." She padded away barefoot in her baggy men's pajamas. Black saw a mellow light go on in the bedroom. His eyes remained on the mellowly lit doorway framed in darkness. Then he rose, went to quickly brush his teeth in the bathroom. He'd made a decision and he had to race sleep. If she got too far she wouldn't want to turn back. He was already as afraid to pursue it as a shy boy asking a beautiful girl for a first date—dreading the very probable rejection. But he'd been aroused earlier in the shower, and he always remained subconsciously aroused for hours, days, until release. Sex was as important to him as anything in life, more important than nearly anything else.

She was curled away from him, small like a clenched fist, to begin with. She knew when he didn't put the lights out, put his hand on her hip instead as he curled beside her, his front almost touching her back.

"I'm tired, Monty. I mean it."

"Just quick. Fifteen minutes, I promise."

"No. Why can't you ever respect my 'no'?"

"I have, many times."

"Yeah, after I had to say 'no' a half-dozen times. Maybe some day I'll say 'no' once and you'll respect it."

"Maybe some day you'll say 'yes' without me having to ask a half-dozen times."

"There's been plenty of times I've said 'yes' right away, and plenty of times when it was my idea."

"Not lately."

"I'm not your wife; it's not my obligation to keep up with your needs. I do it when I want to. Why should I sacrifice?"

"Where's the fucking sacrifice?"

"Making myself a fist for you to masturbate in. Fifteen minutes. You just want to use me to get yourself off."

"Only when you don't want to participate. It's not my preference. I get nervous, stressed out easily. It builds up. Getting off calms me down. It all goes out in my sperm."

"And into me. Then you make me tense and upset."

"Hey, I'm sorry I aggravate you so much." He had already taken his hand off her. Now he rolled the other way, presenting his back to hers.

"You're selfish."

"Only because you won't let me *give* to you."

"Yeah, blame me for all your problems."

"Maybe we shouldn't live together."

"Oh, I see. You can't live with someone unless they fuck you, huh? I'll leave if you really want, Monty."

"No—I don't. Go to sleep. I'm sorry. Man. Fifteen fucking minutes."

"Alright, here." Opal rolled onto her back, arched her hips in the air to jerk down her pajama bottoms. She kicked them off, pushed the ball away with her feet. The bed rocked. She lay with her bare legs scissored out. "Come on, here I am."

"You're being cruel now. Forget it."

"I'll do it, alright? Fifteen minutes. I don't want to have to say 'no' more than once next time—understand? I shouldn't even have to negotiate with my body."

"I can't do it now if you're gonna be resentful."

"I'm not—I'm just *tired*, can you understand that? I *like* sex but I *need* sleep."

"I *need* sex. I never met a woman, *never*, who liked sex more than a man."

"Oh, you poor tormented species." Black rolled onto her. He had peeled off his underpants, all he'd had on, another sign of his intent. "We just use sex to hook a man for what we really want—to get married, or get the man's money, or have a baby, then we'll never fuck again. Him, anyway. You told me a similar theory once. Well, I admit it, you were right. I've just told you the sacred age-old secret of our society...now I'll have to kill you."

Black smiled. She was dry and tight but she let him in a little, more, more, her tissues still resisting him a bit like a castle door resisting a battering ram, and then he was through, gliding slickly in. Her hair was tousled on the pillow; he smoothed it clear of her forehead so he could look at her face.

It didn't always work out this way when she gave in to him, but she ended up holding him tighter, pulling on his bottom, stripping off her own pajama top and climaxing twice—as first he moved down her body to bury his nose in her scratchy dark blond hair (he couldn't breathe, his brain ballooned with blood, and when she began to writhe and buck, twist into him and away from him as if in delicious agony, he was afraid as always she'd injure his neck, but he kept his mouth pressed to her) and then as he rubbed her "love button", as he called it, with his finger and thrust into her simultaneously. But despite tonight's success he knew better than to believe that Opal Cowrie was one to be overpowered at the touch of a button. He hadn't won a battle—she'd shown him mercy, and taken some for herself, too.

As she had said, they weren't married, but she had never insisted for long that he sleep on the guest bed. There was some kind of intimate bond. Whether it had a few last scraps of romance in it, or was just the affection of friends—of two who had chosen to be companions in life—for now, Black felt sure that Opal loved him. He loved her, he felt…but the exact nature of his love was only a little less ambiguous to him than hers, now. That love was some clear-cut, easily identifiable feeling was, to him, an optimistic fantasy perpetuated by song-writers and actors, a lesser reality blown up to mythical proportions, like religion, to make the emptiness of life more endurable.

There things stood for him, and he didn't anticipate a change in his feelings.

Sometimes after sex Black conked right out, sometimes he got up to listen to music, or watch VT and smoke, or read for an hour or two in a hot bubble bath…to soak off the unpleasant residue of sex. He got up, this time. Opal glanced around at him.

"Hey," he told her, "get some sleep, huh? You look tired."

"Asshole."

He shut off the light for her, cast her into darkness.

He resented sleep, anyway. He'd fight it, relent only when fully exhausted. Life was too short.

Of course, often he stayed up fighting sleep and was too tired for any kind of real enthusiasm the next day. So what was he winning by fighting?

Still, he couldn't stop it. He couldn't imagine lying down to sleep with a mind and body still somewhat fresh and hungry for consciousness. How could people mechanically lie down at a precise hour, shut off like a VT? Surrender? He'd squeeze every drop he could out of his consciousness first.

He prepared a hot bubble bath, a lava-like agony to lower himself into before the pain became delicious, and he sighed. Fixed to the pink-tiled wall facing him was a twenty-inch vidscreen. By his slippers on the rug outside the tub lay the remote control and a mug of hot mustard. He took up the remote.

Flip through the stations? Probably fruitless despite the infinity—just boundless junk, music vids and news. He thought to call up the novel he had been wading through for the past few months but was in a slow, drawn-out part and couldn't get past it. He considered calling forth one of the many movies in his chip collection, stored in the master vid unit in the parlor. Finally he held the remote closer to his mouth and said, "Let me see the tape from today—Bum Junket."

No new impressions or feelings came to him. As when he'd killed him, he couldn't see Bum Junket's face when the plasma bullet hit him. It was less dramatic than the fake plasma killings in action movies; again, almost gentle. I only put him out of his misery, Black reflected. Later on, soon enough, his wasting would have become more painful and horrible. He'd just made a dying man die sooner.

Of course, he was dying, too. All life began to die the moment it was born. Nevertheless, it didn't matter if Junket were already dying or not, so much, but that he'd been a threat to the health of the masses. That was the important thing. Black felt nothing but a general, numb strangeness in watching himself kill another person.

Too bad, he further reflected, it had been a homosexual. Again he watched the angry gay organization spokesperson condemn the Health Agency "and its thugs." Women's groups, prostitute alliances (there were united organizations for every type of person except the utterly insane) would have been a little less likely to leap to the fore had it been the fugitive prostitute Auretta Here. But then, it would have been greater groups of the media instead.

Auretta Here.

"My God," said Black, sitting up in the bath, crossing his legs and holding the remote to his lips again. "Give me my filed stories on Auretta Here."

He sat rigid and watched the screen flicker with light, a blizzard blown against a window. Somewhere invisible hands flipped at a crazy speed, but precisely, through his chip collection. It took only seconds. The first story he'd taped on Auretta Here came on, the initial minute or so missing since he'd originally caught it in progress. Black was rapt, and awake.

A very attractive young woman sat in an armchair facing the camera, and was speaking in a haughty, tight voice, one stockinged leg hooked over the other. She wore huge black sunglasses as a disguise. She was a (dyed) blond. She was in someone's apartment and thus wasn't wear a coat.

"I am a free person with a mind and a will and a body that belong to me, and nobody…"

This wasn't the one. Black couldn't remember how many of her vids he had on chip, but he was sure he had the one he was thinking of. He told the VT to fast-scan. People flitted by, spoke and gestured at comical speeds.

"Wait!" The water of the tub sloshed against the sides. "Go back a few tape minutes, then let it play."

Uh-huh. There she was. Black cracked a smile like that which had both frightened and captivated Bum Junket with its suddenness.

"See?" said Auretta Here in a tone of sarcastic disgust, dangling a strip of condom packets from her pocketbook. "I make my customers wear these. But I have to have money to survive…and I *want* to survive until a cure can be found for this thing…"

She stood outside this time, her breath clouding. It was a blasted lot, looking like a bomb had leveled an old building. Maybe one had. Behind her was a charred sign for some kind of shop in Asian characters.

Yes, it was cold, and her (dyed) blond hair fell to the fuzzy shoulders of a short coat of silvery-blue fur.

Auretta Here was the woman struck with the arrow-camera in Toll Loveland's movie *Cupid of Death.*

Blond hair, black glasses, fur coat, even blue jeans. She was dressed for her death now and didn't even know it.

A scrap of paper blew into the scene, around her knees. No; it was a large white moth. He remembered that detail now from when he'd seen this before, but why hadn't he asked himself then—where did a summer insect come from in the winter?

As surely as an artist leaves his signature in the corner of his painting, Black realized, Toll Loveland had sneaked his signature, a moth, into this—one of his movies.

He hadn't woken Opal up, and had waited until today to tell Nedland. After all, this was only one of many, many cases the agency had to deal with.

In Black's helicar, gliding low over the tops of congested early-morning ground traffic, Opal said, "I didn't know if Bum Junket's extermination would scare her into turning herself in, or scare her deeper into hiding so she'd stop with the damn vids. Or, for that matter, if it will scare people into cooperating, or scare them away from HAP."

"Both. People react differently."

"Seeing us liquidate Junket may give other people the idea that it's alright for them to kill the infected. Is that it with Loveland? Why pick her to kill?"

"Ask an art critic. I don't figure him for a vigilante—why tape her and mail her vids to her lawyer, then? It doesn't make sense. Yet."

"Well, we don't have to be afraid that she'll go deeper into hiding, now. But with her murdered, we'll be seeing her old vids on VT all over again. Let's hurry up and bag Loveland so they can get on with the inevitable VT movie about her."

"It may turn out to be a movie about him."

Jose in the guard shack waved them through the back gate, his mask-like face attempting a smile. An ex-health agent, he was lucky to have a face again after losing it during a terrorist attack on the HAP-operated air factory. A weaker plasma than Black and Opal had in their revolvers, but enough to eat a face to the bone. They'd cloned Jose a new face, and it was good for what his insurance company was willing to pay, but he'd remained too shaken up for field duty. Black thought about Vern Woodmere for a moment while lowering his car into a clear spot.

The turquoise building was small by Punktown standards—some of the city's spires lost in the clouds, even from the highway looking like columns supporting the sky—but loomed over them as they approached it in its freezing dark shadow. "I need a coffee before we tell anybody anything," Opal stated.

Black inserted his badge card in a slot by the outer door, which slid open obligingly. A small foyer with potted plastic plants. As the door slid closed behind them, the cold air was shut out, unwelcome. And as the door slid shut, a whooping alarm sprang up like an invisible beast pointing its finger at them, jumping up and down, startling Black as he was slipping out of his overcoat.

Opal looked to him. The whoop was a major scan alarm.

Black didn't advance to the next sliding doors, knowing they were locked. In moments two security guards appeared through the clear plastic, planted themselves threateningly, showing no sign that they recognized these two, though Black and Opal recognized them. A voice entered the sealed vestibule.

"Please enter the door opening on your right."

A door had indeed glided open, and there a man in a white jumpsuit, white gloves and gray boots with a fish-bowl helmet over his head smiled thinly and beckoned them with his arm. "In here, please," he said, again not admitting that he knew them. They knew him as Pablo, a scan technician.

"What is it, Pablo?" Black said, not moving yet. He'd gone through standard decontamination countless times, coming or going, but they had been stopped before they could even get that far. Only upon returning from an investigation at the site of a major biochemical leak or something of that nature had this ever happened to him before—not first thing in the morning. Greenberg—their chemical spill, he thought. He'd gone from Greenberg to the police station to home, no decontamination but for a bubble bath.

"Please come in."

Black followed Opal when she began to move. "What is it, Pablo?" she said this time.

"The scan reads mutstav six-seventy STD."

"What, *in* one of us?" Black stopped face-to-face with Pablo. He looked ready to fight, as if wrongfully accused of a crime.

"In both of you," Pablo said. "Inside, please."

FIVE

There wasn't much on the walls of the little conference room. Montgomery Black stared at a picture titled *Steamboats Passing at Midnight (On Long Island Sound).* Currier and Ives. A faraway, simpler time. Things now were better in some, even many, ways. But they had been content then with Currier and Ives, hadn't needed a Toll Loveland. The picture was on a calendar.

Nedland was on the vidphone, finished up his call when Detective Churchill Jones was admitted into the room. Coffee in hand, Jones nodded to Black and Opal in greeting. "I'm terribly sorry to hear about this—it's awful."

"It was in the moth that bit Agent Black," said Nedland, standing up as Jones sat down. "One of the moths released during the show; a blood-drinking type. I just sent a crew down to Greenberg to spray for any that are left, and hopefully to take a few specimens alive."

"Yes, good, we'd need them for evidence come a trial."

The murder weapon, thought Black.

"One bit Agent Black, and then the disease was passed on to Agent Cowrie in his semen."

"I see," said Detective Jones, obviously a little surprised and embarrassed. "Were agents Beak or Woodmere bitten?"

"Beak was, but he's nonhuman, not of a threatened species. He'll get sick but the virus won't take, and will die of its own. We're printing up circulars to distribute through the art community and running some newspaper articles in the hopes of alerting the others who attended the *Pandora's Box* show and Loveland's earlier show *The Godfucker.* Yesterday on Block Avenue agents Woodmere and Beak investigated a dead mutant found in a vacant lot, with a ticket stub for *The Godfucker* in his wallet, as you know. Genetic disruptor drugs, encoded invader chromes. Mr. Loveland really wants to reach out and affect his audience."

"Infect his audience," said Opal.

"M-670 renders less dramatic results to its victims than what he did to the man on Block Avenue, but the attraction with M-670 is its highly communicable properties and its uncanny resistance to treatment. Probably he didn't think that it would be discovered so quickly, but then he had been told that health agents would be at the show for security, due to the show's location. And anyway, even if we can locate all the other people who saw the show, by then the infected will have probably passed the virus on. It takes hold fast, incorporates itself into the genetic material of the victim, and essentially becomes part of its host. If Black and Cowrie had come here directly after the show, we could have destroyed the virus with little cellular damage to Black, and Cowrie wouldn't have become infected. But it had too many hours to sink in and do its thing while they slept."

"I thought you people have said biting insects couldn't transmit 670. Loveland hasn't adapted this thing, has he?"

"God forbid, no. No need. An insect can't support the virus for long, a matter of hours, a day or two at most, but he could have infected the moths only hours before the show. He's something of a genius, Toll Loveland."

"Mm," grunted Jones, stealing a glance at Opal Cowrie's clamped, rigid profile. "So he was the one who taped Auretta Here's vids for her, then. All along."

Captain Nedland swivelled the vidphone's screen, touched a button. The tape Black had sought out: Auretta Here in the ruin-strewn lot.

"A moth," said Jones.

"Black spotted it at home. He made the connection."

"Good work."

Black didn't reply.

"The lot," said Nedland. "See that old store sign behind her? The others off at the back of the lot? That's the lot in Block Ave. where the mutant was found. The mutated victim was put there on purpose, rather than dying there naturally. So maybe it wasn't contaminated while at *The Godfucker,* and maybe never even went—just had the ticket stub planted on it. Who knows?"

"Playing games. He was giving us clues in Auretta Here's vids of what he was going to do, and laughing at our ignorance of it."

"You've seen all her vids, right? Remember this one?" Nedland scanned forward. He, Black and Opal had spotted this an hour ago. Jones leaned closer, not knowing what to look for as Auretta Here stood in a parking lot speaking to the camera, so much like a movie star in her dark glasses and fur. Shrubs behind her framed the end of the parking lot, and a radically leaning pyramid sculpture poked its slanted tip over the bushes. Jones picked right up on that.

"That's the art museum on, ah, Hill Way...the Hill Way Galleries." A man crossed the lot behind Auretta, hands in pockets, and curiously glanced over at the camera. "Hey!" said Jones, who had viewed Beak's extracted memory of *Pandora's Box.* Nedland hit a button to freeze frame.

As with that film director of old, Alfred Hitchcock, Toll Loveland couldn't resist putting in a cameo appearance.

Nedland enlarged and centered the frame on Loveland's handsome young face. It was smiling.

"I doubt he's in on this, but I'll get a hold of Auretta Here's lawyer," grumbled Jones, disgusted by now with Toll Loveland's antics. "Just a dupe. The question is… was Here a dupe, too, or was she in on it at least up to a point? Pardon the pun."

"I think," Black spoke up quietly, "he knew her or had met her, knew she had M-670 and…"

"Sure he didn't give it to her to start with?"

"No, I doubt it…why the focus on her, killing her on camera and all? She became known to him, she had what he wanted, he prompted her to go on VT to protest her rights, with her not knowing he was directing her in a Toll Loveland VT mini-series. When he was ready he took the M-670 from her to infect the bugs, at the same time killing a witness to his whereabouts and making her a part of his overall artistic statement."

"Is that what all this is?" Jones sneered.

"You should try to find all of Auretta Here's friends and fellow prosties you can," suggested Nedland.

"Precinct 19 is running the Auretta Here case, and P-34 is where she was hit with that dart or whatever and abducted—I called them before I left and they'll send their people here any time now. But I know P-19 has already questioned friends about Auretta Here."

"But not about Toll Loveland. We can show them this vid." Nedland gestured at Loveland's smiling face, filling the VT screen, his smile smug and amused as if he could see and hear them.

Jones punched the button to banish that face. If only it could be so easy. "And what about these two?"

Pacing the tiny room, Nedland lifted the page of the calendar to view the Currier and Ives print for next month. His back to the others, he said, "Agent Black has volunteered to a daily check-in program. Agent Cowrie has opted, as is her right, for a weekly program, since she'll be staying with her parents in the suburbs. Of course they've…both turned in their badges. But we're being optimistic about a cure. Our teleporter filtering efforts will probably come to fruition, especially with people who've been teleported somewhere previously and already have their uninfected code in a computer. We're trying to find codes in the past for Black and Cowrie from a few places."

Jones hated to ask, but agents Black and Cowrie looked to be taking this pretty well…like professionals. After all, certain doctors had contracted the virus also from their infected patients. Hospital patients had the right to ask their doctors if they had M-670. The doctors, however, were not legally obligated to answer. There were infected doctors still practicing. But what Jones asked was, "What's the longest a victim has lived so far—a year, was it?"

"Since the first cases we know of, appearing fourteen months ago, the longest a victim has lived once afflicted was just short of twelve months. People are affected differently, according to their individual physical state. Healthy people usually last longer, but sometimes a drug addict will live eight months and a healthy person will last two. Many factors."

Black noticed that Jones glanced at him again. He had also noticed that not once since Jones had arrived—and even longer than that—had Opal looked at him.

Captain Nedland's meeting with Jones and the detectives from Precincts 34 and 19 was interrupted by a call from Agent Beak.

"I'm in Path-4, Captain. I've been trying to locate family or friends of this guy Tate Hurrea, the mutant from Block Ave.? Well, he's in no phone book, no computer, nothing. In fact, his government index number is a fake…at least, it doesn't belong to him. All his ID in the wallet turned out to be forged."

"Interesting."

"So I kept looking to find his name somewhere, anywhere. Tate Hurrea, Tate Hurrea…"

"Yes?"

"Tate Hurrea." Beak pronounced it slowly.

"So?"

"Auretta Here."

"Shit! Is it?"

"Path-4 has found evidence that the blob on Block Ave. at one time had M-670. The body's in no shape to check for an arrow wound in the behind, but I'd guess she wasn't killed in the street after all. Loveland took the mutstav, and then when he was done with her he gave her the genetic disruptors and mutant chromes and dumped her to die in the lot with the fake wallet."

"Playing games," Jones repeated disdainfully.

"It's his idea of art," said Nedland. "He's weaving patterns."

"He's like a psycho on a rooftop with a paintbrush instead of a rifle," Jones said, admiring his own analogy.

"Good work, Beak," said Captain Nedland. He considered paging Black and Opal in case they were still in the building, but what was the use in that? They were both off the case.

It was no one's break-time, fortunately, and this section's little cafeteria with its six tables was empty. They had come here together; Opal had muttered that she wanted a coffee. Black ordered a juice instead of hot mustard, which sometimes upset his stomach. It wasn't good for his health, and he had to cling to his health now. The more time he bought, the better his chances of being around when they found a vaccine and cure.

He fought not to smoke, chewed at a nail instead. He felt nauseous. He could feel it in him, rotting him, he imagined, could *hear* each cell as it crinkled up black and dead. It made him want to run and scream, run from it, but he had to sit still and listen to it eat him like ants crawling all over his body and face. It was equally maddening watching Opal's shuttered, averted face and trying to read her thoughts. He would have to lance her with probes.

"I'm sorry," he said.

"It wasn't your fault," she said, not looking at him, sounding irritated to talk.

"You didn't want to have sex. I pushed you into it. If I hadn't, the scanners would have detected it in me before I could give it to you."

"If we hadn't fucked last night, we would have this morning, probably. Having sex was normal for us. It was inevitable for me to catch it."

"One night. I should have waited for one fucking night." He wasn't faking it, wasn't manipulating her to sympathize with him or exonerate him for his guilt. He was a little beyond wanting to be reassured that he was innocent. He was convinced that he was guilty, beyond the realm of exoneration. He just wanted her to know he was sorry…forgiveness was too much to ask for. He felt sure he would vomit soon, was conscious of the portable trash zapper near their table. He also wanted to cry. "One fucking night I couldn't wait," he hissed.

"It's *his* fault, not yours. They'll find a cure soon…how long can it be before they find a teleporter filter?" Opal's coffee shivered in her cup as she lifted it to sip. "I'll just pick up a few things at the apartment—I won't need much."

"Do you want me to come with you? Help carry things into your mother's place?"

"No, I can manage."

"I'm sorry." It seemed a race now, vomit or tears. Which would win?

"I know! Alright? I know. They'll find a cure—this is nothing."

"Don't drink coffee, Opal, it isn't good for you," he found himself babbling.

"Yes, doctor." Opal stood and dropped it, barely sipped, in the zapper. The cafeteria door slid open and a guard leaned in a little. He looked like he'd been searching for them.

"Ah, excuse me, but I was asked to tell you not to use the staff cafeteria, please, or wander unescorted in the building. There's a number of visitor and patient caf…"

"We're finished." Opal brushed roughly past him. Black darted after her, forgetting his nausea and tears, but desperate.

"Opal, let me drop you off at the apartment. Then I'll leave you alone, uninterrupted."

She didn't reply but allowed him to walk beside her.

"Idiot," the guard hissed, going to their abandoned table to throw Black's forgotten juice container in the zapper. He sprayed down the tabletop with a bottle of disinfectant from a shelf.

In front of their tenement house, Opal had her door cracked open as soon as Black's vehicle came to rest. "Are you gonna stay here?" she asked.

"Yeah."

"I'll be in touch." She was out of the helicar and walking up their driveway, where her car was parked. She hadn't looked at him directly since the conference, and didn't look back now.

Black was going to call after her to take care, something of that nature, but lifted the helicar high and drove off into the cold air before she could come back and see the tears capping his eyes. He felt certain that for one reason or another, he would never see Opal again.

Just inside the ground floor hall, Opal remembered something and hurried back out into the driveway, but Black's car was gone, no longer in sight even in the air. Well, she could leave him a note, and that was of course better anyway. She had wanted to ask him to keep on putting food and water out for Feral, just in case.

Black both dreaded and hoped to find Opal still at the apartment when he returned from his driving two hours later, and was relieved and disappointed to find that she wasn't. The sight of the note quickened his pulse with dread and hope again, but its message only depressed him, especially its futility. How could she still harbor hope?

He had walked for a time through the park. Last spring he and Opal had come here to walk and had watched a couple being married on a radically arched bridge over a fabricated stream in which aquatic birds bobbed, scudding under the laden bridge which Black had joked might collapse under the congregation. The stream widened and there were a few grassy, bushy, tree-shaded little islands in it almost close enough to jump to, but not quite. The submerged child in him had awakened to yearn for the exploration and temporary colonization of them.

Now they were dismal, the trees like the masts of sunken ships; maybe he could reach them across the frozen stream, but who'd want to? There was still snow gathered around the trees in the park like a photographic negative of shade. Black liked the change of seasons, that it wasn't always artificially warm and temperate like it was in many planet colonies (though violent storms and too extreme blizzards were not allowed despite those who liked even these manifestations of weather), but walking through the park he couldn't see the justification in prolonging this bleak limbo.

Now he was home, and warm, and alone.

She hadn't taken everything, as he'd thought she would despite what she'd said about taking just a few things. She'd left clothes. Things on the walls of the kitchen (but was that because she considered them *their* things, instead of only hers?), decorations elsewhere. She either intended to come back to live here later, or come back to remove the rest of her belongings…or she didn't believe she'd live long enough to need all these things.

No longer crying, numb and tired, Black made himself a drink and sat down in front of the VT, watching it but listening to the soft, soothing bubbling-gurgling of her (their?) aquarium. She had left her fish. Living eyes in the room with him, eyes connected to creatures she cared about. That made him feel both melancholy and a little less alone.

He dozed in the chair, woke, numbly watched VT, dozed, VT, dozed, VT, slept in the chair. In fact, he spent the next three days primarily in that chair, doing the same.

The second day he hadn't taken a shower, and remained in the T-shirt and sweat-pants he'd slept in until the next day, and he didn't shower or change that day either. He scuffed about in slippers. The sharp glinting whiskers on his cheeks were attempting to assimilate his mustache and goatee, a neglected hedge losing its trimmed definition. He had to force himself to eat, a little at a time, fighting the nausea that was mostly psychosomatic, as he still imagined he could feel his organs corroding like spoiled meat inside his refrigerator.

The only time he had left his apartment these three days had been to check into HAP as promised, and for these occasions he had added only socks, sneakers and an overcoat, and to hell with the rest and what anybody thought. He was sick—they'd understand. The first day, Nedland told him about Auretta Here. She was the blob of decaying mutated flesh found in the lot on Block Avenue. Other than that, no developments. The lawyer knew nothing of Toll Loveland, nor did Auretta Here's old friends and fellow prostitutes, even when shown tapes of Loveland's show and his cameo in Auretta's vid message.

"His name obviously isn't Toll Loveland," said Nedland, "It's just his latest 'phase.' Before, he was Vicelord Godfucker. The name he graduated under from P.U. was the same one he used at Paxton Polytech—Manuel Hung. Nothing before that. All previous addresses rented to new tenants; no family, still. No government registration. We're running his picture and voice through census files anyway to see if it eventually rings a bell somewhere, either here or Earth or the other colonies."

"He's still in town," said Black. "It wouldn't be any fun for him if he wasn't close to watch it all. He's got a new name, maybe a new face."

"And a new art project planned for the future, no doubt," muttered Nedland.

Black nodded grimly. "Mm."

On his third check-in visit, Nedland didn't come to see or talk to him. He showered in the decontamination area, the only place he had showered in the past two days, and this time had brought a change of clothes. He even shaved at HAP. Perhaps he was stalling, hoping that Opal would come in. She didn't.

He shaved off his mustache and goatee.

He went home to watch VT, listen to the aquarium and feel his organs rot in the vacant lot of his body like the corpse of Auretta Here.

It couldn't be kept a secret, of course—it was good ratings. Black was mentioned, though not by name, a celebrity again, but his face was not revealed...a reversal of before. This and the Bum Junket incident were not linked, his name not put to the executioner's face. Opal was mentioned... "a young female agent." Toll Loveland's face was shown—indeed, the entire *Cupid of Death* film from his *Pandora's Box* show was run on the news and talk shows. He must be ecstatic, thought Black. Loveland's smile in the vid where he crossed the art museum lot behind Auretta Here seemed broader and more mocking each time he saw it.

Probably all of those who had seen the show at Greenberg eventually came forward, unless some had gone out of town and were unaware of all this. They and as many of their sexual partners as could be rounded-up were tested. Thirty-five of the perhaps eighty people in the audience had been bitten and infected. Not too bad, considering the number who hadn't been. Of the rounded-up lovers and their subsequent lovers as thus far accounted for, however, another fifty-four people were diagnosed as having contracted M-670.

Many of the people who had seen *The Godfucker* came forward in desperation. Only two had M-670, and one had also been to the *Pandora's Box* show, had been bitten, the second being the girlfriend of another infected man who had seen *Pandora's Box,* though she herself hadn't. Nothing else wrong or unusual was detected in the remainder of *The Godfucker*'s audience.

At the Agency they offered to enroll Black in an outside counseling group for M-670 victims and their families and they proffered him a drug that would nullify his sex drive completely for as long as he took it. He turned down both offers, insulted greatly by the latter. After he had infected Opal, did they really think he'd go out and try to get laid? What did they think he was, Bum Junket reincarnated?

He had programmed his VT to tape anything and everything—news, talk shows, specials, even a music benefit—on M-670, and quickly filled up several chips, some shows having to be taped simultaneously, the news especially, on two or more channels. There were too many stations for him to scan himself, even though he spent the next few days in front of the VT as before.

But Black had seen it all before in the past fourteen months, and found himself switching the recorded shows off after a short while, watching some movie instead. The stories concerning Toll Loveland—and thus himself—he watched, of course…and he watched the six-hour music benefit, featuring Del Kahn and a few other favorite performers. But only three items he saw on VT really caught his interest, and these he encountered in random flipping.

The first was a critique of Toll Loveland's performance *Pandora's Box* in the art reviews of a trendy sort of net magazine Opal had subscribed to through their computer service. A little ways into it, Black had to start at the beginning again to believe what he was reading.

Toll Loveland was brilliant. Portraying the candy-like, chemical-ridden children's breakfast cereal *Screaming Pink Nazis* as a Pandora's box of flying poison (in place of the real cereal's rampaging holographic soldiers) was a biting statement on society and its merchandise, a stroke of genius. That Toll Loveland showed his face during the show only on a VT screen was further criticism of society's flat, VT-oriented presentation of life, shallow and inorganic and product-obsessed…not to mention a clever echo of the Auretta Here vids, his cameo appearance there. The symmetry between those vids and the blob on Block Avenue and the *Cupid of Death* film was praised. Loveland's so-called one-night-only show had actually been unveiled and running earlier in Here's vid messages, and still continued on through the infected M-670 victims. Loveland's creation was a pyramid, this critic said, growing higher and more awesome as the M-670 victims multiplied…though he correctly observed that the pyramid's growth would have been radically curbed by the Health Agency by now.

Holding the performance in the old Greenberg Products plant, retired after a chemical spill, was a splendid choice of stage. Again, that Loveland never once revealed his own flesh during the show was a brilliant comment on the passionless plastic of society. And *Cupid of Death* was "an encapsulated artwork all its own, a gem within a gem, a stunning masterpiece of erotic horror. The audience watched Loveland's arrow pierce Auretta Here's body full of M-670 even as moths filled like syringes with her infection pierced their unsuspecting flesh…"

All in all, Toll Loveland's *Pandora's Box* was a "masterwork of existential art."

The critic, incidentally, had not personally been to the show but had watched the entire piece played on various VT programs, as extracted from the memories of health agent Beak and others.

Black had a brief, harmless fantasy of showing up at the critic's door at midnight to let him know how he felt to be a block in Toll Loveland's brilliant pyramid. He imagined cutting himself and forcing the man at gunpoint to drink his blood…then he could be a part of the masterwork, too!

Browsing channels, Black came upon a face which filled the screen and halted him. It was a face that made Bum Junket's look well-nourished, and Black couldn't believe the man was still alive at this point…but he was in a hospital bed, obviously, a portion of a glowing monitor screen showing behind him. The eggshell of a skull, its hair only a few last wisps like cobwebs, rested on a pillow…the teeth grinned horribly from shrunken-back gums…the eyes were glazed and quietly, wearily frantic in skull socket pits. There were sores, one on the forehead patched with a bandage. Of course Black had seen worse things. Addicts of the drug "fish" deteriorated to something like this, their whole bodies shrinking but their arms and legs—mere sticks—lengthening, the skin going purple-black…ending up looking like mummified gibbons, and little larger than that. And he and Opal had found a headless corpse lying on the sidewalk outside the house in the gentle tree shade one morning when they were leaving for work. But this was personal. Black felt his nausea rise to the occasion. This might be a mirror of the future.

There was a phone number superimposed at the bottom of the screen, and the man was croaking words. Black listened, like a priest to a confession.

"I used to live for sex…it was my whole life. My job meant very little to me. I didn't have any male *friends*…if you were my friend, you were my lover. I didn't… hang around bathrooms or anything, but bars, clubs. I didn't know names, sometimes. I…couldn't tell you how many…"

A photograph of the victim as a boy replaced the face, and then one of the man as an adult, good-looking and smiling a smooth-skinned, chubby-cheeked boyish smile. Black heard himself groan. Back to the skeleton. A caption read *Two Days Later.* Days were years for this man. Black could see the patient had only hours to live. The eyes had no life, could have been glass. The clenched teeth could barely part, but still the man confessed his guilt, laid out his sins.

"My life…was wrong. Don't go to bed…with anyone unless you love them. Get married. Just one partner. I brought this on myself. You can't…don't let this happen to you. Even if they find a cure, there are so many other diseases…it's just not safe. Find one person…get tested…get married if you love each other. Being a homosexual…is wrong…it's a lie…it's unnatural. I'm sorry now."

The man's despair seemed to be the only strength holding these bones together now. Despair and utter self-loathing.

But Black knew what this was by now, and cursed under his breath. It was *very* much like a confession…sins admitted to be forgiven, and the soul thus cleansed for death.

Four hours later, read a caption on a black screen, *Martin died.*

"Scum," Black said, but not to Martin, feeling like he was the one who had been exploited.

Sure enough, a new face filled the screen. This one appeared shockingly broad and fleshy by comparison, so much so that the man's black little eyes were almost swallowed up in it. It seemed to contain a colossal fury, and Black recognized it, had seen it twisted and raging, spitting its venom as its owner—the Reverend Matt Cotton—paced his stage on VT.

"Martin did not die in vain. Martin realized his life's mistakes, and luckily our ministers found him out in his need and were there to guide him in his final months. He did not die in vain if he could be of help…to you. But what about you? Martin was able to free his soul from its shackles—you saw him. But he was lucky…"

A caption explained how the vid of this program, containing the interview with Martin, was available for a fifteen-munit contribution to Matt Cotton's ministry.

They had found him out, Black thought, like vultures found out a starving cow. Angels of mercy with buzzard wings.

"We can't magically be there at the last minute to save all of you, can we? So what about you?"

"Shut the fuck up." Black didn't change the channel; he shut the VT off entirely, pressing the button with such force that he might have been launching an atomic bomb on Matt Cotton's ministry. The colossal face vaporized.

He couldn't feel disgust with Martin for cooperating with them. The man was facing death without solace, and obviously with little hope of an afterlife until they came along and offered him that hope…for a price. The price of telling his story, so that others might come forward to be saved before death, be redeemed, they told him. And mostly, to prevent people from catching the virus in the first place.

But to do that they had to first make him resent himself, hate himself for the lifestyle that had brought him to this. He had to renounce his former self, like a criminal. Being a homosexual had been the crime.

And being promiscuous, too. Those were the two diseases Matt Cotton sought to save people from; M-670 was just a related consequence. A curse from God, Black had remembered seeing Cotton call it before, delivered to punish those sinners who were stupid and immoral enough to open up their arms and invite its embrace. Didn't they bring it on themselves, as Martin had been taught to say? Sure, thought Black. These people deserved to die of M-670…they *wanted* to die of it. Right down to the children born of M-670-infected parents, right down to doctors accidentally infected during their contact with victims. Oh, these people hadn't brought it on themselves? Well, that couldn't be helped. God had his work to do; he had sinners to gun down with his machine-gun, and it was regrettable if innocent bystanders were standing too close. Hey, it wasn't God's fault—it was the sinners who were spreading this thing.

Matt Cotton didn't want to stop M-670, Black mused, he *loved* it. It was the righteous wrath of God, it was God's golden sword, and no doubt Cotton would have loved to personally wield that sword. The disease was good, as Martin's eagerly exhibited suffering illustrated…it would help cut down on casual sex and prostitution

and discredit homosexuality more effectively than Matt Cotton's fifteen years of
televised preaching ever had.

Yes, Black thought, people did need to be warned about casual sex, prostitution.
But there were promiscuous homosexuals and there were monogamous homosexuals—
homosexuality in itself was no more a dangerous or immoral condition than
heterosexuality. And it wasn't even rampant promiscuous sex alone that Cotton railed
against, but premarital sex, living together out of religious wedlock, just sex in general.
Repressed, frightened little maggot. Probably dressed up in women's underwear while
he watched kiddie porn vids. His business wasn't preaching love and brotherhood
(Jesus? Jesus who?), but bullying people into hating themselves as much as he hated
them, and as much as he hated himself.

The third piece he chanced upon (when he reactivated the VT) lifted Black's
spirits a little, helped him to feel not so alone in his disgust and cold, steaming hatred.
It was more than the plastic concern of newscasters, some of whom might really
deeply care though it wasn't their job to show it. It was another magazine review of
Toll Loveland's show *Pandora's Box*…and this critic, Yancy Mays, *had* attended the
Greenberg plant performance in person.

He had attended *The Godfucker,* too, Black soon realized, and he knew then
who Yancy Mays was—the man Nedland had mentioned who had been checked for
abnormalities resulting from his attendance at *The Godfucker,* but who had only tested
positive for one thing…the M-670 he contracted from a moth bite while viewing
Pandora's Box.

Black wondered if he'd recognize his face if he met him. He began reading.

"I know what you're thinking…this guy isn't *exactly* unbiased, here. The
show was so bad it killed him. Assuming a cure can't be found in time to undo Toll
Loveland's artistry, but there's no sign of that yet and I've seen too many scary death
tolls to feel much optimism. However, I'm going to leave the moral issue out of it.
Yes, tempting as it is to vent my own individual fury and fear, I'll leave the outrage
to others. It's obvious how I feel anyway, isn't it? I will try to be as detached as I can
be. Not objective—I'm a critic of art, not a judge of a court trial. Criticism should be
approached and thought of as subjective, not objective…a personal viewpoint based
on the critic's opinions and tastes, not an attempt to manipulate the reader into the role
of a programmed sheep. But I will do my best to approach Toll Loveland's piece as art,
as he intended it, and not as an act of mass murder, which it is but which he obviously
also intended it to be. It may be best to remember that I also hated *The Godfucker,* at
which I wasn't murdered, and I would encourage doubters of my integrity as a critic to
search out that previous review.

"To detach *Pandora's Box* entirely from its evil is impossible. Killing is not an
art. The martial arts are not art but a way to defend yourself at best, to kill people

at their worst. A horse accidentally killed in a movie battle is a sad thing. A horse killed purposely in a movie changes the movie into news footage of an atrocity being committed. No film of a woman being actually raped, even if filmed by the finest director and camera crew, could be art. I attended a play entitled *Shit for Breakfast* (also to be found reviewed in a previous issue, in which I did vent my full fury), during the course of which a goat that had been standing at the back of the stage for a half hour was hoisted up by its rear legs and had its throat cut. The naked actors stood under the pouring blood, and I'm told the goat was hanging there throughout the remaining three and a half hours of the show. Normally I wouldn't think it fair to review a play or film I'd walked out on, but I was too busy summoning police and animal rights groups. (That performance was not stopped, nor was the next night's, but there was no third performance of *Shit for Breakfast* in Punktown. Did I, a mere critic, overstep my boundaries by preventing a piece of art from reaching an audience? Perhaps to some. I'd prefer to think I intervened to prevent a criminal act from taking place. What if it had been a cow that would have been slaughtered anyway? I eat meat. I don't know—don't confuse me with questions like that.)

"But Toll Loveland seems to have really felt that *Pandora's Box* was art. The moral issue aside—or at least viewing in a dispassionate way the use of M-670 as an extension of his art—and my own feelings as a victim of a murderer put aside, *Pandora's Box* is *still* bad art. Pretentious as it is pompous (you have to be a little bit pompous to think you have a right to kill people for the sake of your art). The use of *Screaming Pink Nazis* cereal as representative of society's ridiculous and obnoxious products, especially those aimed at the young, was tired even when spoofed in Dop Limzy's recent film *Uh-oh.* It's a cliché and I groaned when I saw the monolithic box on Toll Loveland's stage.

"*Cupid of Death* was no more than a snuff film shot with an expensive trick camera. The moths as symbols of the evils unleashed from Pandora's (Auretta's) box? An offensive myth to begin with, as offensive as Eve plucking the apple: it is women who invited evil (Eve-ill) into the garden, those rotten bitches. Mr. Loveland doesn't love women. That isn't an angry observation on my part—it's what he's saying in his art, isn't it? He fears them, so he must act in such a way as to feel he's in control of his fear. By cowardly firing an arrow (or activating a robot probe—same thing) into a woman's back. By reaching out and killing women in his audience.

"He obviously fears and hates critics. They hadn't been too kind, in general, with *The Godfucker* and others before that. So why not reach out and get some of them, too? Even *that's* a cliché. Search out, if you can, a twentieth century horror film called *Theater of Blood*, starring Vincent Price as a mad actor out to kill his many negative critics.

"The use of VT as a symbol of the impersonal nature of society, as suggested by certain enthusiastic critics who did not, I must stress, view the performance in person?

Oh come on! Cliché after cliché. The show was short. It had no focus but to serve as a smug, self-amused prelude to Loveland's crime—merely the grandiose gesturing and brandishing of a madman's gun before he finally uses it.

"The Auretta Here VT messages? Merely broken-up bits of the snuff film run as a series building up to the finale. Somewhat clever. (I'm shocked to say that, but I did say I'd be detached.)

"And the use of M-670 as a continuance of the show…of his creation? Original, I suppose…if feeding a baby to a pack of starved dogs could also be considered art. I've heard of a snuff film, shot in slow motion, featuring this—but I shouldn't mention that. Some of you will want to seek it out.

"I hope to be around for a follow-up review, in which I might include as final a death toll as can be determined (right now I hear it stands at about ninety *infected* by Toll Loveland's art—no deaths yet, and I can only pray there won't be.) But like I said, I'm not sure I'll be around long enough to see the conclusion of *Pandora's Box*.

"As I stated earlier, I hate to review a play or film if I haven't seen the entire thing. But his time I may have no choice."

Black thought: I'd like to meet this Yancy Mays.

Ninety people.

Black ran a computer search to seek out more reviews. He copied the articles from every magazine and major newspaper on Oasis and Earth, even from every local paper consisting of ninety percent advertisements, that had reviewed *Pandora's Box*. There were too many to read for now. Some had liked it. Most didn't—reviewed it as a criminal act, not as art as Yancy Mays had attempted (with only partial success, Black felt, but he'd tried.)

One reviewer who liked the show *had* been to Greenberg, and *had* been bitten and infected. He seemed rather proud to be part of the notoriety. Black was sickened. But Yancy Mays stayed with him…an encouragement.

Ninety people…no doubt more to come. Infected…maybe killed. By bad art.

Black thought about *Shit for Breakfast*. The goat. And Yancy Mays stepping over his boundaries.

SIX

Vern Woodmere lived in a basement apartment beneath the parking garage to an immense movie and holograph theater. It was all one long room but seemed to be more, broken up as it was by four pillars of bright yellow plastic marbled with black clouds and veins, each so thick around that four men could have easily hidden behind each one. The walls and floors were tiled in a checkerboard of yellow and black, though Black remembered that the pillared parking lot above had tiles on its walls only. The mortar between the glossy tiles was a grimy black, the floor tiles sticky (perhaps due to the proximity of sticky theater floors), and a bucket in a shadowy corner caught a slow drip of oil from a ceiling so low that Black's head nearly brushed it.

Vern had been expecting him; he'd called, but hadn't elaborated. Still, Vern had employed the camera eye and microphone outside his door before admitting him. "Damn, man," Vern had drawled in his Outback Colonies accent, looking genuinely haunted for Black's sake, "it's terrible what happened…I'm sorry, man. I'm an old fart—I shoulda gotten it instead of a kid like you."

"How are you doing, Vern? You need a shave."

"I always need a shave."

"Especially now."

"You've never been to my place before, have you?"

"No."

"You sure?"

"Never. I like it. No—really." He did. He liked the eccentric layout and its décor…it made him imagine how Vern must live, made him feel like Vern a little. Black had artistic inclinations, sketched a little, though not for almost a year now. While he and Opal had combined their tastes in furnishing and decorating their apartment, Black's tastes had usually dominated and often overruled Opal's, even in the kitchen, though he didn't cook. Art was one thing, cooking another. Black liked the torn movie posters (war films) pasted around two of the squat, broad pillars, and the framed lobby stills from one of Vern's favorite films about the Red War. The fold-out sofa was still unfolded and covered with clothes, the VT played in spite of the bullet hole through the screen. On the tiled wall in the area designated as the kitchen, a giant slug was glued, orange and yellow like a huge mushroom, a flower-like red blossom on its back. Big as a big cat. Black was very surprised—he had never taken Vern to be a pet owner.

Black liked his solitude—when it was chosen, of course, not forced as lately—and this secret subterranean place was very homey to him. He *did* feel like he'd been here before.

"You want a drink or something?" Vern held a can of Zub.

"No thanks—I'm fine."

"How do you feel? You feel alright so far?"

"I've got some cold sores. I bite them when I eat. They hurt so bad it's hard to sleep. Very sudden. They gave me some medication at HAP…with all their technology, you'd think they could find something that doesn't bring tears to your eyes when you put it on."

"I thought you were talking funny. Man." The haunted shadow patches on Vern's face must have been absorbed from the shadows of his lair, the way others tanned from the sun. His concern made Black feel good—he hadn't really seen anyone but for the HAP people, and not even Nedland for a while. He and Woodmere had never been close, either. Now they had more in common, it seemed. They weren't friends, but felt like old friends. "How do you feel otherwise?"

"Weak, tired, physically depressed. Nauseous, headaches. But then I haven't been eating or sleeping right."

"Stress, man; you've got to be good to your body, you've got to last. Right now it's probably emotional depression more than physical."

"True." Black glanced around the sprawling crawlspace of an apartment. A red parachute meant to blend with the red sky Vern had fought in and under hung from the ceiling to partition off the bathroom area. "You keeping busy?"

"No. Busy at what? Waxing my trophy? I'm lost, man. What am I gonna do now, become a security guard? Freakin' accident, man, I'm sorry—you know?"

"I believe you."

"I'm lost. What am I gonna do?"

"I've got something you might wanna do for a while."

"What's that?"

"Help me find Toll Loveland."

For a few moments Woodmere stared dazedly, his eyes half-bulging, though that was a common expression for him. This wasn't his first Zub of the day. Then a smile sparked up and spread fast. It was a nasty one.

"I'm your man, kid. Damn right I'll help you find Toll fucking Loveland. I already thought about it. Together we stand a better chance."

"That's my thinking."

Something about Black's manner gave Vern pause. Vern was an explosion ever rumbling to get out of a weary skin. Black was an electric hum twitching inside a cool shell. Right now he seemed positively cold. It was almost scary even to Vern.

His sculpted-bone face looking at home camouflaged in these shadows. Those heavy-lidded, far-spaced eyes looking flat, dispassionate…dead.

Vern got a little sober. "Look…I know you wanna kill him, but that's not a good idea."

"Why?"

"Premeditated murder, that's why."

"No one has to know it was us."

"Everyone's looking for him. If we're close to him, chances are good we'll be seen…"

"I don't want to get you in trouble—just help me find him and I'll do it."

"No. *Look.* Say you kill him…they cuff you…toss you in a cell…"

"I'm dying, Vern."

"Listen! They toss you in a cell. A month later they find the cure for M-670."

"Owing to my state of mind at the time, I'd plead extenuating circumstances."

"You'd be a hero, but the law doesn't give a fuck! Look…Christ, I can't believe I'm saying this. I sound like you and you sound like me. I thought you played it by the books."

"I'm not a health agent any more…am I?"

"Kid, I don't wanna see you destroy yourself! They could find a cure tomorrow, but you've already given up! Come on! I know you broke up with your girl, I heard—but when you both get cured you can try to work it out, right? Right? So why go to prison when we can catch this freak and turn him over to HAP and that'll be just as good? You know if he's caught this psycho isn't gonna hit the streets again in this lifetime."

"People adapt very easily. In prison he can eat, read, work if he wants, watch VT, make friends, take drugs and fuck. He's got guaranteed food and bed—a lot more than many people."

"He'll get death!"

"No, he's a psycho—unbalanced."

"He'll be put away, isn't that what counts? The public will be safe. Think of Opal, man…think of your woman. Think pink." Vern tried to chuckle, make a joke of it.

Black looked away with a kind of sullen pout, his tensed jaw a little thrust. One poster showed a soldier cutting the throat of another soldier with a huge knife. Actors.

"Alright."

"Great, man—that's great. We'll kill him if we *have* to. Only if we have to."

"I hope we have to."

"He is dangerous," Vern admitted.

"Good."

"Just don't push it to that. Promise me, Black. Or I won't help you. Believe me I'd love to smoke that fuck. But we can't. Too many eyes. *Promise* me."

"I promise you," Black said like a robot.

"Beautiful." Vern threw his head back, sucked the suds out of his Zub can, crushed the metal and tossed it at a wastebasket. It missed. "You got a civilian gun?"

Black was dressed all in black but for his robin's egg blue tweed jacket, which he held away from his left side. Glints on a dark form in the darkness there. "Lead-slinger. Decimator 220, snub."

"Ballsy old piece. I been lookin' for the 340 all my life. You got good plasma for it?"

"No."

"We want HAP-style plasma. This fuck plays with M-670 and God knows what else...we can't risk splashing him. Innocents might be around. We got to do it pro."

"Our plasma is illegal. If we get caught with it on us..."

"I know, but what else can we do? Here." Vern moved to a plastic footlocker, swept it clear of clothes and magazines, punched in its code to unlock it. He lifted out a pistol in a holster. Before returning to Black he retrieved the pistol he'd worn in his waistband when he'd answered the door but had then set aside. "Take this." He extended the holstered handgun. "I've got a good plasma for it...my own little stash."

Accepting the gun, Black unsheathed it from its scratched old holster. It was a squat, more compact version of Vern's gun, a semi-automatic made from a glassy red plastic. This one was more scuffed and dulled than Vern's longer version. It felt nice in the hand—not light and ineffective like so many guns these days.

"I've got lead for it, too. Keep the lead clip in it in case we get checked out along the way. Keep the plasma clip hidden...sew a pocket in the lining of your jacket or something. Quick to get at if you need it."

"Thanks."

"What else will we need?" Woodmere pivoted to glance around the apartment, enthused despite his previous caution. "Ahh..."

"I put my tools in my trunk in case we have to break in somewhere."

Vern snapped back to Black. "Hey, now...let's not be reckless, huh? Think of me, too, will ya?"

"I am, I'm sorry...just in case, you know? You never know."

"Yeah, right, just be careful, huh? We have to stay calm with this. We gotta do it clean and pro. Like we were still health agents."

"Some places we'll wanna go will have weapon scans. I want to pull surveillance on the Hill Way Galleries, where he made that Auretta Here vid with his cameo appearance. He's got a painting there, too, I found out. A place like that will have a scan."

"True. Hm."

"Can you shield us?"

"Yeah, maybe—no. No…look. The syringes they use at HAP, plasma-proof syringes they use to inject and dispose of contaminated lab animals? I can get something just like it from the black market goons where I got my plasma. It's a pen. You put a plasma bullet inside, you push the plunger and the capsule breaks, the plasma gets injected. You have to get close, but that will pass a normal scan looking at weapon *shapes*. Unless they got one *looking* for plasma."

"We can't go against him weaponless at any time."

"True. Look, I'll get four pens—two each. Right? Two blue and two red. In the red will be the plasma. In blue we'll put remonil to knock him out and take him alive if we can. Sound good?"

"Very good. I knew I could count on you to work these things out."

"Weaponry is my life, my man."

"I'd love to get into Greenberg and look for a trap-door, an air vent, something. See how he made his exit."

"Forget that. Forget those tools of yours—we break in there and we blow it. Too obvious; HAP could be around. Anyway, don't you think they already picked that place clean? Let's try new angles, man…the museum and Greenberg have already been done."

"It's just a start to get our feet wet. Anyway, our perspectives aren't the same as other perspectives. We might find things the others missed."

"There's no trap-door. Loveland was either a hologram or he teleported out."

"Where would he get a teleporter…on the black market?"

"Maybe. Maybe he made one. He's supposed to be this freakin' genius, right?"

The blue pen was clipped in the spiral binding of Black's sketchbook and the red one holstered in his shirt pocket—and the scan at the Hill Way Galleries let him pass. Last night Vern had also acquired two miniature, powerful communication devices disguised as rings (tacky rings, Black thought) from his black market contacts. They went in together for now; if any HAP people spotted either one of them alone, it would arouse just as much suspicion anyway. If Loveland ever saw them both together, it was doubtful he'd remember them from his show—and anyway, Black had shaved off his mustache and goatee since then. Even Vern had shaved.

After selecting a number of museum guides and brochures at the reception area, Black located Toll Loveland's painting *Matter of Life and Death* in an index, took note of its floor and wing location. If nothing more came of this—and what might, anyway?—Black had to see this painting. *The title.* His heartbeat grew more pronounced as they made their way upstairs in the nearly empty building, more pronounced down every hallway, as if when he finally turned into the room they sought, there would stand the handsome Toll Loveland. Smiling. Expecting them. He wasn't there; the room empty, though a stern gray-suited man strolling in an adjacent gallery gave them a look, resembling a strict teacher presiding over an exam and keeping an eye out for cheaters. "There it is," said Vern. "I remember seeing that on VT, now."

"I didn't." Though he must have had it in his hours upon hours of unwatched vid files. Black followed Vern to the painting, his heart still beating with anticipation.

It was a moderate-sized light painting, portraying a moldering skeleton against a black background. A baby boy was trapped in the rib-cage of the skeleton but the ribs were beginning to break outward. Both skeleton and baby were in the exact same pose, to the tilt of head and spread of fingers, one of the boy's hands reaching through the ribs. The skeleton just reached at air.

"Pretty good," murmured Black. "Pretty damn realistic."

"Hey, it says here the picture changes every hour…it has four stages. For the sake of surprise, it won't describe what they look like. I guess it has different layers of projected light operating on a timer."

"Ha." Just when Black was beginning to feel safe near it. He found himself squinting at the artwork, changing his angle, though he knew he wouldn't be able to discern the hidden, alternating layers. "Let's look around for an hour, come back."

"Let's look for a men's room."

"Well, we'll split up for a while—meet me here in exactly an hour."

"All we're gonna meet here is a health agent with questions."

"Hey, we're art lovers, Vern—that's no crime."

Black was back first, but only by seconds; Vern joined him outside the gallery. Too bad—he'd have liked to look at it for a few moments alone. As it turned out, however, the room was no longer empty. A group of five figures, all dressed entirely in black, had gathered at Toll Loveland's light painting.

They were a particular college type, or an emulation of that type: the black clothing, black slippers without socks (but a therm rub on the skin, no doubt, owing to the chilly weather), mops of spiky blacker-than-black hair shaved almost to a stubble below the temples, and whiter-than-white flesh that looked as smooth and soft and fragile as mushroom flesh…you could imagine pushing your finger through it. A familiar style in Punktown, so normally Black wouldn't have looked twice. But they were gazing at and talking about *Matter of Life and Death.*

Black placed a hand on Vern's arm to warn him into silence. He took in the painting's mutation at the same time he tried to sort their soft conversation. He was aware that as he and Vern stood off behind the five young people, the stern gray-suited guard stood off behind him and Vern, grimly observing one and all.

The moldering skeleton in the painting had taken on hard, living flesh. Not just any flesh. It was unmistakably a self-portrait of Toll Loveland, extending his arms as if to reach out of the painting. All that was left visible of the baby in the skeleton's rib-cage was an arm reaching bloodlessly out of Toll's hard belly…only now it was the tiny arm of a skeleton child.

The black background remained empty. Black had expected to see some white moths there, maybe just one. Nothing of the kind. Still, two stages to go.

From what the black-garbed group related, a special exhibit of paintings, sculptures and film strips by Toll Loveland was coming to the Hill Way Galleries, collected from various small galleries here and in Miniosis and from private collectors…including the giant *Screaming Pink Nazis* carton from *Pandora's Box,* recovered by police and safety-scanned by the Health Agency, plus the two plastic skeletons on fork-lifts. The film *Cupid of Death* would be shown. Black was gladder than ever that it was from Beak and not himself that the film had been extracted for release to the VT networks, and now this.

"That'll be something to keep an eye on," Black muttered.

"Are you crazy? That twisto won't come within ten miles of it."

"Excuse me." Black approached the group; they all turned. Black lipstick, mascara, black beauty mark tattoos. Two or three were probably girls. Whether to let the hair fall down to hide the left eye or right eye was probably a major issue with them, and that was the only major difference Black could see in them.

"Didst I detect the tones of one in inquiry of me?" one asked of his fellows, who chuckled approvingly at his wittiness. "Didst a blond entity address us, in such like a manner as to elicit a response to said inquiry hereto?"

"Do any of you know a girl named Ivory Ebon?" The ticket girl at *Pandora's Box* hadn't known anything, but maybe one of these people could be of help in some way. She could have been one of them—but then, there were thousands of their ilk in Punktown. Probably millions in Miniosis.

"What is this blond person asking of thee, I mean me, I mean we? *We?"*

"Oui," chuckled a girl, presumably.

Vern stepped closer. "Just answer the man's question, you glow-in-the-dark fucking cave fish."

His eyes could have set them on fire. A vein snaked under his taut forehead skin. The chuckle trickled down the witty boy's throat like ice water. "Who is it?"

"*Ivory Ebon,*" drawled Vern.

"No…who is that? Oh, oh…the girl from *Pandora's Box?* I saw her on VT."

"None of you know her personally?"

All shook their heads or muttered in the negative. No one smiled.

"Any of you fucking little ghouls know Toll Loveland personally?"

All said no. "We're just looking at his painting," a girl said quietly, the only protest the group offered to Vern's murderous blaze. Boy, can he turn it on, Black smiled to himself. But was it part fake or all real? This was the old Vern. He'd seemed so mellowed, so tired since Black had gone to see him at his basement apartment yesterday.

"Well, you're in my way. Go get a tan or something."

The five young people obliged, drifted silently off like a black cloud. The gray-suited man, less intimidated, stepped up to take their place.

"Can I ask what you two gentlemen are doing?"

"We're from the Health Agency," said Vern.

"Oh, I see—what can I do for you?" The sternness lightened.

"When is that Loveland exhibit coming?" asked Black.

"We have the pieces already but we need another week for promotion. The exhibit opens on the first of the month."

"Where are all these little galleries and who are the private collectors?"

"I thought you people had that information."

"We're a separate branch of investigation," said Vern. "The other team holds out on us; they want the cuff and the glory all to themselves."

"Well, I'm not sure about the galleries…I know one or two were on Newbury Street. And I wouldn't know anything about private collectors. Shall I buzz the office?"

"Ah…not yet. We'll do that ourselves if we have to," said Black. HAP obviously had that angle covered for now, were probably concentrated on it…best to try to find new, unthought-of angles, as Vern had said. "Was this painting here scanned for dangerous substances or properties?"

"Oh yes, all Toll Loveland's work has been exhaustively scanned."

"Alright, thanks for your help."

More trusting now, the guard strolled out into the hall to leave them alone.

"Now what?" asked Vern.

"I wonder if anyone's thought to extract Ivory Ebon's memories of Toll Loveland approaching her to do the tickets, or her approaching him, however that went. I'd like to see him in the non-performing mode. Mrs. Greenberg's memories, too."

"He wouldn't reveal anything to them. The kid was truth scanned, right?"

"Just to observe him. Study him unguarded, you know?"

"He wouldn't have been unguarded with them. It was still acting."

"True."

"Anyway, we don't have access to that kind of gear."

"Was Mrs. Greenberg truth scanned?"

"I don't know. You still get inside HAP, not me."

Black pouted at the painting. "Well, time to split up again."

"He's not coming here no matter how much he likes to tease us. Just ask the guard what the other two phases are. Maybe he can adjust the timer and run through them."

"He can't do that…hey. Wait. Your glasses. You got your sunglasses?"

"Yeah. Shit." Woodmere reached inside his leather flight jacket for a small case, opened it and handed over the glasses he had worn inside the Greenberg plant to see in the dark. "Give it a try. Want me to show ya?"

"I got it." Black placed the glasses on his face, touched a button near the frame hinge. A red spot of light came on in each lens. He turned to the painting. No difference—dimmer if anything, colors faded to ghost light. There were tiny dials, and a switch he flicked with his fingernail. The colors jumped up in intensity. He adjusted a toothed dial. Toll Loveland's flesh became insubstantial. Bones showed through. "I got it!" He moved the dial the other way. The entire picture surface clouded over. New flesh. It became solid, a chest with nipples and a trim, steely belly filling up the entire frame. Baby in man, now man inside this man. What was last? A baby inside the baby?

He moved the dial and watched for moths.

"So what do ya see?" asked Vern, impatient.

Back to the skeleton, the baby in the rib-cage breaking out, and no moths. Only one thing was different. No one had noted its significance, Black was sure. He had known his individual perspective would benefit him. The painting had reached out to him; maybe some obscure faculty of his *had* perceived the hidden layers. He smiled.

In the previously empty, sightless sockets of the skull were now two spheres like bulbous eyes. Crystalline globes filled with a glowing, translucent milky liquid. And inside the globes, one in each like pupils, were beautiful metallic blue fish.

Navigator globes. From a tran.

"Come on, let me see—what is it?"

"I think we've found our teleporter," Black said at last.

SEVEN

"For all intents and purposes, a tran is a teleporter between dimensions for the Bedbugs," Black observed. He was piloting his helicar.

"And how the hell would Loveland know about Bedbug technology?"

"Like you said, he's a freakin' genius."

"Yeah, but he's not God. Maybe he got a book out of the library, huh?"

"Maybe he did."

"Shit, man."

"Maybe they helped him."

"Who?"

"Some Bedbugs."

"They don't associate with humans. We don't like them and they don't like us."

"But some of them live in our dimension, right? They have to function here. So they need money. You need money, you can be bought. Right?"

"True."

The gate was locked at Greenberg Products, the barbed wire-garlanded fence charged with a strong but nonlethal current. A uniformed young guard came to meet them on the outside of the gate, both fists on the handles of an automatic blaster that moments earlier had been slung over his shoulder. Black kept his own hands still and in sight on his helicar's console. "Who are you?" the guard demanded. A second guard was approaching, too.

"Health agents." Black slowly flipped open a badge I.D. that Vern had also acquired from his black market friends. He'd had it at the museum but the guard there hadn't asked to see credentials. If he ever got caught by the authorities with this on him, it would be as bad as the plasma.

The guard looked convinced, but his companion leaned in the window and focused on Vern. "Hey, wait a minute—you see him? That guy? He's the guy who killed Gato."

"Who, him?"

"I was there that night, I saw his face! I thought they were gonna expel that guy! What is this, huh? You can kill anybody you want and…"

"They did expel him," Black said calmly, before Vern could speak. "He's out of the agency…but he was there that night and I'm using him as a source of information in my investigation. I want him to show me around the grounds, and inside too if we can."

"You can't, not without an appointment," said the first guard. "The place was sold and they're cleaning it all up inside."

"Sold?" Black looked toward the plant through his windshield. "To who?"

"Some pharmaceutical company."

"The place stood here empty for years and now suddenly, of all times, it's bought?"

"Maybe all that Toll Loveland controversy attracted the attention of a buyer," the guard suggested.

"Maybe. But we can look at the grounds?"

"Yes."

"Are there any other health agents on the property right now, inside or out?"

"No."

Good.

The guards let them in and they parked in the lot close to the Beds. There were a dozen or so other vehicles in the lot, but closer to the plant. Stepping out, Black heard the hum and rumble of heavy machinery from the other side of the plant, and then a great crashing as of cars colliding. He pictured the old mechanical guts of the Greenberg company being extracted and unloaded at the docks into great scrap-eating robots, to be recycled.

"I seriously doubt Loveland's still hiding in there," said Woodmere.

Black said nothing, but why had he imagined that Loveland might be?

Together they walked toward the odd track beds of the extra-dimensional Bedbugs. In the light of day, Black took note of the fact that there was no length of charged fence separating the property of the Greenberg plant from the Beds. Odd—he and Opal hadn't thought of that before. Had there ever been? It wasn't likely that anyone could enter the Beds and thus walk onto the Greenberg property that way, however—surrounding the Beds there was still a fifteen-foot high fence of what looked to be wrought iron, each of its bars covered in razor-edged black knife blades. Only a helicar could get over that. But there was no length of frightening metal bars separating the two properties, either. Had there ever been?

"Come on," said Black.

At the end of the Beds the wall of knives rose high, and—less high—the charged fence hummed. From here, at the rear border of the Greenberg property, they watched fork-lifts on the loading docks dump tangled masses of machinery into hungry yellow robots as Black had imagined. Then, returning to the matter at hand, he inspected the ends of both the towering metal fence and the charged fence.

On both end posts were the scarred indications that there had once been sections blocking the two properties off from each other. Now gone.

"Did one side remove both walls, or did they both remove their own, and why?" asked Black.

"You don't think Loveland would do all that."

"No…not necessarily. I don't know what to think. Let's go look at that tran."

The tran which Black and Opal had climbed up into on that night was an old, lonely thing in the daylight. Tentacle-like weeds had woven themselves inch by inch through and around the wheels and underbelly of the complex black machine, securing it, claiming it as a captive. Bird turds stood out as bold graffiti on its riveted back. A sad, beached whale corpse. The two men hoisted themselves up inside its carcass.

Thick porthole-like windows let in the light. And up front there was the soft glow of the two globes filled with their Navigator fluid. Within them writhed the shadowy forms of the twin metallic blue fish. Just like the painting. Vern grunted.

Below the globes, those six silver metal rings like miniature steering wheels, one for each of a Bedbug's whip-like pincered arms. To one side, six small glass balls were set into a wall section. A greenish-yellow glowing fluid half-filled them, and floating in each one was a smaller silver metal ball. Gauges of some kind. There were rows of yet tinier silver rings, some large black levers set in the floor and ceiling, but hardly enough controls, it would appear, for a machine that traveled through dimensions. Vern had crouched to look under the front console with its six metal wheels while Black tried to pry a wall panel open without breaking off his nails.

"Black…hey, Black."

Black came to crouch beside Vern. Vern shifted to let Black twist lower and gaze up under the hollow console. He could see inside clearly by the light from the exposed undersides of the two Navigator spheres. There were rows of metal rings with alien characters etched beside them in silver. And there was a plastic box the size of a thick paperback book fixed to the inner wall. Cables from it were clamped to a few rings… but most notably, two cables ending in sticky disks were adhered to the undersides of both Navigator balls. A tiny red light blinked alive on the plastic box.

"Doesn't look like Bedbug technology," Vern observed.

"It isn't." Black smiled with grim satisfaction.

"Smart boy."

Black didn't know if Vern voiced the compliment for him or for Loveland. He straightened up to face the older man. "I don't want to fuck with it. It's obvious it's still active. It must operate by a hand remote…he's probably still using it. If we fuck with it we could ruin it."

"So what, then? We report it?"

"No. Maybe we can make it work for us. Who do we know who could understand it, maybe manipulate it to our needs? What about Bubba Hernandez? He's a whiz."

Bubba was yet another expelled Health Agency employee, but a technician, not a field agent. His drug habits had led to his dismissal, especially after a near hazardous spill in his lab. Woodmere laughed. "Man, Bubba is a burn-out."

What are we? thought Black. "Well…"

"Listen, lemme think a minute, here. There's a guy I know from the Teeb family—his name's Dirge." The Teeb organization was the biggest illegal arms and black market dealer in Punktown, and with their illicit cloning and manifold other services was considered a threat the Health Agency had been trying to crack for years. Those agency people who weren't paid off, that is. "Dirge is a freaking whiz…he'd be our best bet. But it'll cost."

"I'll pay it. What else good is my money now?"

"Don't' keep talkin' that way, man!"

"I'll take you home. Go find this Dirge…see if you can get him down here tomorrow. I'll call you tonight."

"Right." They both rose and departed from the tran.

Black's lips hurt—he hated to talk. Before he got on the vidphone in his apartment he dabbed a numbing ointment on them. It was numbing *after* the initial acidic fire, which made him moan, nearly swoon. He felt extremely nauseous.

He took his weight off gelatin legs, sat before the screen. In a moment it was filled with a woman's face and he swallowed ointment-tainted saliva, which didn't help his nausea. The woman had a severe look. Humorless gray eyes, a small twisty sneer of a mouth in a doughy face. She looked surprisingly old for her forty-some-odd years. Would Opal appear this old if she lived long enough to double her life?

"Mrs. Cowrie, can I speak to your daughter?"

"She isn't here right now."

"I know she told me she'd call me, but she hasn't…and, um…I have some very interesting developments to tell her about the Loveland case."

"I'll tell her you called."

"Do you know where she went or when she'll be back?"

"No. I'll tell her you called."

"Could you have her call me tonight? I'll be here all night."

"She'll call you when and if she's ready. I'm sorry. Goodbye."

The screen went dead. Probably sitting right there beside her, Black thought.

He was both dismally disappointed and shamefully relieved.

In the guard shack at the entrance to the Health Agency's back parking lot, Jose the ex-health agent received a call on his vidphone at the same moment Black pulled up in his helicar. Rather than make the caller wait, Jose made Black wait. Black groaned, shifted his weight in his plush seat. He found himself becoming more and more impatient with little things. Life was short.

"You can see my fucking face, Jose," he muttered under his breath, "just let me in, will ya?" He could see the vidscreen in the shack from here, a man with a crewcut and black handlebar mustache. The man seemed to turn his head a little to glance back at Black a few times over Jose's shoulder.

Black lit a black-papered cigarette. Brain damage, he thought about Jose, and regretted it a moment later. Probably was, from when he'd lost his face. Jose had once been electric, an energetic agent. Now he seemed to shamble in his booth, move and speak as if inside a tank of thick liquid. The man with the handlebar mustache definitely was craning his neck to see Black over Jose's shoulder.

A shocking-pink hovercar pulled up alongside the helicar on its left; Black looked out his window, saw the two men inside the vehicle and threw himself across his passenger seat, raising an arm to shield his face as his driver's side window exploded.

One of the men in the pink hovercar had used a metal tube to shatter the window, touching it to the surface and activating a sound vibration. Tubes like these were used by car thieves to gain access. But this was no parked car.

Crystal pebbles covered Black; he bucked on the seat, thrashed in his tight coffin as the man with the tube now leaned out far to point a pistol. The pistol barrel actually entered into Black's car. The health agent had finally yanked free his own gun but it snagged his jacket lining and he cried out, kicked at the pistol uselessly as it went off.

A tiny dart hit him in the face beside his nostril, spiking deep. Still crying out, one cry on the tail of the next, Black brought up his civilian, licensed Decimator 220 and emptied three of its six revolving chambers, hardly aiming. The blasts inside the car were ear-splitting.

The man was hit squarely in the face by one of the projectiles, directly on the left eyebrow. He pitched back.

Insane screams from the other car; Black quit his firing and sat up, the crystal pebbles flying off him. The other man, the hovercar's driver, had been hit by one of the strays. In the ear. Even as Black rose to look, the screaming had stopped, the ear having become a crater filled with steaming bluish glow. The weak plasma available to the licensed public. Black looked back to the first man. God, he was still alive. A little. Head tossed back, his face was melting like glowing blue wax, the holes for the eyes and nose stretching out into long slits, and his mouth gaped open wide to accept it all as it ran off the more slowly dissolving bone. The man choked a little softly; Black saw his throat move as he swallowed his face.

A moment later the man was dead but the plasma still hissed, spread inside him a little longer. Black felt a trickle of blood tickling down his face from the dart embedded near his nose, and then black flowers sprouted in profusion before his eyes and he pitched back on the pebbly car seats before Jose could get to him.

Black heard the man on the vidscreen yelling and cursing—at him, it seemed—and then it went blank, and so did he.

The Currier and Ives calendar had been advanced to a new picture since Black had sat in this conference room last. Opal had been here then.

Captain Nedland came in, as before. He smiled at Black and put a coffee in front of him. "Thought you could use this. I remember it right, black and two sugars?"

Black could drink it black or with milk and sugar but not black with sugar. "Close enough," he said. "Thanks." He could use it, just the same.

"We played back the call from the guard shack. The caller was in police files—Granite Buttercup. He belongs to a homosexual militant group, the Gay United Liberation Party. A bunch of psychos. Did you see the news last night?"

"I haven't been watching VT."

"Two of them infected with M-670 killed themselves on the steps of Town Hall last night after spraying policemen with squirt guns filled with their urine and blood. One forcer got squirted in the mouth. I haven't heard how he'd made out—they got him to the hospital fast and may have had time to clean him up before the virus took hold. Before the forcers could get their hands on the two of them, one shot himself in the head and the other slashed his own throat. Contaminated blood all over, just what they wanted. Protestors."

"Because of the Bum Junket thing."

"That's why they came after you. They must have been watching you for a while."

"Do they know my name, where I live?"

"Very doubtful, or they would have attacked you there where the risk is less."

"Well, they're suicide squads, right? It's more symbolic to attack me here."

"Yeah, but the two you killed didn't have M-670…I'll bet they wanted to make it out alive. They don't know your name, I'm sure, but be careful. I'm having your car held for now and we'll have the window fixed for you. We'll lend you an agency car. Dye your hair or something."

"So the dart was what I think?"

Nedland nodded. "Mutstav six-seventy."

Black had to laugh out loud. "Those stupid fucks. Threw their lives away for nothing."

"Scary intentions, nonetheless. How do you feel?"

"My face is numb. I just got queasy and passed out."

"You aren't eating or sleeping right, I hear. Don't do that."

Black had stopped laughing. "I haven't seen you in a while. I haven't seen Opal, either. Has she been coming in?"

"Once a week."

"What day and time?"

"I don't think she wants to see you."

"Dammit, man…" Black sprang out of his chair, spun on his heel and shot into a tiger's angry, caged pacing.

"Give her time."

"We don't have time!"

"We'll find a cure soon."

"Mutant shit!"

Nedland sipped his own coffee. Waited instead of arguing.

In a softer voice, facing the calendar, Black asked, "So how's she doing?"

Nedland sighed a little. Black didn't like that. "She doesn't feel too good. It affects people in different ways, according to many personal factors. She's been eating and sleeping right, she mostly just stays home in her mother's care. But she's not doing as well as you are."

"Great." Black felt like a drunk driver who in a collision with another car had killed the driver but had only received minor scratches himself. And he had chosen to drink. His responsibility. His fault.

"A cure is within reach, Monty. That isn't the standard VT line like you think."

"I can't afford to get my hopes up."

"At least calm down."

"Go stick that dart in your arm and then tell me to calm down. I wanna rip right out of my skin. I want to run and scream. Can you understand that?"

"I think I can, yes." Nedland studied the back of the standing man. "I hate to change the subject, but I'm not, really. One of our people saw you and Vern Woodmere down at the Hill Way Galleries."

"Yeah, we went there. I looked him up for lunch, then I wanted to see Toll Loveland's painting they have there. And when they have that big exhibit of his work they're planning, I'll go and see that, too."

"You're being awfully defensive, Monty."

"Well, you seem to be implying something."

"Only that you should be careful."

Black faced his former commander. "Don't threaten me, please."

"Good Lord, I'm not threatening you! I'm concerned for you, Monty, can't you believe that? I'm on your side; we want the same thing. But let us handle this, alright? You know what I mean. When I say be careful it's *concern*. In fact, look here. You aren't taking care of yourself, and now you're in danger from that bunch of psycho-terrorists. Why don't you come stay with us here in the ward? We'll take care of you and protect you. It won't be long, I know it."

"No. Absolutely not."

"Monty, what are you now, Auretta Here? You think we're going to throw you in a zapper and disintegrate you?"

"I don't want to be a prisoner in a white smock. I'm not a lab rat."

"Monty, for your own good…"

"Don't tell me my own good. I'm not interested in spending what could very well be the last few months of my life in a hospital room. I come here every day; that's enough."

"You're twisting this all around. We can keep you fit! Look at you, look at your eyes! You're losing weight fast. Your skin looks yellowish to me."

"I'm dying."

"You're sick. You don't have to die; you've got to get that into your skull."

"You just want to study me and keep a health hazard off the street. You're mad because I won't take the libido blockers you offered me…like you think I'm gonna go out and seduce school children."

"You're the one talking mutant shit, Monty. This is all Bum Junket-style paranoia. You're talking Bum Junket."

"I know about Bum Junket, man. You had me kill him, remember? We could have taken the selfish bastard in here by force and studied him and made his last days comfortable. That would have been a fair compromise. But you had me kill him."

"You were all for it, as I remember."

"Things have changed. Extremes aren't good."

"We have to protect the public."

"I am the public! Bum Junket was the public!"

"That sounds good, Monty. And Toll Loveland? Isn't he also the public, then?"

"I'm no threat. I'm no Bum Junket or Auretta Here and I'm no fucking Toll Loveland. I'll come in and give you my damn blood and cell samples. And that's it. You understand me? I'm a free man."

"You also have a responsibility to society."

"And society has a responsibility to me!"

"Yes. And that's why I want to help you."

"I don't need your kind of help." Black went to the door, pushed its button. It wouldn't open. He stabbed the button again, again. "Let me out! Let me the fuck *out!*" He glared at Nedland, his face twitching, ready to rip out of its skin. He looked like Vern Woodmere.

"Let him out," Captain Nedland said softly, and the door opened.

Monty Black plunged through it, and the next day he didn't show up for his daily appointment at the Health Agency.

EIGHT

Extremes weren't good. But didn't he want, and intend, to kill Toll Loveland—as he had killed Bum Junket?

He had demanded back his helicar and driven away in that, demolished window and all, instead of in their proffered agency car. Had checked the helicar into a repair garage and rented a nondescript-looking, black, wheeled car, which Vern had just let himself into in front of a café where they'd agreed to meet. From now on Black couldn't afford to be caught at Vern's apartment.

He told Vern what had happened. And that they'd been seen.

"You still with me?" he asked.

"I knew they'd catch on sooner or later…I just hoped it'd be later. We're not hurting anybody…they can't touch us yet. Fuck it."

"Did you contact that guy Dirge?"

"He can't come until tomorrow afternoon."

"Damn. Now what?" Black watched traffic pass, a skinny gray dog drifting dejectedly along the sidewalk. Collar hanging loosely. He felt contempt for the smartly-dressed business types and students from a nearby university who strutted past it without looking. Opal would be cursing now. "I'd like to find the Bedbugs' new track-bed, see if I can meet with some of them. Maybe we could get them to look at Loveland's hook-up, and sniff them out while we're at it…see if it looks like any of them might've been paid to help him."

"It's something, but they don't care for humans…I say they didn't help him and they won't help us."

"What about the widow Greenberg? You wanna go talk to her, or is that too obvious for you? Too risky?"

"Well, that's not so much the thing…it's just that she's probably been all questioned out already."

"But not by *us,* Vern. Remember the painting?"

"Alright, whiz, do it. I just wish I'd shaved today."

A handsome dark-haired student expensively dressed all in black looked over his shoulder at the dog, turned, crouched down beside it amidst the busy throngs of people to look at its license and I.D. tags. A feeble ray of sun found its way to Black's heart as he pulled into the flow of traffic.

Despite its great size, Paxton was called a town to Miniosis's city, and on Earth both of them together would be like a city block by comparison. But to Black, Punktown was huge even with his lifetime of familiarity. So it was ironic that he should have been so familiar with Mrs. Greenberg's house for years without ever realizing that she lived there. He could remember staring at it, even, with Opal once or twice from a path in the park he had wandered through recently alone, which the house overlooked.

It rested atop a mint green, exclusive apartment building with only ten stories, a rather simple design but elegant. The Greenberg house sat upon it like a leafy hat, not a connected piece. Leafy because three-quarters of the three-story building atop-a-building were engulfed in a thick green ivy, green even now though probably not synthetic, neatly trimmed around the rectangles of windows. The box-shaped, flat-roofed building was covered—as patches in the ivy revealed—in glossy checkered tiles of peach and jade, a beautiful design to be so largely obscured, but also beautiful in its obscurity. The roof was no heliport (vehicles parked there would be crassly intrusive) so ivy covered it instead.

Black and Vern checked into the guard station outside the mint green larger structure. Black had called an hour ago to make an appointment to see Mrs. Greenberg. She hadn't been able to come to the screen—she was bathing—but she relayed the message to her servant that they were welcome. Beyond the guard stop Black and Vern caught an elevator to the roof of the host building, where its beautiful scaled parasite waited.

Vern rang the bell while Black stood at the high scrolled parapet watching tiny figures stroll through the ant farm of the park.

The glossy jade door opened and the servant from the vidphone was there—a friendly, pretty young woman with red hair in a frizzy flood down the back of her black uniform. Black couldn't remember the last time he'd seen an actual—as she appeared, at least—redhead. She talked more like a waitress than a rich widow's servant.

"She's just gotten dressed and put together, finally. Mrs. G. doesn't like to get up before noon, usually. Sorry for the wait. Hope you haven't had lunch."

"We just did, while we were waiting," Vern said. They'd been told on the phone to give Mrs. Greenberg an hour. "No problem, hon." Vern was all smiles for this succulent redhead.

"Damn…my fault…I forgot to tell you she asked me to invite you to join her. I remembered just after you hung up. She'll kill me."

"We'll tell her we ate before we even called," said Black.

"Thanks, guys. At least will you have coffee? Great. Alright, follow me."

Even Black watched her ample hips roll inside her tight black skirt. But for him the stimulation brought the confusing torture of guilt.

Glinting coppery red hair. Black stockings, heels. Perfumed alabaster flesh, the so-soft cleavage up front like a child's rear poking out of its pants. It was almost like looking at a corpse for him, however, and drooling over that. His nausea awakened to boil in his gut. He should have accepted Nedland's fucking pills after all.

Many potted plants, native Choom antiques of polished wood and sparkling crystal and glowing metal. Down a wide courtyard-like corridor, its ceiling, floor and walls all tiled in peach and jade, flanked on either side by tropical plants in museum-style jungle dioramas, miniature pools filled with darting coppery fish. But Black only had eyes for their guide. He'd never taken a sex suppressor; how could one see and smell a woman like that without feeling anything? Without wanting to see and smell more? He supposed that it would feel like looking at an elderly woman, or mutated or nonhuman alien woman, or a man, felt to him now. A dismal concept. But still, if he'd had one pill in his pocket today he'd have popped it in his mouth.

And the worst, to his surprise and displeasure, was yet to come.

The redhead rapped on a glossy peach door, opened it. "Your guests, Mrs. G.—are you ready for lunch?"

"Yes. Will our guests be joining me?"

"For coffee; they already ate."

"Thank you, Linda. Gentlemen, please come in and be comfortable."

Black and Woodmere entered, Linda closing the door after them. It was a combination office and book-lined study, and Mrs. Greenberg sat behind a desk of black marble or perhaps crystal, with blood-red veins or striations—very expensive, whatever its material. She got up from behind it to come offer her hand.

She saw their amazement, an almost gaping shock, at her appearance…and explained good-naturedly, "Yes, I'm Mrs. Greenberg—Helga Greenberg—not her daughter. I don't have any children. And no, this isn't the result of illegal longevity drugs or treatments…I suffer from a metabolic mutation that greatly slows my aging process naturally. If you can call this natural." She gestured at herself with an apologetic chuckle. "Sometimes I feel lucky, sometimes I don't."

"How old are you?" asked Vern. "If I can ask?"

"You just did. No problem. I'm forty-two. Physically, I'm thirty years younger than that. Before puberty my rate of aging was normal. Then I changed. I've aged only months in decades. My old schoolmates have children older than me, physically. Like I said, it can be a mixed blessing."

"You must get tired of talking about it," said Black.

"I'm used to it, don't feel bad."

"Is your *mind* twelve?"

"My *brain* is twelve. My *mind* is forty-two. I have forty-two years of memories and experiences. I don't have temper tantrums or play with dolls, Agent Black, I promise you." She laughed again, as friendly as her servant. Black was surprised. But more surprising, as startling as her physical age, was her physical beauty. That had dazzled these men into their initial gaping just as much.

Had she been this beautiful at twelve, or had the years of inner maturity lent her youthful form its aristocratic grace and sophistication? Had to be—not your standard twelve-year-old's face. But maturity couldn't have done it alone—couldn't give her eyes of so pale a blue, disturbing as the rare blue eyes of a dog, under their fleshy, almost Asian folds. Black was familiar with the old Earth movie actress Lauren Bacall, and Mrs. Greenberg looked like an adolescent version, a tadpole. Her nose hadn't lengthened, was still a button close below her eyes. When smiling she was a casual, open gamine, but normally her features fell into a model's sullen, pouty frown, her brow frowning over the far-spaced, icy, unsettling eyes. Tangled wavy hair, dark blond and parted on the side to half hang over one eye, fell to her waist. She was tall for twelve but still small, and wore a black woolen sweater that fell to mid thigh, her legs bare, thin, white. She didn't have much for breasts; maybe not much, if anything, for pubic hair.

But Black had the start of an erection, and it was rare for him to be so moved primarily by a face. It had to be many factors at work, conspiring. Her physical age linked with her womanly beauty. The hint of pedophilia, no matter how justified, still made his flesh crawl. And perhaps now that he couldn't have sex, he wanted it a little bit more, was more aware of the sexual stimulations he was encountering. Had to be. He had seen beautiful girls and women, some stark naked on the street, every day of his life and seldom been so moved—you became jaded. You looked, you hungered, if you didn't have a lover you ached—but the stirrings of an erection? Despite his body's arousal, Black was greatly dismayed. He felt almost certain, too, that Mrs. Greenberg was aware of his swelling.

He was grateful when she returned to her desk, hid her slim bare legs, and he could sit to take the weight off his own rubbery legs and hide his erection. Problem was, when he sat it seemed to swell a bit larger. The nausea lapped against his inner walls in a storm-edged surf. His head fizzed, bloodless. The blood was all down low, pounding at his crotch door, some of it seeping under the crack. Vern was going to have to carry this one.

"I don't mean to be rude or uncooperative but I don't know what more I can tell you guys…I've talked to others from the Health Agency and police force."

They hadn't had to show their bogus badges, or relinquish their weapons. Vern replied, "Well, we're a separate HAP branch running our own investigation and I'm afraid there's a little too much in-house competition…you know how it is. Our comrades are keeping us in the dark so they can get their faces on the news."

"Speaking of faces on the news, I remember seeing you on VT, Agent Black. You're the one who terminated that male prostitute in Red Station."

Black had had enough of being recognized for that accomplishment today. "Yes, I'm afraid I am. Just following unsavory orders."

"I won't hold it against you, I promise." Gamine smile again. Then the pout. "Did you hurt your face today? Looks like a bite."

It was swollen, red and shiny, near his nose from the dart. "Just a stupid accident."

"Well, anyway, I will tell you whatever I can—everything I told your greedy comrades, I promise." Linda came then, set Mrs. Greenberg's lunch tray before her on the desk, and left the men their coffee on a wheeled cart between them. She winked at Black for protecting her secret on her way out.

"So Toll Loveland approached you directly to ask to use your old plant...not through an agent or associate or anything?" Vern asked, slurping coffee.

"He made an appointment and met me here, where you sit. He paid me for the privilege of using Greenberg Products as a theater for one night. Needless to say, I had no idea of his intentions. He described the performance but not the so-called *Cupid of Death* film, or the infected moths. I never saw any associates, if he had them. I'd never met him before that and I haven't met him since. After what happened I had myself tested for M-670, in the thought that somehow during our meeting he had infected me, too. He hadn't."

"You're a lucky one," said Black.

"You didn't attend the performance yourself?" asked Woodmere.

"Well," Mrs. Greenberg bit in half a huge shrimp dipped in cocktail sauce, "he had shown me a vid of his last show...you know...the one in which he cut off his finger and cloned it back?"

"*The Godfucker.*" Vern wasn't afraid to say it.

She smiled, a shy twelve-year-old. "Yes. A little too gruesome, not for me. My instincts may have saved me."

"Have, ah, any of our associates approached you to have your memories of that play and your meeting with Loveland recorded for them to view?"

"They asked me—I'm afraid I declined. A creepy thought; I've never cared for the idea of someone paging through my private life like that."

"Why let him perform, if you didn't like his art?"

"Well, Agent Woodmere," the widow Greenberg giggled, "just because I don't care for a man's approach to art doesn't mean I won't help support the arts. It isn't for me to judge what should and shouldn't be seen. I could hardly turn him down. In fact, I felt guilty at the time for accepting his money instead of simply lending him the plant. Now, of course," she grew solemnly pouty, "I blame myself for this tragedy. If I had only turned him down...I feel like an accomplice."

"No one blames you, ma'am," Vern reassured her. "He would've held it someplace else with the same effect, that's all."

Mrs. Greenberg sighed, picked the shell off a soft shrimp body. "I was receptive to the idea because I love art, as you might tell from my home. My husband Emmanuel and I were always supportive of it, and my husband himself was a fine painter—did you know that?"

"No, I didn't."

"Oh my, yes. This picture." She swivelled her chair to point. "He did that."

Both men had noticed it. It was a lovely, stately, highly realistic oil painting of Helga Greenberg, her small hands clasped on her black lap. It could have been painted today…or thirty years ago.

"He was very gifted," Black spoke up.

"How did he die again, ma'am?" Vern asked reluctantly. "Not in the chem spill…"

"No, no, a common misconception. He did die shortly thereafter, however—Garland Syndrome."

"Oh," said Vern.

"Yes, it was terrible. He mutated absolutely beyond recognition in two weeks. Thank God when it got that bad it was like he was in a walking coma. When he died he was more fungus than man. I can talk about it now, but I've never remarried…never will, I suspect. We don't do too well with mutation around here, do we?" she tried to joke. "Both Emmanuel and me."

"I'm really sorry," Vern said, profoundly gentle. Vern—*gentle?* A first for Black.

"I'm fine, but thank you for your concern, Agent Woodmere."

Black dared speak up again (his erection had dwindled back to nothing). "We hear you were able to finally sell Greenberg Products—to a pharmaceutical company."

"Yes. I think previous buyers were reluctant about the site after the spill, but I was also reluctant to sell the business my husband loved so much, put so much into—it was *him*. But I suppose all the controversy surrounding my plant recently attracted the attention of these people, and I decided it was finally time to sell. This incident kind of soiled it for me anyway, you know? Best to put the plant behind me."

"Who are they?"

"A new group, Cugok Pharmaceuticals. In full, the Fredrick V. Cugok Pharmaceutical Research and Manufacturing Company, Inc. They just got their research and manufacturing licenses this year but they've got a lot of fine minds fresh out of the best schools. I felt good passing the plant on to them."

"Mrs. Greenberg," said Black.

"Helga." Smile.

"Helga. Ah…was there once a fence between your plant and the Beds of the Bedbugs?"

"Yes—two fences, theirs and ours. They were removed after the spill to connect the two properties because my husband once owned the land the Beds were built on, and after the spill the Coleopteroids sold it back to us."

"They bought that land from your husband?"

"Yes, and sold it back when they moved."

"Coleopteroids?" said Vern.

"They don't like to be called Bedbugs. Coleopteroids—it means beetle beings."

"They left a lot of stuff. Some of it looks salvageable," said Black.

"I wouldn't know about that. How can we tell what they need and don't? Emmanuel had as good a relationship with them as any human ever has—he found them very intriguing."

"Do you know if Toll Loveland had any contact with them?"

"I have no idea. They seldom come 'round now to the Beds near Greenberg. Is there a problem with the Coleopteroids?"

"We don't know yet. Maybe a connection to Loveland."

"Hm—I see." She sipped her tea, weirdly lovely eyes on Black over the rim of her cup. Hard to read, more so even than Opal's.

"Well," he broke their gaze to look at Vern, "nothing else really comes to mind."

"I'm here if you ever need to return, gentlemen. I'll do anything to assist you...as I said, I can't help but feel partly responsible for all this. Some more coffee?"

They declined. "You got a bathroom, ma'am?" asked Vern.

"No...sorry. Just kidding." Helga rang for Linda, who took Vern away. Black and Helga rose, and she came out from behind her desk.

"Natural blond?" she smiled.

"Me? Yeah. You?"

"Yes. Nice to see another one—it gets lonely."

He was going to say that his girlfriend had blond hair, too, but didn't feel comfortable thinking of Opal, thinking of her as his girlfriend. And maybe, he recognized, he simply didn't want the widow Greenberg to know that he had a pseudo-girlfriend, semi-lover. Guilt bubbled. Nausea rolled over in him like a baby he was carrying...growing, wanting to burst out of him.

"I was hoping we'd have the opportunity to talk alone." Her eyes didn't flinch or coyly divert from his. She was forty-two. "I was wondering if you'd care to have dinner with me tonight or some other, Mr. Black?"

"Why?"

"Why?" She couldn't help but giggle a little. "Well, I find you to be an attractive man. Why else do people ask to see other people?"

"I, ah." He looked to the oil painting, which was only a little less disquieting in its appraisal of him. "I'd like to but I really can't..." A sickly embarrassed grin.

"Married?"

"I, ah, contracted M-670 at Toll Loveland's *Pandora's Box*."

"Oh, good Lord!"

"Yeah."

"Oh, you poor, poor man—I had no idea! That's horrible! Oh, I feel so bad for you…I feel like it's my fault."

"It isn't, don't say that. So…I…assume that dinner might lead to other things, as it often will…and I can't."

"Yes, I suppose sex would have been on the agenda. I'm so sorry. Please don't despair, I'm sure a cure is right around the corner."

He made himself look back at her, smile again. "That's what they say. Thanks, anyway."

"Maybe in the near future, eh? Hang on for me—put that in your head. I want to take you to dinner." She smiled to comfort him.

"I will." He liked her.

She gave his hand a squeeze and then finished off her coffee.

Vern returned. "Ready to go, man?"

"Thank you for the coffee," Black told Helga.

"Remember."

"I will."

"Goodbye for now, gentlemen, and good luck in your search. I enjoyed your company."

"Likewise." Vern waved. Black didn't look back. As they followed Linda down the jungle-lined corridor again, Vern whispered, "I asked Red out for a date. No go, dammit. I knew I shoulda shaved today. We'll have to think of a good reason to come back, huh?"

"Yeah." The study door remained open behind him and he was sure he felt Helga Greenberg's eyes on his back like two ice cubes melting down his spine.

NINE

When Black got home that evening, there was someone in the hall waiting for him, stepping out of the shadows.

It was Ruichi, the landlord, dusky-skinned and pock-faced—of indeterminately mixed heritage, unknownable even to himself maybe. He never seemed to bathe, or use deodorant, and Black was not startled to see him there. The cloud had announced him.

"Mr. Black, I need a word with you."

"What is it?" Black didn't care for the tone of voice. He didn't care for Ruichi.

"You have it."

"Have what?"

Ruichi kept a safe distance. "Mutstav six-seventy."

"Who told you that?"

"You have it. I know."

"Who told you, man? You got a call, did you? From a Captain Nedland, maybe? He wants me at HAP in a hospital bed so he called you, right? So I'll have no place else to go, or so he thinks."

"I don't want you here."

"Fuck you. You can't discriminate against me!"

"I own this building."

"I'm no threat to anybody, moron!"

"If my other tenants find out..."

"They won't, and so what if they do? I'm not leaving."

"I will have you thrown out by the police."

"HAP. Don't you mean your buddies at HAP? Go ahead...I'll have housing officials, fire marshals, building inspectors, and the works down here to go over your buildings with a fine-toothed comb, asshole." Black stabbed a finger in Ruichi's face, backing him against the wall. "Don't fuck with me or I'll sneak in your house and puke down your throat, fuck—then you'll have something to worry about."

"You can't threaten me...you'll be sorry."

"I'll get a lawyer, Ruichi, and I'll own your fucking building when I'm done. Now stay outta my face. And go take a shower, huh? You're more a health hazard than I am." And Black passed the landlord to thump upstairs, before his anger could mount to a dangerous level.

Bastards. Those slimy bastards. No more check-ins at HAP…none…that was a promise. And before he let them lock him in their hospital dungeon they'd have to kill him. Another promise.

The tran was gone.

Massive yellow robots and tiny human (and humanoid) figures moved across the strange overlapping configurations of tracks. The hum, buzz, grinding of their activity resounded out there.

Greenberg had owned the land originally, sold it to the Bedbugs, bought it back—and now sold it to Cugok Pharmaceuticals. And Cugok was cleaning up its new property.

"Shit. Bloody fucking steaming shit," snarled Vern. Beside him stood Dirge of the black market Teeb organization.

"Nothing can come easy for me, can it?" Black said to himself as he strode with such determination toward two of the workers that they prepared themselves for trouble. When he got close enough for them to see, he flipped his badge. "Health Agency. Where's this junk going…to the other Bedbug trackyard?"

"Some of it," said a Choom woman in a hard-hat, clipboard under her arm. "Some of it they're paying us to dump."

"What about that intact old tran that was close to the Greenberg lot?"

"Ah, we brought that to their new location. All the trans, except one burnt-out shell…that we'll dump."

"So where is this place?"

She told him, cowed by the flash in his eyes.

They went there, Black and Woodmere and Dirge.

It was an old airport—Black couldn't remember the name but remembered now his father and mother bringing him here as a boy to watch the many various vehicles come and go on a lazy summer Sunday. The buildings and hangars were now used by the Bedbugs, it looked like—hangars with tracks vanishing into them, obviously storing trans. The old office and administration buildings were low, flat-roofed and in need of paint, and every window was bolted over with black slabs of metal. A huge spiked fence like the one around the abandoned yard surrounded this space, too. Black brought his rented car to the gate, but there was no one at it, no guard shack. He hooted his horn repeatedly, got out of the car to yell and wave his arms.

He saw a small black figure scurry from behind one building to behind another, and maybe some more scrambling in the cave mouth of a hangar. A large, black metal sphere appeared from behind the main office building, floating on repulsor beams, or maybe an antigrav, six inches above the ground. It approached the gate. Black took a few wary steps back from it, and Vern had his gun in his lap in the car.

The implacable, almost featureless black globe hovered beyond the gate. A lifeless, robot-like voice came from a grille—probably a translator.

"Are you of the Cugok Company?"

Badge again, held up for eyes that weren't apparent. "No, Health Agency. A derelict tran from the old Greenberg property was brought here and we'd like to take a look at it—it's very important."

"Are we considered to be in violation of health ordinances?"

"No, no, it doesn't concern any wrongdoing on your part. A human placed something in the tran and I have to find it. It's evidence in an investigation." If they demanded to see a search warrant it was over. Also, there was still the possibility that the Bedbugs, or at least some opportunistic rogues among them, had aided Loveland in constructing the teleporter. The chances were good they'd be turned away until the Bedbugs visited the old vehicle themselves, destroyed the evidence of their participation.

The lifeless voice droned, "You may come in and look. No weapons."

Black glanced back at Vern. No problem. They still had their blue and red pens in their pockets, if an emergency arose. A little something.

The ball opened upwards like a blackened orange peeling itself, two figures emerging as the vehicle remained suspended. One was a Bedbug. Bipedal, small, black and armored, four slim tentacle-like arms ending in pincers, the lower two of the original six removed and replaced with jointed, intricate black metal prosthetic arms which actually looked more appropriately insect-like than the wavering whip arms.

The other figure was as tall as Black; that was because it was a human. Apparently. Black-robed, the colorless bald head atop the black cone waxy and as lifeless as the voice from the sphere, which had come from its lips. The eyes didn't seem to see Black as they looked at him. Atop the bald head was a black cap. No, he realized: a black metal plate in the human's skull. No names were offered, none asked for.

The bluish lips moved slightly. "This way, please." As it pivoted and moved away, the Bedbug with it, Black realized the human's feet—if it had them—didn't touch the ground. Vern elbowed Black. "Trick or treat," he said.

The gate closed and bolted by itself behind them, as in a horror movie.

Black described the tran they sought to the human's back, not getting into too much detail. They were led to a group of trans outside one of the hangars in which the functioning trans were stored. For a few minutes Black and Vern were in doubt; the first one they tried had no Navigation globes and Black began to worry. But the next one was it. Vern peeked under the front console, gave Black the thumb's up. Dirge moved down beside him.

The robed human stood to the rear of the vehicle with Black. "What is it that has been placed aboard our craft?" it droned. Black had hoped it would leave them to their work, but why not ask it some questions since it intended to remain with them?

"An illegal teleportation device has been tapped into the tran, to the Navigator spheres…I don't know the how. It was used in the escape of a criminal from a crime scene, and he's probably still using it by remote control. Do you know anything about this, or an artist named Toll Loveland?"

"We have no knowledge of that person or of an illegal teleportation device aboard our craft. We would not cooperate in the installation or utilization of such a device."

Black didn't know whether to believe his cadaver-like host or not. "Is it possible some of the Bed…the Coleopteroids could have cooperated on their own?"

"They would not."

Yeah, right. Black thought of the Dimensionals, the errant gang of Bedbug criminals said to live in the subway tunnels and forgotten grottoes far below Punktown, sealed off by humans after the destruction of the great earthquake.

"I will examine the device." The human glided forward, Vern and Dirge backing off to give it room. They stared in horror as the black cone crumpled and telescoped, the white head lowering to look up under the console. There could be no full body inside those robes. A black mechanical arm emerged to gently probe the hidden device.

"Trick or treat is right," muttered Black. "Dirge, what I want is to see if we can tap into Loveland's device, get in its mind. Then work in our own remote control. Home in on him, and teleport him right here into our arms."

"A tall order."

"It's important."

Dirge was an odd being himself—a white salamander thing, no bigger than Black's finger, in a box riding atop three silver legs like a camera on a robot tripod. Three little silver arms were retracted under the box. Like the prosthetic limbs of the Bedbugs, an adaptation to humanoid-based society. Black could see the bright-eyed little creature in a window of its tiny cockpit. In there earlier, Vern had pointed out a wall calendar featuring a photograph of a nude salamander female. Odd, but at least he wasn't trying to look human, or be partially human, like that thing up front.

Dirge replied, "If he's got his molecular pattern on file in the thing's memory, maybe…*maybe* I can snatch him. Otherwise, all I could zero in on would be the remote control. I could teleport that here. Or maybe let you know where it is. That way you'd know where he lives, or where he is if it's on his person."

"Beautiful. Either way."

"Maybe, I said. Either way. This guy's not stupid; he may be prepared for this. No memory pattern. A scan blocker where he is. Whatever."

"So if he had no pattern on file, what would he have to do, scan himself and transmit that information to the teleporter before he teleported?"

"Yeah. His remote unit might be a scan, too, though that could be getting unwieldy, more something in an apartment than something you carry in your pocket. Who knows? This is a smart boy. It looks tough."

"I am afraid," said the seemingly disembodied head, floating back to the level of Black's own head, pivoting to face him, "you are correct. Some of our kind must have assisted the criminal you seek. But not one of us here."

"The Dimensionals?"

"It must be."

"Shit," said Dirge, "this is gonna be a pain in the gills."

"Give it your best go, man," Vern reassured him.

"I must report this to my superiors," said the mock-human liaison. "Proceed with your investigation—I shall return." It left the tran.

"I shall return," Vern mimicked its voice exaggeratedly.

Dirge's telescopic legs collapsed enough for him to work under the console, his tiny robot arms coming into play. Vern and Black hunkered down to watch him. Vern lit up a smoke. Dirge said, "Ah, guys…could you give me some room—you make me nervous. I don't like an audience."

"Let us know if you're onto something." Black moved to the door, hopped down to the ground and lit up his own smoke.

"Ya wonder just how bad the relationship is between the Dimensionals and this ant farm," mused Vern, squinting toward the old administration buildings. "I never hear about them going after the Dimensionals."

"They don't like to talk about them—they're an embarrassment. Like you said, they've got an ant farm mentality. I'm sure they try to deal with the problem in their own secretive way."

"Can't blame them, though—the Dimensionals. I wouldn't want to live like these freakin' cockroaches."

"It's a wonder there are the Dimensionals. I guess we decadent humans just have a corruptive influence, huh?"

"Well, they can just keep the fuck out of our dimension if they don't like it."

Black began choking as if he had swallowed the wrong way; doubled over. Vern clapped him on the back. "I'm okay," Black hacked, waving him off. He flicked away his cigarette. "I inhaled too deeply."

"You shouldn't be smokin', man."

"What's it gonna do, kill me?"

"Enough of that talk—I told you! You can't have that kind of attitude!"

"I'm gonna *die*, Vern…I'm dying now."

"So am I…but I want to prolong it as long as I can, right?"

"So why are you smoking?"

"Well, you gotta enjoy life, too."

"My brand's milder." Black tucked his cigarette package into Vern's leather flight jacket. "There. I quit. Happy?"

"That's better. You're learning."

Black grinned. But it was a bloodless grin. His eyes had the puffy bareness of a model without makeup. Vern hadn't been close with Black in the past, but it was apparent nonetheless that he had lost weight and was still losing it fast. His skin had a light but unmistakable yellow cast. Not Asian yellowish-brown. *Yellow* yellow, like they painted Asians in comic books. The stark sunlight was not flattering. Black suddenly looked to Vern like a fluorescent-lit corpse on a morgue table.

"Hey," they heard Dirge calling from inside, "hey *guys!*"

"What?" Vern said, starting to turn as the tran exploded.

They were close to the machine, but it was thick metal firmly bolted and contained most of the blast. Still, pieces flew; a chunk of something smashed across Black's left shoulder, spinning him to the ground. A more treacherous piece of shrapnel hit Vern. He managed to stay on his feet, but he howled. Black heard him howling up there, rolled groggily onto his back to look, shielding his face with his arm although the metal hail had ended.

Black smoke billowed out of the tran's door and portholes and ruptures, and inside those thunder-heads flickered purple tongues of lightning. Vern was dancing, a marionette in the hands of a child. A jagged plate of metal was embedded in his cheekbone, splitting his nose in half sideways. A bolt from the pouring smoke clouds had reached out to the shrapnel, making Vern dance spasmodically, shaking out his howl while it flashed like a strobe jump-rope, the marionette's string that kept him on his feet. It was a nightmare image which transfixed Black.

Then the electric flashes tapered off, withdrew, and dropped Vern onto his face. His moan in response was high-pitched and horrifying.

Black struggled to his feet, staggered backward, fell. He lost sight of Vern…saw only the thick smoke above him, beginning to spread and disperse. But he heard the sphere's door open, and an excited chittering. Then the voice of the pseudo-human representative of the Bedbugs. The words were urgent if the tone was not.

"Take them, they may be saboteurs, take them…"

Pincered claws caught hold of Black's jacket. "He left a trap…it was a fucking trap," he protested. He thrashed weakly as he was hauled to his feet, a Bedbug at either side, remarkably strong for their size. Like all bugs. Now he could see Vern. "Help my friend—help him!"

Vern was on hands and knees. Moaning. He could rise no further. No blood, when

Vern lifted his head to gaze (could he see?) toward Black. The edges of the wound around the jagged plate were black and cauterized. The Bedbugs took hold of his arms but his head fell forward limply, heavy with its alien weight. Black was convinced that he had just seen Vern Woodmere die. He was wrong.

Only moments after he was bundled into the black sphere, Black lost consciousness, watching the door come down and the sky disappear.

"Where am I?" Clichéd questions didn't come into existence for no good reason. Black did have a damn good idea, however. The real question should have been, "Why am I here and not in a hospital for humans?"

"You are still with us. You have been examined and treated for your injuries." The human-headed, black-robed being by the door was a woman. The red wavy hair that covered her black skull plate was obviously a wig but helped a great deal anyway. She was waxenly attractive. Her eyes didn't seem to be quite on Black, however. He was strapped to a cot in a white, undecorated room with one window covered by a metal plate. His first irrational idea was that they were going to make him into one of these beings like the red-haired woman now addressing him. "You have the virus called mutstav six-seventy—are you aware?"

"Yes—what have you done with my friend?"

"The tiny one aboard the destroyed tran is dead. The human is alive but in need of further care."

"Vern's *alive?* Thank God! Look, let me go, I'm no fucking saboteur—he left a booby trap! The man I'm after—Toll Loveland! You must have heard of him on the news; he did this, not us! Why would we blow ourselves up?"

"An accident, perhaps, while setting a greater explosion, having fabricated the story of the teleporter and having previously installed the teleporter so as to gain admittance here. That was our…"

"It isn't true! Call my boss! Look…"

"As I say, that was our first assumption, for the sake of caution. But the device on the table beside you is a human truth scan, as you can see." Black twisted his head to look. "It indicates that you are telling no lies."

"Then let me go!"

"Of course. Pardon our security measures."

A Bedbug entered the room and unstrapped him, removed the truth scan's sticky disc from Black's forehead. Black swung his legs over the side of the cot. He'd been given a heavy painkiller, felt cloudy but pleasant. "Thanks for helping my friend and me. Can you please summon an ambulance to come get him immediately?"

The redhead chittered. The Bedbug scurried away. "It is done. We must now speak with your police force."

"Good idea. Tell them what happened. I'll go downtown and fill out my own report with the Health Agency." Black risked standing.

"Very well. We must be kept informed of your findings."

"Of course. What are my friend's chances?"

"Chances of survival?"

"Yes."

"Fairly promising."

"I got him into this. I did this to him. It's my fault."

"Then you confess that you are a saboteur?" It didn't sound alarmed, but telescoped an inch or so taller alertly.

"No, no...I mean...I feel guilty. I convinced my friend to help me. I confess my guilt."

Black's pallid, black-frocked confessor offered him no absolution.

He wanted to look in on Vern but couldn't afford the time. Black left the administration complex in a sphere piloted by a Bedbug, with no one to translate for him. He told it "thanks" anyway as it let him out through the gate.

Inside his black rental car, Black folded his arms across the console and laid his cloud-filled forehead on them. But then he heard the ambulance. He sat up straight. They mustn't catch him. They'd come after him now, with Vern in their hands...there could be no question of his activities. The Bedbugs had his name to give the authorities. He must not go home.

He didn't know where to go. But the ambulance was coming—so he went.

TEN

His left fist knotted in his sheet, the unfeeling pillow squashed beneath him, Montgomery Black vomited off the side of his bed into a plastic basin. He may as well have been vomiting into the void, which seethed all around this bed, so vertiginous was the combination of nausea and the sleep the nausea had wrenched him from. He clung to the bed for all his worth, even hooking his feet off the side. The tornado would subside, the bed would lower. Already it was slowing, casting the last of his dream's debris out of his reach.

His throat was seared, and the last loud retches produced nothing; it was like gargling up his shattered rib-cage. The effort brought tears to his eyes and the front of his skull filled up with the fluid of agony, heavy and pressing against his brain and down on his eyeballs. Black curled at last into a naked, trembling fetus which had just narrowly survived another attempted abortion.

He shook with low, mindless sobs of self-pity, degradation and fear. The fetus had no one. In his extremity Black might have called out for his mother, but he was not close to his parents, might as well have called out for the computers which had educated him, so even in his delirium it didn't occur to him. One person's name waited to be said, however, and he didn't so much want to call out for her to help as to beg to be forgiven. This pain, also, was ever growing…

Vern, too. He remembered what he'd done to Vern. Dirge—well, he hadn't known him but it was extra weight he didn't need.

It was all too much. He might have remained there in bed, crawled back into his dreams to escape, but he had already slept for twelve hours by the clock on the side table. And he must take something for this headache, he really must. Yes, definitely. In a minute, when he could regain some strength.

After an hour of lying in his sweaty womb of pain at last he let himself onto the floor and stood up.

God—the cramps. They stooped him. He had to shamble to the bathroom. The only light came from in there. He kept it lit at all times for emergency needs, though now he seldom rushed for it when his basin was near.

The mirrored cabinet was already wide open, the mirror turned to the wall. Black shook out two pills for his headache. He had stopped taking the stronger pills which kept headaches at bay for a week or a month or more at a time, depending on the strength level; they aggravated his nausea and thank God he'd purged the last one out of his system by now. These mild things deadened it sufficiently without too much nausea, and without fogging his brain…though he'd had to take six over the course of the day, a few times recently, and that left him nauseous enough.

For the nausea he had a half-effective syrup he'd bought at a local pharmacy. Without a prescription his resources were limited; he didn't even dare check into a street clinic. No—no way. If he stepped into one of those they wouldn't let him step out. You didn't need to administer a test now to see.

Black shut the cabinet, morbidly, to see for himself. Masochistically. How much more degraded could it make him feel?

Still, he shivered nakedly, almost drew back, as if—in gazing out a window into a graveyard—a corpse had raised its head to peer back at him, nose to nose. The white-green fluorescent wasn't kind. He hadn't looked at his face for several days, though he had brushed his teeth and hadn't neglected shaving—a mindless fastidiousness he recognized for its irony. But he did have to go out occasionally, after all. And he bathed at least every other day—womb-warm bubble baths, for hours. Sometimes reading a novel someone had left in the apartment, sometimes sleeping. The tub too small, luckily, for him to slip under the water level. Hours of floating tranquility, like a drug.

But now, confronting his face, he felt a surge of desperate fear that was almost panic. He wanted to give up, to die then and there. He also wanted to burst out into the street, run and yell for help, run and scream, run and sob, run. But he stood mesmerized by himself, gripping the sink for support.

His already prominently-boned face was cadaverous, eyes sunken into sockets so purple he might have been beaten recently. The yellowness of his skin was unmistakable even from a distance. He could scarcely close his mouth; even to suck lukewarm soup through a straw was a misery. The sores had spread past the borders of his cracked and bloated lips, caked hard with blood and dried pus and scabs. They had spread up to his nostrils, which were red, inflamed. He had nosebleeds, even now the blood a rocky crust in there so that he had to breathe out of his mouth.

"You need a shave, fucker," he mumbled, the effort further tearing lips ripped by the vomiting. Black reached in the cabinet for his shaver, this time watched the foolish, meaningless ritual. Today he must confront some things, he told himself. But then, he always told himself that. And then went back to bed, or filled his bath.

He wouldn't put on his lip ointment—that was it. Maybe the pain would keep him on his toes…if it didn't bring him to his knees.

Today, he told himself.

It had been a month and three quarters since he had left the Bedbugs, withdrawing all his money from his bank account and renting this tiny apartment. Directly after withdrawing his money he had made just one quick stop to the apartment of Vern Woodmere with its pillars and black and yellow tiles, using the tools from his trunk to gain admittance. He had worn gloves, for all that was worth. He had taken all of Vern's weapons for safekeeping. Anyway, he was doing Vern a favor; he wouldn't want the forcers to find that collection.

Vern's huge orange and yellow slug with the red blossom on its back was contentedly glued to the tiled wall of Black's shower stall.

The Canberra Mall was a ten-minute ride from his apartment, and had everything he or anyone in Punktown could need; it was the largest and most popular shopping area in town. Black remembered it from his boyhood as the Canberra Circus Mall. It had covered less area then, though still being five floors in height. The ground floor had the carnival rides, games and sideshows, the second was an immense arcade and billiards parlor, floor three was a parking mall, four had a movie theater, shops and gift stores, a few bars, a legal gambling parlor and a legal brothel. The top floor with its domed roof window had a more upper-class version of the floor below, with a cocktail lounge, nice restaurant, swimming pool, saunas and a better quality movie theater where plays and concerts were also performed. Over the years the stores and shops had greatly proliferated, and the legal brothel and gambling den had been done away with.

As a boy he had come here with his friend Dover and Dover's parents and older sister and her friends. Black had liked Dover's parents very much, had envied him their warmth and patience. He was drawn to the sideshows but would find their inhabitants following him to his bedroom that night in dream form. Even today he could envision, as if those specters had taken residence in the carnival of his mind, the rather pretty woman whose face looked out of the huge mouth of another, insensate giant head with hair growing out of its nose and eyes. A black man who was nothing but a huge human head, yellowed eyeballs as big as Black's fists were now, ever drooling, with only two feeble arms to drag itself about. And the Lava Man, who looked like a figure from Pompeii that had come to life, naked and stiff, cracked and breaking away at the joints from what little movement he could manage. Later Black had felt guilty for staring so directly. But next time he'd stare again. Despite the guilt, despite the hauntings. Despite the fear. Because it was also the fear that made him look. The unspoken philosophizing of children. "Flesh is clay," he might have said to himself if he'd been able to articulate his feelings. "This could have been me…"

The pet store was his first stop. In the wild, the slug's red blossom attracted flies, the flower opened and consumed them, but there weren't enough flies in his apartment to leave it at that, and he had consulted this store a month and a half ago on what to feed the creature. The first box of pellets, one hand-fed to the slug's flower-mouth a day, had lasted this long. Black was more attentive to the slug's feeding than to his own.

He couldn't help himself from gazing in at the puppies. The various rodents and such he didn't pity so much—they were indifferent to humans, it seemed, but the puppies made him feel guilty for not taking all of them home. He could imagine any one of them as his pet and companion, and was even a little tempted now, half out of pity for them and half out of pity for himself.

One cage had a sign boasting: PUPPY OF THE WEEK! HALF PRICE! The "puppy" filled the cage, gnawing innocently on a plastic bone, apparently not as concerned for his fate as Black suddenly was. He beckoned to a woman who worked here, she came, when he spoke she withdrew a little. His breath told of the dying of his body.

"What happens if you can't find homes—do you kill them?"

"They go to animal shelters—I wouldn't work for this place if they did that." Her answer was brusque and she moved away.

Yeah, Black wondered, but do the animal shelters kill them?

He let some kittens in a stinky cage bite and seize his index finger through the mesh. If I wasn't gonna die, he thought. But what good could he be to them now? They should feel sorry for *him.*

At times—*at times*—he could even look forward to death…like now. He wouldn't have to worry about all the pain of living things, wouldn't feel this intense impotence.

He left the pet store.

He was in a vast, high-ceilinged single chamber, divided on either side into shops of seemingly infinite variety. This would be as great a heaven as many people could imagine. Even as they thronged here to yearn for all that they couldn't afford or even contain, they seemed to take pleasure simply in their proximity to it. This was their culture encapsulated; they were closest to themselves here. In his new state, Black felt like an alien to this culture…he could step back and view it from a new perspective; the perspective of one who didn't dream of new furniture to buy, new clothes, better toys, because soon he wouldn't be here. He already felt like a spirit, without a body (except for the pain), moving amongst the living, observing their ways for a short while.

This immense cathedral with its neon and laser signs in place of stained glass was sufficiently dark to lend Black this feeling of ghostly anonymity. In the bright pet store he had been nervous, too revealed. Not to mention that bright light made his eyes burn and water. Stupid to have left his dark glasses in the car—they could have hidden his sockets, also. He would pick up a new pair in the pharmacy when he went for fresh drugs.

The *girls.* Everywhere; he didn't know where to look. The Canberra Mall was a favored youth hang-out. As many milled about amongst the stores as in the arcade and carnival areas still in existence here. Boys of eight to thirteen with ridiculous, elaborately spray-molded pompadours (when Black was a boy he had hated to even comb his hair, had feared having his hair cut), affecting sulky Elvis-like expressions to match their coiffures, zoomed about overhead on hoverboards, endangering all. Their colorful costumes repulsed Black; unrefined, erratic, an anarchy of color and design.

How much more obnoxious could children look, short of wearing vests made of rat heads, and that was a fashion in other parts of Punktown.

But the girls weren't hard to look at. Hard *not* to look at. Black would follow one with his eyes as long as he could, afraid to lose sight of her, only to hitch his eyes suddenly to another, and on. Leotards, tight jeans, tight skirts, some in skimpy bikini-type bottoms. Round smooth horse-like haunches, tiny tight child-like asses. Smooth, hard-skinned fruit without the sag and ripples and dimples of age—*glowingly* smooth and hard. Apple-skinned youth. Eyeing them, Black felt vastly old. He was rotting, his rot slowly oozing out of every orifice. With age the doors of the body were flung open to accept every vile invasion. Black's doors had been wrenched open early and the rot had been quick to come live here, to be fruitful and multiply, maggots in his apple.

He felt ashamed of his decay, of his lewd voyeurism, prematurely old man that he was, his slimy stare defiling young buttocks. When a long-haired teenager caught his gaze on her lovely peach-skinned face as she stood chatting outside a music store with friends, she scrunched her nose at him in disgust like she could smell him coming, smell his filthy stare. Black lowered his head in shame as he passed her.

As old as he felt, it also seemed decades since he had last had sex. Sex. That imperative hunger had gotten him into this nightmare. Well, Toll Loveland had, but aside from the obvious. The nightmare wouldn't have spread without the hunger. And still he hungered. He had to force his mouth to eat but his penis needed no prompting. Why did the urge seem even greater now than before he'd become sick? Because he knew he couldn't have sex? Certainly. But was it also the primal biological urge to procreate, more urgent as his own extinction drew near? The narcissistic aspiration to fleshly immortality by leaving a part of yourself alive to eat, and fuck, and buy things when you no longer could? Black had never much thought of being a father. Lately, though, several times, he had regretted not having children. Was that vanity, instinctual…or, less cynically, the sadness of not having experienced all the wonders life had to offer?

Better this way, he thought. No children to mourn him.

How sad, he thought. No children to mourn him.

He wandered, putting off his errands. Especially the major chore to be done. In a men's room he broke down and, hidden in a stall, smeared ointment on his lips. The agony made him lean his forehead against the cool stall wall, tears streaming down his cheeks—not just from the harsh light—before the welcome numbness came. While it lasted he went out to buy a coffee to carry in his wanderings. He could wander here all day, despite the temptations and regrets. Though he couldn't be part of this society much longer, he felt soothed by his proximity to it.

I'm dying, he thought. No cure will come in time. There's no hope, no reprieve. I will die soon.

There was no chance of his catching Loveland. No attempt was worth the effort;

he was out of time and ideas. Others would have to do it. But for him, Loveland had won. And he had to accept that.

To rest his wobbly legs he bought a newspaper and sat on a stone bench under a basin of giant ferns. New movies, new wars, new marriages and divorces, birth announcements and obituaries and every day a new paper. It's not like I'm the first to die, he thought. I'm not special. I haven't been married or had children. So what? On page nine it said a ten-year-old girl had been killed in the crossfire of a youth gang war.

He wished he believed more firmly in a God. That would ease his pain, give him something to look forward to. He'd be ecstatic, maybe, to be dying. But it was because of his pain that he didn't firmly believe. Black wouldn't make any child of his suffer like this. So was he more loving than all-loving God? Maybe God was an energy more than an entity, but Black couldn't feel loved by it.

Idly he scanned the personal columns. Nothing like, "M-670 victim, female, young, attractive (once), seeks similarly afflicted male with whom to fuck away what little time we have left." Why not? And what was keeping him from submitting his own ad? There had to be plenty of compatible people out there. She didn't even have to be too young or attractive. And it wasn't just sex he wanted, either. Vern's slug wasn't a good conversationalist.

The first half of the paper he mostly avoided. He was living enough bad news. Black watched three very tall teenage boys with platinum-blond pompadours strut by. One of them thrust his face in the face of a black boy of about twelve and roared, "Boo!" The boy shrank, the assholes strutted away laughing. Ten-year-olds killed in gang wars. Why wasn't Black out there with Vern's arsenal, cleaning up some of this mess with what time he had left? Here he'd wasted his time pursuing Loveland when he could have been blowing away drug dealers and child pornographers who were only too easy to find.

Well, sorry, but he didn't feel up to it now. Or even up to placing that ad, really, despite the hunger. Best to just run his errands, wander around a little while more, go home and take a long, long bath.

He finally reached the end of the great hall, entered a huge department store to cut through that to a nearby supermarket where he would pick up some groceries. Shit; the lights in here. He'd bought his drugs and the paper in the pharmacy and had forgotten his sunglasses. Oh well, they had them in the market. How could he have forgotten?

A young teen with long, wavy red hair and tight white leotards walked in front of him in the department store. He thought of Helga Greenberg. Sorry, Helga. He wouldn't be keeping that date. He wondered, though, if she even remembered him.

To reach the exits he had to go through the children's clothing department, but on its outer boundary Black came to a halt.

His eyes were already watering, but now these colors, explosively bright in the full glare of store lights. Yellow screamed, orange, green, red. In hideous combinations, in hideous designs. Had they found a way to make colors brighter, more colorful? There seemed to be colors he had no names for. Had it always been this way? How could people look down at themselves enveloped in this garishness, how could parents bring these shrieking colors into their homes, dress their children in them, and why? Black stared at the expanse before him, unwilling to venture into it, disgusted with the human need for bolder stimuli, brighter peacock plumage, even as he recognized the ridiculous extreme of his reaction, even as the colors got through his eyes, poured down his throat and into his belly in a noxious mix of candy liquids. He staggered a few steps in another direction, fell to hands and knees and vomited up his coffee.

No longer the anonymous spirit. A rotten apple fallen from its shelter of cool leaves.

"Drunk," someone above him hissed.

"Oh for Christ's sake," sneered a teenage girl who worked here, abandoning her register as if afraid someone would ask her to clean it up.

"Yuck," said a child. Black could hear the wrinkled-up nose in its voice.

Considering how revolting people found him, many were willing to stare. No one took his arm; Black pulled himself to his feet, tottering. No one handed him his dropped bags; he had to stoop for them. Meeting the sneering gaze of the red-haired girl in white leotards, who stood a safe distance from him, Black wiped his lips on the back of his sleeve and spat some of his tainted saliva on the floor. "What'sa matter? Never seen the Lava Man before?"

"Disgusting." The girl tossed her hair and strutted off, insulted in her youth and beauty by the visage of death.

Black gulped some medicine for nausea from his bag and skirted the children's clothing department on his way outside.

It was cool, dusk, drizzling. The supermarket was near, a boy out front collecting hovercarts from the parking lot, corralling them. There were four pay vidphones in a row of booths. Black stood outside them. A teenage girl occupied one booth, laughing, a teenage boy's naked rear-end filling the screen of her phone.

I'll shop first, Black thought. That girl might listen. After I shop. Later...

Now, he ordered himself. *Now.* It's already later. *Too* later.

He didn't have a hand phone, or a vidphone at his flat. If he waited until tomorrow he might not be able to rouse himself to leave the apartment. He had taken a few steps toward the phone. The laughing girl put him off—maybe he'd wait until she was gone. Maybe he'd have a cigarette first. The corner of his right eye twitched with a rhythmic pulse; he squinted hard and subdued it. His right eye felt swollen—it hurt to blink his lid across it. He was unconsciously feeling the change in his pocket. He couldn't stand this girl. She was squashing her nose and lips into the screen, where the naked rear had returned. The boy broke wind, the girl leaping back with a squeal of delighted mock disgust.

Black had drifted two uncertain steps away when the girl emerged from the booth. She eyed him suspiciously, grin vanishing, casually slid a hand into her pocketbook as she passed him. Probably a gun, Black thought, eyes downcast as he moved forward bloodlessly into one of the phone booths.

No excuses. No time. He had to look up Opal's mother's number before he punched it in. As he waited for the call to be answered he thought he might vomit, nausea medicine or no.

Maybe they're not home.

Her mother's face filled the screen and Black flinched at its hugeness so close to his face. "Hello," she said, before she could recognize him.

"Hello, Mrs.—"

He saw the face withdraw as she reached to touch a button.

"No, wait! Please!" Black cried at her.

For a second, before it was gone, he noticed the change in the woman's face. Tired, even haggard. Did she now have it, too? he wondered for a foolish moment.

"Wait!" he cried again, but it was too late already. And yet the call hadn't been disconnected, after all. Black was startled by what he saw next.

It was obviously Opal. There was a dim lamp on a table behind her but she was silhouetted, her face in darkness. He knew the patterns of her tangled, thick hair. Some of it, highlighted like filaments, even glowed with a soft blond incandescence.

But the voice wasn't familiar to Black. It made him want to recoil. It was a gravelly, painful wheeze, just a thin trickle of air through a bricked-up tunnel.

"Monty," it said. "There's a few things…I want to tell you…"

"Opal." Tears were rising in him, as he felt his own throat closing up. "I'm so sorry…"

"Please listen to me…"

"I'm listening."

The head swayed, heavy, sunken into its shoulders. As it moved slightly a little light found its way around to the edge of her face for a moment. Black almost cried out. Her *eye*. It was sealed shut, swollen into a ball as large as a lemon, black and crusted. It had to have been an illusion…now gone.

"I…it's wrong for me to be mad at you…I know. I'm scared…"

"I understand."

"I know you didn't do this to me on purpose. I know it isn't your fault. I'm mad at you because…I'm so scared…"

"I understand, Opal…"

"I was looking for him for a while…"

"Loveland?"

"I thought maybe...I don't know."

"I was after him, too! I..."

"I traced him back to his various identities, but I never got far with any of them. But I found out something weird...that happened when he was...when he was...at school." She was straining to remember. Head swaying. "Paxton Polytech," she said at last. "When he was Manuel Hung. I went down there and spoke to people...they told me a funny story." She began to cough, coughed for a good two minutes, her shoulders jerking. She moaned. She croaked out words through the chinks again. "During his stay at the school some animals disappeared from the labs. They pinned it on him, but I guess...charges were never brought. He paid for their replacement..."

"Animals? What kind? How many?"

"I never could trace his identity back to his childhood. HAP and the police can't trace him. Who knows where he came from. I'm too...I can't do anything any more. I'm dying."

"Can I come see you?"

"I got it real good, huh?" she snorted, a half chuckle, more like a hiss.

"I'm sorry, Opal." The tears were here.

"If you find him before it gets you, too, kill him for me. But try to hang on. A cure is just around the corner—right?" He heard the sarcasm in her voice as she echoed the line they had both heard endlessly.

"It's too late," Black sobbed. "I'm dying, too..."

"I've got to go," she croaked.

"Can't I see you?"

"My poor mother..." Opal said, a wafting sounded thought.

"Oh my God, no! No! No!" At last, Black had realized. The realization lifted him out of his own fog. He pounded a fist on the phone console. "No, no! Opal! Opal!" he screamed at her hoarsely...even as he knew she was already dead.

"Best of luck to you, Monty. God bless you. It wouldn't hurt you to look for just a little faith...even if it's just a painkiller..."

"Opal..."

"I'm sorry—I was selfish not to see you in person while I still could. This is the best I could do. I had to be mad at somebody. Please understand...I wanted to say goodbye but this is the best I could do."

As she prepared to end the recording she sat back a little in her chair. Though she had sought to spare him the sight of her, she now accidentally allowed the light to unveil her. It had been no illusion. Both eyes were swollen, black, crusted...like skull sockets turned inside-out. One sealed, a solid rock. The other one's ossified lids open, the eyeball itself blackish-purple with a silvery pupil. Huge. The rest of the face was shrunken, wasted, festering, rotting. A monster with an Opal Cowrie wig on.

"Monty…" it resumed in its corpse voice.

This time when he slammed his fist down the screen went dead.

Black slid to the floor of the booth, hugging his knees, sobbing. It was almost dark outside; rain came in earnest. He was curled in this sarcophagus a long time.

"This is ridiculous!" the man laughed, his hovercart bumping into the shelf of toilet paper rolls. He fought to wheel it around, point and guide it evenly.

"Maybe it's…uneven weight distribution!" his female companion laughed, and moved some things around inside the cart.

"Oh, come *on!*" the man laughed back. He had short, neat hair, a bulky pink sweater over a high-collared white shirt, pink jeans and white high-top sneakers. The woman had neat silken hair, a gray blazer with huge shoulder pads over a white blouse, a gray skirt, black sneakers. He wore glasses with thick pink frames, hers thick and black. Neither had a vision problem; it was more a sort of jewelry, or statement of social status, like a primitive's facial scarring.

"It has a mind of its own," the man exclaimed. "Surely it's possessed by the soul of its previous shopper!"

"Surely this is a sign of the apocalypse!" the woman gasped, clutching her chest. She tossed a four-pack of toilet paper into the clear plastic cart.

"Which one?"

"Which what? Sign?" She tossed in another four-pack.

"No—which apocalypse?"

"*The* apocalypse." Another.

"Oh—*that* apocalypse!" He tossed in a six-pack, and then another.

She laughed, looked to see if the man at the end of the aisle appreciated their performance of wit, fine-tuned to the level of VT commercials. To live as did those grinning, droll, hip commercial beings. To live in the houses and apartments of those commercial beings. To buy the products of those commercial beings. Life.

The man was studiously ignoring them, picking out paper plates and plastic eating utensils. He obviously wasn't watching enough commercials to plot his life by. He was tall, the collar of his long black coat turned up, his hair plastered dark by the rain, his face white and bony.

"There's another sign of the apocalypse," she whispered to her companion.

He sniggered. "The Antichrist."

"Which one?"

They saw the man incline his head ever-so-slightly, aware of their attention if not of their words. They saw how red his eyes looked, even from this far.

"Want to buy a used hovercart?" the pink man called to the tall man.

The woman slapped the pink man's arm, suppressing laughter.

"Fuck off," the tall man said. He dropped a double roll of paper towels into his cart.

"No sense of humor," the pink man muttered, intentionally loudly enough for it to be heard.

"I told you to fuck off." Now the man faced them down the aisle. "Life's too short for me to waste my time dealing with you."

"That's right, you have better things to do, like sift through garbage cans."

"Brent," the woman said.

The man left his cart to come toward them. "Hey," Brent said, holding up a hand, "don't get belligerent with me, pal…I haven't done anything to you."

The man stood a few steps from their cart. He looked even more terrible up close. His lips bloated, cracked, one eye twitching at the corner, both watering from the bright light. "And I haven't done anything to you. So why couldn't you just leave me alone? Why couldn't you just respect my existence without commenting on it?"

"*What* comment?"

"Aren't you afraid of me? *Look* at me. Can't you see what's in me? Can't you *see* that? Are you insane? Do you think your money and imagined security will protect you from me? You think you're watching VT? I can *hear* you, man. And I don't like it. I shouldn't have to put up with this."

"You need a doctor, I think."

"You're just too smug and perfect and in control to back down, aren't you? You're so stupid. It's too late for a doctor…"

"I can see that. Come on, Jhayne." The man was shaky but resolute in his stance. He started to turn the cart to make a dignified exit. The thing fought him. His face was reddening.

"How did you get to live this long in Punktown?"

"So nice to chat with you, sir…so sorry to have intruded on your time with our meager existence."

"*Brent.*" The woman was wiser.

"You're gonna get to stay and see trees and snow and new movies and drink coffee and I have to go?"

"Yeah, you just be a good derelict and wax philosophical and we'll be on our way. Shit!" The basket veered against the shelves again.

"Here, the decent thing to do would be to put that poor thing out of its misery." Black stepped forward and drew the red plastic semi-auto from inside his coat and blasted off a round which punched through the clear cart and into a melon. Orange meat was exposed, glistening. The next shot hit a jug of synthetic milk. The cart began filling. One shot went clear through the cart into the floor. The fourth shot tore through two rolls of toilet paper and dove into a big cake of expensive cheese.

Brent and Jhayne screamed, covering their faces, babbled for mercy.

Black felt like he had just shot his VT set. He left the store empty-handed. What did it matter?

They kicked in his door. They knew knocking would only alert him.

Black was in the bathroom, naked. Out of bubble-bath liquid; the clear water in the tub steamed. His clothing was in a pile on the toilet lid. Atop the clothing was the glossy red compact semi-automatic Vern Woodmere had given him.

Captain Nedland had a gun in his hand, loaded with sleep darts. The other two health agents also had sleep darts. The three black-uniformed, helmeted forcers, however, had automatic two-fisted ray blasters. One agent followed a forcer into the bedroom. The other agent followed a forcer into the kitchen. In the small parlor, Nedland looked behind the sofa.

"I'm in the bathroom!" Black yelled out into the kitchen when he heard their feet stomp in there. "I've got a gun!"

"We've got him!" called a voice. "The john! He has a gun!"

Black was plastered naked to the cold wall tiles to one side of the door he had quickly closed and locked when he first heard them enter. The pistol was in his fist. Four shots left. They were big, fat slugs in these guns Vern favored.

"Let me through," Nedland hissed. He crouched behind the stove, poking only his head and gun around it to address the closed, blistered door. "Monty! It's me—Nedland!"

"Wow—what a surprise!"

"I'm glad you're still alive, Monty. I mean that. We weren't sure. We locked onto your trail after that incident tonight in the market."

"Then you know I'm not in very good spirits lately and you'll back off. Let me die in peace!"

"You'll want to hear what I've got to say, Monty. But some of it is good news and some is very bad news…"

"Opal is dead. I know."

"How? Her mother?"

"Yes. When was it?"

"That was, ah, ten days ago. I'm sorry."

"What other bad news? They're gonna make me pay for the shopping cart?"

"Enough bad news. I've got good news. Come out here and talk to me…it doesn't have to be this crazy!"

"I can hear you fine."

Nedland sighed, glanced at a forcer ready to blast through the door at the slightest provocation. "You haven't been watching VT, Monty."

"Why?"

"It was in the news two nights ago. We've found a cure for M-670."

"Mutant shit."

"It isn't. It isn't, Monty."

"You're baiting me."

"Toby," Nedland ordered one of the agents, "go find somebody with a VT with a paper subscription, go back to two days ago and bring me back a hard copy. We'll just wait here nice and calm until you return."

"You could fake that," Black called.

"For God's sake, man!" Nedland replied. Toby dashed out, hunched over. "Why are you so paranoid? We're not here to harm you or even *arrest* you! We came to take you to be cured!"

"I used to be one of you, remember? Health hazards are to be done away with. I'm a health hazard."

"Right. Which is why I'm here to take you to be cured."

"I was in the mall today. I didn't see anything about a cure."

"You didn't look. So there's a cure—what's the difference? The whole world is gonna stop and talk about it? The fun is over…the fear, the human interest stories, the dead. The cure is the dull part."

"I'm not stupid."

"You're dying, though. What have you got to lose coming out here, man? You're gonna die *anyway!"*

A long pause. "I want to see that paper."

"Alright." Nedland felt he had a hand-hold now. "Are you ready for the next good news?"

"Speak."

"Toll Loveland is dead."

Silence. Blank blistered door. Finally a soft, muffled, "How?"

"It all makes sense, now. It was M-670."

"How did you find him?"

"A man in the Blueflame Apartments on Convex Ave. complained to the super that his neighbor's VT was running too loud, night and day. The super went in. The police were called. There was Toll Loveland, dead for four days, wasted to skin and bones by M-670. His face looked like a skull. That was why he hid his face at the show you saw, obviously…only appeared on the VT monitor. He was already showing it. Like I said, it all makes perfect sense now. Motivation and all. It wasn't just art—it was revenge. Against Auretta Here, at first…the prosty he must have hooked up with and originally caught it from. Then it was revenge against the healthy, the people who would outlive him, who weren't suffering with him. A drowning man likes company, right? So he pulls you with him."

"I don't believe it…"

"I'm not *lying* to you, damn it!"

"I believe you. I didn't mean it like that. I mean…I don't believe *it*."

"Oh…oh, I see. Yeah, I know. I'd liked to have blown his face off, too, Monty, believe me. But it's better this way. If we'd caught him we'd have to cure him. He died good and slow."

"Yeah—like Opal."

"I know how you feel. Anyway…case closed."

They waited for Toby. There was no exchange for a while. Then Black asked, "How's Vern?"

"Not too good. He's alive. That was stupid, Monty. Very stupid. You should have passed your info on to us. When this is over…and it is, believe me or not…I'm sorry, but you aren't getting your old job back."

"Oh well," said Black.

"What's he gone out for, a coffee?" one of the forcers grumbled five minutes later. His gun rested across his leg now, no longer trained so keenly on the door. They all knew it was over. Even Black. When Toby came and the print-out was slipped under the bathroom door, it was just a formality. Black merely glanced at the page. They were right—what did it matter if he stepped out and was hit with a plasma bullet, anyway? Better than becoming the one-eyed creature he had glimpsed on the vidphone.

"I'm coming out," he announced, stepping back into his clothing from that day. He placed the gun on the floor. When he opened the door, saw the guns aimed at him, he kicked the pistol across the kitchen tiles, hands held up empty.

Nedland straightened, holstered his weapon. "Stupid, Monty, but I appreciate the strain you're under. I've been your friend all along whether you care to acknowledge that or not. I told them I didn't want you arrested or charged for endangering the public. I wanted to be here myself when they took you. And I'll be there when they give you the cure tonight. Until we get there I'm afraid we'll have to take you in cuffs, though. Now this is the HAP labs, Monty, not a furnace. Trust me."

Black did. He wasn't concerned anymore. He said, "Eight days."

"What?"

"She died eight days before they found the cure."

"Oh. Yeah. Just over a week. How sad and ironic, huh?"

"Yeah," said Black. He let a forcer cuff him.

Two new men entered the apartment. They wore baggy black rubbery suits, black hoods with face plates, orange tanks on their backs connected to orange spray guns.

"Don't hurt my snail," Black warned them as he was taken away.

Part Two:

Meathearts

ELEVEN

The Fekahs wore red-tinted fish-bowl helmets, not so much to protect their sensitive eyes as to protect human ears from the sound of their respiration, which was nearly deafening otherwise. Monty had heard one breathing off in the night, once—far away—and had pitied those close by. Human ambassadors on their world had to wear helmets at all times also. To remove these in a city full of Fekahs would mean instant deafness, perhaps even death. Monty sold this one its newspaper and watched it waddle clumsily away like a giant albino toad on two legs, the lacy pink gills vibrating inside the helmet. It rolled its paper into a tube and stuffed it into its handbag for the ride to wherever it was headed.

Two teenage human girls browsed the teen music and movie star mags. No doubt in emulation of one, or many, of the predigested celebrities inside, they both wore their hair in a wild, spiky disarray they spent hours weekly to make appear so disorderly. They both used *Swell,* a lipstick that harmlessly caused the lips to bloat to sexy overstated fullness. Black leotards on one, leopard-spotted on the other, and both with T-shirts with plastic toy propellers over their nipples. Monty had seen a lot of these lately. When those wearing such shirts stood close to the edge and a train passed, the propellers twirled and the girls would laugh.

Their spiky hair in all directions seemed to work as antennae, for these girls would glance up to catch him eyeing them, as such girls always did, guaranteed. And Monty would feel guilty for looking. Even with the leopard spots and nipple propellers.

Of course, antennae can't receive unless there are transmissions. Yesterday he'd been outside his booth, squatting to arrange magazines, and that new teenage girl who worked at the food stand had walked by, and glanced back at him over her shoulder to catch him drinking in her eye-level ass. He'd felt guilty, but also excited that she'd caught him. Did she glance at him from the food stand so often because she was disturbed at his glances, or to attract them? He was consciously transmitting to her, trying to catch her eye—though he'd then look away. One minute he thought they had a flirtation growing…the next he felt like a dog with its nose in her crack.

Today, only a year or so older than the propeller twins, still present and giggling, she wore a leopard top and tight black dress slacks while she served food at the counter—no white smock. Thick curly dark hair, a pretty face with heavy eyebrows. He might have eyed her all day had there not been so very much else to look at during his shift, from three-thirty to midnight.

He fell in love (all right, lust—but a lust so intense and greedy and possessive that it seemed very much like love) at least once a day. Today it had been that blond. A curly mane down the back of her white business suit. Skin as pale and flawless as porcelain. A delicate, serious face—sexy because she looked tired. Glamorous, radiating intelligence. Then yesterday it had been that Hispanic teenage girl in the canary yellow mini-skirt and black turtleneck jersey, white socks bunched around her brown ankles and a yellow bow in her lush black curls. She'd glanced at him several times, where the blond hadn't noticed him. Both had left him with a twitching hollowness in his groin when their trains whisked them away, leaving him bolted down here in his pen.

His eyes flitted from one to the next to the next ceaselessly, barely noticed, an eager fly's presence at best. It had been over a year since Opal Cowrie had died.

Even during the periods of slow traffic he spread pornography in front of him on the counter, or trashy tabloids with photos of celebrities taken by terrorist photographers with sniper cameras that could pierce through their clothing. Many celebrities now, though, wore material the cameras couldn't penetrate. The technology was ever improving on both sides in a kind of arms race.

He read women's magazines. Fashionable faces, fashionable bodies. In one, a fourteen-year-old finalist in the magazine's annual contest to discover a new cover model from among its readers sighed that modeling could be such hard work, all that waiting for camera set-ups. Daily, Monty watched people coming off trains between three-thirty and five who looked like they'd been dredged up from the bowels of hell. That poor tormented model.

It was five-thirty now, already slowing down greatly. From here on it would be mostly dinner- and theater-goers, the theater district being close by along with Punktown's major museums. The slowest traffic would be from ten to twelve; people getting out of movies, plays, restaurants. From eleven to twelve it was people getting off their own second shift jobs. There was no third shift at the newsstand. There were some paper machines nearby for the late denizens, though hardly of the variety Monty offered. He carried news from other planets. The Kodju in their other dimension were represented.

Monty hadn't had time to slow down for two hours, and waited impatiently for a late flux of Japanese businessmen to exhaust itself before he left his circular booth to buy a coffee at a nearby stand that sold pretzels and dilkies, a fried native root. The hotdog stand the cute new girl worked at was farther away, and he wasn't ready for speaking with her anyway. He lit a black-papered herb cigarette as he waited for his coffee, keeping an eye on his neglected station.

Two people at the pretzel stand, two or three at the hotdog stand, but he didn't envy them their company. He liked it this way. When he needed a little socializing he could come here for a coffee, chat a minute. Funny how few people struck up a casual conversation with him at the booth; very little bartender patter. People in a hurry. He was mostly just a human dispenser machine.

"Need to take a leak?" chirped Midge, the Choom woman behind the counter.

"Nope; all set, thanks." Midge or her male Choom partner Belly would keep an eye on his stall…fill in for him, if it was busy, when he had to go. He had never really become too friendly with the crew over at the hotdog/food stand but that was okay— he hadn't taken the job to make friends. Hadn't intended Midge and Belly.

"How many dispersers are you taking?"

"One a day…mom." The pills controlled the need to urinate and defecate by doing away with the wastes while still within the body. He would have felt nervous and vulnerable having to deal with people on a full bladder, and felt funny about bothering these two all the time, but the three dispersers a day he'd been taking had started giving him an upset stomach, cramps. His body had been through a lot.

"You watch yourself," Midge threatened him.

"Just give me my freakin' coffee, huh? Man, the service in this place."

"That's the thanks I get for worrying about you. No cards, no flowers, no love limo in my greasy garage."

Monty laughed, a little embarrassed. Belly, busy, was chuckling. A year, and Monty still couldn't tell how much of Midge's racy talk was just joking around and how much might be flirtation. Invitation. She was cute enough—with her glossy black bowl haircut, large hazel eyes behind big cosmetic eyeglasses with yellow frames, a short perky body—but Monty just could never find the ear-to-ear Choom grin attractive. It was too huge a factor to ignore. So Midge was appealing enough to want to bed, and yet she wasn't enough to make him want to form a relationship. Maybe personality-wise. Not physically. That made him feel somewhat ashamed—but hey, he reasoned, if he wanted a friend, appearance didn't matter. Lovers had to stir the blood, not make you reluctant to look at them squarely, right? He didn't ask for perfection, but a mouth that when gasping in ecstasy would appear like it might swallow his head was hard to overlook. Other human men took Chooms as girlfriends, wives. Despite his artistic inclinations and sensitivities, however, Choom women simply didn't appeal to his sense of aesthetics.

He sipped his coffee, kept his eye on a lingering Japanese businessman who was paging through a child bondage mag at the booth. You couldn't trust anybody; not suits, not old ladies. Every day he lost magazines and papers right under his nose, and when it was busy he probably lost twice the amount behind his back. Stupid, a circular stand, but he hadn't designed it.

The businessman peered over the abandoned counter, then from side to side. Monty waved at him. "Right here. What's it say for price?"

"Three ninety-five," the man called shyly.

"Throw four munits behind the counter, on the floor. I'll get it in a minute."

The man held up the bills for Monty to see, tossed them and scurried off with the magazine in his briefcase.

Midge had just sold a bagel and coffee to a customer, now turned to Monty and said, "There's some of your buddies here again."

Monty swivelled around to peer between Midge and Belly. Hissing sounds. A figure had appeared around the escalator banks, and another could be heard back there. Baggy black rubbery suits, hoods with face plates, orange tanks and orange spray guns. Ghosts, haunting him.

A thick white ooze that smelled strongly fish-like had appeared a few weeks ago, creeping upward from the base of the escalator banks. If it had started to come back, Monty hadn't noticed...maybe just a follow-up check. Did he know these men (women?), he wondered. Did they know him? Had they spotted him, recognized him? Why should they even look long enough to notice?

"Vermin patrol," Monty joked quietly.

"Here's one for them." Midge jabbed a thumb toward Belly.

Blue Station was one of the very cleanest of Punktown's subway stations. Forcers were often in view. In some stations forcers, and these suited sprayers, might be a rare sight—though much more warranted. The spray graffiti that filled almost every available inch of wall and pillar and floor (and train, inside and out) in some areas was quite subdued here, the blue tiles of the walls and thick hexagonal support beams glowing with their glossiness. Though the station forever had the sweaty laundry smell of a gym locker room, even in the height of summer it was tolerable. The tunnel wall was decorated with huge framed advertisements for hotels, restaurants, movies and plays. The escalators worked. A robot sweeper, glossy blue, was in constant roaming motion sucking up trash. In each blue tile was an actual insect like an ant in amber, magnified by the substance of the tile. Insects from many planets, no two insects of the exact same kind represented in all these many tiles. No labels, though Monty accepted their word for it.

Dragging on his cigarette, Monty watched the suited men spray the encased insects as if they were the infesting invaders.

One seemed to look his way; Monty turned his head from him. He saw a human-like Tikkihotto walking off with a Tikkihotto news magazine, some of his swimming ocular tendrils taking in the complex multi-holographic hieroglyphics while others watched where he was walking. "Hey!" Monty shouted. One clear tendril looked back at the newsstand worker as the humanoid quickened his pace. Monty didn't pursue. "Ass-wipe," he muttered.

His employer, who ran the booth from five to three-thirty himself, forbade Monty from using a stinger, stun gun or knock-out darts to deal with thefts. Actually, those were the terms of the contract with the Paxton Transit Authority, the rationale being that a weapon employed by Monty might inspire the thief to retaliate with a much more lethal weapon, whereas otherwise he would have just run off with his prize. Monty appreciated this point, but also felt that people would be less apt to steal if they thought they might get zapped or stung or knocked out for it.

And according to his terms of probation with the Health Agency and the police, he was not permitted to carry a lethal handgun at any time. He still had Vern Woodmere's collection at home, but could only bring them to a firing range unloaded and in a suitcase or gym bag.

But now, as always, Monty wore two pens inside the lining pocket of his tweed turquoise jacket. One blue, one red. Remonil, a knock-out drug, in the blue. A plasma bullet in the red.

"I should get back—I'm neglecting my job."

"More than a year of that and suddenly you're worried?"

"Need something to read to get you through the slow chunk?"

"I'm all set, thanks." Midge held up the disc she would stick to her temple to directly pick up VT transmissions in her brain. She would sit and "see" the program, "hear" it, but still hear if a customer came, and Belly would be there anyway. Many people on the trains used these rather than read a paper, could view the news that way but more likely chose a game show or rerun of a sitcom. A lower level setting could be adjusted so that a person could still receive the transmissions but also walk about and function fairly well simultaneously, the mind doing its best to keep its tasks separate, as when a person drives a car but daydreams or chats on the phone. Still, Monty saw people with discs on their temples or foreheads bumping into each other every day. Sometimes teenagers stumbling dazedly with three or more stuck to their foreheads. Sometimes a man with a shaved head covered in discs would sit on a tiled bench and grin at the passing trains.

Monty preferred reading from a material object in his hands—had always loved books, libraries, magazines; no doubt a great contributor to his acceptance of this work. He seldom used a computer to read the paper, now, and didn't subscribe to such a news service at home. He didn't own a disc to paste to his head, rarely watched VT at all, though he enjoyed a good movie. He liked paintings painted with brushes, not computer programs. Mistakes were harder to correct with paints, the challenge thus greater—skill more necessary, whether the end result was more beautiful or not. A robot could paint a picture. If it were better than a man's picture, Monty was not impressed. The technology might impress him…not the art.

Just an old-fashioned guy, he thought. More so all the time. He saluted to Midge and Belly as he walked away. Midge blew him a kiss, puckering the front of her long Choom lips, lipsticked a soft pink. Monty had changed her mind from her previous electric red.

He entered his booth, sighed. No people to watch. Another great contributor to his acceptance of this job; he loved to watch them. A library of books rapidly flipping their pages at him so he could catch glimpse of a few words—some bland, some tantalizing—before the covers closed and new ones opened. They said you couldn't judge a book by its cover. Nonsense, utterly. Of course you could, for the most part. People dressed like book covers, complete with title, a brief description of the contents and a series of blurbs. The golden-haired woman in white hadn't been a waitress in a truck stop. The Hispanic girl in the yellow dress, a concert pianist.

Well, but out of his newsstand, what were others to make of him? Then again, occupation and station in life were not the only factors to be divined. A perceptive observer might detect the mix of brittle sensitivity and angry toughness in his face. He had floated in his clothes for awhile, but had gained back all his lost weight and then some. He had the start of a paunch, disquieting, and a weary pale puffiness to his face. The artistic, almost delicate bone structure fighting through this lazy swollen puffiness echoed his inner state. He was still narcissistic, taking care to dress as he liked best, brush back his proud dark blond hair, shave and shower daily. But he had also become increasingly ashamed of his added weight, self-conscious around females, as if his face were still yellow and bony, lips crusted in sores. He found himself sucking in his belly around people, holding it in for hours at times, used to it, until he ached with gas. One minute he looked in the mirror and was desperate for someone to appreciate how good he looked just then, comment on it, enjoy it while he was still young, still here. Another minute, while naked perhaps, he dreaded that anyone should see him this way. Such is life in the flesh.

He paged through a teen celebrity mag, in which he could ogle pretty young girls less self-consciously than when he watched them at his counter, but still their eyes on him made him squirm a little, and he didn't dare open to the fold-out holographic posters. Mm, a picture of pristine Dora Deering, cute and dimpled, ever-smiling, a bogus blond. Her image and selling point as a singer was her clean-cut image, whereas her current rival Topaz (just Topaz), also sixteen, was her polar opposite, dark and sexy. It was therefore Dora that Monty now fantasized making sweaty love to.

The older he felt, the more he was attracted, uneasily, to teenage girls—as if, vampire-like, he could draw youth and vitality from them. For he did, though not even forty, feel quite ancient. Dried-out, bloated with decomposition. Close to death. As if he had never even been cured.

He had taken home one teen magazine, scanned a picture of Dora into his computer and had it strip down her clothing to her underwear (shielded from cameras and this kind of technology), then print out a color hard copy for him to tack on his apartment wall. Life-size. Dimpled Dora Deering, the unknowing virgin sacrifice to one man's silent volcano.

Around nine-thirty the traffic was heavy; those just leaving the movies, those coming in for the next show. Things were orderly and peaceful, despite the traffic. On a Sunday afternoon after a sports game let out, particularly in the height of summer, the station would fill wall to wall with people, pressed right up to the edge of the platform, waiting to flood the cars to the bursting point, and the tension would seethe like the smell and the heat, and sometimes fights would spread—once to a near riot. Midge and Belly had closed themselves safe inside their stall. Monty had watched from his circular booth, ignored in the battle like a fish in a bowl watching a murder.

Two people had been pushed accidentally into the path of a train, that time, squeezed out like tubes of paint by its powerful repulsor field as it passed above them. Another time, at the close of his shift, he had seen a train go by from which came wails, cries, screams, shouts. Blood could be seen splashed inside, obscuring the windows. Frenzied bodies inside, thrashing, flailing, flashes of light, cracks of shots. Then gone. He'd read the next day in his papers that it had been a gang war—common enough, but its hellish mysteriousness at the time had shaken him a little and he hadn't forgotten it.

Nice and quiet tonight. People coming and going as docile as cattle. A little laughter, a little noise from the young, as always…no big deal. No one stole any papers from him. No seething tension. It was cool—autumn up there. But he knew the suddenness of danger. That train of the damned that had flashed by and gone. As when he held his stomach in, Monty held himself tight…never fully relaxing himself until he got home.

Some women bought magazines from him, politely smiling to acknowledge his existence, dressed in the geisha style right down to lacquered wigs, white face, high painted brows and black-painted teeth—though not Asian. One even appeared to be black. Hiding the true covers of their books? Oh no, just the opposite. This was them. A mask can be the self, even when the expression is different from what it hides. Their fakery told much of them. Not repulsive to Monty, altogether. But still, fake.

Already the traffic began to peter out as the cinemas prepared to open their curtains, screen their movies, and the trains whisked away those already sated. Late dinner-goers trickled about; it would be that way for a time yet. Another night, its rhythms as familiar to him as the tides. From his lighthouse tower he could see many of the storms before they hit. Who needed VT?

Two fresh-faced young men waited on the platform, one's thumb hooked in the rear pocket of the other. It was a tender scene, like seeing a boy and girl together. The more overtly affectionate of the two nuzzled his boyfriend's neck. They didn't sense Monty. He remembered Bum Junket, though he didn't take these boys for hookers. The memory made him restless.

He'd killed men before in the line of duty. One of those mobsters who disposed of hazardous waste illegally for ostensibly legitimate businesses had opened up on him and Opal; Monty had killed him, Opal one of his partners, and the others had been taken alive. He had exterminated men before. A bunch of mutants, crackling with radiation, had refused to surrender themselves into HAP custody once and the agents had had to storm their crumbling tenement fort, Monty himself in one of those black rubbery suits. He'd killed two mutants who came at them with crude swords, the rest rounded up alive but for a few pitiful creatures no longer vaguely human, close to death in their dark corners, whom he and his fellows had exterminated. But that hadn't felt so much like execution, then.

He asked himself again: would they really have resorted to rounding up those infected with M-670 for mass extermination, if the plague had gone on—as they had confided to him they might, before he'd even gotten it? Himself included, had he surrendered to them?

Oh no, not you, Nedland had assured him after his surrender. Never him.

Well, even if that were true—so what, not him? So what?

Several months after his cure, after he'd started working here, an amazing story had come to his newspapers. A former associate of the popular VT evangelist Matt Cotton had come forward to reveal what he claimed he'd been threatened with death to hide…that Matt Cotton's ministry had hired a group of brilliant bioengineers still in college to create the deadly STD mutstar-six seventy, and begin its spread to the homosexual community and amongst drug users, in some popular singles bars and brothels both legal and illegal. Matt Cotton had taken his battle on sin very seriously. He was now an historic mass murderer of thousands of evildoers. He was currently free on bail, hiding from the public in his fortress of a home, pending trial.

Monty had allowed himself to derive one guilty pleasure from this amazing and horrid revelation. That Toll Loveland, so pleased with his grand artistic statement, his impressive body count and the technical expertise that had rendered it, had been so grossly dwarfed by Matt Cotton and his achievement. What a laugh on poor Toll. If only he were alive to know it.

Monty lit a cigarette, kept his eye on a pretty Asian girl waiting for her train. No geisha makeup for her. They hadn't found one of the three students Cotton had hired, Monty mused. Escaped. Probably starting his own company under a new identity on some far colony. Or Earth. Easy to lose yourself in that teeming ruined hell.

He thought these same things many nights. His life had become all dull, predictable rhythms. Maybe, in fact, he *had* died.

A helmeted Fekah slapped up to the platform on its frog feet. A Blue Line train docked and the Fekah hopped in with the Asian girl and the gay men. And there went the cute girl from the food stand; she left this early every night—maybe went to school or college in the day. She didn't look at him. Was whisked away. The trained whooshed in the distance, a lonely sound.

Monty glanced off toward Midge. Sitting down, eyes glazed, disc to temple. Oh well…maybe he didn't feel like talking anyway, just thought he did. He sold a few papers and read from a comic book for awhile.

A new knot congregated for the next train. Idly Monty looked up. This group proved quite surprising and held his attention. There were two Stems at the rear of the group, most saliently. He'd only seen their kind on VT, but they were easy to identify.

Seven feet tall, no part of their body larger around than a drinking straw, they consisted of a long central section jointed once at the middle, three jointed legs and three jointed upper limbs. Their bark-rough skin was a brilliant red, and though he couldn't see their tiny faces he knew the sunken black triangular eye sockets, triangular single nostrils and black toothless grins looked like the features of miniature jack-o'-lanterns. Their plump women (as thick around as broom handles) were a foot to two feet shorter, glossy smooth and pure white—and no other race but the Stems were allowed to view them (though pictures and film footage had been sneaked of their sacred beauty). The women who were soiled by the eyes of others had to be purified by death. Those who stole a look must be punished by death. The Stems were a hard, violent people, their warrior class renowned, sometimes hired as bodyguards or assassins here and on other colonies. Monty didn't feel comfortable near them, despite his curiosity.

Once his attention shifted from the two silent Stems, he saw the scarred woman for the first time.

She was beautiful. Only the Stems could have made him notice her second She looked taller than she must have truly been in her high heels and trim, blue satin business suit with padded shoulders, her body slender. Her long straight hair was a silken auburn, the hue probably artificial, parted on the side in a chic scattered wave. Lipstick vivid red in her slim, pale face…her skin flawless but for the monstrous scars.

He thought there was just the one on her right cheek at first. It might not have been apparent to him at this distance except that the way the light fell on her, the scar's deep outline stood out sharply. It curved, with just a few irregular waves, from the middle point of her ear down to the very corner of her mouth, which seemed to have drawn up a little there. But then a train passed on the other, farther side of Blue Station and she offered Monty her other profile as she watched it. An identical scar, but it didn't draw up the corner of her full lips on the left side.

A Choom, recovering from an operation to look human? He doubted it—there should be no scars, if it had been done right. Had she been attacked, maimed? There was only one possibility, he decided. She was a willfully disfigured hooker. There was quite a market for these things. Mutants, amputees, scarred women, deformed women—some having been born that way, others making themselves that way. There was a lot of money to be made, especially around this part of town.

She never once noticed him while she waited. Two men approached and conversed with her; she smiled and tossed her hair out of her face constantly, a nervous mannerism. She wrote something in a little pad one of the business-suited men produced. A phone number? The men left her to cross the station.

Her train came, she boarded, the Stems boarding after her. By the time she was gone, Monty had fallen in pseudo-love again.

TWELVE

The second time, three days later, she had considerably healed; in fact, the scars were completely gone, unless it was just the light. Maybe he'd been wrong about her. A surgery she'd recovered from? *Was* she a Choom? He wondered what Midge would look like after such surgery, but only briefly...he was too taken with the scarred woman. The more so now that he'd seen her again.

She wore a black leather jacket, a black sweater and a black miniskirt revealing long, slim, black-nyloned legs ending in black high heels. She had a coffee and a cigarette in her hands and a woman was with her, older and not beautiful so he barely took her in. There were too many customers to attend for him to stare at her; he took quick bites. When a train docked and he turned from a customer to see her climbing up into it he felt irritated, resentful of his impotence inside his circular cell. He hadn't noticed them before but now he saw two Stems board the train. Did they work around here now? It was about the same time of night that he'd seen her the last time, but funny he should see both her and the Stems again at the same time on the same night after three days.

Well, he wouldn't totally despair. He'd seen her twice in four days; he was fairly certain he would see her again. And as the night closed, and in the next few days, other enticing creatures materialized to distract him, tantalize him, so that by the time six days had passed from the first time he had seen her he had largely forgotten the woman. Largely.

Business was good, as usual on a Sunday night around this time, hard to keep up with. He juggled customers in the circle around him, saw a businessman type strolling away casually reading a paper he'd lifted. "Hey," Monty said over the heads of other customers but he went unheard or else ignored. He wondered how smug that man would feel if they were the only two people down here and Monty vaulted over the counter as he wanted to now, just to show that he wasn't impotent...to prove it as much to himself as to the man. But he didn't; he let it go.

At last the flood began to recede and he was coming up for air.

"Who do you like better, Dora Deering or Topaz?"

"Huh?" Monty turned around behind him.

Here she was before him, her eyes on him and she was smiling, tapping with a finger the magazine he'd left open on the counter. A flash of embarrassment, as if he'd been caught jerking off to his Dora Deering poster. But a greater flash through him of shock. The scars curving from the corners of her mouth to her ears were distinct pinkish creases in her soft pale flesh. He wouldn't have reacted this strongly to them, stared so blatantly, except that—light or no—he could have *sworn* that three days ago the scars had been gone. Had she simply been too far away? Wearing thick makeup?

"Ahh...who do I like better?" A customer bought a paper from him as he groped blindly for an answer. "Well, the standard cliché answer...Dora Deering writes her own songs but Topaz has a better voice. Dora's sweet and Topaz is sexy."

"Sweet isn't sexy?" Now the scarred woman presented a paper for him to key in on his register.

"Well, ideally one would be both...but one quality doesn't, ah, depend on the other."

"I can't stand either of them. All the real artists in the world who never get a shot."

"The public likes them."

"The public would like peanut butter and jelly sandwiches more than filet mignon if that was all they were exposed to."

"Or if the public were vegetarians," he smiled, recovering himself now, doing good. "I don't mean to defend them too strenuously...it's not like I'm their manager or something."

"It's a trend, all these teen music and film stars...it'll die down again soon. For a while. Thanks." She gave him money.

"Dora's my favorite. She's stuck on herself—that's natural, she's a kid. But she is sweet and sexy, I think."

"I like Topaz better, if I had to choose. She isn't so publicity-conscious and plastic that she won't let herself look nasty and jealous of Dora."

"I say we give them swords and tridents and let them fight it out in an arena. Imagine the box office!"

The scarred woman laughed, brushed aside her ragged wave of hair. "Thanks. Bye, now."

"Um—yeah, bye." Monty grinned.

An old woman, her face creased with the maiming scars of time, took her place at the counter. The scarred woman drifted toward the platform. A knot of people surrounded her suddenly, greeted her warmly, enthusiastically. Friends? She didn't look as though she'd expected them. Someone handed her a piece of paper and a pen for her to write something down.

Her train came in. He had hoped she'd look back at him, wave (as he was prepared to do), but not so much as a glance.

Two brilliant red Stems boarded the train shortly after her.

Monty was starting to become concerned. Never before had he seen a Stem. Now, three times.

Each time after he'd seen the beautiful scarred woman.

Were they following her? If so, hadn't she noticed? She hadn't seemed nervous, suspicious. He didn't like the way they'd just mysteriously appeared these two most recent times, as if they'd been keeping out of sight until she mounted the step into the train. Maybe she didn't suspect a thing, maybe she figured they came and rode the train every night. He should tell her they didn't.

The train sailed away into the endless dark maze below Punktown.

Traffic gradually tapered away to the point where Monty could remember the paper she'd bought, and he pulled one of the same toward him. Just a standard all-purpose Punktown newspaper. He didn't open it. He still worried about her.

She hadn't seemed to mind his blatant staring at her scars, though she had to have noticed. Then, maybe she'd even *wanted* him to stare. Now that her scars were back, so was the idea that she might be a hooker. Not *necessarily*. What constituted beauty for one person, group or culture might represent hideousness to another. Monty had read about the ancient races and peoples of Earth having bound women's feet to keep them from growing, binding their heads to shape their skulls, stretching their earlobes, stretching their necks ridiculously with stacks of rings, stretching their lips with huge plates in their mouths, impaling their noses with bones, becoming ritually tattooed or scarred, suffering clitorectomies and circumcisions and castration, swallowing tapeworms to keep from gaining weight, becoming anorexic in the obsession to remain fashionably thin. And the most extreme of these measures usually seemed to be reserved for the women of these peoples.

Maybe she'd had herself scarred like this for the sake of her own aesthetics…or, having been maimed, had decided that she accepted or liked herself this way.

He had been just a little bit unnerved by the sudden appearance of her marred face so close to his, even with his excitement and his embarrassment. He couldn't help but think how she must have bled, how the wounds must have gaped in a hideous imitation of a Choom. He was very sensitive, lately, to deformities of the face. A few weeks ago he'd seen a woman with the top front of her skull flattened at a radical angle, her brow pressed in accordion folds down into her slits for eyes, her ears barely formed and her lips immense and purple-blackish. A pretty tame kind of mutation, common enough, but he didn't see many mutants in Blue Station, and that night as he lay reading in a drowsy bubble bath he had become strangely nervous about suddenly looking up to find that flattened-headed woman standing in the doorway.

Some nights he awoke with a jolt or a gasp or a cry. He'd taken to sleeping with a dim light on in his bedroom at night…for he had been able, in his dreams, to gaze longer and more clearly at Opal Cowrie's face than he had during the message she'd made for him.

Sometimes, crazily, he even dreaded looking into a mirror, for a brief moment. Afraid his face would have been transformed. He had confronted the instability of the flesh, face to face. His own. And he couldn't forget that. Was that so crazy?

Still embarrassed about the teen mag he'd been paging through ("Dora and Topaz—Who is the Queen?"), Monty idly flipped through the paper the scarred woman had bought, idly wondered what kind of things in it would draw her attention, what she cared and thought about.

In her early to mid twenties, he ventured. The scars kept coming back, a focal point. No accident, he felt sure. She hadn't looked ashamed. Maybe it was a fashion statement. Caucasian warriors had shaped their heads so as to slant their eyes and widen their noses to resemble their Mongolian comrades, and later Asians had had their eyes operated on to resemble Caucasians. Blacks had once straightened their hair and narrowed their noses to look "white," and whites had tanned themselves dark, while sometimes hating blacks. No, no accident. Whether by surgeon's scalpel or madman's blade, those scars—so symmetrical, their effect in conjunction with her beauty so *designed*—were an act of someone's expression.

Friendly, natural…not overtly flirtatious. She hadn't been trying to "wow" him; her beauty, at least then, hadn't been flaunted at him. The scars humbled her, maybe, made her more human.

But why? Was she a prosty or not? And what about those Stems? Too many frustrating questions. He mustn't let her get away again.

He welcomed a nice, compelling infatuation. It was something to think about during those endless hours in his little fish bowl.

"Someone threw up—I could smell it," said a sharply-dressed woman to another as they neared his bowl.

"Well, they should know better than to go to a show like that. There was a sign out front warning people and a warning on every ticket."

"It was still hard to watch even when I expected it and had read all about it…I felt terribly woozy."

"I thought it was powerful and brilliant." This second woman bought from Monty a copy of the paper the scarred woman had purchased. The two women wandered away.

The rest of the night remained busy enough that Monty could avoid visiting Midge, and thus be left alone with his new focus. He didn't even notice when that girl from the food stand went home.

The next night he saw her face again…this time in the trash barrel in the men's room. Midge had taken over at his booth for him. He had to use the toilet, and liked to read and take his time, but he had brought his own *clean* magazine and put clean paper towels down on the seat. He was an ex-health agent and knew better than to handle a newspaper in the trash and then clean up after himself.

But he saw her face, and the scars like centipedes crawling on it, and for a moment thought it must be a story about how she had originally been attacked; the paper must be a week or so old, at least. The scars were prickly black with stitches (of all things, in this day!).

As it turned out, it was last night's paper, the same one she'd bought, the one he'd flipped through. But he hadn't gotten as far in as this. It wasn't up front with the other crimes, but in the entertainment section.

The photo was large, hard to miss—a big story. He had seen only part of her face, one eye and one scar, peeking out from around the sports section, but that had been enough. He had been so close last night…but now he read and all his questions were answered.

The photo attended a review of a play, and the review had been written by Yancy Mays. Monty's eyes zoomed past this name but screeched to a halt and flew in reverse. He remembered that name. He had never heard or been told whether or not the critic, whose scathing review of Toll Loveland's *Pandora's Box* he had read, had survived or died from the disease he had contracted at that same show Monty attended.

Yancy Mays. So he had survived, God bless him. Monty remembered how he had dumped on Loveland's *The Godfucker* as well, and that other play by some other artist…*Shit for Breakfast*, that was it…in which a goat was hung upside-down by its legs and had its throat cut while naked actors basked in the hot pouring blood. Yancy Mays had helped shut that nightmare down. Monty hated some critics with a passion, thought that there were too many of them (one for every movie, it seemed), hated the very word critic ("movie reviewer" was vastly preferable), and wasn't crazy about any form of censorship. But so far he liked this guy Yancy Mays.

Let's see what he had to say about Monty's mystery girl.

The name of the review was: *Meatheartlessness.*

"If you've come for thrills, you don't have long to wait: in the opening scene of director Ferule Cangue's production of *Meathearts*, a scene not present in Josh Reymeffat's original play, a beautiful woman in a white dress in a white room has her face slashed by a man with a scalpel. Later we will find that this is the woman's boyfriend. As the lights go down the other half of the stage is illumined and we witness a woman in a white dress on a white set attacked and viciously raped by two thugs as she is attempting to unlock her (white) car. She is raped atop the car's hood, and then her right arm is hacked off with a machete.

"These two violent acts are not special effects. The blood and mayhem in this piece of not-so-Grand Guignol are authentic acts of violence.

"The next half-hour of the two-hour play focuses on two mutant hookers played by actual mutant actresses who are seen chatting after hours in a brothel which deals in deformity and disfigurement. Then return the two victimized women, stitched and partially healed backstage, who turn out to be hookers now also. Both traumatized, degraded by men but trained by a patriarchal society to be victims, they have surrendered themselves to utter degradation; in becoming prostitutes, using the very disfigurements which have reduced them to this point. The remainder of the play consists of the four women sitting and talking of their lives, opening up to their hidden emotions. At the end, one of them who has confronted herself finds the strength to leave…a triumphant climax, perhaps, but no doubt an anticlimax for the thrill-seekers.

"Josh Reymeffat's original play, previously staged elsewhere to less success, was a brilliant and poignant portrayal of women's submission to man's timeless domination of them through victimization and humiliation…but as translated by Ferule Cangue, it has become exactly that which it was meant to attack: a horrifying degradation of women, reducing the actresses involved to the level of the disfigured prostitutes they portray, freakishly exhibited for the morbid interests of the audience, with the heinous opening scenes resembling nothing so much as scenes from a snuff film…and no more redeeming.

"For every performance the rapists are 'played' by different 'actors' not previously known to the actress whose arm is hacked off, so as to keep the actress's reaction authentic and to make the scene all the more realistic and terrifying. I'm impressed. Of course, the audience is warned of the authentic rape and violence on the posters and signs outside the theater. Warned—or enticed? That the rapists are different every performance has been publicized to a sufficient extent to convince me that the motivation for this little bit of gritty realism is purely one of cunning and sleazy titillation.

"The actor who portrays the slasher of the first woman is an uncredited surgeon, due to the greater precision required for the mutilation of that actress (Mauve Pond). Our mystery surgeon is also responsible for partially repairing his handiwork backstage. The actresses have previously been administered drugs to prevent pain throughout; nevertheless their courage and enthusiasm for their roles is extraordinary. Their performances (particularly by Aurora Lehrman, whose arm is severed every show) are highly commendable…if not their judgment in contributing to such an exploitative, drooling piece of gleeful sadism, hiding its ugly face behind the mask of art. With all respect to the skill of these women, this reviewer cynically ventures that the attention they knew the play would receive for its violence was as much an attraction as the challenge of the roles. But that's show business.

"The play is performed only once a week on Sunday nights at the Jason Scarborough Theater. It takes a week for Lehrman's arm to be cloned back and Pond's pretty face made smooth. There have been two performances as of this writing, and the box office has been so good that the show is already booked solid for the next four months (that's at least sixteen more right arms for the plucky Aurora). Already a movie is being discussed—but how well would that fare, I wonder, when the action is primarily limited to talk in one room, and the thrill to which the play owes its new success is to be there when the blood is spilled?

"Director Cangue has previously staged in Punktown the rather less sensationalistic but similarly mean-spirited musical *Jack the Ripper*; after this perhaps he'll update his interpretation and mutilate women on stage for real once more (I shouldn't give him ideas if it hasn't occurred to him already). He also directed *Some Black Girls Sittin' Around Talkin' About Life, Love, And the Way Their Men Snore*, very similar to this play in approach and subject matter, without the blood. Somewhere along the line he was no doubt bizarrely inspired to combine these two previous efforts within the vehicle of Reymeffat's play, much superior to LaShawna Tempest's pretentious and self-conscious *Black Girls*. Why Cangue was attracted to *Black Girls* in view of these other two major projects seems mysterious—until you remember that for the sake of 'earthy gritty naturalism' Cangue had his five black actresses perform naked. He was praised for symbolically baring the hearts and souls of the women, at that time. Quite impressive. That he also bared (un-symbolically) their breasts and pubic regions was of no consideration in his motives, naturally. Thus do some artists lie to themselves. Thus do the audiences of such artists lie to themselves, enabling these artists to go on as they do. Not that a sexual element in itself is wrong. I don't feel ashamed of admiring the physiques of ballet artists in a less than professional way, and ballet is very consciously sensual, erotic. But you realize that. No one is exploited. You can *sense* exploitation. At least, you should. (And if a ballerina lied to me that there was no sexual element in her work I'd be critical of her, too.)

"And finally, back to playwright Josh Reymeffat. Reymeffat wrote his play with the intention and assumption that the roles would be played by actresses in makeup. There is no reason but for the sake of exploitation that this production has sought to 'capture a powerful sense of raw realism as these acts are committed before the audience's eyes,' in the words of the publicity people. If it were economically feasible I wouldn't doubt that Cangue would have a woman beheaded in a play and cloned for the second act—all for the sake of the violent pornography he disguises as art. Ferule Cangue would, if he could paint, copy a Renoir nude but position her in a gynecological beaver shot and call that art as well. A slight reinterpretation of Renoir's intentions.

"So how does Reymeffat feel about the liberties Cangue has taken with him? In a recent interview he said that while his play was not meant to be presented this way, he finds it interesting. This is greatly disturbing and disappointing to someone like myself who respects his work, and even shocking. Can't the man see how his play, intended to criticize the victimization of women, has been distorted into just another weapon against women? Perhaps he is drunk on his new success…but his credibility, in my eyes, has been done much damage.

"For this execrable production is of the Toll Loveland school of art. But then some are still calling *him* a genius, aren't they?"

Whew, thought Monty.

Mauve Pond, huh?

All the rest had engrossed him just as much, however. He knew he had to see this play, but Christ—booked four months solid! Who did he know who could help him? He didn't really have much in the way of contacts of any kind, anymore.

That explained the vanishing scars. He'd first seen her on a Monday night, her wounds still fresh from *Meathearts'* opening night. By the middle of the week they were gone. And then he'd seen her again on a Sunday, going home from her second performance, stitches out but her flesh still undergoing its accelerated healing process.

He absorbed the large close-up of Mauve Pond more intently, now.

The caption read: "Actress Mauve Pond, now starring in *Meathearts* Sundays only at the Scarborough Theater, has her lovely face sliced on stage and then stitched for the rest of the play. Here she is backstage, minutes before going back on. The play has opened here to much success, but critic Yancy Mays isn't in stitches (see review)."

In the photo, she looked too exhausted by her ordeal already to go on for the remaining hour and a half of the play. Her eyes appeared puffy, tired, but she was wearing no makeup and that was part of it. She couldn't be in pain, but surely the ordeal itself was unsettling. How many dress rehearsals had there been? Monty couldn't imagine that the first time she was slashed, and Lehrman hacked, had occurred on opening night...but then again, after reading about Ferule Cangue, maybe it had—for the sake of realism. Her slender face looked swollen and battered, the lines of black stitches trailing from her ears into the corners of her mouth like strands of barbed wire. Her hair was mussed. She looked very young, vulnerable and weak. Suitably victimized. But she was smiling, her weary eyes narrowed as when she had smiled unabashedly at Monty.

She wasn't weak—she was strong. He wouldn't be able to let anyone do that to him.

He kept the picture and review.

At the booth he scoured the ephemeral library around him for more. Last week had been opening night and the fanfare had rushed by behind him like a train. Then again, the play had been picking up more attention since then through word of mouth and in response to its box office. His boss had tossed out all of Sunday's papers, and evening papers replaced morning papers, but he still found a review in a magazine—favorable—featuring a photo of Aurora Lehrman on stage, her stitched stump of a right arm poking out of a T-shirt. And he found plenty of printed ads for the play in the theater sections of papers, the artwork featuring a severed arm holding a teacup. Monty stacked his collection under the counter for later snipping.

Booked for four months already, huh? Unless Yancy Mays helped shut this production down, also...but it looked too big for that. Monty smiled, less frantic now inside. He was confident he would see her again.

THIRTEEN

When he did, he was ready with a half-dozen witty, just flirty enough ways to get a conversation flowing should she buy a paper at his stand. He'd thought about having a flower ready, too, but he didn't. As it was, however, she didn't approach him to buy a paper, or even glance at him, as far as he'd seen. He had come up with a few ideas in case of this, but none of them seemed good now, and the confidence he'd found began to look a little frayed around the edges.

It was Sunday, eleven-fifteen, close to the end of his shift—midnight. He'd been looking up alertly at every footfall, every peripheral movement, for hours now. And there she was at last, her high heels telegraphing her arrival—and what an entrance, as if this were her stage for him. She wore a tight black miniskirt, baring long slim legs encased in black nylons, black heels, her black jacket square-shouldered and the blouse underneath black, too. She wore a red flower in her lapel, the red of her lipstick shining like a petal from that flower on the snow of her face. Snow etched with a stick to make the scars he briefly saw.

He considered asking her if she had the review that he'd found two days ago; he had a copy of it with him. It was in a Miniosis newspaper, said her work showed "impressive dedication." She must already have it, he rebuked himself disgustedly...if I walk up to her she'll think I'm just some drooling fan...

Aren't I? he countered.

It was the Stems who inspired him to action.

The woman stood at the platform edge, toes to the safety line, lighting a cigarette with her back to Monty, alone there but for a female Choom dwarf lost in a huge man's coat. She handed the croaking dwarf a cigarette, and then the peripheral, stealthy approach of the Stems made Monty turn his head. Like red mantises they moved, all but soundless. As in the past, they wore small black pouches for belongings.

They only approached so far, and then hung back. They were definitely tailing her.

Monty started closing up his booth. Fast. He tried not to look panicky as he began unfolding the portions of the circular stand's security screens.

"Hey Blondie," cried a voice. It was Midge at the coffee stand. "You shutting down a little early, aren't ya?"

Monty saw the scarred woman twist at the waist to look at him.

The Stems looked, too.

Monty tried to ignore them, called back, "My customers have dried up…I don't feel good, either. What are you gonna do, report me to my boss?" He'd never shut down a minute early before.

"Not immediately, but now I've got something on you for the rest of your life."

Shut up and leave me alone, Monty told his friend in his mind.

Get her over here, he ordered himself, *warn* her. Maybe they meant her some real harm. Maybe it hadn't been clear for hem to strike before. Call her over.

How? he argued back with himself, impatiently.

The last screen was locked and he began tossing bundles of papers roughly into the storage compartments running around the outside of the booth. He heard a train coming. He was only halfway around the booth.

The train pulled in. His face was hot. Fuck it. He straightened up.

She was already in the train; he saw her in the windows, and the dwarf. The Stems were now boarding…

"Monty," called Midge.

Ducking behind his booth, Monty bolted off down the platform to the right, hoping she (or they) didn't glance out the windows just then…and if they did, that they didn't spot him.

"Hey *Monty!*" called Midge. Shut the hell *up*, he called back inside.

He launched himself up into the car two cars over from the one she had entered. One of the closing doors hit his shoulder coming in; he stumbled in the door well as the train pulled out of the station. He smiled nervously.

Three teenage boys sitting opposite the door well were laughing at him. When Monty stepped up out of it and loomed over them for a moment they quit laughing. They saw too much of the dying he'd lived in his eyes.

Monty cautiously peeked down into the car she had entered, the doors which could separate these cars now parted open. The car beyond this one had a homeless person sleeping in a seat—that was all. In her car, he saw the back of her head, and behind her the two Stems, their backs to him. Smoke rose from where the dwarf sat, giving her away. One of the Stems started to turn around in his seat and Monty lowered himself swiftly back into the recessed door well, out of sight.

It was a fairly long ride to her stop. Along the way the train pulled into four stations, losing the three subdued teen boys and the dwarf, gaining two couples, young and loud and drunk, in the car behind Monty, plus an obese black man with a huge yellow-white bony growth above his left eye, in the car with the homeless person. The black man took the papers covering the slumbering derelict to read, and gave him a cuff across the head before he sat, giggling. Even if he'd known Monty was watching he probably wouldn't have cared. The homeless man only moaned as if at a bad dream.

When the train pulled into Beaumonde Station, with its dark green and metallic gold checkerboard tiles, Monty saw her disembark from her car out his own car's door as it whooshed automatically open. He leaped out, landing lightly like a cat, stepping immediately behind a great circular green marble pillar. He was vaguely conscious of a few people boarding or leaving the train, but when he casually moved around the pillar the woman was nowhere in sight. Nor were the Stems.

Had that pair gotten off? He hadn't seen them. The train was already gone, leaving only a few student-types on the platform, Paxton University being very close by. Monty walked on, turning the corner to a row of turnstiles. Beyond them, the path forked. The right fork ended in escalator banks. The left curved to who-knew-where. He was sure he heard high heels clacking hollowly around the bend in this left fork. Monty pushed through a turnstile and down the left-hand branch.

Around the bend he saw doors to restrooms for men and women. He no longer heard footfalls, but neither had he heard a door open. Uncertain, he hesitated outside the ladies' room door. He began to reach for the pen inside his jacket, the red one with the plasma capsule inside.

The door to the men's room burst open and the Stem snatched his hand at the wrist just as he took hold of his pen. It bore down on him, pushing him up against the opposite wall, its other two tiny hands gripping his jacket. Monty cried out, thrashed. His wrist was bleeding, pinched, the pen slipping back into his pocket. With his free hand he chopped and pushed at the arms. He kicked at the three legs. It was not nearly so brittle as it looked. And now the second one was emerging from the men's room, holding an object from its black pouch. It extended the object, obviously a weapon, at Monty's face. He yelled, crazily, desperately, fought so hard that he managed to free both his arms and shove the Stem away from him with his foot. He knew, however, that he would die.

Peripherally he saw the ladies' room door open. Then, a voice. "Hold it or I'll shoot."

He had to look. Another gun was now trained on him. Mauve Pond held a small, orange plastic pistol in both hands, in an experienced stance. Monty calmed himself down. He let the first Stem pin his arms.

"All right, don't shoot."

"Who are you?"

"You know who—I'm the paper man from Blue Station."

"I know that. Are you following me?"

"Yes."

"Why?"

"I thought these two Stems were following you."

"They are—they're my bodyguards. I'm an actress."

"I know; Mauve Pond. I read the papers. I thought they meant to hurt you…they weren't with you, they were behind you."

"They keep back a bit so they won't draw too much attention and make me conspicuous, but they keep me in sight."

"How'd you know I was tailing you?"

"I looked when I heard that girl calling you and I saw you jump on the train. You acted very suspicious, I thought."

"You're sharp. Sorry. I used to be a health agent and got paid to chase people around. Old habits die hard."

"A health agent, huh?" She lowered the gun a bit but looked leery. The Stem wasn't drawing any more blood, but then Monty was keeping perfectly still, even if his heart wasn't.

"My name's Montgomery Black. I got dismissed when I contracted M-670 during Toll Loveland's show *Pandora's Box.* You remember all that? Last year?"

"I've heard of him. I'm in the arts. So you were cured, right? Why are you selling papers?"

"I was a bad boy. I kept looking for Loveland on my own, didn't turn myself over to the HAP containment and research program."

"Can my bodyguards see your ID?"

"Sure."

"Go ahead," Mauve Pond told the one with the alien hand weapon.

Monty's wallet was produced. Handed to Mauve. She flipped through it, nodded and pouted and handed it back to him. "Let him go, boys. Sorry, Mr. Black."

"No prob." Monty straightened his jacket, slipped his wallet away.

"You're bleeding." She touched his arm.

"I'll live."

Mauve withdrew her hand and smiled. Her eyes narrowed warmly. "You would've taken on these two guys to help me? I'm impressed."

"With my stupidity?"

"Whatever it is."

"I thought I was dead. Good thing I didn't soil my pants or I'd be pretty embarrassed right now. I considered it for a minute." Monty was nervous, but weirdly elated at conversing with Mauve Pond face-to-face and at still being alive. "Do these things live with you?"

"No, just escort me home. I've been mugged before and I was raped by two men in my apartment once. And that was even before I made the papers."

"Popular girl."

Mauve was a little shocked at his making so light of her ordeals, but was smart enough to know that he wasn't unconcerned. He wouldn't be here, with blood on his wrist and very nearly with shit in his pants, would he?

"Sorry, just kidding."

"I know. Can I reward your attempt at heroism with a cup of coffee? There's a nice little place not far from here."

"That's awfully kind. Love to."

"It's still early yet. Come on, boys."

The mute gun-wielding Stem finally, reluctantly, put its weapon away.

Beaumonde Square was one of the nicer areas of Punktown, since the Blue Line mostly only stopped at the nicer areas, to as safely as possible transport Punktown's "nicer" people from one spot to another without having to pass through areas like Red Station, and those far, far worse. The expensive Beaumonde Women's College was here, P.U. was near, and so Beaumonde Square was cobblestoned, with trees and stone benches and bookshops and coffeehouses. Mauve told Monty she had a nice little attic apartment across from some of the P.U. dorms. She obviously trusted him now. What a turn of events, tonight…more than his fantasies had allowed.

"You a native P-towner?" he asked over frothy cappuccino.

"No—I'm from Enceinte. My father's a career military man. A colonel in the Colonial Security Forces, stationed on Earth right now."

"Ever been?"

"No thanks. Enceinte's close to the Outback Colonies. I'm a bit of a hick."

"You handle yourself well in the city."

"My dad taught me how to shoot. Bought me my gun."

"Can these things understand us?" Monty nodded at the Stems seated at the next table, voice lowered.

"They've got implanted translators—so yes, they can—but they can't answer back unless they use the translator mikes in their pouches."

"Scary critters."

"They're okay." They sat without eating or conversing, watching the humans with their tiny jack-o'-lantern faces. "So, you seen my play?"

"No, but I'd love to. Booked solid. You think if I paid you, you could dig me up a ticket someplace? I hate to ask…"

"I'm sure I can. And don't worry about paying…"

"Oh, come on…"

"No, I mean it. You tried to save my life, right?" Narrowed eyes again, so sincere. He found it surprisingly easy to forget the scars.

"A lot of good I would have done you if you'd really been in danger."

"It's the thought that counts. I'll find you tickets; my treat. I mean it."

"You are most kind." Without a sweet dessert to go with his bitter cappuccino he had to spoon some sugar in. "So," he said as he stirred, trying to seem casual and not morbid, "you're never in pain from your wounds, huh?"

"Nope. I'm good with pain, but I don't need this; a little excessive, you know?"

"Takes a few days to heal all the way? How do they do it?"

"My most popular question. You sure you don't work for a newspaper?"

"Just selling 'em."

"Why not ask me how I psych into my role?"

"Okay, then, how do you psych into your role?""I'll tell you about the scars; it's inevitable."

"No—really—it isn't important."

"I don't mind, I was just teasing. They're hard to ignore, so let's get them out of the way. First off, I get sliced on stage by a doctor in the part of a mugger. He's not a doctor, actually, he's a medical researcher named…and this is top-secret, now. He isn't supposed to be named, for the sake of his reputation—all the controversy, and all."

"Word of honor."

"Westy Dwork. So he slashes me. Then backstage he stitches my face and stitches up Aurora Lehrman's stump. He regenerates the cells *somewhat* with a full cell cloner setup he has backstage, then we go on. It has to look like we were attacked a few months ago; we don't become hookers overnight."

"Then why do your characters have stitches, still?"

"Just for cosmetic reasons, so to speak…to appeal to our customers. We work in a freak show brothel."

"I read that. So why doesn't this Dwork guy just clone you and Aurora fully after the show instead of only accelerating the healing…too expensive?"

"'Friendly flesh.'"

"Excuse me?"

Mauve laughed, brushed her hair from her face. "Westy works for a company called Cugok Pharmaceuticals."

"I've heard of them." A tiny vertiginous thrill of déjà vu.

"Really? They're very new."

"I know."

"They're really into research and innovation; Westy's one of their top people. Aurora and I are sort of guinea pigs for something he's nicknamed 'friendly flesh,' a new inexpensive concept in cell regeneration that doesn't require hospitalization, necessarily, or intense cloning. It could very well make people immortal. Kind of."

"Kind of immortal, huh? Sort of invincible? How's it work?"

"Your body is scanned like it is for a teleportation record. This is your cellular blueprint. Then you take these pills, one a day, to maintain a certain level of a drug in you which will instantly begin rapid cell regeneration once you get injured. Your cellular blueprint, which will be on file at a specially equipped participating hospital, is alerted by the activity of the regenerative drug and transmits its blueprint information to the drug's 'memory.' If Aurora's arm was cloned in the traditional way it would only take a day or so. It takes a week right now with this...*but,* this would be cheaper, ideally, and outpatient...no prolonged hospital stay. Her stump would just be sealed, then she'd be released. The regenerative drug stimulates rapid cell growth, and the cellular blueprint being transmitted insures that the arm will be restored just as it once was...right down to every last mole."

"Fantastic. This will be big."

"Well, Westy is a little wary about it. He thinks the medical profession might try to buy the rights and then sit on it. Hospitals are big business. They might only let it sneak by for those who can shell out the big money, though the process itself isn't really all that costly."

"How far does the immortality possibility go? Can they perfect it to the point where the cells refresh themselves constantly and the aging process doesn't take place?"

"There's already various approaches to that, but I'm talking about this thing getting to the point where you can be shot with a gun and heal a moment later. Get beheaded and grow your head back in seconds. Wild, huh?" Mauve sipped from her tiny cup. "But the hospitals are like corporations, if not owned by them. You'll see it stomped on, squelched. Why do you think cloning after death is illegal? Religious pressure and colonial security alone, like they say? Mutant shit, pardon my language."

"You're a conspiracy nut. Paranoid."

"Why does everyone think I'm paranoid?" Mauve bulged her eyes, an eager actress.

"So if you cut your finger off right now you wouldn't feel pain because of your painkillers, and you'd grow it back entirely because of the drug and this Dwork with your molecular scan on file?"

"Right. Except my fingernail wouldn't be painted red."

"Hey, give them time. Before long they'll regenerate the ring along with it." Monty shook his head. "This is all pretty fascinating."

"But you've heard of Cugok before?"

"Their building used to be the Greenberg food plant. That's where Toll Loveland held his show *Pandora's Box.*"

"Is it really? Wow, I didn't know that. What a coincidence."

"Fate works in wondrous ways."

"I guess." Mauve killed off the last of the rich exotic dessert she'd had with her cappuccino. "So, I could cut my face open for you right now as a preview for the show, Montgomery, except I'd bleed to death before my cells could regenerate enough."

"I guess I can wait. Does it spook you at all, looking in the mirror?"

"No, but that first scene in the play does. Dwork really gets into the role." Mauve appeared subdued a moment, smiled faintly…an odd expression. "He's a little strange. It looks like something romantic is developing between him and Aurora."

"Oh? What's so strange?"

"Well, I heard he slept with one of the two mutant actresses in the play already. I've seen him flirt with the other. And he's tried to pick me up, too, I think."

"You think?"

"He's asked me to dinner. I've declined. And he's excessively physical, in my opinion…hand on the shoulder a lot, stroking the hair, et cetera. He's kind of stroked my face while punching the stitches in. I've never said anything. He just makes me rather uncomfortable. I hope he sticks to Aurora with his romantic impulses, now."

"Just send your two bodyguards, here, after that Lothario."

"They work for him. For Cugok, that is, not for the theater. It was Westy's idea to have them escort me home every night."

Monty glanced at the silent, unblinking creatures again. "Ah…so…you will try to get me that ticket, then?"

"Certainly."

"Do you think maybe we could get together for lunch during the week?" A big shy grin.

"Sure."

"I'm not trying to be a pest…"

"I know. Health agents exterminate pests."

"Right."

"Sure, that sounds like fun. You're my hero."

Monty laughed, giddy. Did she really like him as much as it appeared? "Yeah, right," he responded sarcastically.

FOURTEEN

OPENING SOON, the advertisement announced, *THE BIG FROWN*.

Monty had seen a huge billboard with this same advertisement for the first time today while coming into work. It had caught his eye because it reminded him of Mauve. It showed a man's face with the corners of his mouth turned down in an enormous grimace. He looked like a Choom, but in the painting there was a drop of blood running down from both corners of the big frown, and the man's eyes looked bewildered and pained.

The ad was in the entertainment section of the paper, amongst those for plays, and the billboard amongst others advertising plays in the theater district, and so it mustn't be a film...but when exactly would it open, and where, and who had written it? Obviously the ambiguity of the ad was a form of hype meant to garner the play advance attention.

Monty scanned for more on *Meathearts*, sipping his first coffee of the shift. His boss had been irritated that he'd left early, especially since those bundles of papers Monty had neglected to put away had been strewn throughout Blue Station by kids on their way to school. Monty didn't let it bother him. Mauve Pond had agreed to meet him for lunch two days from now. She hadn't elaborated on why then, specifically. Busy schedule? Other men-friends to see? Or did she want her scars to be pretty much gone for their next encounter?

Mulling this over, Monty flipped the page to a shock.

PAXTON THEATER CRITIC FOUND SLAIN.

It was attached to the entertainment section. And it was Yancy Mays.

"My God," muttered Monty, his eyes racing down the column. He had to break away for a moment, impatiently, to sell a magazine.

"My God," he said again.

Yancy Mays' roommate (male lover, Monty conjectured) Isaac Angeles had found the body upon returning home from work in the early evening, last night. Poor Isaac must have had a horrible shock, much worse than Monty's now, to find Yancy hanging upside-down by his ankles from a ceiling fixture, naked, his throat cut.

Like the goat in the play *Shit for Breakfast*...the play Yancy Mays had helped shut down, in his outrage. Monty recognized the similarity immediately, but found no mention of that play. A motive was unknown, as of yet, the article said—robbery ruled out.

Who had written that play, directed it? Monty couldn't remember now if Yancy had mentioned this in the review he'd read of *Pandora's Box*. Would someone connected with that play have come after Yancy for revenge?

Why after all this time, a year and more?

Monty thought about calling the police with his observation.

Then he thought about Yancy Mays' scathing recent review of the Ferule Cangue production of *Meathearts*.

And he remembered the scathing review of *Pandora's Box*, back when he and Opal Cowrie and Yancy Mays were all dying of M-670...filled with these memories, and surrounded in his prison of headlines.

"I'm Detective Juarez, heading the investigation into the murder of Yancy Mays," the round-faced, cold-eyed man on the vidscreen introduced himself. "So who are you, again?"

Monty had called Police Central, asked to speak to the lead officer investigating Yancy Mays' murder in whatever precinct that fell under. Now he introduced himself. "My name's Montgomery Black; I'm an ex-health agent, dismissed after I contracted M-670 at Toll Loveland's presentation *Pandora's Box*. Mays contracted M-670 at the same show and reviewed *Pandora's Box,* and in that review he made mention of a play called *Shit for Breakfast*, in which..."

"A live goat is strung up and has its throat cut. I know."

"Oh, good, I wanted to be sure..."

"Good observation. I appreciate your calling."

"So do you think the director or writer of that might have...you know..."

"The writer/director Twitch Member has already been questioned and he has an alibi. He submitted eagerly to a truth scan because he knows how bad this looks. He's innocent. He thinks someone's trying to frame him but I doubt it. Right now we're trying to track down the cast for questioning. It could even be a fan who liked that play and resented Mays for shutting it down. Whoever it is, is a psycho."

"It might be the director or writer of another play Mays attacked," Monty suggested. "But he doesn't want to give himself away, so he killed Mays in a way that suggests he wants revenge for his criticism...but not in a way that reveals his identity."

"Maybe. But Mays has reviewed a lot of plays and movies and dance productions, and his reviews are often unkind. Could be some walk-on actor Mays said two words about in a play five years ago—who knows?"

"Well, it seems to me he would have killed Mays before this. Mays must have recently stirred things up with someone. Some of these plays he's cut up have been made by very disturbed people...violent people. Look at *Pandora's Box.*"

"Yeah. Well, at least we can rule out Toll Loveland as a suspect, huh?"

"Mm," said Monty.

"Like I said, I appreciate your calling. Sorry to hear you lost your job over that fuck, Loveland. Call me again if you think of anything helpful. You didn't know Mays yourself, did you? Or speak with him at *Pandora's Box*?"

"Never even saw him." Christ, thought Monty, I'm not stupid, pal. I didn't fucking kill Yancy Mays. But he said nothing. Juarez was just doing his job…but no doubt now he'd poke into Monty's background a little. Oh well; Monty would do the same in his position.

Monty disconnected without getting specific about Mays' bad review of *Meathearts*. After all, he hadn't wanted so much to help the police investigation as to rule out the creator of *Shit for Breakfast* in his own.

"Beak."

The tall, weasel-like being with the little black bird's beak, wearing a bulky jacket and a purple ski hat against the morning cold, spun at the voice, ripping his zipper open. Two small children were with him.

"Hey!" Monty said, holding up his spread hands.

Beak had torn his pistol free and shoved it out on level with Monty's face. "Get in the house, kids—*move!*" They hesitated, uncomprehending. "*Now!*"

"It's me, Monty, Beak—take it slow!"

"I know who you are, man." The kids ran to the tenement steps, up them. They had longer, lighter, fluffier fur than Beak, and their black beaks were three times as long as his—like hummingbird bills. They disappeared inside.

"Cute kids. Why the animosity, Beak?"

"I heard about your shooting spree in the supermarket and your stand-off with the forcers, man. I'm taking no chances. How do you know where I live and what the hell are you doing sneaking up on me?"

"You snuck up on me and Opal the night of Toll Loveland's show, remember? And do you forget, you yourself invited me and Opal over here once with the rest of Organic Control to celebrate your marriage to the mother of those cute little chicks of yours?"

"The mother of those cute little kids was raped and stabbed to death last year, Black…and like I said, I take no chances."

"What—are you kidding? Oh my God, man, I'm sorry…"

"That's fucking life, right? That's fucking life. So you still haven't told me why you're here, Black." Beak hadn't lowered his pistol an inch and cars were going by. No one had stopped, though. That was fucking life.

"I didn't mean to upset you, Beak…I didn't know…"

"Why?"

"It's about Toll Loveland."

The gun wavered a little like it was getting heavy. Then it lowered, slowly, to Beak's side as he straightened up from his tense firing stance. "Yeah?"

"Did you ever get to see his body when they brought it in?"

"No. Why?"

"Did you see photos or vids of it?"

"Photos."

"Was it really him, Beak? The same guy from *Pandora's Box*?"

"Yeah, you could tell it was him. He was dead four days and he was practically a skeleton from M-670, but he had the same high forehead and slicked-back hair and whatever. And he had some ID…"

"Let's stick to the physical body."

"What's this about?"

"I have this feeling he's alive."

Beak squinted at Monty, who stood near the end of Beak's car, his hands still held out of his pockets so Beak could see them, despite the chill. Beak asked, again, "Why?"

"The theater critic Yancy Mays was murdered in the same way a goat was killed in a play. The writer of that play has an alibi, but the play was mentioned in Mays' review of *Pandora's Box*. And just recently Mays mentioned Loveland again, in a not-too-kind way, in a review of a new play."

"So you think Loveland is still alive and killed a critic?"

"Maybe he was cloned."

"By who?"

"A black market outfit. The Teeb Family will do that. Or maybe he did it himself."

"Himself?" Beak sounded like he thought Monty might be mad.

"He majored in bioengineering at Paxton Polytech before he went on to P.U. for his Liberal Arts degree. In his play *The Godfucker* he cut off his left hand's little finger, swallowed it, and at the end of the play cloned it back himself on stage in three minutes."

"Yeah, I remember that, now."

"Me and Vern went to the Hill Way Galleries to see a Loveland painting called *Matter of Life and Death.* It's a light painting that changes at various times of the day. First it showed a baby boy inside the rib-cage of a skeleton, trying to break out, his arms in the same pose as the skeleton. Next I saw it, the skeleton had changed into a man: Toll Loveland. This time the child had turned into a skeleton but only his arm was reaching out of Loveland's chest. Next it showed a huge naked chest—baby within Toll, and Toll within this third body."

Yeah—so?"

Matter of Life and Death. Flesh. Bones. Rebirth." Monty let it sink in. "Cloning."

Come on, man, this mutant shit kind of art can be interpreted a million fuckin' ways."

Loveland likes to leave clues. In the same painting he had Bedbug Navigator globes in the eye sockets of the skull, in reference to the teleporter he had rigged up that me and Vern found..."

Yeah, and Vern found his way into a hospital for that one, thanks to Toll Loveland *and* you," Beak hissed.

Let me finish, dammit. He gave himself a cameo appearance in Auretta Here's vid to the news people, remember? Then he killed Here in his movie *Cupid of Death*, turned her to sludge and planted a ticket for *The Godfucker* on her. Having his fun, playing his games..."

And?"

And so maybe he wanted us to *think* he died of M-670, and left an infected clone of himself for us to find so we'd believe it was all over..."

Beak was already wagging his head. "Mutant shit. Crazy paranoid mutant feces, man. It's been a year. We'd have heard about this psycho already, he'd have struck again—that's his passion. *Was.*"

Maybe he has, and we haven't realized it was him. He's got a new identity; he was Manuel Hung in school and Vicelord Godfucker after that. Maybe he's in Miniosis, or went to Earth. Or maybe he's here...just been taking his time and working on his next project."

Man, I know what you're going through." Beak sighed, cold steam puffing out. Frost sparkled on his car; winter was on its way, striding in on huge white legs taller than Punktown's towering buildings. Most of them, anyway. "On weekends I leave my kids with my brother and his wife for a couple of hours and look for the punks who killed my wife. Every weekend since it happened. Some weeknights, too. My people mate for life, man. *For life.* Your people laugh at us, but that's your fucking problem. I'll never stop until I find those fucks and skin them alive. Never. My kids don't understand...they still ask me when she's coming home, or will she come on their birthdays, or whatever. They don't know what a fucking afterlife is any better than I do, but I do my best, and my brother's wife draws for children's books, so she draws pictures of their mother playing in heaven, or wherever. That's my biggest help. So I try not to let them see how hate-filled and despairing I am...I gotta be strong for them, I can't be selfish and irresponsible. But when they're not around, I look. And some day, when they're not around, I'll find those two human punks. And my kids won't be there to see what I do to them."

Monty sniffed from the cold. "I'm so sorry, man," he breathed.

I know you are. And I'm sorry for you and Opal. I know what you're after. Same thing as me. Only difference is, my boys are probably still alive. And your boy isn't. You wish he was, so you yourself could kill him. But Toll Loveland is dead."

Monty let out more than he'd first intended to let Beak know. "A new play just opened; *Meathearts.* In it, on stage, a woman has her face carved up and another one gets her arm hacked off. Then backstage, for their next act, they get patched up—and for the rest of the week until the next show, the slashed woman heals and the armless woman grows her arm back, using a new long-distance cloning technique. Sounds Lovelandish to me."

Sounds to me like a Loveland emulation. I'm not surprised, Black. You'll see more of this. People hopping on the Loveland bus. The controversy. The publicity. He's a genius and a hero to some sick fucks."

The playwright is fairly well-known and established, but the director sounds suspicious, Beak. His name..."

Black."

His name is Ferule Cangue. I know a ferule is a stick or ruler you punish children with, and today I looked up 'cangue.' It's a heavy wooden yoke they made you wear in ancient China, on Earth, as punishment. It isn't his real name, Beak. Ferule Cangue is the Punisher. And Yancy Mays has been punished."

And my name isn't Beak, and half the people in this fucking town, at least, don't use their real names, Black—you know that. A Toll Loveland *fan*, maybe. Look into this guy if you have to...you'll see. But I'm telling you. You're chasing a ghost, Black."

I'm haunted by ghosts, Monty thought. Opal's. Maybe his own. And while he was on the subject of ghosts...

Where's Vern at, now? You must have heard from him."

Leave him alone."

Beak."

I mean it. Leave him alone. I'm sorry what I said about the tran incident—nobody held a gun to his head to get involved—but I don't want you going up to him with this crazy obsessive shit you're throwing at me."

I just want to know if he's all right, dammit. I haven't heard from him or seen him in a year. I have to know he's all right."

He's all right. That's all I'll say. I mean it. He's all right."

Monty sighed, calming a bit. "Thank you." Though he wasn't sure how much he could believe Beak on this.

I have to go; my kids'll be late for school, and I've gotta get to HAP. Don't worry, Black, I won't mention our little talk. Especially the stuff about Loveland."

Thanks, Beak. I can't tell you how sorry I am about your wife. Why don't you let me come with you sometimes on weekends? We can cover more ground..."

Beak wagged his head, chuckled a little. "I'm honored, man, I'm honored you'd suggest that. And it's tempting to have somebody along to lean on and to understand my pain. But I *have* to be alone. It's personal, it's a private thing, it's *my* thing. And I'm afraid that if you were with me I'd talk too much of it out of my system. You'd talk me into staying home with the kids. You'd try to get me to take a new mate in the human way. I can't, man. I've got to stay alone and stay sad and stay full of hate."

Just let me know if you ever need any kind of help. If you change your mind, at least give me enough info that I can hunt for them on my own."

Nobody's ever offered me so much help. I can't believe you, Black. People tell you they feel sorry for you, and two weeks later they've forgotten you had a problem; at least they ignore it 'cause it makes them uncomfortable 'cause they got their own problems. And here you are with your own problems, and you're offering to help me. You're empathizing with me. I'm impressed, man, and I'm touched. Only my old buddy Woodsy, I think, would have done that for me."

He did it for me," Monty said, smiling.

Beak stuffed his gun away and held out his small furry hand. "I won't forget this. You let me know if you ever need help. But drop the ghost, buddy, drop it. All right?"

As soon as I can. Look after those cute little chicks, Beak. That has to be your top priority."

Always."

They let go of each other's hands. Monty patted Beak's arm and turned to walk back the two blocks to the subway kiosk he'd emerged from.

He felt sorry for Beak and his kids, sorrier now than for his own loss. He and Opal hadn't been married, nor had children. He almost felt guilty, as if his obsession were trivial. But Opal wasn't the only one who needed vengeance, was she? Many others had died as a result of the opening of *Pandora's Box*. There was Auretta Here, however tainted her innocence had been, and of course Yancy Mays to be avenged.

But even if it had only been Opal, that didn't mean Monty had no right to feel his own pain. A person with a cut-off finger needn't feel guilty that the pain of a person with his entire arm cut off is greater.

This was his pain. His personal, private thing.

And if someone, anyone, were still alive to be punished, then Monty would designate himself the Punisher.

Mauve had no scars today. More unusual to Monty was that every other time he'd seen her she'd been glamorously attired in skirts, stockings, heels—but today she was wearing faded blue jeans, sneakers, a heavy gray sweater over a white blouse and an oversized, drab green military rain parka, the hood up over her head. "Incognito," she explained as they walked, side-by-side.

Is it that bad already?"

The play is doing really well—the best box office right now for a non-musical in Punktown. The movie talk is big. But I won't get it…watch them give it to Malka Tribe or Patricia Gates…"

Or Lhinda Sanchez."

Right. They always get the juicy parts."

But do they have the guts to let your pal Dwork cut their faces open?"

I really hope they ask me, but I won't bank on it. My agent is letting them know I want it. But even if I don't get it, I'll have got enough attention to maybe nab a nice film role someplace."

So are you dressed like this only as a disguise, or am I seeing the real Mauve Pond?"

Mauve laughed. "This is the real me. The real me *is* my disguise. I don't mind the recognition, signing autographs, but some days I still like to just disappear. And get rid of my two skinny shadows. When I mentioned to Westy that I had a lunch date with you today he wanted me to take the Stems. He was pretty insistent, but I blew him off. Anyway, I told him you were an ex-health agent, not some drooling psycho."

Please don't tell anybody else I was an ex-health agent…all right, Mauve? It's personal. They ask you why you're an ex, and I'd rather not get into it."

Sorry."

That's all right." No, shit, it wasn't. Now what if Westy Dwork mentioned to Ferule Cangue that Mauve had just been befriended by an ex-health agent?

Did you mention I caught M-670 at the Toll Loveland thing?"

"Ah…sorry."

Don't worry about it."

The cold from this morning had let up a bit but it was still dark, and now raining. The cobblestones of Beaumonde Square glistened like scales, and the warm lights of the shops that flanked this long strip they strolled down were reflected in the water gathering in the spaces between the stones. In friendlier weather, lovers would stroll here, sit on the stone benches or under the huge potted plants. In summer this strip would be full of ice cream eaters, baby carriages loitering. Now it was sparsely populated and hunched figures moved quickly.

The rain's getting heavy, you poor guy," Mauve laughed. Monty had his neck scrunched into the upturned collar of his overcoat. "Wanna poke around in some shops, or are you ready to eat?"

Whatever you want…I'm in no hurry."

"I won't subject you to my shop-browsing; you have to get to work."

Actually, I was thinking of calling in sick today."

Will your boss get mad?"

"I've never missed a day, but probably. If he wasn't such an asshole, maybe I'd worry about what he'll do to replace me, but I won't 'cause he is."

Well, let's eat first anyway, just in case you don't call in. One of these restaurants, or would you rather we hit Quidd's Market?"

Would you mind Quidd's?"

I was hoping you'd say that. You passed the test."

The immense structure housing Quidd's Market was just one cobblestoned strip over from where they were, so they passed through the intervening mall building to reach the strip bordering the market. The pre-colonial Choom style was much in evidence, though the building had been restored and enlarged upon. The great central rotunda was meant to look like this planet, Oasis, as an invitation to the Earth people who initially settled here, and Quidd's Market had been the major spot in this area for the Chooms to sell their wares and crafts and produce to the first of the military and civilian colonists so long ago. Nowadays the market rented its many tiny booths and stands to Earth people, Tikkihottos, people from many different worlds and even other dimensions, such as the Kodju with their popular stir-fried vegetables. All of the stands sold foodstuffs now, except for one tobacco shop, some stands quite old but many renting for only a year or so. Rents were high and a fad food might not be popular enough to pay the fees a year later.

The vast hall could be entered at either end, but Mauve and Monty climbed up the marble front steps. In a glass-roofed outer hall—a more modern addition—portable booths offered gifts, curios and souvenirs, clothing and leather goods. Mauve tried to get Monty to buy an umbrella but he resisted. They passed into the rotunda. Amplified voices blended into one echoing rumble. Faces peered down from a circular balcony above. The translucent, shell-like material of the dome wasn't letting in more than a feeble luminescence today, and no amount of cleaning had restored it to its once bright glow.

The hall of Quidd's Market now stretched off to left and right, seemingly endless. It was thronged, as always, though on weekends one could scarcely move. A real tourist site, but also the favorite shopping spot for the wealthy locals for whom these exotic selections, a treat to outsiders, were a staple. "Which way?" said Mauve.

Ohhh…why not left?"

Why not?" Mauve pushed her hood back from her head and smiled at him.

The espresso machine made a loud sound like an old-style aircraft coming in for a landing. This had to be Monty's first stop, as always at Quidd's Market, all other treats secondary. Next came desserts; they figured they'd work their way backwards. Picking out a dessert—as with anything here—was difficult in that you were afraid to make a choice, lest further along you discovered something better. They settled on a rich, fudge-like Tikkihotto candy, sweet enough to complement and offset the bitter espresso, and retreated from the crowds to talk a little, sheltering close to a broad support column between two stands and using the top of a trash zapper for a table.

I've got your tickets, by the way. Hope you're free this Sunday night."

Of course—thank you. That's great."

Row E. That's fifth row."

Wow. I'm much obliged."

I have to warn you, we have our pukers every show."

It will just add to the air of gritty realism, as Ferule Cangue might say."

That sounds derogatory."

Well, I do feel a little uncomfortable about seeing you mutilated. I mean, are we an audience or bystanders?"

You sound like Yancy Mays now. I feel sorry he was murdered but I didn't care for his review. I know when I'm being victimized, and I'm not a victim if I'm scarred willingly, am I? And even if the rapists are different each night, Aurora isn't *really* being raped...since she's subjecting herself to it voluntarily."

I think Mays meant that Cangue is making you a victim of exploitation."

I *want* to do this. It's powerful, and I believe in it. Yeah, it's tough stuff. It isn't some candy-coated musical. We're rubbing noses in it. I'm part of it; I'm not exploited." Mauve looked defensive, wary of him now. "So do you agree with Yancy Mays—that I'm no better than a real freak prosty letting herself be humiliated for money?"

A little bit. I know you honestly believe in it. I just think maybe your enthusiasm is blinding you a little to Cangue's kinky ugliness."

Life is ugly, Monty, and I don't think I'm all that blind."

I'm sorry. I haven't seen it yet...I shouldn't say anything. I'm just concerned for you, that's all."

They didn't talk for a while. Monty eyed the milling people, many of them making hostile or blandly curious eye contact with him as they oozed past. Rather than drop the subject, he went back to it. "I may not like the play, Mauve, but I can still enjoy your work in it. I hope I haven't insulted you, but I have to be honest to my feelings."

I know...I'm sorry. It's just that I'm so into the play."

Things were better. "I understand."

I know you told me you don't like discussing how you became an ex, but you already told me a little so I assume you don't mind telling me some more of it. Why the hell are you working at a newsstand in Blue Station? And don't give me some crack about meeting interesting people."

After what happened to me I wanted a job where I'd be alone—and something mindless. I just wanted to make enough to live and be numb and vegetate."

So...what happened to you? With Toll Loveland and all that?"

Monty met her gaze. It wasn't easy opening up after all this time of solitude and silence. He'd barely told Midge any of it in the year he'd known her. But all the noise and people made it easier to confess; just the two of them alone in a quiet place would have made him more unsettled.

He told her. About the night of *Pandora's Box*. About Auretta Here. About Opal, the hardest part. How she'd become infected. About the vid message she'd left him.

He told her about Vern and the Bedbugs' tran. He told her everything he'd told

Beak today, except for his suspicions about Ferule Cangue. He told her about *Shit for Breakfast*, the sacrifice of the goat and of Yancy Mays, about the cloned finger in *The Godfucker*. He could tell that she saw what he was closing in on.

You think Toll Loveland is still alive…and you see a similarity between his work and my play…"

Mauve. Can you possibly arrange for me to meet Ferule Cangue?"

You think he knows whether Toll Loveland is alive or not?"

He might know just that." Monty didn't unveil his ultimate suspicion.

Oh come on, Monty…"

Where's the harm? I'll do my best not to embarrass you or hurt your position with the play, I swear…but if Loveland is still alive, then he's a dangerous mass murderer who's gotta be stopped."

Have you told the Health Agency or the police all this?"

Not really. If I'm wrong about Cangue, I'll turn it over to them—if they believe me. My friend today was less than convinced."

It is a pretty far-fetched idea."

It suits Toll Loveland. How about Westy Dwork; can I meet him, too?"

Now, why him?"

Monty's delivery was cold and matter-of-fact, and afterwards Mauve stared at him blankly, soaking it in. He said, "Westy Dwork is a researcher for Cugok Pharmaceuticals. Cugok is the old Greenberg Products plant, and that's where Toll Loveland presented *Pandora's Box*."

Oh my God," Mauve breathed at last.

Monty exchanged glares with passing people. Mauve watched him a few moments. "Worth looking into?" he asked, without glancing at her.

I'll arrange it. Wow. So…" she chuckled a little, "I can see now why you wanted to befriend me. Rescue me from the Stems and all that."

Monty faced her abruptly, his brow furrowed. "No…I didn't know you were even an actress…I really did think you were in danger. It was your scars that caught my attention, but it was all just a remarkable coincidence."

Let's hope it stays that way, just a remarkable coincidence."

Monty didn't respond to that. He realized he'd be quite disappointed if Toll Loveland were not alive.

You know," Mauve said, "I thought I sensed a difference in you today. In the coffeehouse you were focused on me. Today you've been distracted, focused on something else."

I'm sorry. Now that I've got it all out in the open, I'll focus on you again." He grinned.

That's the flirty ex-health agent I know. I'll tell Westy and Ferule you're my new boyfriend and that's how I'll get you backstage. How do you like *that* for flirty?"

"Sounds good to me. I just hope you're a method actress."

Now this is more like it. Why don't you call in sick at work before we go on any further in our food binge?"

Good idea." He did feel lighter, even with Opal fresh from his lips. Maybe because of it.

Mauve couldn't find her hand phone in her pocketbook, cursing lightly as she burrowed in vain for it, apparently having left it at home, so they moved on in search of a pay phone.

Maybe we should take the train someplace for lunch," Monty said as they pushed along through and with the crowd.

Ohhh—*why?*"

To lose our tail."

What tail?"

Take it easy, don't be obvious. Look behind you. There's a very tall man in some kind of breathing apparatus."

Mauve looked over her shoulder as an actress, pretending to glance at the food stand they'd just passed. Indeed, not far behind them a figure loomed above the river of bobbing heads. Bulky black plastic jacket, a black helmet with a black visor and black rubbery tubes connecting it to a device on the figure's back. She faced front again. "He does look sinister, but I think you're getting paranoid."

He walked past us twice at the trash zapper back there and he looked toward us both times."

So? I'm seeing a lot of people again and again."

Just humor me a minute, then." Monty took Mauve's hand and hurried her along. The left-hand end of Quidd's Market gaped open before them, the rain still pouring down out there, umbrellas dragging people along, wealthier people utilizing electromagnetic repulsor shields (also good for light muggings), a strange sight in such a heavy downpour as these individuals remained dry inside their expensive invisible bubbles, the rain exploding off the outlines. Mauve pulled up her simple hood.

The black-garbed giant stepped out into the torrents. Awkwardly weaving, as if inexperienced with this planet's gravity, it turned from right to left. On the left, flat against the building, stood Monty and Mauve lighting cigarettes.

Hello," Monty said. "Care for one?" He held out his cigarette.

The ungainly giant ambled on, down the slick marble steps, across slippery cobblestones like a drunken robot. Mauve pressed against Monty's arm, shivering a bit. "Do you really think he was following us?"

You told me Dwork was insistent, didn't you? You'd walk like that too if you had one leg in one boot and two in the other."

What do you mean?"

We just saw the fattest Stem you're ever likely to see."

Oh…my…God. That bastard."

You told Dwork too much about me, Mauve. Ex-health agent. Contracted M-670 at the old Greenberg plant. He's worried."

He always worries about me anyway, Monty…I told you how seductive he is with me. I think he's jealous. He looked unhappy when I told him I was meeting you today."

Maybe this is too dangerous for you. Christ, what am I thinking of, involving you in this? Forget backstage; I'll find out about Dwork and Cangue on my own…"

No, Monty, you come backstage. I'm a big girl; I know when to be scared. That creepy worm Westy, having me followed after I told him no. I *owe* him one."

Let's go back inside. We can at least eat in peace, now."

FIFTEEN

Monty was suspicious about opening the large envelope he signed for at the door to his apartment; it had no return address, and the only mail he normally received was bills and the mountains of glossy junk he tossed without ennobling with more than a glance. He held it to the light, sniffed it. What the fuck. He sliced the bottom of it open. It was from Beak, whom he'd seen only yesterday. He must have acquired Monty's current address at HAP after Monty had foolishly neglected to leave it with him after Beak's reluctance to accept help.

There were computer-generated portraits of two young human men in the envelope. There had been a witness to the flight of the men who had raped and killed Beak's wife in the parking garage under the bank at which she had worked. Had she survived long enough, the exact faces and voices of the men—indeed the attack itself, as she had lived it—could have been reproduced from her memory as *Pandora's Box* had been reproduced from Beak's…but she hadn't. It was too expensive and involved a process to be utilized in every rape or attack, certainly, but this victim having been the wife of a health agent, it could have been done.

Beak had enclosed a police autopsy report. Monty was appalled. Being stabbed was bad enough a thing, mutilated even worse. Her throat had finally been cut.

Monty went back to the photos. One looked like a typical mongrel punk; part white, part Hispanic or black, part Asian, with more tender care administered to his greasy black bouffant than to anything else the punk was ever likely to encounter. The other had black features but white skin and a blond crewcut. Monty imagined that the witness hadn't seen them well enough or long enough to warrant having his memories recorded, played back, blown up or enhanced, and so these were only loose sketches really, but Monty was sure they were true to the spirit of the killers. Brutally emotionless and utterly repellant.

Both had been wearing red plastic jackets, the report went on, indicating a possible gang association. In reference to this, Beak had added a notation for Monty: "Have questioned and investigated three gangs that wear red jackets. One had nearly same jackets but no one matches the suspects and they profess no knowledge. I keep an eye on them from time to time—the Menses, they're called. You don't need to cover them."

Monty set the reports and photos aside, finally read Beak's letter to him.

"We work separately, Black. I had to send this out fast before I changed my mind.

If you change your mind, I understand. Don't feel pressured—go at your own pace, if you go. Whether you help or not, thanks again for your concern and offer. I won't forget it, I mean that. One thing: if you ever did find the monsters, they're mine, understand? I insist on that. You know what this is to me. Thanks, buddy."

Monty sat back, sighed. He felt guilty. The thing was, he was partly sorry for offering to help Beak right now. He was absorbed in his own mission, and trying to nurture the embryo of a relationship he'd created with Mauve. He had meant his offer, but he had expected, for the most part, to be turned down.

Later, man, he told Beak in his mind, I promise.

Mauve's apartment was on the third floor of a large old house across from a Paxton University dormitory building—easy to find. She opened the door to the front porch as he came up the wooden steps. "Right on time," she smiled. She was very casually attired: a loose-fitting charcoal top with short sleeves, baring several inches of midriff, and dark gray sweat pants that smoothly defined the gentle contours of her slim hips and legs. Following her up to the third floor was not unpleasant.

On the second floor was a single tiny room off the stairs which, in the sectioning of the old house into distinct tenements, had oddly been appended to her apartment—occupied by a sofa-bed and a bookcase, plants. The flight to the third floor took them to the apartment proper, a large single room but for a partially partitioned kitchen and the bathroom. A huge waterbed, sofa and two armchairs close by, a small kitchen table, many plants, many framed posters from movies and plays. The walls and ceiling were broken into odd, interesting angles in correspondence with the roof, and the floor was covered in dark red and green plastic tiles with an unusual emblem or symbol incorporated into the tiles in the center of the room. Mauve explained that this had once been a frat house and that was their insignia.

"The landlord told me he won't rent to students now after the damage they used to do. You should hear them at night across the street. I've almost called the forcers a few nights myself, but the cold weather seems to be slowing them down a little."

"I love it. Very artistic place, nice mood."

"And it's nice and warm and toasty, so take your coat off, why don't ya?"

He wore entirely black under his black overcoat. It slimmed him, and he knew he looked good in it—it showcased and contrasted his pale skin and dirty blond hair, light eyes. He played to the physical attraction he knew Mauve felt for him, obvious from her quick interest and receptiveness to him. But also it was his no-nonsense, down-to-business look; it was Sunday afternoon, and tonight Mauve would take him backstage to meet the director of *Meathearts.*

She'd invited him for lunch before the play, set it out for them now as he poked around on her combined VT/home computer/vidphone. He called up the titles of movies she had recorded in the memory and read through them. Most were less than ten years old but some were quite old, pre-colonial. One recent movie was based on the true story of a woman who'd died of M-670, played, of course, by Lhinda Sanchez, one of the top juicy role snatchers. Monty had seen it. The movie briefly portrayed Matt Cotton, the VT evangelist who had financed the creation of M-670.

Calling him to the table, Mauve poured wine. It was a light dinner of fish and vegetables, and quite good. "You'll make some man a good wife," Monty said, half smiling.

"Oh please, Monty. I'd rather make myself a good actress, right now. Anyway, you should see this place when I'm not expecting company—I'm a slob. Clothes everywhere. Can't you still smell the socks I picked up before you came?"

"Hey, I'll have to turn you over to the Health Agency for producing hazardous waste."

"They'll never take you back, huh? Have you tried?"

Monty poked his fish, flipped open the silvery skin to the feathery white inner flesh. Steam curled out. "No. I'm not so sure I'd want to try. Outside them now, I can see them a little better for their hypocrisy and corruption and all that shit you find in an institution, whether it's private or government run. Inside, you feel this loyalty 'cause you're part of them. I knew, then, that HAP looks the other way when the price is right. They'll nail a little printing company to the wall for dumping some sludge but they'll just slap a major corporation with a fine and you'll never see it in the press, though there might have been a violation endangering thousands. Politics and business are inseparable…we live in a plutocracy."

"But like you say, every place, private or government run, is full of hypocrisy and corruption…so where do you go?"

"To sell newspapers in Blue Station."

"That answer disappoints me, Monty."

"Sorry." He wasn't looking at her. "I don't feel like being a HAP goon. Hired assassin."

"Come on—you did some real good, didn't you? The police force is corrupt, to a huge extent, but they do good, and there are good forcers and bad forcers. It's all we got. Good guys like you have to be strong and hold on against the bad ones…not give up."

"I assassinated a male prosty with M-670 in Red Station. It was on VT—you don't remember seeing that?" She shook her head. "I made him go to his knees and then I melted him with plasma. I executed him. I could have cuffed him and taken him in by force. Selfish hazard or not, he wasn't given a trial. I didn't question my orders. And if I had, if I'd refused, it would have gone down against me and someone else would have executed him."

"All right, that was bad—but it bothers you, right? You regret it. It wouldn't bother a bad man."

"Regret doesn't bring a dead person back to life."

Mauve dropped the subject, prodded her own fish. "I don't want to upset you."

"You aren't. I was upset before I met you." He hadn't dropped the subject. After a few moments he said, "Matt Cotton won't be executed. He may not even spend the rest of his life in prison..."

"Oh, come on now, Monty."

"Well, he's got VT, decent food, recreation. He's already been allowed to preach his shit to the inmates at the cushy rest home they call a prison. I'd like to commit a crime and get put in there with him, to ream his ass myself, but that's probably already been done and he probably likes it."

"How's the fish?"

Monty finally looked at Mauve and smiled, embarrassed. "I'm sorry. It's great. Fantastic. No more ranting."

"You've got good reason to, but not right now, all right?" She smiled at him, one corner of her mouth pulling down without the scars, this characteristic not caused by them as he had originally believed. She looked beguiling. But he missed the scars, he was ashamed to admit to himself. They were what he'd originally noticed, what had originally defined her for him, he argued to himself in justification.

It was only twenty minutes from the end of the meal to the waterbed. Why postpone the inevitable? His ardor was real and strong in the beginning, frenzied even, his right hand alternately up under her loose top or slipping under the elastic rim of her sweat pants, their mouths locked. Her tongue in his mouth. But his was timid, and he preferred kissing her jaw and neck. When they were naked his kisses didn't stray any lower than her ribs. She didn't complain or pull him lower but he felt guilty, a little inadequate, for the omission. Her ardor was so much stronger than Opal's had been but for rarely. He had had to ask Opal to wrap her legs around him like this, Mauve's feet propped on the ottoman of his ass. Opal had usually been dry at first; he had glided instantly into Mauve. She moaned heartily, and at her climax she thumped him on the back with the heel of her hand, startling him for a moment, making him think she wanted him to stop, but she didn't.

And he didn't. He couldn't. He had been soft at first, and afraid it wouldn't progress beyond that, was relieved when it did—but he couldn't climax, couldn't ejaculate. A full hour after she had climaxed a second time he knew he was no closer to release. He sweated. They tried various positions. His heart hammering, his brain starved for blood, he rolled off of her slick flesh and curled in a sweat-chilly ball.

She lightly touched the wall of his back. "I know," she said.

"Sorry."

"I understand, Monty. You can't because you're thinking of Opal. You're afraid you're going to hurt me. But that's all over now. You don't have to feel guilty—you didn't kill her. Matt Cotton and Toll Loveland did."

"Let's drop it for now."

"You've got to *face* it. Don't be humiliated, Monty, I'm not upset. I had a great time. I know it's been a long time for you…next time will be much better, I'm sure. Just be patient. But Opal wouldn't blame you for what happened, you know that."

"She did blame me. She wouldn't see me. Even in her message she admitted she felt that I did this to her and it was my fault…"

"She was probably apologizing, admitting her guilt, from the sound of it."

"You didn't hear it."

"So call her mom. Show me."

"Drop it, Mauve. This is my shit. Drop it."

"It's the same reason why you work that empty newsstand job. It's self-punishment. You don't feel worthy of a better job or going back to HAP and asking for your job back because you failed in catching Toll Loveland…"

"Oh? So why am I looking for him now, if I'm so defeated?"

"Because you're struggling to be yourself again."

Monty slid his legs from the bed, sat up. "Are you an undercover therapist hired by HAP to plague me?"

"I'm not trying to plague you." Mauve sounded hurt, bitter. "I'm trying to help you."

Twisting around to look down at her, Monty took her hand and kissed it. "I'm sorry. I know. Thanks for your help. You're very special…not many people care about other people's problems for long."

"I'm not from around here—we're a little warmer down south, like the climate." Mauve got out of bed. "I'm gonna grab a shower; I feel like a glob of hazardous waste. Why don't you relieve yourself while I'm gone…don't be proud. I know how you guys are—you don't get it out now, it'll be backed up in your brain until you get another chance."

It was backed up in his eyes; he'd almost cried from the frustration that had left him this exhausted and shaken. "Take your shower, doctor."

She ruffled his hair, strode naked across the cold tiles toward the bathroom. How beautiful she'd been in bed, he reflected as he heard the water go on. Women sought to prepare their hair just so, their makeup and clothing, to compose their expressions into sly seductiveness, but to him nothing matched the mussed hair, the flush of blood and the weighted lids and slack mouth of the sex act, the exhausted dizzy sheen to the eyes and lazy smile afterwards. The primal, natural abandonment of pretense and posing.

He wondered if the scars would have been able to push him over the edge to release. He confronted their allure more directly now that she was safely away from him, blocked off by water. That photo of her in the paper had seized him—the yin/yang her face had presented so distinctly and compellingly. Ugly black stitches in a beautiful soft face. A weariness there from the arduous performance, as after sex. How a face could still be so lovely with such ugliness within its borders fascinated him, made her more intriguing and striking than she was normally. He longed to have her naked before him now, the stitches bold in her face, weary and vulnerable and softly smiling, lids heavy. Could he possibly convince her to convince Dwork to leave the stitches in for one night? How? He didn't see how...

Well, tonight her scars even without stitches would be raw and distinct. That would be quite close. He was certain she'd let him sleep here tonight. He wouldn't release himself now; he'd save it for then.

On top of all his other guilt, this new guilt perched. But why be guilty? he struggled to argue to himself. She isn't a victim—she chooses to accept these wounds and brands, doesn't she?

They reached the Jason Scarborough Theater good and early. Mauve left Monty only briefly to change into her white dress for the opening scene, and when she returned introduced Monty first to Westy Dwork.

Dwork's work area, contained within a small dressing room, was much less exotic and bizarre than Monty had envisioned, resembled more closely a miniature dentist's office. There was a central reclining chair to seat patients, various glittery instruments poised over it like statues of Stems, and a counter against one wall—a large mirror behind it—covered with devices with colored jewels of light attempting to enliven their blandness. The two Stems were here, keeping to the corners like something you'd toss your coat over.

Dwork was Stem-like himself for a human, very tall and very thin. Dark hair in boyish bangs over wide eyes. He had a nervous flicker of a smile and a twitchy sort of nervous energy. He wore a white lab smock, open to show his gray suit, gray shirt and gray tie.

"Westy," said Mauve, "this is my friend Montgomery Black."

"Mr. Black." They shook hands. "You're a lucky man to be a close friend to this lovely creature."

"I understand it's your job every Sunday to make her not so lovely."

"Oh yes, I have the distinction of hacking her up every performance, but I'm *also* the one who restores her loveliness."

"It's a remarkable process...Mauve told me some of the future potential. She didn't give away the technical aspects, though—don't worry."

"I haven't given away the technical aspects to her, so don't you worry, either. I do have to ask you, though, Mr. Black, not to reveal my name to any newspapers or such. Mauve tells me you're in the newspaper business. Not as a writer?"

"Oh no. Sales and distribution."

"It's just that the process is still rather experimental and I don't want to discredit the research company I work for. It was kind of difficult getting them to let me use the 'friendly flesh' process in the play. Ah, Mauve tells me you're an ex-health agent. That's intriguing. You're fully out of the Agency now?"

"Yep. I caught M-670 at Toll Loveland's *Pandora's Box*, performed in the old Greenberg plant where your Cugok place is now."

"I remember hearing about you, but they didn't release your identity. Good—now you don't release my identity and I won't release yours. Sound fair?" Dwork chuckled a bit in his tall man's deep bass voice. "I, ah, I remember that your partner died…a woman?"

"That's right." Monty ignored Mauve's glance at him.

"A terrible thing. Good to see you're all right now."

"Is 'friendly flesh' primarily your own invention?"

"Yes, it is, which is why I had the leverage to get Cugok to let me do *Meathearts*. I'm the Chief of Research at Cugok, in fact, which is why any controversy with me would reflect badly on them. I wear a blond wig and mustache on stage. I wish I had a bigger part," Dwork chuckled again. "The acting bug has bit me."

Is the acting bug a moth, in this case? thought Monty, not amused but showing a smile. "You must have had some pretty rigorous schooling—you're not an old man." Monty figured Dwork to be in his twenties, but you could never be sure. He briefly remembered the child-like Helga Greenberg.

"Oh, I sure did," chuckled Dwork, nervously pulling his tie taut, jerking on it. "I'm not some lab monkey bio-technician but a full-scale bio-researcher, as I said. I studied just as rigorously as the best doctors—much more so than the common mechanics they call surgeons. The medical training is similar. You had to be very, very aggressive and driven. In dissection we'd have ten cadavers going on and one instructor patrolling; you had to hog him for questions so he couldn't get to anybody else. If he was at your stiff I'd come over to ask my question and nudge you out of the way to point out my question on your stiff. Very cutthroat, pardon the pun. You have to be a vulture and pounce first to do the cutting and poking before your work partners can go at it. Several times I deleted names off posted project rosters and put my name in. I was reported once, but the complainer was told some mutant shit and I wasn't even spoken to. They *like* that aggression."

Monty imitated Dwork's enthused chuckling. "Well, they knew they really had something in you, obviously."

"I was imaginative. You can't *teach* imagination. That was my greatest edge. For my master thesis on radical functional mutation I extended the body of a lab beagle, in *four days*, to sixty-two feet in length, while still keeping it alive and functioning without artificial means. On a playing field it even showed clumsy efforts at locomotion. We called him Hotdog—he'd put a dachshund to shame, believe me!"

"Amazing," said Monty. He meant it. He found Dwork's cruelty quite amazing. "Where'd you go to school?"

"Earth. Ever been?"

"Nope."

"It's a lot more provincial here, but that's what I like. Forgive me for saying this, Mr. Black, but you're interviewing me, aren't you? Are you sure you aren't a reporter…or still with the Health Agency?"

"Don't apologize; I admire your honesty." Monty ignored Mauve's glance again. "I assure you I'm merely curious about you—I don't mean to seem so nosy. It's a habit from my old line of work. Please forgive me."

"Forgive *me*. I'm just on edge after this Cugok scandal."

"Cugok scandal? What is this?"

"You haven't heard? Oh come on, Mr. Black. Didn't you read last night's paper?"

"I sell them, I don't read them—what happened?"

"You either?" Dwork asked Mauve. "Oh shit, wait 'til you get a look at this." Dwork motioned them toward a monitor on his workbench and deftly punched up a story on the third page of last night's copy of Punktown's lead newspaper. Monty leaned in intensely, not hiding the concern in his tight face.

There had been a labeling mix-up at the Fredrick V. Cugok Pharmaceutical Research and Manufacturing Company, Inc. Two one-thousand-unit lots of a vitamin with an added formula which helped prevent radioactive poisoning and mutation had accidentally been sent out with the wrong bottles in the boxes. The substance in these two thousand mislabeled bottles was the drug Cugok called "friendly flesh." Several people medically scanned for routine problems had been shown to contain an odd drug in their systems and it had been identified, as had the drug's source. Cugok was ordering a recall on the vitamin and had already reclaimed five hundred units from area stores, but the error had taken place last spring and it was expected that at least half of the mislabeled drugs had been consumed by now…

"Is this dangerous?" Monty asked Westy Dwork.

"Oh, not at all, thank God. How could it be? It doesn't conflict with other common drugs or medical procedures. Of course, it won't aid in the healing of anyone, either— not without their molecular pattern on file in my computer."

"Why was an experimental drug produced in such amounts?"

"To experiment with. It won't harm anyone, but it's a fucking shame it had to happen…it makes Cugok look like idiots. A research drug goes out in vitamin packages, no less. They still haven't traced back whose error it was but I'd love to strangle them myself for the damage this could do. Your friends at the Health Agency are supposed to come down today to talk to Mr. Cugok."

Monty tried on a playful little smile for Dwork. "This wouldn't in any way be an experiment on Cugok's part, would it? Utilizing unknowing guinea pigs?"

"That would be impossible. For one, this was bound to be detected and traced to Cugok sooner or later…"

"It could be said, 'hey, it's only an accident.'"

"But for what purpose? Without the molecular blueprints of these people on file, what could we do to them for the sake of monitoring? No, this was all just a terrible ironic farce, and it concerns my 'friendly flesh,' of all things, calls too much advance publicity to it. So now you can understand why I was a bit wary of you, Mr. Black."

"I sure can. What a terrible coincidence. Could someone have done it on purpose, as a joke, or as industrial sabotage to discredit you and Cugok?"

"Maybe, but it looks like an honest fuck-up to me."

"Can it be withdrawn or neutralized in the people who took it?"

"No need; it will run its course and disperse naturally a few weeks, at the most, after the drug is no longer taken. Without a trace."

"Whew…what a strange thing to happen. Especially right now, with *Meathearts* in the news. But maybe it will sell more tickets, huh? Scandals are good publicity."

"It hasn't been revealed that the 'friendly flesh' technique is used in *Meathearts*, yet. Please, Mr. Black…do I have your confidence on that? One scandal for Cugok is enough right now. The Health Agency will be told about its use in *Meathearts*, anyway."

"Word of honor. After all, you've got something on me, now, too…don't you?" Monty held out his hand. "Mauve is going to introduce me to Mr. Cangue before the show so I should run. A pleasure to meet you, Mr. Dwork…you're a fascinating person."

"Pleasure to meet you. Hope to see you again."

Monty encircled Mauve's waist with his arm. "I'll be around."

"An accident?" Mauve whispered.

"I'll check in with HAP tomorrow just to make certain they have Dwork by name to look into."

"Then again, he did point out the accident to you himself."

"I would have heard; it made him look good and upset. Also, he seems to have a bad habit of pointing out and boasting about his own sick achievements…"

They walked up to a man whose back was toward them, as he was absorbed in conversation with a pretty, plumpish woman Monty recognized from photos as Aurora

Lehrman. He remembered that she was currently romantically involved with Dwork. She smiled over the man's head as Monty and Mauve approached.

"Ferule?" Mauve said.

The man turned about. "Hello, Mauve."

"Hi, Mauve," said Aurora.

Introductions were traded. Monty shook hands with Aurora Lehrman, and then with the director of *Meathearts*, Ferule Cangue.

He was a dwarf, huge-headed and stub-bodied, with his hair cut in a monk's crown-of-thorns wreath, dyed platinum blond and combed to his eyebrows in even bangs. His irises were metallic chrome. Even without the cut and color of his hair and his dyed eyes…he sure wasn't Toll Loveland. Monty was a bit amused, but then he'd never seen a photo of Cangue or revealed to Mauve his suspicion that Cangue could be Loveland.

Then again, Monty remembered Dwork's beagle, "imaginatively" stretched like a rubber band. Why not compressed?

"Heard a lot about you, Mr. Cangue. As the cliché goes."

"Good things, I hope, as the cliché goes."

"Well, not from Yancy Mays…but then we won't be hearing from him again."

"That was a horrible thing, whether he disapproved of my work or not."

"He liked *you*," Monty said to Aurora.

"Mauve says you haven't seen the play yet, but that you have prime seating for tonight," said the actress.

"Yup. I forgot my rain slicker and umbrella, though."

"Oh, it isn't that bad."

"I heard people are scalping the front rows for up to five hundred munits. I think some people want to get sprayed."

"I saw a man in the front row lean forward with his mouth open last time when I got my arm whacked off, and I was told he jerked off while I was raped, but usually the sickos don't get in the top seats up front. They can go and see this stuff for real in the alleys, anyway. You're always gonna attract a few sickos; it's inevitable. Makes us look bad, but you can't stop because of a few morons."

"I introduced Monty to Westy. They had a nice talk," said Mauve.

"Mauve tells me that you caught M-670 at *Pandora's Box*, so you're a bit of an actor now too, Mr. Black," observed Cangue in his dwarf's voice.

"An unwilling one…for a while, anyway. But that show's over now, isn't it? I'm sure your show is a lot more…tasteful and meaningful than Loveland's psychotic masturbation, eh Mr. Cangue?"

"Now you sound like Yancy Mays. I'm sure you won't care for my opinion, but I found Toll Loveland's show to be quite brilliant and ingenious in its own horrifying way."

"Many psychotic killers are brilliant and ingenious. You sound like you were there, Mr. Cangue."

"No—fortunately," Cangue laughed. "I saw the vid. Was that derived from your memory?"

"Another agent's."

"I've got to get changed," said Aurora. "Curtain in forty-five minutes." She kissed the hand that would soon be lying away from her on the stage. "See you next week, pal," she said to it for Monty's amusement. He found it blackly humorous, he supposed. "Nice to meet you, Monty. Hey, why don't you and Mauve join me for a drink after the show?"

"That would be nice. Monty?" said Mauve.

"Great." Maybe Dwork would be there, hoped Monty, but as it turned out he wouldn't be. The Stems would silently accompany them, however, at Dwork's insistence.

"I have to get cracking now, too," said Ferule Cangue, shaking Monty's hand once more. "See you again, Mr. Black?"

"I would imagine so."

"Good. Mauve, I think you should psych up a bit now, too."

"Right." Cangue waddled off after Lehrman, and Mauve took Monty as far as she could go toward seating him in the audience without revealing herself to the loudly mumbling influx of people. She kissed Monty. "See you after the show. Stay at my place tonight?"

"I'd like that. Good luck, tonight. Break a leg, don't they say?"

"Rip a face. Hack an arm, in this case. See ya."

"See ya," he said, then turned to go find his seat in the audience.

Monty didn't know how much stage fright Mauve might be experiencing, but he himself gripped the arms of his chair tightly as if strapped in it, as if it were the chair he had seen backstage in Westy Dwork's work area, as if it were he who was waiting to be mutilated. The show would begin any moment now, he guessed. The drone of the audience, all settled in (nobody being stupid enough to miss the opening scene), was great; the theater was the inside of a giant beehive. Monty could single out a conversation from it, however, and more so when he focused on it to distract himself from his anxiety: the two women seated to his right.

From them he learned that in two weeks it was going to snow black snow in Punktown. It was an artwork conceived by the well-known Eric Hughes, who some years back had made the sky over his hometown, nearby Miniosis—which actually dwarfed Punktown—a vivid blood red for the entire length of a day, so as to commemorate the fiftieth anniversary of the infamous street riots there that had been slowly spreading ever since, changing the once fashionable, sophisticated city into a smoldering and increasingly gutted husk, now a close rival to Punktown for violence and squalor—where before, Punktown had been like a rotting corpse to Miniosis' misty ethereal splendor. Still, the rich and powerful clung to their city in heavily fortified areas, and colonial security forces from Earth had reduced the so-called "freedom fighters" to splintered terrorist gangs, but the battles went on, buildings were taken or burned, the cancer slowly spread. The fighters hid out in Punktown at times to recruit fresh soldiers from the underworld ranks of mutants; they seduced the surly roaming street gangs, the homeless, the teenaged girl and boy freelance prosties, the disgruntled among the Chooms, lost souls of endless types woven into one crazy quilt, united by their anger and fear into some sort of effort that gave them a direction, a sense of purpose, an enemy to engage, an identity. They were steadily taking a giant city for themselves. Creating a new society. It was, to Monty, both horrifying and inspirational. At times he had alternately fantasized about dropping a bomb on Miniosis or going there to disappear into the army in its haunts of rubble and ruins.

This year, to commemorate the anniversary of last year's takeover of an atmosphere control station at the planet Echo's Earth colony-town of Oracle by a schism branch of the Red Jihad—in which thirty-seven thousand colonists had been killed by the sabotage of the station, the poisoning of the atmosphere causing extensive damage to the planet's overall environment as well—Eric Hughes was going to make it snow a blizzard in Punktown, and the blizzard would be black. In fact, Monty overheard, Hughes would be utilizing Punktown's own atmosphere recycling facility to a great extent to accomplish this feat. Naturally the Health Agency would be working very closely with him to keep an eye on things. And stores everywhere would be selling cheap Halloween skull masks, which the population of Punktown would be urged to wear for the entire length of the day. Already the striking image of this took hold of Monty's mind. If you can't bring people to the art, bring the art to the people, he thought. But where Toll Loveland had followed this theory by spreading death, Hughes was using it as a protest against it. Monty smiled. He liked it. Hughes was a bold, *true* artist, he decided.

"Too ostentatious, for my taste," said one of the two women. "Does he think we haven't all heard about Oracle by now? God, we were *inundated* with it for months. If I want art I'll go seek it out myself; don't shove it down my throat. And all we need is to have our town bogged down in a foot of black snow. Terrible, pretentious fatuousness. All I can say is they'd better melt the stuff away the next day."

Monty hoped not. He hoped it would be cold, so the snow would stay. And he hoped the woman to his right slipped and fell in it, too.

The lights dimmed, the curtain rose, the hive fell into an instant hush. A totally white room representing an apartment. In the center of the stage stood Mauve Pond in a white dress, stiff and composed like a statue in a shrine commanding their reverence. A minute passed; she didn't move. A sacrifice, waiting. It was excruciating for Monty. It was as if a noose were around Mauve's throat and the crowd waited for the trapdoor to fall through. Very much like that.

The door was kicked in…Monty flinched with the audience…Mauve came to whirling life…a tall man in a white suit burst in. A blond wig and mustache, but Monty knew him as Westy Dwork.

The struggle. She screamed. His scalpel. And now blood. *Blood.* It sprayed. Splashed. The audience gasped, cried out. A wave of *"Ohhh!"* fell down on Monty from behind. Mauve's shrieks and now gurgles made him dizzy; the white dazzled him. Dwork made sure that at no time did he block the audience's view of his slicing. Monty wanted to pull out a gun and shoot him whether Mauve felt the pain or not.

At last it was over, the room darkened, vanished. Monty felt too close; he didn't want to see the rest, he wanted space, but he knew he must stay…and the second half of the stage became lit. A white set, a white car, Aurora Lehrman in a white dress poised as if to unlock the door. Ticking seconds…she didn't move. This suspense disgusted Monty; he realized he was furious.

The rapists burst onto the stage, and Monty's heart leaped higher than the hearts of the rest of the audience…even before Aurora was struck, slapped, slammed onto the hood of the car, even before her dress was torn away, even before she was viciously raped by first one and then the other man and then had her right arm hacked off with two chops of a machete…

He felt blasted, and barely heard or absorbed the rest of the play, barely acknowledged Mauve's acting, though he could tell it was good (but Aurora was much better).

"Brilliant," sighed the woman at his right when it was over, breathless as if from sex. The audience applauded loudly, and Monty trembled amidst their standing ovation.

Monty showed a pass to get backstage. People were smoking cigarettes and drinking wine. He hoped to get to Mauve directly but Westy Dwork, devoid of his disguise and scrubbed of blood, intercepted him.

"How'd you like it?"

"A little violent for my taste."

"Oh—everyone's a critic. But haven't you yourself *killed* people, Mr. Black?"

"I didn't call it art. Excuse me." Monty brushed past him to find Mauve.

He spotted her, plowed toward her, crowded her into a safe corner. Her scars had never looked so deep, raw, frightening—as if they might split open and bleed if she so much as smiled, but they didn't when she did. "How'd you like it?"

"You were great, powerful. It was very disturbing. You're a brave lady—braver than me."

She had on a silk robe, her hair was mussed, she looked spent. "You do look drained," she noted, smiling still. "I didn't know you were so squeamish."

"It was Aurora, mostly. Those rapists."

"Oh, yeah, that is powerful." Mauve appeared somewhat disappointed, probably wanting her ordeal to seem the more powerful of the two to him. "So…is it still on for tonight?"

"I'm sorry, I can't. Really." He had someplace to go now. Also, he knew the scars wouldn't enhance his sexual performance, after all. Not after this.

Mauve's disappointment grew. "Why can't you? You look turned off."

"Yeah, all right, I'll be over…but later…I don't know when. I can't explain it right now—I will when I can, trust me." It would be good if he stayed with her. She could very well be in danger. Again. He knew what had happened to her in the past, but he still wanted the confirmation. "You told me the first night we talked that two guys raped you in your apartment…"

"Yes."

"Did Cangue use your experience as a model for the rape in the play? For more 'gritty realism'?"

"Yes, he did. He patterned the two rapists after them…"

"Right down to their red plastic jackets?"

"Yes."

Monty nodded.

SIXTEEN

Only one other of the six little cafeteria tables was occupied, by a short dark-skinned Indian woman in a white lab smock eating an off-schedule lunch, an insectoid helmet on the table by her plate. Monty had a hot cup of mustard in front of him and nervously smoked a black-papered herbal cigarette.

Monty looked up sharply as Captain Nedland entered, thin and morose-looking as ever, dressed all in black as Monty was. Soft-spoken as ever, too. "You're back in, if you want it."

A purely vain part of him wanted to smile, but too many other parts of him didn't. "I think I do."

"You do or you don't, my man…we're not going to beg you. The big man is much impressed by what you've dug up…though like me, he wishes very much that you'd come forward sooner."

"You wouldn't have believed it if I didn't have substantial info."

"Well, he's impressed and he's grateful. See, Monty, we aren't the reptiles you seemed to have thought we are, but of course we realize you were under a lot of duress when you had M-670. Like I say, we're willing to take you on under ninety-day probation, but you have to want it—I'm not going to push you. I'd *like* to have you, but…" Finally Nedland sat across from him. He glanced over at the Indian technician. "Are you almost done, Anu?"

"Oh yes, yes, pardon me, Captain." Anu went to rinse off her plate, gathered up her lunch bag and the helmet she wore in her work.

"Sorry," Nedland told her. "Don't mean to rush you, but…"

"No problem, no problem." Anu scurried out.

"Do I get to continue on this case?" Monty asked.

"Naturally. You're inside, close to the questionable individuals, and you've done very well so far."

"I'll take it," said Monty.

"Good. I knew you would. But after this you *will* stay with us, won't you? This has to be work first, revenge second."

"I'll be a pro."

"Good."

"It beats selling newspapers, I guess."

"Well, I was hoping for a little more enthusiasm than that. So, you didn't tell the girl that Beak's wife was raped and hacked up by two punks in red jackets..."

"No—I didn't want to endanger her any more than I already have. If she shows a new fear or disgust at the opening scenes involving her and Aurora, they might get really suspicious of her. I will try to find out about her rape, though, in a more casual way. But now I'm not sure I even want to see her at all...not until it's all over. If anything happened to her because of me..."

"Well, wait, Monty, we can't defeat our purpose, here. She's what got you close to these people..."

"They know I was a health agent...they already followed us once."

"But didn't she say she still wanted to pursue this even after you suggested the risk to her? She's a plucky girl, Monty. Besides, I realize you have feelings for her, but many other lives could be at risk, whether this is Loveland or a Loveland imitator."

"I still won't tell her about the red jackets for now."

"Fair enough."

"It isn't an imitator, it's Loveland. He knew of Beak because Beak was the one whose memories of *Pandora's Box* were used to view it, and they showed him on the news several times. He waited a while, then punished Beak by killing his wife. Mauve was raped before the show opened but obviously after having won the role, and then the staging of the rape in the play was supposedly inspired by that. It's all just more of Loveland's games with symmetry and echoes. He's amusing himself by leaving all these clues floating out there in the open...he thinks we're too inferior to catch them."

"What about this 'accidental' mix-up at Cugok—that looks odd."

"It does. Dwork says it's harmless, but I don't know. It's too strange. He made sure to point it out to me himself so he'd look innocent and properly concerned. Another arrogant asshole underestimating me."

"Why would a sick artist have so many accomplices? They can't all be deranged fans of his."

"It's a deranged world," was all Monty could offer at this point.

"I've already got Tanabe and Giddry on the Cugok mix-up, so I'll put them on the case. I don't want you going down to Cugok or that'll blow your closeness to the theater people..."

"I want Beak for my partner."

"Monty...I told you...work first, revenge second."

"If you deny him this he'll quit, I guarantee it. Then he'll just pursue it on his own anyway."

"He doesn't have to find out until it's over."

"Come on, Captain. I'll keep a rein on him, I promise. Beak's a good man, and he was on the original Loveland case."

Nedland sighed, played with Monty's ashtray. "All right. I'll talk to him about controlling himself. I'll tell him the connection between his wife and the other stuff."

"Thanks."

"Next you'll be asking me to put Woodmere on the case."

"Is that fully out of the question?"

"More than fully. He's lent his experience and expertise to the organized crime network of Neptune Teeb, and I regard him currently as an enemy to HAP."

"Jesus. Shit."

"Other than that I guess he's doing pretty good. I just hope I never get my hands on him. He always had loose ties to them, I guess…buying illegal weapons, and he recruited that individual to help you investigate Loveland's teleporter from the Teeb bunch. Many of Teeb's activities represent legitimate health hazards. He offers illegal cloning. Crimes too numerous to mention. I wouldn't doubt that Beak knows where to find Woodmere, but he says he doesn't and I haven't pushed him. Yet."

Monty diverted the conversation from his friends. "How quick can you get me my badge and a permit to carry?"

"It's in the works now. You're on probation, my friend, but I'm gonna take a chance and put you senior on this. Beak, Giddry and Tanabe will answer to you. Don't disappoint me. Keep Beak in line. And keep yourself in line."

Monty needed some sleep and wanted to get back to Mauve—tomorrow he'd confer at headquarters with Beak, Tanabe and Giddry—but before he left HAP he checked into the armory with his new permit to carry and a pass from Nedland ordering a health agent's camera-equipped pistol to be put at Monty's disposal.

It was late so it was a security robot that let him in. He took his time, knowing a robot wouldn't grow impatient. The fact was, Monty loved guns. It wasn't that he loved to kill, but they did give him a feeling of strength and security, and there was that perverse romance they held. Also, he loved them from an aesthetic standpoint, their form and color and feel in his hand, artistically sensitive as he was. One man might not care about his coffee mug so long as it was practical, but Monty chose his carefully and had an interesting variegated collection from which to choose, according to his mood. He would have liked to approach guns the same way now, carrying whatever struck his fancy that particular day, and he had Vern's collection to select from, but on duty he was required to carry only a health agent's gun, which would take a picture of the target when the weapon discharged. There were, at least, many makes to choose from.

He recognized among them the very revolver he had killed Bum Junket with, picked it up and handled it. Yes, this had been the one. He put it back down and finally settled on a woman's gun, a short and chunky compact semi-auto with a magazine that could hold twelve tiny bullets, but that wouldn't matter much if he used a good plasma—which of course he could, now. Like the orange plastic pistol Mauve carried in her purse, women's guns were usually bright colors, easy to find in a pocketbook in a dark parking lot or apartment, or softer aesthetically appealing colors to make the weapons seem less intimidating. The gun Monty chose was a glossy coral pink color. Despite Nedland's warnings about priorities and conduct—about revenge—he thought a woman's gun was appropriate.

He used his new hand phone to call Mauve downstairs to unlock the door. She was sleepy and amorous, warm and smotheringly cat-like—he ended up making love with her, but it was dark and he couldn't see the scars well and he didn't kiss her lower face. To his relief, he didn't do badly and after an hour was able to release within her. Mauve was pleased, stroked his back and purred to him, "So you can't tell me where you were?"

"The Health Agency. I'm an agent again."

"You *are?*" She pushed him away to see his face. "Really?"

"Yes."

"That's great! Why didn't you tell me? You must be proud."

"Be careful with these people, Mauve. Dwork, the Stems, Cangue. They're dangerous. I'll try not to involve you, as much as I can. Don't tell *anyone*, Aurora or anyone, that I'm an active agent again."

"Of course not. So you're totally forgiven?"

"I'm on probation but I'm heading the case."

"God. Well, they must think highly of you even if you don't think so highly of them. They *do* a lot of good, Monty, they do…you know that. Things are bad, but you do the best you can with what you got."

"You've got an aphorism fetish." Monty rolled off her, lay belly up exhausted. "Always carry your gun. You got lead or plasma?"

"Lead."

"Crap. I'll get you some legal plasma…it'll do the trick, so don't be trigger-happy."

"I told you about my dad; I know how to handle a gun just fine. Monty…you're thinking about Opal too much, I'm afraid. You're worried that I'm gonna die, too, and then you'll have two deaths to feel responsible for…"

"I *would* have two deaths I'd be responsible for."

"You *wouldn't*…"

"Enough, all right? Let's just sleep. I've been through this with people a hundred times." Silence for a few minutes.

"Well, I'm not through with it yet…I'll just let it go for now."

For a moment Monty felt irritated and defensive, in the next he felt a warm flow of affection and pride. He realized, through all the clouds of distraction, that he was falling in love with her.

Before he knew it he was softly confessing, "I don't know if I'm trying to do a job well, or if it's just totally revenge, or a commitment to society. I don't know if I want to avenge Opal because I loved her and miss her and want justice, or if it's mostly to alleviate my sense of guilt…to redeem myself."

"I'm sure it's all of those things, but maybe one thing more than the others depending on the moment. Don't be ashamed—it's just the different parts of you. At least they all want the same thing."

"You're very soothing." Monty closed his eyes. Sighed, tired.

"I'm an actress—I can do these things." Mauve settled back.

Monty opened his eyes. "So you're just acting concerned but not really feeling it?"

"What? No, of course I feel it…I'm not *faking* my concern! I was just making a joke…" Mauve watched him swing his legs out of bed and sit on the edge, naked back to her.

"You're an actress."

"*Yes*, Monty, but I'm not acting now. You're hurting my feelings and I'm getting mad…"

"The coincidence makes me uncomfortable. That you just happened to be connected to a play that's obviously connected to Loveland…that you just happened to become involved with me…"

"My *God!*" Mauve scrambled naked out of bed. "I get it, I see—you're saying I'm one of them!"

"I'm just saying it's odd…"

"No, you're not, you *suspect* me! You don't trust me—you think I'm part of this, don't you? *Look* at me!"

He didn't. "It's odd, that's all."

"You followed *me!* You looked into me and came after *me!* What did I do, squirt a magic perfume on you when I bought a magazine? Yes, Monty, I admit Westy concocted this super pheromone spray, a magic potion, and I put you under my spell. I'm part of them, Monty, I'm luring you to your doom. *Look* at me, Monty, don't turn your back on the enemy."

"I'm just thinking of Beak…I'm paranoid, I admit it, I'm sorry…"

"I don't believe you." Mauve slapped barefoot across the tiled floor to thrust her arms into her robe. "Thank you. Thank you."

Monty got up, faced her, face pained. "I'm sorry. I mean it. It was just a crazy thought, I admit it. Please."

"Why don't you go home? I need to be alone." Mauve began making herself tea.

"I know you're for real. You're risking your life to help me…"

"I love this play—it's the best thing to happen to me in years. You think this is easy for me?"

"There'll be others." He tried to joke, "When this is over you'll get all the more attention because of it."

"Have me truth scanned." Mauve glared at him, deeply scar-faced in the unpleasant kitchen light. "I mean it. I will. I won't have you suspecting me even subconsciously."

"I was thinking of my friend Beak, who was on the Loveland thing before. His wife was murdered last year. I'm sure Loveland did it to get at him. That's why I got paranoid. And Loveland likes playing intricate tricks."

"I'm no trick. Scan me."

"Not necessary—I believe you." Monty wanted to tell her about the rapists but fought the temptation. "Later, though, I may want to record your memories. I could find some clues in them." He was already fairly certain, however, that the faces of Mauve's rapists would match the computer-generated faces Beak had sent him. What he must find out was if any of the "actors" Cangue had hired to play the rapists, different each show, matched those faces also.

"Now I don't trust you. I don't trust you that you trust me."

Monty sighed. "I'm sorry. Tomorrow I'll scan you, then, down at HAP. Just to clear the air. And I'll copy your memories, too—all right?"

"Fine." Mauve stopped making tea and returned to bed. "I'm going to sleep."

"I *am* sorry, Mauve."

"Mm," she grunted.

He read a magazine at the kitchen table and didn't guiltily sneak back into bed until she was asleep.

Haz Tanabe was crewcut, youngish, of Japanese extraction—solemn and solemn-suited, a dependable machine. Baf Giddry was a white, burly forcer-type in his early fifties, his graying hair slicked back and clinched into a braid down to the middle of his back. Monty quickly sensed resentment from Giddry that Nedland had placed him in command of the field investigation. While Mauve was having her memories recorded, Tanabe and Giddry filled Monty and Beak in on their investigation of the mix-up at Cugok, where "friendly flesh" had gone out labeled as vitamins in two thousand bottles. The source of the accident was still rather ambiguous, but no evidence as yet pointed to a deliberate act. No workers or supervisors had as yet been asked to submit to truth scan.

"How'd your girly fare under truth scan?" Giddry asked.

"She isn't lying," Monty intoned. "She's not involved in anything weird."

"How involved are you with her?"

"That has no immediate bearing on this case."

"You drilling her, though, huh?"

"Baf, I want a professional and cooperative working relationship with you. If I can't have it, I'll ask Nedland to pull you off this."

"You're on probation, you sludge, and you threaten *me?*"

"Shut it, Baf—*now*," Beak growled. "I back him up. One more word and I go to Ned myself. Let's drop this now before it gets bad."

"*Dropped.*" Giddry sneered and lit a cigar.

"Good," Monty hissed, his gaze on Giddry cold. "Now, what I'm having recorded from Mauve is every show they've done so far. I want to see if any of the rapists who've attacked Aurora Lehrman on stage match up with the two who raped Mauve, or the sketches of the two who raped Beak's wife."

Beak said tightly, trying to sound composed and professional, "But you haven't told her, for now, what you're recording and looking at."

"Right."

"Remember how I figured out that the mutated body with the ID identifying it as Tate Hurrea turned out to be Auretta Here?" Beak said. "Well, I've started a list of names…Westy Dwork, Ferule Cangue, for now…to see if they're really something else coded or scrambled up, too. Loveland does have a certain style."

"It has to be an *imitator*," Giddry groaned. "You give that psycho too much credit."

"Don't underestimate him," said Monty. "Don't close your mind to any possibility regarding him."

Giddry just sighed out cigar smoke.

Tanabe said, "Why would a prominent researcher like Dwork assist Loveland? For money? There's enough money to be made at Cugok, with 'friendly flesh.'"

"Some people never have enough money. And Dwork's a psycho, too. He's a freak lover and he loves what he's doing in *Meathearts*. During last night's show he cut Mauve so deep the scalpel scraped her teeth. And…what if Loveland helped Dwork develop 'friendly flesh?'"

"Come on, Black," said Giddry.

"He majored in bioengineering at Paxton Polytech, and in *The Godfucker* he cloned his finger back on stage after cutting it off. Sound familiar?"

"You still think Cangue is Loveland?" Tanabe said.

"Maybe. He may think coming back as a dwarf will keep us off his scent."

"Cangue is doing these freaky plays because he *is* a freak," Giddry said.

"If all I'm gonna get out of you is negative shit, Giddry…"

"Hey, you need to hear the opposing view, too, don't ya? If all you want to hear is somebody parrot your theories I'll *gladly* get off the case…"

"Gentlemen?" The Indian technician Anu was leaning in the room. "We're ready to show you what we've got…"

The rapists in the debut performance of *Meathearts* didn't match Beak's computer sketches. Monty stole a sideways glance at Beak. The agent's eyes were riveted into the screen, and blazing. His hands squeezed the arms of his chair. "Enough," Monty told Anu. "Forward to the second show." He leaned toward Beak. "Easy, man. Why don't you go? I can do this."

"Then why'd you ask me to come on the case? I can handle it."

Aurora Lehrman stood intact on stage again…but as in the premier show, Mauve saw only a brief glimpse before she was whisked backstage to be repaired. It was in the work area of Westy Dwork, however, that Mauve witnessed Aurora's rape and mutilation—on a monitor screen. They watched a panting, gore-spattered Dwork toss his wig and mustache onto a counter. "Got you good that time, love." He smiled directly at the four men. He touched buttons on his devices, meanwhile distracted by Aurora's ordeal on the monitor.

Anu froze one rapist's face as it appeared on the screen, blew it up. No match. Then the other. No match…just the red plastic jackets.

It was the same with the next show. Finally, the performance Monty had attended. No—none of the rapists resembled either the dark or light-skinned mongrel from the computer composites. Monty sighed. "Take us to Mauve's rape," he now told the technician…with dread.

She'd been sleeping. Vague dream images, then the invading boom, the invading light. Monty realized that she had moved since then to her current apartment; the walls here were alien despite familiar decorations. She sat up. Through her eyes the four men saw the two men, plunging at her. One leaped as she screamed. Cuffed her. The camera angle abruptly whipped away…

"It's them," breathed Beak.

"I know," said Monty. "Freeze it," he ordered the tech.

Mauve's nightshirt was seen being raised over her head, blocking the screen for a moment. One face was close, well-framed. "*Freeze it!*" Monty barked.

It was frozen. They didn't have to blow it up. The sneering face looked like that of a typical heterogeneous punk: part white, part Hispanic or black, part Asian, all lost in one unpleasant mix topped with a greasy elaborate bouffant.

"Hard copy," Monty instructed. A glossy printed copy whirred out of a machine. Anu set it aside. "Go on," Monty said.

They watched the mixed-breed rape Mauve, his hand over her mouth. He glared at his audience. He spat on the camera in contempt. They heard Mauve sob and gurgle.

"Make a sound and I cut you," said the off-screen second man. A knife must have been held nearby, maybe its edge or tip pressed against her cheek in a kind of dress rehearsal…

Finally the other one came into view. The tech froze a good look at him and made a copy. He was a white-skinned punk with black features and a blond crewcut.

"Should we go on?" asked Anu meekly.

"Absolutely not," said Monty, shaking, bloodless. "Kill it."

"Scum," observed Giddry.

"They killed my wife. Those are the monsters who killed my wife," Beak whispered, his eyes filling, hands still locked as claws on the arms of his chair.

The lights came up—show over.

SEVENTEEN

"What did the blackies say?" said Giddry, referring to the police. Monty had just returned from a meeting in which he and Nedland had informed their police liaisons and the former chief investigators of the Toll Loveland case of these new, bizarre developments.

Monty sat at a computer screen, tapping keys, in the small workroom handed over to them at HAP for their investigation. "They say the involvement of Westy Dwork in the drug mix-up at Cugok and in any weird activities connected to Loveland is too tenuous for an arrest..."

"Tenuous?"

"Insubstantial. *Weak.*"

"Yeah, yeah—so?"

"We can bring him in for questioning, but I said no, I don't want to tip him off yet. Ned urged them not to bring him in, either. Let's hope they don't stick their noses into this too far and scare these people away."

"They shouldn't even be involved."

"It's unavoidable, if there's any connection to Loveland."

"So what are you looking for?" Tanabe came wheeling closer in his chair. Beak had been given the rest of the day off to spend with his children.

"Dwork bragged to me about his extensive schooling, but I didn't get to push it enough to find out where he went. Loveland majored in bioengineering at Paxton Polytech..."

"You think they met in school," said Tanabe.

Monty had to pass several security blocks before he was admitted into the files of Paxton Polytech. "They're about the same age, it looks like—mid-twenties." He called up the file of Manuel Hung, the name Loveland had used in school. Loveland looked back at him from the screen. His hair, usually short and slicked back so far as Monty had seen, fell below his shoulders in a mussed tangle, but his forehead was still bared and broad...his strikingly handsome, brooding, subtly smirking features unmistakable. Society was usually too kind to such an attractive person to allow such a disturbed personality to develop.

Monty punched up a list of clubs and activities. A few—enough to fulfill expectations, but not the kind of manic overkill seen in many ambitious students.

Monty asked to see a group photo of each club, which he knew would exist for the graduation book. The computer told him these photos weren't stored within Manuel Hung's file, but it quickly drew them from the graduation book itself for him to view.

No Westy Dwork. He had the photos enlarged, scanned each face. Loveland was there, smiling as seductively and confidently as a model. Monty asked the computer if Paxton Polytech had ever known a Westy Dwork. No, it hadn't. Of course.

"Maybe they met at Paxton University," Tanabe suggested, "where Loveland took Liberal Arts…"

"Wait a fucking minute," Monty breathed, jerking forward at the screen.

"What?"

"This guy in back." He tapped at the screen, a photo of a bioengineering club. Loveland-Hung sat in front. In the last row, looming conspicuous, stood a very tall, very thin young man. "He's tall…"

"And?"

"Dwork is tall. Very tall." Monty zoomed in. The face filled the screen. It wasn't familiar.

"Is it him?"

"Not immediately." Monty asked the computer for the man's name. It appeared across the bottom of the screen. PILTER DE VARD.

"I know that name. Where do I know him from?"

Giddry leaned in between them. "Pilter De Vard, De Vard…*shit!*"

"Who is he?" snapped Monty.

"Those…those three college kids who Matt Cotton hired to develop and spread M-670…that's one of them. Pilter De Vard—he was one of them…"

"The one they didn't catch," said Tanabe.

"Okay, okay, stay calm," Monty chanted, "stay calm." He was chanting it more to himself than to anyone else as his heart stomped heavily, eagerly up a staircase in his chest. He punched into the file of Pilter De Vard.

He bypassed the ID photo—it told him nothing. But the file itself was another matter…

"You stupid fuck," Monty snorted, smiling, wagging his head. It hadn't taken him long to find it. "You stupid over-confident bragging fuck."

"*What?*"

Monty swivelled to his men. "For his master thesis, Westy Dwork extended the body of a living dog to sixty feet in length while keeping it alive without artificial support. Funny. Pilter De Vard did the same thing for his thesis."

"Let's go cuff this sludge," rumbled Giddry.

"Shouldn't we call the forcers?" Tanabe said.

"Now why the hell would we wanna do that?" Giddry said. "They're on the case now…let them follow their own leads. We don't need them to do our job for us, man… we're health agents."

Monty was up and slipping on his long black overcoat. The blood throbbed in his cheeks. "He'll be at Cugok."

"Should we give Beak a call, let him know we've hit it?" said Giddry.

"He's in no shape," said Tanabe.

Monty hesitated only a moment. "Call him."

"Monty…"

"I can't deny him part of this. He'll be all right. Ring him up, quickly."

Beak came on; Monty nudged in past Tanabe. "We've got Westy Dwork on a platter, man—he's Pilter De Vard, one of the college punks who designed M-670 for Matt Cotton…the one they never found. He was also a classmate of Toll Loveland's at Paxton Polytech. We're going down to Cugok to take him. You think you're up to it?"

"Meet you there," Beak said grimly.

Beak leaned against the side of his car waiting for them in the parking lot, his ski hat pulled low and collar turned up against the chill of oncoming evening. He straightened up as his three partners crossed to join him.

"I'm going to stay out here 'til you have him cuffed," said Monty, removing his hand phone from his pocket. "If he sees me he might get spooked. I want this smooth. This bastard is directly responsible for the death of *thousands*…he makes Toll Loveland look like a shoplifter."

"Unless Loveland was part of that, too," said Tanabe.

"We'll know just what their relationship was soon enough." Monty lit a cigarette. "Call me inside the minute you've cuffed him…and I mean literally cuff him. If he resists arrest, Tanabe, drug him."

Agent Tanabe had taken along a dart pistol. Giddry carried a professional-looking businessman's valise containing only one thing—a powerful military ray blaster with folding stock. Monty and Beak had their plasma-loaded handguns with a spare clip each of solid projectiles. Despite Dwork's careless bravado, they did not want to underestimate his capabilities.

"Don't you get trigger-happy, Baf," Monty warned Giddry.

"Hey, I'm not your traitor friend Vern Woodmere, Black. Is everybody ready now or what?"

"Go on in," Monty told them.

He watched the three agents disappear through the company's glass front door. Over that door, gold letters protruded from the building:

FREDRICK V. CUGOK PHARMACEUTICAL RESEARCH
AND MANUFACTURING COMPANY, INC.

He was too tense to lean against Beak's car while he waited…

The handsome reception area featured a miniature garden with trickling waterfall. The decor throughout the office areas and cafeterias of the plant—and even in the plant proper, to a lesser extent—was in the realm of old Earth's Art Deco. Behind the receptionist's desk, a huge glossy sculpture filled the wall, a yin and yang portraying two stylized dolphins, one red and one black, chasing each other's tails. By now the receptionist knew the health agents Tanabe and Giddry, and greeted them cheerily by name. She was young and plumply pretty.

"We're sorry to come in like this without advance notice, Alise," smiled Tanabe, "but do you think we could see Mr. Dwork for a few moments, if he's still here?"

"Well, we've started our second shift, but he *usually* stays a few hours into it, at least. Let me page him."

Beak glanced about the reception area. Dark austere walls with grainy lighter speckles, the floor black marble and the ceiling metallic gold. Quite an artistic interior designer they'd brought in, he thought, impressed. He looked down an off-branching hall toward office sounds, distant chatter and chuckling. The hall had gold archways spaced along it, reflecting in the marble.

"Westy Dwork, call two-nine-six, please. Westy Dwork, two-nine-six."

"Cold out there," Giddry said to Alise.

"Oh I know, huh? They shouldn't let it get this cold so fast." Her phone rang; she answered it. "Mr. Dwork? Agents Tanabe and Giddry are here from the Health Agency…they'd like a word with you?"

The screen faced Alise so the three men couldn't see Dwork on it, but they listened to his voice, deep and resonant with his height despite his narrow frame.

"Ahh…well, I was hoping to go home soon. If it's another tour they want, I can have someone take them…"

"Just a brief word—no tours," Tanabe spoke up.

"Of course, gentlemen. Send them in to my office, Alise."

Alise rose from her desk. "Do you know where Mr. Dwork's office is?"

"Um…I don't believe so," said Tanabe. Previously they had interviewed the plant superintendent under Mr. Cugok, and the captains of manufacturing beneath him.

"Okay, this way please." Giddry watched Alise's generous rump roll in her white dress as they followed her down the hall of arches, Beak flicking his narrowed eyes nervously from door to door. They passed an open office area partitioned into cubicles, turned down another hall. One open door showed a vast conference table within, presently deactivated wall screens. Then, at the end of the hall, a door labeled:

WESTY DWORK—CHIEF OF RESEARCH. Alise rang a buzzer. They heard the door unlock by remote; Alise cracked it to lean her head in. "The health agents, Mr. Dwork?"

"Send them in," they heard. Alise smiled, cherubic, as she passed them, left them, high heels clicking on marble.

Giddry let Tanabe and Beak go before him so that he had time to bring out the ray blaster, unfold its skeleton stock. He leaned the empty valise against the wall.

Dwork stood up smiling behind his desk to greet Tanabe first.

Alise glanced back over her shoulder. Giddry and his new friend.

"Oh my God!" Dwork heard Alise shriek in the hall beyond.

"Get him!" Giddry roared, spinning away from Alise to plunge into the room.

Tanabe fumbled for his dart pistol inside his prim jacket.

Dwork touched a button on his desk. A transparent pane slid up from the floor to bisect the room like one of the partitions in the office area they'd passed. "Shit!" Beak barked, his gun out. He aimed away from Dwork and fired. The plasma bullet exploded across the pane, but it wouldn't hold. It quickly ran down the barrier, a glowing ooze. It did, however, melt the carpet quite nicely where it pooled.

Dwork lifted a pistol from a drawer in his desk. Giddry had his blaster leveled but didn't dare let loose for fear of ricochets.

"Open it, Dwork!" Beak shouted. "You can't stay in there forever...we'll get people in here to rip the walls down if we have to!"

Dwork pointed his gun at Beak, and the health agent realized the situation in time to duck as a green ray bolt streaked from the pistol, through the barrier without leaving a hole, and into the wall behind Beak where it *did* leave a scorched hole. His blaster utilized a beam that could pass through the screen as sunlight passes through a window.

Giddry's more impressive-looking weapon could not, nevertheless, reciprocate in kind, and he leaped out of the room in time to avoid a second hurriedly aimed bolt, which struck the doorframe. Giddry plastered himself to the wall outside, gulping at air.

Tanabe and Beak scrambled for the door, both for a lethal moment unprotected. One of them would be hit. It was up to Dwork to decide which.

The third emerald arrow struck Tanabe in the back of the head, at an angle which sent a raw mass of its material up over the top of his skull to hang across his face on a hinge of skin. Tanabe pitched across a chair, smoking...pulled the chair to the floor across his chest as if for a shield even in death.

Beak jumped over his legs, out the door. Giddry yanked him over by the arm. A silent green bolt struck the wall opposite the open door, leaving a smoking star-shaped impact point on the austere grain-speckled surface.

Beak tore his hand phone from his pocket. "Monty—we're under fire! We're outside Dwork's office…Tanabe is dead…"

"Didn't catch you," Monty responded tensely, probably having heard only the last bit about Tanabe. "Repeat!"

"We're outside Dwork's office, man, hurry! He's killed Tanabe! Fucking *hurry!*"

"Jesus," Beak heard, and then the connection clicked off on the other end.

Alise was standing at her desk punching up a number on the vidphone when the front door opened and a tall man in a long black coat and carrying a pink handgun burst in. She screamed, and he deftly flipped open a badge—something Monty had guiltily caught himself practicing in the mirror from time to time. "Health Agency—who are you calling?"

"The forcers," Alise whimpered.

"Good…tell them we need assistance in arresting a dangerous criminal—Westy Dwork. Which way did my friends go?"

"Down that way. Westy *Dwork?*"

"Sound a fire alarm or get on the intercom—get everybody out of the building, quickly."

"Yes, sir."

Monty bolted into the hall, cape-like coat billowing out behind him. He had come into the building too late to hear Alise call a security alert over the intercom system.

Into the pink semi-auto he'd slapped his clip of solid bullets in place of the plasma. He wanted to take Dwork alive if possible, and if he used the plasma there'd be nothing left to take. Dwork's body and blood probably didn't present a biohazard, and there was the risk, too, of hitting an innocent or fellow agent. Bullets it was.

Giddry poked the two-fisted blaster around the corner and let loose an automatic spray of short red ray bolts. He heard them zing off the barrier, hiss like angry insects around the room, burning some things and knocking other things over. A few came back out into the hall. "Enough!" Beak snapped.

On his hands and knees now, Giddry pressed his cheek against the wall, pushed one reluctant eye quickly past the doorframe before jerking back. Then he looked again, longer. Withdrew again. "*Fuck!*"

"What?"

"He's either down behind his desk or he went through that door in the back of the room…"

"Great—I'll give you one fucking guess. Where does that door go?"

"How the hell should I know?" Giddry peeked again.

"You've been here before several times."

"They didn't give me blueprints for the goddamn place…"

Beak held his hand phone to his bill. "Monty…"

A blue ray bolt passed through the air between Beak's mouth and the device in his palm. The bright flash dazzled him. He turned his head to see a figure at the end of the hall, dressed in a uniform of black.

It was a security guard in an ostentatious black uniform with gold trim, a gold-trimmed black cap; he looked more like a cross between a chauffeur and a gay man in leather bar regalia. He had a blaster at the ends of his outstretched arms. And now the guard turned his head, unintentionally saving Beak's life.

Monty recognized the man even as he was pumping two bullets into his face at point-blank range. The ridiculous cap flew off, the heavy black blaster clattered. Monty stood over the gaudy corpse.

"I'm sorry, Beak."

"Sorry shit—you saved my fuckin' life, man!"

"He's one of your boys."

"One of my…boys." Beak then came running while Giddry kept to the door. Beak looked down now, too. "My *God*," he breathed, and trembled.

The dislodged cap had revealed a blond crewcut. Even with the two leaking bullet holes, they could distinguish the white-skinned black man's features.

"No red jacket, but…" said Monty.

"You're dead, you worthless monster." Beak let a glob of saliva drop onto the gaping dead man's forehead. "How do you like it, *fuck*?" He almost kicked that vulnerable slack face.

"What happened to Tanabe?"

"A screen came up…it cut us off from Dwork, but he has a blaster that can project through it. He nailed Haz in the head. Now he's ducked out a back door in the office."

"Shit." The fire alarm blared to life, making Monty flinch. He raised his voice above it. "The forcers are on the way and I had the receptionist pull an alarm. Dwork might slip out with the crew—we need someone outside until the forcers come. Baf!"

"Yeah?" Giddry scrambled over to them.

"Beak and me are splitting up to look around. I had a fire alarm set off; go outside and make sure Dwork doesn't sneak out with everybody else. The forcers are on the way."

"Let Beak go outside—I want that sludge! He killed my partner!"

"They killed my *wife*!"

"They killed my partner, too," Monty snapped. "Go outside, Baf, *move*. He could be in his car right now!"

"Well, he'd better come out to me." Giddry pounded off down the hall after leaping over the sprawled security guard/part-time actor-rapist.

Monty just naturally assumed, logically or not, that the rapist's partner must also be on the premises somewhere.

"Keep in touch," he told Beak. "Okay—let's make like amebas and split."

Beak darted back toward the reception area. Monty headed toward the doorway opening into the partitioned stalls of mini-offices.

He felt potent and a little high after killing Mauve's rapist. Lightheaded but vital. No Bum Junket doubts. There was, unfortunately, a necessary time for killing.

From the reception area, Beak found his way into the plant proper. It hummed with its hidden life…and throbbed with its dangers. He almost hesitated before embarking into its already abandoned maze.

The fire alarm droned on as Monty entered the bright offices. He saw that they extended on for quite a distance, dozens of dinky mini-offices. A sound in one nearby made him whirl with his gun; a man stepped out from the cubicle and froze, raised his hands. "Don't shoot—please!"

"I'm a health agent—who are you?"

"Sean Ahmed…I'm the chief expeditor."

"What are you doing, having a coffee? Get outta the building."

"I was just securing my terminals, sir…I'm on my way."

"Where does the door in the back of Westy Dwork's office go?"

"Westy Dwork? Oh, ah, that would go into a hall that takes you into the Research and Development Department."

"How do I get there?"

"A couple ways. Through the plant. From here, ah…you can't just go through his office?"

"If I could I would, right?"

"Well…there's another way near here. I can take you."

Monty didn't want to endanger the man, but Westy Dwork had proved more than a danger to thousands. "All right, quick, show me."

While they walked Monty used his hand phone to call HAP. He asked for reinforcements to be sent to Cugok, and for Captain Nedland to be notified at home. They came to a door with gold letters projecting above it: RESEARCH AND DEVELOPMENT DEPARTMENT.

"Thanks—you can go," said Monty.

"Ah, a number of labs in there are bound to be locked and require special clearance codes. Security has override keys."

"Forget security. If you see anyone outside who knows the codes send them in with a forcer, but have them wait until the forcers come."

"Who are you after?"

"Westy Dwork."

"Why?"

"He's an asshole." Monty moved through the automatic sliding door.

Beak peered into a huge bin filled with green pills like peas. The next one had orange tablets like Halloween candy. Dirty pills of assorted colors were scattered under a huge machine nearby. A radio on a table beside the machine still played, photos of someone's children were taped to a support column. Ahead of Beak was a low corridor lined on either side with thick red pipes, and it drew him toward it, pistol ready. He was jumpy; the fire alarm masked potential sounds which might otherwise alert him and save his life. He had a layer of bulletproof mesh inside his jacket, also impervious to moderate ray blasts, but the skin of his scalp crawled vulnerable inside his purple ski hat. He thought of poor Tanabe.

He entered the tunnel. They let him get halfway down it, trapped exactly in the middle.

The Stem stepped before him at the tunnel's end, pointing a tubular black object—which it discharged as Beak was dropping into a crouch...

...unfortunately for the black-garbed human security guard who had just stepped into place at the end of the tunnel behind Beak. The Stem's weapon fired a black crystal bullet, which struck the man in the thigh. Immediately on contact with flesh the crystal branched out, multiplied its mass in black obsidian spears. Even as he dropped howling, the guard saw that his leg was being forced away from his body by the crystals tearing out through flesh and cloth.

From his crouch, Beak fired crazily at the Stem, shot after shot of plasma. The odds of hitting the stick figure were slim and Beak knew it. Five shots missed. One hit the Stem on the elbow of one of its three arms.

The two good arms and the smoking, melting third arm flailed wildly in the air, a high-pitched whistle of agony coming from the tiny jack-o'-lantern face. Plasma drops sprayed from the melting arm the creature flapped as if to extinguish the fire. Snapping off two more crystal projectiles without aiming, the Stem darted away out of view.

One bullet missed, the other hit Beak in the chest. He flew onto his back with a grunt. The fire alarm and the wounded guard kept wailing.

"Shit," Beak grunted, but he was okay. He rolled to his feet. He couldn't hear the Stem's whistling shrieks any more. From his jacket pocket he pulled his balled-up winter gloves. Then, glancing at the writhing guard, Beak dug in the hole in his jacket, fingered a tiny object wedged into the lightweight armor mesh.

The bullet in the guard's leg had quit expanding but the pool of blood was enormous; only crystal linked leg to body now and the man's face was gray and glassy-eyed. Beak stood over him. The man's cap had come off to reveal, no surprise to Beak, a greasy black bouffant.

The man's eyes rolled to meet Beak's. Beak liked the fearful recognition he saw dawn in them through the fog. "You know me, huh? You know my wife? A good fuck, huh, tough guy? Ready to pay for it?"

The mongrel moaned, just minutes from death anyway. Beak almost hesitated; why perform a mercy killing—wasn't it better to let him suffer? No. He was bleeding to death, slipping away, now. Better to give him a nice fat jolt, however brief.

Beak knelt by the man, hooked a finger in his mouth and dropped in the crystal bullet he'd pulled from his jacket. Then Beak stepped back to watch.

It was fast. Glassy black spears plunged out of the mouth, which stretched and stretched to accommodate them until it split at the corners. Spears out the throat, out the nostrils and eyes. The mongrel's head split apart in all directions, and now he had a jagged black crystal globe for a head. Beak considered it to be an improvement.

Beak could now say he had killed the man himself. He was satisfied, didn't even feel the need to spit on the remains. Prudently scooping up the security guard's ray blaster, Beak moved on after the Stem.

A number of the rooms in the Research Department were open and accessible. Monty observed abandoned desks, monitor screens still exhibiting data, coffees still steaming, a radio playing top-forty trash (a revoltingly bouncy tune from Dora Deering at the moment). Other doors were locked, wouldn't open to his manipulation of their inset keyboards…

He turned at a noise in an open room further along the hallway.

Monty peeked into the room to see a work area filled with machines, the functions and duties of which were beyond his immediate speculation. He was too distracted from speculation, anyway, by the actions of the person within this room.

The Stem had an arm missing, the end of the stump still smoking and dripping glowing drops of plasma. Beak had hit it. But had it hit Beak? Its back was to Monty, and as he watched it inserted its melting arm into an oblong opening in the front of a refrigerator-sized gray device. The Stem touched some keypads. A glare of red light shone inside the oblong opening, then a sharp buzz and the Stem reeled back with a whistle of pain, its melted arm neatly trimmed back to the shoulder, the slowing spread of plasma arrested.

Monty had his pistol on it. "Freeze right there, skinny!"

The Stem whirled and launched itself at him. Monty's heart catapulted into his throat and he fired; once, twice, and by the third time—having missed even at this range with all three bullets—the creature was on him.

It swung one of the two remaining arms, the hard little fingers at the end raking his face, almost catching him in the eye. The other arm and an upraised foot took hold of his clothing. Stick-like though it was, it was still tremendously strong and it seemed like a great heavy being was forcing its weight upon him. Monty fired a fourth bullet as his sleeve was gripped and his arm wrenched to one side; once again he missed. He cried out as its other arm switched grips to seize him by the hair, forcing his head into an agonizing angle. The grip on his sleeve now leapt to his hand. Hard fingers dug into the meat of his thumb, bringing blood, and the pink semi-automatic clunked to the floor.

Monty pushed at the insectoid limbs, chopped at the body with his free hand, to no effect. He went onto his knees. He felt blood trickling down his face. With a surge of strength he propelled them both forward, the Stem bumping roughly into a counter edge, knocking a tray of instruments to the floor in a loud clatter. Would someone hear? Monty kept crying out, and tucked his face into his shoulder as the upraised foot released his coat to make swipes at it, one gashing his chin.

Monty remembered his hand phone at last, and had it out in a moment. "Beak, help me, help, I'm in Research, a Stem has me!" he shouted, half hysterical. A finger hooked the corner of his mouth then, but before it could rip he shoved out his hand that gripped the phone to push it away, and raised himself up to his feet with a cry. The Stem left the ground for a second before Monty twisted and toppled onto his back. He dropped the hand phone.

The Stem loomed over him, the inane carved jack-o'-lantern face—ridiculously small in its pencil-thin body—gazing down at him, grinning emptily like a shark. It still had his right hand pinned, but Monty had caught its other arm between his knees, hooking one leg over its elbow. That wouldn't last for long; as it was, he'd have been dead already if the thing hadn't been so badly wounded, in such pain. He could feel the arm about to free itself from his legs, and saw the foremost of its three legs readying to fold up and lash out at his face again.

From inside his jacket Monty withdrew a red pen. Vern Woodmere had given it to him. The night he had thought he was rescuing Mauve from her bodyguards he had come close to using it, but the Stem—this one?—had overpowered him.

His luck was better now. He jammed its point into the triangular, single black nostril of the tiny unmoving face and thumbed its button. A syringe.

There was a single capsule of plasma inside. The Stem's grip on him flew instantly away. Monty let go of the pen and rolled out of the way of any deadly overflow or dripping.

The whistling was incomparable to any sound he'd ever heard, the dance of the Stem as incomparable an image; all frenzied thrashing spider limbs. Both impressions were very brief, however. The top of the Stem's head, containing the eyes, dropped away from the rest of the body. The creature folded up to quiver and jerk and melt down further—so much more slowly than a soft-bodied human, but the prime objective had been achieved. Death.

Rubbing away the drops of blood from his chin with the back of his hand, Monty scooped up the Stem's weapon from where it had set it down on a counter—thank God, rather than replacing it in its holster, where it would have had it handy during their struggle—and tossed it into the zapper slot which had clipped off its ruined stump. A buzz and the gun was no more. Monty now retrieved his hand phone and blipped Beak.

Beak came on. "Monty, I heard you call—where are you?"

"Research, I said; it's over. I nailed it. I'm all right."

"I nailed the other punk, the one with the Elvis-do. Come on down to the loading docks; I got Dwork pinned down. We can hold him 'til the forcers get here, then we can close in."

"Jesus—good work, man."

"He almost made it out but I spotted him. Hurry up and help me. Rear docks, back of the building."

"I know—I've been here before." Monty bolted.

Monty saw a flash of green streak by in the distance, heard a hollow clang of punctured metal. He ducked down, darted from cover to cover, from support column to pill bin. Behind some machinery he blipped Beak again.

"You all right? I saw him fire."

"I'm fine. He's closer to the doors than I am but he's afraid to make a dash for it. Get between him and the doors if you can. I'll let off some shots to keep him occupied."

"Do it."

Solid bullets whined off metal, slammed into less resistant material. Beak had thought it safer to slap in this clip in place of plasma, where Monty was getting too near the line of his fire. Monty crawled on hands and knees to a robot hover-lift, quietly humming as it recharged, and gingerly peered over the top of it. A flash of green as Dwork returned Beak's fire. Monty was able to get his bearings on Dwork's position. He dashed again.

"Give up, Dwork!" Beak called out. "The forcers are probably surrounding the building this very minute, asshole. You step out there and you're gone...and I don't mean escaped."

"Why are you after me? What have I done?"

"Oh, gee—you killed one of our agents a few minutes ago..."

"Self-defense! I was confused—you stormed my office!"

"You had my wife raped and killed!"

"I don't know what you're talking about!"

"They're both dead, your security guard punks, Dwork. If you want the same that's fine with me. Fight us and you die. Fight us in court if you're so damn innocent... maybe you got a chance. Right?"

Monty crouched under a huge, clear plastic tray filled with red pills. He could see Westy Dwork squatting behind another charging robot lift. He was reaching up into it, touching controls. Activating it. Monty knew he meant to power it up, fling himself inside and escape in it. A control on the dash would automatically open the dock doors, no doubt, when he was ready.

Monty extended his pistol in both hands to take careful aim, squinted his left eye shut.

He fired four times. Two bullets struck Dwork in the side, knocking him away from the sleeping robot. Dwork barked once loudly in surprised pain. Blood had flecked the yellow, scuffed robot. Dwork kicked on his back, disoriented like a fallen ice skater. He lifted his pistol in Monty's direction...

The half-dozen arrows of green light streaked mostly off to the left of him, but one hit the clear tray of pills above him. The plastic began melting rapidly around the puncture, the widening edges of the hole glowing green. A rain of red pills poured down in front of Monty, obscuring his view. Before he could turn and go out the other way the bottom of the basin opened up and an avalanche of pills poured down on him.

Dwork pulled himself up the side of the robot. Blood was spreading across his white shirt and long white lab smock.

Beak skidded into view. He and Dwork sighted each other, fired almost simultaneously. Both missed. Beak dove behind a shipping rack full of cartons ready to leave the plant. Dwork kept firing to cover his retreat. Cartons burst and a Halloween rain of colored candy pattered across Beak's back.

Spitting out red vitamin pills, Monty pulled himself from the mound beneath the melted basin. Glancing toward the robot Dwork had crouched behind, he now saw only blood. And then Beak, through the rack beyond the robot. Monty blipped him. "Where'd he go?" he hissed.

"Not out the doors."

"Keep them covered...I'll follow the blood."

Monty expected the second Stem to spring up at any moment, but he went unmolested as he traced the trail of blood drops back into the Research and Development Department. There he reached a door. No doubt the blood continued on past it, but the door wouldn't open at Monty's urging.

By now the police had come. In minutes they had joined Monty at the door. In several more minutes they brought in a top technician from Research and Development who knew all the security code.

He unlocked the door for them, the forcers then pushing him out of the way of danger. The first of them let Monty come right after him.

A half-dozen guns pointed. None fired. None had to.

Dwork was slumped against a desk, sitting on the floor, legs splayed, head slung to one side on a slack, dead neck. Blood had saturated much of his white smock. He'd pulled papers to the floor with him, a portable keyboard lying across one knee.

Monty looked at the activated monitor screen atop the desk. It took him only seconds to guess Dwork's final intentions. After all, he recognized much of this equipment from backstage at the Jason Scarborough Theater.

"'Friendly flesh,'" Monty said. "He had his own molecular pattern on file. He was trying to repair himself but he didn't make it."

No one at the moment understood what he was talking about. Monty holstered his pistol.

The building was searched thoroughly, without turning up the second Stem. Captain Nedland came at last, joining Monty, Beak and Giddry. The paramedics who'd arrived to cart bodies had treated and taped up the lacerations in Monty's face. They'd heal without scars.

At Monty's request, Nedland called in one of the top computer techs at HAP.

They had coffee in the cafeteria while they waited. The forcers interviewed certain employees, particularly those from Research, but made no arrests. The corpse of Westy Dwork/Pilter De Vard had been removed. The computer tech, Olive Slate, arrived; an attractive black woman who greeted Monty warmly. Besides her extensive research and library duties at HAP, Olive was specially trained to decipher corporate computer codes during the investigation of various sorts of organized wrongdoing. Nedland set her to work at Westy Dwork's equipment.

"Watch it for booby-traps," Monty warned her, not joking; remembering Vern.

"A little messy, Captain, wouldn't you say?" the police officer in charge commented, hands on hips. "You lost a man, and three suspects are far beyond questioning. Why didn't you call us in before you moved?"

"We acted well within our legal authority, Lieutenant," Nedland droned calmly.

"You just wanted to nab Dwork before we could, that's all. Big game—the prize lion. The boy who made M-670 for Matt Cotton."

"We just wanted the job done right," snarled Giddry.

"Oh, you did it right, pal…just ask your dead partner."

Giddry took a step forward. Nedland blocked him with an arm. "Sludge," Giddry growled.

Monty ignored them, took a seat beside Olive but said nothing to distract her as he watched her work. "Mm…we do have some encryption as we get in here," she murmured, mostly to herself. "Looks basic, though. Mm-hm. Not that this boy wasn't smart enough to do better, but he obviously didn't expect anyone to look…"

"What are we looking for?" the police lieutenant said.

"Proof of Dwork's involvement with Matt Cotton, his creation of M-670 with his dead partners," said Nedland.

Proof of his involvement with Toll Loveland, thought Monty. "Are we still into 'friendly flesh?'" he asked Olive. She'd been briefed on the subject first, Monty explaining about Mauve and *Meathearts*.

"Yes…but it's…just hold on. Let me turn this into English—I know I can clear it pretty easy. Yeah. Here we go…" Monty held his breath, expected the computer to explode. It didn't. Meaningless symbols on the monitor screen were replaced by three words in English.

THE BIG FROWN.

"Jesus," said Monty. "Hold it."

"What?" Nedland came closer.

"*The Big Frown.* That's a billboard I've seen. An ad in the papers, too. 'Opening soon—*The Big Frown.*' That's all it says. Doesn't say if it's a film or a play or what. Or when. It just shows a guy's face with his mouth in a huge grimace, like a Choom's mouth, but with blood running down from the corners like his mouth's been split open…like Mauve in her play, but more of a frown than her grin."

"Go on," instructed Nedland, leaning in over Olive's shoulder.

"It's a program name," she announced coolly.

And now the program lay unveiled, explained by Olive along the way.

"Montgomery." Olive looked up from the screen for only a second. "When Dwork explained his 'friendly flesh' process to you and to Mauve Pond, he said only that the injured body could be rapidly regenerated…nothing along the lines of the reverse of that?"

"Reverse of what? Of regeneration?"

"No, then?"

"No—why?"

"Well…apparently he didn't tell either of you about a whole other range of his invention. And his intended uses for it." Olive punched up a full-length illustration of a human being on the screen, not much more than an outline. More work, however, laid in the brain and nervous system, or the internal organs, the muscles or circulatory system or the skeleton, or all in combination. Monty was reminded of the changing of Toll Loveland's light painting *Matter of Life and Death.* Olive zoomed in on the head so that alone filled the monitor screen. "Not only could Dwork use his drug to repair injuries long-distance, but to inflict them long-distance. By slashing this figure—don't worry, I know what I'm doing—he could inflict a matching wound on whoever's molecular code he had punched up, and the 'friendly flesh' would respond and obey." She demonstrated by drawing a red line down from the edges of the illustration's mouth.

"My word," breathed Nedland. "And that was what *The Big Frown* was going to be, in some way?"

"I believe I know in what way. It would have been his long-distance maiming on a mass scale…"

"The 'friendly flesh' mix-up," Monty cut in, as it came to him. "Two thousand bottles of vitamins with 'friendly flesh' instead…and only five hundred have been recalled."

"It's obvious Dwork switched the drugs on purpose," said Nedland.

"*The Big Frown*," Olive said. "A thousand, fifteen hundred people maimed with two brief strokes. Instantly slashed open, wherever they are, so long as they're in the transmission range, which must obviously be very wide…slashed open as if by an invisible person." Olive seemed to appreciate the depraved awesomeness of the image, but Monty was shaking his head.

"Impossible," he argued. "All those people don't have their individual molecular codes on file in Dwork's computer—how could they? It was a random contamination; he didn't have personal contact…"

"Access to medical files?" said Beak.

"No—this." Olive indicated the slashed face on the monitor. "Dwork has this labeled his *Skeleton Key*. Apparently he'd need your code to put you back the way you were before, as a surgeon would, but why should a maimer need to know your body's particulars? All he had to do was slash his one 'skeleton key' model to wound all those people simultaneously."

"One sick fuck," Giddry commented.

"And when was this to have been done—*The Big Frown*'s opening date?" Nedland asked her.

"None given. Maybe waiting for the right time, playing it by ear. Otherwise a date probably would have been given on the poster Montgomery mentions."

Nedland turned to him. "Congratulations, Monty. Not only did you take down a tremendous mass murderer, but you inadvertently stopped this from happening."

"A lot of those people might have died from shock or blood loss before they could get patched up," Giddry noted. "That sick, sick fuck. Man, if only they'd let us clone him to stand trial."

"He's dead," Nedland said. "His dog-stretching days are over."

He suffered a few agonizing minutes, Monty thought. But he had suffered, too. Opal had suffered worse, before her death. *Thousands.* Even to clone Dwork and execute him again wouldn't be enough. Killing those two punks who'd murdered Beak's wife wasn't good enough. Nothing could be.

"At least he died," Beak told Giddry. "If he'd still been alive when we came in we'd have to save his life, right?"

"I wouldn't have. I'd have kicked that keyboard right out of his hands and told him to wait for his ambulance. See how friendly his flesh was then."

"This is all over my head," the police lieutenant confessed bitterly to Captain Nedland. "I expect a full report."

"Just go see the movie in six months," Giddry told him.

Nedland worked his way to Monty in the milling confusion. "You did good, Black. We did the wisest thing we could do when we let you come home. You sure didn't waste any time, did you? Of course, I would have liked to have him alive for questioning, but dead is the next best thing."

"I'd have liked to have him alive for questioning, too. Very much so. This isn't over. *The Big Frown*, maybe. Probably. But there'll come something else."

"Something else like what?"

"Toll Loveland is still alive."

"Oh, Monty, I really doubt that now. Dwork was just carrying on with Loveland's type of thing, probably following through with an old plan of Loveland's..."

"Why would he do that? He's not an artist. They didn't go to any art courses together at Polytech; Loveland went on to P.U. for his liberal arts study, and Dwork didn't."

"But they were friends."

"You think Dwork did this out of loyalty to his friend's memory—as a tribute? Threw away a chance at raking in a fortune? Threw away his life?"

"He was a psycho, like Loveland—that's why they *were* friends."

"Yes, I know—I'm sure the thrill was a lot of it. But Dwork wouldn't do this alone...he'd just focus on making money. Just like he didn't invent 'friendly flesh' alone. That was the bond. They developed it and perfected it together, as friends, but had to accommodate the other's needs. Dwork's need to make money from it here at Cugok, and Loveland's need to use it in his art. If Loveland is dead, why is Dwork still accommodating him?"

"Why not out of friendship? Why not just for the thrill? Look at his role in *Meathearts*, personally carving up your girlfriend. And that thing with Matt Cotton. Loveland didn't have anything to do with that. You still want Loveland so bad you refuse to see that regardless of all he did, the more dangerous of the two turned out to be Pilter De Vard."

"Loveland is the more dangerous. Dwork had the skills, but Loveland has the vision. How do we know that he and Loveland didn't come up with M-670 for Matt Cotton together?"

"Oh, Christ, Monty—come on, now. That was Matt Cotton's vision and De Vard just executed it. You don't think Matt Cotton was friends with Toll Loveland, too, I hope."

"No, I don't. But I still think you're underestimating Toll Loveland."

"And I think Toll Loveland has become blown out of proportion in your mind.

I can't fault you for that, Monty, but I'd hate to see you not make use of this new opportunity we've given you, beyond this case. Your work so far makes you look good, but this excess of speculation doesn't."

"I've been right so far, haven't I? You can't think this case is over."

"Not fully. Of course I'll let you tie up all the loose ends; take all the time you realistically need. This will be big with the public, anyway, and it's in our best interest to keep it up front. I'll leave you free of other commitments until you're ready. You can keep Beak."

"You can keep Giddry."

"Well, Monty, he's been on the Cugok mix-up and he knows it well. You'll need him to help you figure out how Dwork...De Vard, rather...got the mislabeled drugs past Cugok's Q.C.. At least finish that up first, and then maybe I'll pull him. Also, you need to figure out how involved Cangue was in all this...hopefully the forcers will find him. And find out how Dwork managed to have the two Stems and those two punks working for him like that...whether he brought them with him to Cugok, or if they already worked here and he bought them."

"I'll interview Cugok myself. Tanabe and Giddry never were able to speak with him directly and I don't like that."

"Monty, enough paranoia for now, huh? Is Cugok a psycho out for thrills, too—is that why he developed this multi-million-munit business?"

"Maybe not, but Dwork just happened to get a major position in a building once owned by the Greenberg Company, where Toll Loveland presented *Pandora's Box*?"

Nedland didn't know what to say to that. He sighed and glanced at Beak. "He's taking it all well. A good man. He got his boys, and within proper context. I'll put his name out there...the media will want some front man from our team, and I'd rather it not be you."

"Good."

"They'll like the angle about his wife and all. They'd like the angle about you and Mauve but I won't feed 'em that. Sound good?"

"Good."

"Looks like your lady is out a job."

"Good," said Monty.

EIGHTEEN

Captain Nedland had been right about the media explosion, but not about Mauve. The next showing of *Meathearts* went on without the direction of Ferule Cangue and the magic of Westy Dwork. A makeup effects artist was rushed in to handle the prologue, which it was decided by all to retain despite its absence from the original play. Actually the bloody attacks were no less horrifying *looking*, but everyone knew it wasn't real this time. Box office hadn't suffered, however—all those with tickets showed up. And phone reservations even increased. There was a new attraction to *Meathearts* now: backstage horror on a grander scale than the previous brief prologue violence. Mauve and Aurora Lehrman would surely become stars, though Aurora had to fend off many questions about her romantic involvement with Dwork, and suffer the truth scans and interrogations of health agents and forcers alike. She showed Monty no hostility, however, as he'd feared; she even seemed shyly embarrassed or ashamed of herself for having gone to bed with the greatest mass murderer in the history of Punktown.

Fredrick V. Cugok was on a vacation/business trip out in the far province of Kaihany, but was at last reached by Monty on vidphone for an interview. He told Monty he had only just learned of the story and of Dwork's death last night and had called the police himself this morning. Monty assured him that he needed to answer the Health Agency's questions as well.

"I had no idea, of course, of Mr. Dwork's activities…though I was very aware of his 'friendly flesh' experiments, and of his participation in *Meathearts*. I most certainly did not approve of his role in that, his being the top Cugok researcher, or his use of an experimental drug in a play…but he was persistent and I was frankly afraid that he'd leave us if I didn't give in." Cugok was white-haired and deeply tanned, quite seamed and wrinkled though his hoarse voice still carried an inner strength. Behind him was a window showing a rolling golf green and vivid blue sky, rivaling each other for artificiality. "He did have a great influence over me, I'm sorry to admit. Now, to the detriment of my company. This will be a hard blow to recover from. I have to dissociate myself from that bastard's name as best I can. It would kill me to sell the company…but after this, and that Matt Cotton business, people may not want to *touch* my products. Of course, we could go into research exclusively, and I still own the rights to Dwork's creations…"

"Getting back to his influence over you, sir—did you yourself hire the Stems for security? And the security guards Terrence Melendez and Viz Johnson?"

"Well…unfortunately, there I allowed Dwork to dominate me, as well. The Stems were his idea; he brought them in. Same with Melendez and Johnson."

"Why, when you already had a contract with Airtite Security?"

"He had his reasons for them, obviously, and he simply used his leverage with me. Told me I needed tougher men to protect his work from industrial spies. That sounded fairly reasonable. I don't know where he met them; he told me the humans came from Fog Security but the forcers told me this morning that Fog has never heard of them. Just some thugs he hired."

"Have you ever met or seen this man?" Monty touched a key. He could still see Cugok, but Cugok's screen would be running through various photos of the handsome Toll Loveland. Monty came back on.

"No, except on VT. He's Toll Loveland, right?"

"Yes."

"It's your belief that Dwork and Loveland were partners?"

"Yes. Money and art aren't always strange bedfellows, but in this case I can't see Dwork going on with or inventing an 'artwork' like *The Big Frown* or even participating in *Meathearts* without Loveland's influence."

"Good God, you mean to suggest he's still alive?"

"Please, Mr. Cugok—your utter confidentiality on this."

"Of course, of course. God. This is all so strange."

"When you come back here I'd like to interview you in person, sir."

"Mm—as do the police. I understand. Of course, Mr. Black."

"Did you ever see this man at Cugok?" Monty punched up a photo of the dwarf director Ferule Cangue for Fredrick Cugok, then returned.

"No, never."

Ferule Cangue was captured by the forcers the next day. He was sincerely shocked to be arrested. A hospital had called the police to inform them that Cangue had come there in a state of alarm—suffering amnesia. He had no recollections of directing *Meathearts*. No recollections of Westy Dwork. No recollections of the entire past year.

Naturally the forcers extensively truth scanned him, with Monty, Beak and Giddry present. He had recollections of *Pandora's Box*, and the truth scan revealed that he found Toll Loveland and his work to be thrilling, but he did not know Toll Loveland. And now, of course, Monty could be certain that Ferule Cangue was not himself Toll Loveland in radical disguise.

It was evident from the scans and interrogation that Cangue *believed* he could be responsible for collaboration with Dwork and Loveland, though he had no memories of it. The possibility of it agitated him greatly.

Reluctantly, they had to let him go free until such time as they had witnesses or evidence to prove that he had intended anyone harm from his association with Dwork. Giddry vocalized the frustration Monty felt. His having had a year's worth of memories erased from him indicated either that he was guilty or knew too much about those who were.

He was advised to remain within Punktown, and informed that he would be prosecuted and imprisoned, if proven sufficiently guilty, whether his memories were wiped out or not.

Despite his nervousness, before he was allowed to leave Cangue expressed an anxiousness to attend the next presentation of *Meathearts*.

"That little piece of sludge," Giddry hissed to his partners. "Let me follow him for a few days, Black."

"All right." Monty didn't think anyone would contact Cangue—the point of the memory erasure was to clear him from associations. His surviving partners, if any, must have cared for him enough not to kill him, which indicated the extent of the knowledge he'd possessed before erased, his intimacy with them. Nedland, though, would probably say that no partners survived to contact or pose a threat to Cangue, and that he'd simply had his memories deleted to protect himself and no one else. Still, it couldn't hurt to keep an eye on him and it would keep Giddry out of Monty's way until he needed him.

"Maybe Loveland wasn't part of *The Big Frown*," Beak hypothesized now. "Maybe it was Cangue the artist, obsessed with Loveland, and Dwork the scientist in a new partnership."

"Cangue was just invited in to stage *Meathearts*, an echo of *The Big Frown*—and Loveland loves echoes, the intricate relationship of one thing to another, to weave all his patterns and symmetries. Games upon games. I'm sure Cangue became a friend, but he wasn't in it like Dwork and Loveland."

"So who wiped out his memories and left him at his apartment? Loveland?"

"Most likely."

"Well, still, the Teeb Family will clean memories for a price. Remember when Michael Suzerain was indicted for polluting, and he had his memory wiped? He was still proved guilty and his company fined..."

"Not hardly enough."

"...but he tried it, and I heard Neptune Teeb's people wiped him. Remember when Selectman Leone 'hit his head on his dashboard' in a minor accident and forgot all about receiving illegal funds? Teeb's people wiped him, too."

"Well, we can look at it, I guess."

"Vern works for them, is what I'm thinking. Why not make use of it?"

"You're the one who didn't want me to look up Vern and endanger him. If the

Teebs find out he's talking to us they could kill him."

"Let's just talk to him and see what he thinks."

"You know where to contact him?"

"Yeah."

"All right. Let's dump Giddry on Cangue's ass and go have a look."

It took an hour of calling attempts, between which Beak and Monty ate their lunch in a cheap family restaurant, before Beak finally got an answer on Vern Woodmere's hand phone. Beak came back to the table to tell Monty that Vern had anxiously agreed to meet them in an hour at a restaurant/pub for a beer.

It wasn't a good part of town, but then most of Punktown wasn't a good part of town; at least it wasn't downright awful. The *Bone Club* boasted a decor obvious from its name: animal skulls ranked row after row, more rows below that, entirely covering certain walls, human skulls on shelves within the transparent bar counter like museum pieces, dinosaur-like leg bones framing doors, whale-like rib bones lining the length of the arched ceiling over the restaurant section. The background for this profusion of specimens was black to set them off, for more of that museum feel. The bar was too crowded; Monty and Beak took a table behind a thick support column made from glassy-surfaced, stacked giant vertebrae from a creature unknown to Monty, black but with an oil-slick-like red iridescent quality in certain light. He touched it, envisioned having a pillar like this in his dream apartment some day.

Smoky air, a jukebox booming loudly: "*I'm a Kama Sutra for your love, darlin'... wanna Kama in your Sutra all night long...*"

Beak returned with two golden meads. "Thanks much," said Monty. He was eyeing a woman at the bar, generally Asian in appearance, in a black silk dress slit to showcase her crossed legs. He thought about Mauve. They'd barely seen each other since the night of their argument. And so the knot of tension hadn't been untied yet. He felt a little frightened about it now; maybe it was all going to slip away.

"*Said I'm a Kama Sutra for your love, darlin', gonna Kama in your Sutra all night long...*"

Monty diverted his thoughts to Beak, regarded him a moment over the rim of his mug. "How you feeling now, man? Is the burden off?"

"The burden off? No. The mission is accomplished. The hunt is over. The burden's never off."

"You were right about me. I want to tell you to go find yourself a new girl..."

"I can't. It's not our way, though some give in nowadays. But the kind of female I'd want wouldn't accept me, because I had a mate before."

"How did that ever evolve? It isn't biologically practical in terms of guaranteeing procreation and the continuance of your race. What if a disease wiped out a lot of people...what about a war?"

"My people don't war each other. And our behavior didn't evolve biologically—we *chose* to be this way. It's love, honor, respect. Loyalty. Loyalty is big with us, man, it's everything. You can't see the beauty in that?"

"Yes, I can."

"In the afterlife, if one exists, I want it to be me and her, not some three-way scene. Yeah, smile...that's heaven for you, not for me. My wife is indispensable. It's not like a job you fill again. You mustn't forget that person—she's part of your soul."

Monty nodded, stared into his glass. "I can't shake Opal. I love Mauve—I'm sure I do. I want a thing with her...I want us to live together. And Mauve cares more for me romantically than Opal ever did. But I can't shake her. A lot of it's guilt, I know. A lot of it isn't. I loved her. I don't want to forget...abandon her. That's what it feels like. That sound to you like I should have a bird beak?"

"Yeah, but you don't. My advice to you, man, is to go on. Go for Mauve...leave Opal in the past. You don't have to forget her. But go on...'cause your people do. You can't be like me. You have to do like your people."

"Do your folk look down on us for that?"

"My people realize that different beings have different needs."

"I'm sick of your fucking perfect people, Beak. Is there anything wrong with your people, is there any intolerance or selfishness?"

Beak laughed. "Nope."

"Right." Monty sipped his mead.

"Gonna Kama in your Sutra, darlin'... 'til the break of dawn... "

A hand fell on Monty's shoulder and he jolted. "You boys can't even wait 'til I get here to start drinkin'?"

"Whoa, look at this guy!" Beak exclaimed, holding out his hand for his ex-partner to squeeze. "We're in the wrong business I guess, huh, Monty?"

Standing over them, Vern Woodmere looked strikingly good. He wore a square-shouldered blazer in alternating bands of metallic red and gold over a black silk shirt and black high-waisted trousers, fashionably baggy like Monty preferred. Metallic gold slippers. His grayish hair was neatly cut and slicked back; he was even clean-shaven. Though all the ravaged look could never be painted over, he appeared relaxed and healthy and happy. No trace of the hideous shrapnel wound Monty remembered from the last time he'd seen him, so long ago.

"Well, since you guys got a head start on me, I'll have to make up for it." A waiter came as Vern seated himself. Vern ordered a yaupon—a powerful drink as black and opaque as India ink. Vern shook Monty's hand across the table. "Blackie. Shit, man, you look better than last time I saw you."

"You too."

Vern returned his attention to Beak, and some of the old intensity revealed itself in the hatchet-wound creases between his eyebrows. "You did good nailing those fucks, man. I knew you'd get them someday. Who'd have believed it had anything to do with all this other dung?"

"Monty bagged one of them, but he did a good job so I'm not complaining."

Vern looked from one to the other. "So…fill me in on this, huh?"

They talked. The waiter brought Vern's drink, another mead for the other two, a plate of appetizers to go with their drinks. Beak did most of the talking, except where Monty knew the details better or from closer experience. They brought things up to the gun battle—battles—at Cugok, though Vern had caught a lot of that on VT this past week. He'd seen Beak on VT but not Monty, as Nedland had said it would be.

"I was afraid to meet you in public, where I've been on the screen," Beak said quietly. "What if one of the Teebs see me with you and recognizes me? We shoulda met in private, don't you think?"

"Hey, my last name isn't Teeb—I do what I want. I'm not hurting them. I'm still me and this is more important."

"Glad to hear that," said Monty. "Nedland calls you an enemy to HAP."

"Hey, Teeb isn't into illegal hazardous dumping like some of the other crime orgs are. He's careful what he gets into and he's even got a conscience about what he does, believe it or not. I like him. I'm not close, of course…but I've got a comfortable future. Anyway, don't worry, Beak—this is a big town and it's not like Teeb's got gorillas in every fucking bar, right? If I can't have some drinks with my best friends then I'd rather they *did* waste me."

"Did you find out if they had anything to do with Ferule Cangue having a memory wipe?" Beak asked him.

Vern munched a salty dilky root. "I didn't dare poke into their computer files, but I do have a few reliable and trustworthy friends in there, some of 'em even from when I was at HAP. My old buddy—and don't let this name go *anyplace*—is Blud Fulcrum, one of Teeb's two top weapons boys. He's the one who got me into Teeb, though he didn't have to work hard to convince him, with my HAP experience. Anyway—yeah, Blud told me. We did do Cangue's wipe."

Monty sat up and forward, frankly surprised that Beak's theory had been correct. "Jesus, they did? All this stuff Dwork and Loveland can do but they have Cangue wiped by Teeb?"

"Well, Dwork is dead and who knows about Loveland. Anyway, Cangue might not have been sent by anybody but himself, his own idea. Blud doesn't know much about it and I can't press him, you know? They make a lot of money wiping big shots and they can't let anything happen to jeopardize business…weaken their customers' confidence in them."

"That's it? No word on what Cangue knew?"

"Nothing specific—the obvious. Affiliation to some extent with that Dwork fuck. I'll tell you anything I can safely learn, believe me."

"Safely," Monty stressed. "I almost got you killed once—that's enough."

"Hey, shut that right now, pal, I mean it. Don't *ever* let me hear those words coming out of your mouth again or I'll push 'em back in with my fist. It was *my* choice to help you before…just like it's my choice now. You think I'm not a part of this? I am. We all lost. We all want revenge. Don't you even *think* about not counting me in on that."

"I've got your slug," Monty smiled.

"How's it doing?"

"Great. Want it back?"

"You don't like it?"

"I do—I talk to it. I love that stupid thing."

"Keep it. I'll visit it sometime and bring some flies. Me and Yas got a cat, anyway…I'm afraid the cat might hurt it."

"Yas? Is Yas what I think it is?" Beak said.

"She's gorgeous, man—I wish I had a picture. You'll have to meet her. I thought I told you about her; it's been three months now. So far, so good. And there I used to hate hebs. *Ginzburg.*" Vern laughed.

"You hate everybody," Beak observed.

"True. Maybe I'll turn Ginzburg to Woodmere…we'll wait and see, huh?"

Monty wanted to tell Vern about his relationship with Mauve but didn't, out of deference to Beak, a widower. Later. Anyway, he wasn't so sure where things stood anymore.

Beak clapped Vern on the back, and they all ordered a mead—Vern wisely resisting a second yaupon. For now they drank and laughed. In the general anxiety and gloom of life, brief islands of happiness like this were to be embarked upon and enjoyed, and meager supplies collected to last through another stretch of seemingly endless black ocean.

Vern departed from them with promises of further information when and if he got it. Monty was glad he was back in his life, even though the danger Vern seemed to radiate and attract simultaneously was still there, only partially disguised under his expensive cologne.

Monty tried on a jacket like Vern had worn yesterday, only with wide horizontal bands of metallic green and silver instead.

"I don't like it," Mauve commented.

"Black and orange." He took that one down in his size. "Yeah." He tried it on. "Nice and Halloweeny. This is the latest style."

"Try pink and gray—you look like a bee." She watched him. "That's better. It'll be time to Christmas shop before you know it, you know…I should really start now."

"Mm," agreed Monty. He had suggested they make time for each other today. It was he who hadn't been able to make time lately, really. Her show was still only once a week—despite the fact that a week was no longer needed for the healing of wounds—since the theater schedule was filled with other productions…though another performance or two a week would be added later if its popularity still warranted it. It appeared that it would. In any case, they had had lunch today and Mauve had needed to go to a store for a few items. It was the Canberra Mall, where Monty had wandered philosophically in his dying.

"Red and green—for Christmas." He held it out from the rack.

"Hideous."

"Agreed." They moved on, Monty with the pink and gray jacket draped over his arm. "Mauve…I hope I didn't hurt your show in any way. I know you know Dwork was a sick dangerous monster, and you aren't sad to see him gone, but I appreciate that the prologue thing was a real challenge to you and everything…"

"You and your guilt, Monty. Don't worry about that. I did it—I proved my commitment. After finding out about Dwork I don't think I'd want anybody slicing my face again. Everything's fine. I'm getting more attention than ever, right?"

"I'm sorry, too, that I didn't tell you what I knew about those two punks, but I didn't want to make you so afraid that Dwork suspected you knew something…"

"Monty, I *understand*. You think I'm mad you found those two scum?"

Killed, she meant, him and Beak. He'd killed one of the Stems, and Westy Dwork himself, he knew she knew…and he wondered if she viewed him any differently for it. Not that killing in Punktown was a unique achievement, but Monty had claimed three unique victims in one day.

"You seem cold." He came out with it.

"I'm just tense."

"Are you mad at me?"

"Hurt."

"I told you I was sorry. You aren't jealous about…my thing about Opal…"

She stopped, he stopped. People were close by; he hated fighting with a woman in public but Mauve was uninhibited. "I *understand* your thing about Opal, Monty…I *want* you to follow it through to some kind of a conclusion so you can get her out of your system enough to make room for me!"

"Don't hate her."

"I *don't*, you jerk, I just told you—I *understand!*"

"I'm sorry. I just can't seem to give you enough credit."

"I noticed. Or trust."

"I don't blame you for being hurt. But I've gone through a lot of hurt, too. Just soften up a little…bear with me—*please.*"

Mauve sighed, brushed her hair out of her eye. "All right." She blinked, breathing deeply and slowly. "I'm sorry."

He took in her smooth beauty. The scary thought came that had come before, since the raid on Westy Dwork's lab: just as on the day of *The Big Frown*, had he lived to see it, at any time Dwork could have reversed the healing effect on Mauve. With a few strokes on his computer screen, reopened her face wounds. Or slit her throat. Or mutilated her beyond recognition, perhaps. The picture in Monty's mind sent a chill through him. As did the idea—the possibility—that Dwork had had another lab other than the one at Cugok. A lab with Loveland. Where there might be duplicates of the "friendly flesh" equipment…

How frail was her smooth, pale tissue. Vulnerable, a mist of cells. Mortality. He wanted to protect her.

"I was wondering if we could start thinking more serious," he said. "Like moving in, serious?"

"Me with you?"

"Well, I like yours better."

Mauve smiled, embarrassed at her earlier bitterness. "Sounds good."

"We can enact pagan beer-drinking and sex rituals on that mysterious fraternity emblem on the floor, summon up the spirits. I hope you like slugs." He'd throw away his poster of Dora Deering.

"Do you want to wait until this is over…you know what I mean? Until it's all out of your system?"

"It'll never be *all* out of my system. Like you said, I just want some kind of definite conclusion. But that could take a while. Besides, I worry about you. If Loveland is truly alive, he could still want to involve you in this again in some way. Always keep your gun handy…"

"You don't know if you believe he's alive any more?"

"Who knows? Who knows what to think?" he sighed.

Mauve leaned up to kiss him—another thing which embarrassed him in public. "We can spend a nice Christmas together, huh?"

"Looks like it."

A Choom woman had floated up to them, her huge mouth in a grin of recognition. "Excuse me—aren't you Mauve Pond?"

Monty slapped across the tiles in bare feet, naked and muss-haired, to activate Mauve's loudly beeping vidphone. "*Hello?*" he growled, bleary-eyed.

"You're of the circumcised persuasion, eh, Monty?" It was Beak.

Monty pulled over a chair and sat to hide his body. "I know this is too much to wait until tomorrow, but convince me of it."

"Remember I told you I was trying to reassemble names to see if I could find any significance in them—like Tate Hurrea was Auretta Here? Well, I wished I did this before. I asked my computer to take names like Vicelord Godfucker, Toll Loveland, Manuel Hung, Ferule Cangue, those punks Johnson and Melendez and everybody, and see if they match up with any other names of people in the Loveland and Dwork case files, in a rearranged fashion."

"And?"

"Get ready."

"Yeah?"

"Godfucker. As in *The Godfucker?*"

"Yes, yes—come *on!*"

"Drop the 'ick' from Fredrick. Fred Cugok…"

"*What?*"

"Fred V. Cugok becomes V. Godfucker, as in Vicelord Godfucker, as in Toll Loveland."

"Jesus, Beak…Jesus, man!"

"What? What?" Mauve mumbled from bed.

"Let me write this down." Monty scrawled on the corner of a newspaper. "My God," he breathed. It was confirmed.

"He's alive," said Beak. "He has to be."

"But I spoke to Cugok on the phone; he's an old guy. Makeup?"

"A stand-in. Did you record your call?"

"Yeah—right. I know…we'll compare Cugok to actors who attended P.U. while Loveland was there…have the computer run through school records to look for a match. My God, Beak…an entire fucking company. Just another part of his crazy fucking games."

"Well, I'm sure he didn't mind making the money. And Dwork, too. They were going to ride it for as long as it held, then go underground."

"Come back as somebody else. Shit, I've got to call Nedland! That place has to be seized, everything from it recalled immediately—*everything!* Everybody there has to be questioned. I'm sure this Cugok person, whoever he is, has gone back to his real self and vanished, but we have to send a bulletin out to Kai-hany anyway. *Shit,* man!

You know, I thought that fuckin' place was a wee bit too artsy-looking inside…"

"The scariest part of it all is that this nonexistent Fredrick V. Cugok was able to fake his way into opening a pharmaceutical research company to begin with," noted Beak.

"Fucking terrifying," Monty agreed.

"I was just playing around, mostly—I couldn't sleep," Beak explained, proud of his discovery. They drank coffee. It was an hour yet until dawn.

"Nope—sorry; no match." Olive pushed away from her computer. "This man you spoke with doesn't match anybody who attended Paxton University while Manuel Hung a.k.a. Toll Loveland did. He could be anyone, any friend…not even an actor. I'll have the image broken down to see under the makeup he's obviously wearing—you should get a good accurate picture."

"You think it is makeup, then…that he really is younger?" Monty said.

"Unquestionably. The wealthy head of an experimental pharmaceutical company wouldn't have wrinkles like that. They overdid it to make him look old. Have a tech read his voice, too. It sounds younger…faked."

"Thanks, Olive."

Monty and Beak left the phone recording with a lab tech for further examination, and then responded to a page instructing them to report to Captain Nedland's office. He had just arrived, but had called ahead to have a raiding party gathered. Giddry was in Nedland's office, rumpled and irritable, more about having been notified of this development last than by the early hour.

"Coming along?" Nedland asked the health agents when they came in.

"Wouldn't miss it," said Monty.

Those four went in one hovercar, and a van full of men and women in black rubbery suits followed. The security people from the Fog Agency were, to say the least, surprised…but calling ahead might have alerted one or more of them (if so inclined) to destroy evidence or escape. Giddry removed their weapons and cuffed the four men together pending questioning, remained outside in the cold with them. "Always the sludge work," he grumbled at them accusingly.

The Fredrick V. Cugok Pharmaceutical Research and Manufacturing Company was swarmed, and seized.

Within two hours, much had been ascertained. The plant had thus far registered negative in every toxins test administered. Of course, many more tests would be performed yet—for days, no doubt. And even if all the drug products tested negative, they would still be destroyed.

So far, the only thing amiss besides Dwork's office and personal laboratory was, naturally, the office of Fred V. Cugok.

There were files, progress reports, the like, as one would anticipate…and that was just the point. One would expect to see such details, and so they'd been provided for. Even down to a photograph of Cugok with a white-haired wife. Another overdone effort at disguise: wouldn't a man of Cugok's wealth have a gorgeous young wife? Probably, Monty thought cynically.

But the office, the desk, when observed more closely, did begin to resemble a movie set: flat, a facade. Props. Dwork had run the show, with a few obligatory appearances from the front-man Cugok now and then. Later, interviews with the higher personnel—the plant foreman and the department supervisors (truth scanned to prove their innocence)—confirmed this. Though only the head of Research, Dwork had seemed to them many times to have an inordinate amount of influence in the company.

"Loveland made a mistake," said Beak. "Why hire somebody to play Cugok, risk involving another person, when Dwork could have played the boss himself?"

"It made sense. If Dwork was caught or had to run, Cugok could still stay in business. That's what happened, right? Though, thank God, only for a short time." Monty held onto the desktop photograph of Cugok and his wife so the wife's identity could be investigated. "I've got to drop in on Helga Greenberg again. She sold this property to these people—maybe she met Cugok. Most likely. Dwork, too, maybe. She might be of some help."

Monty was staring hatefully at a series of framed diplomas and certificates of achievement on the wall, cheerily gleaming gold seals on them. All obvious fakes. Fucking terrifying. Money had to have had a lot to do with this place coming into being. The right palms had been papered. Only such an evil substance could have provided for such an extent of evil. The plant was polluted with it, even if it didn't show up on any toxin scan.

At this point, Monty experienced the disheartening feeling that all the world was in some way part of Toll Loveland's sick, passionately heinous vision.

Part Three:

Black Blizzard

NINETEEN

"Jesus *Christ!*"

"Like it?"

Mauve stood at the foot of the bed, naked but for the cheap plastic skull mask over her face. Monty sighed and wagged his head. "Cute. Losing weight, huh?"

"You forget today is Eric Hughes' *Black Blizzard*? I'm so excited."

"I hadn't forgotten. I just didn't expect to wake up to this. Please, Mauve, take it off."

"All day we're supposed to wear masks and I intend to do it. I bought something for you, too."

"No. Forget it. Sorry."

She tossed a gift onto the bed. It was a skull head pin. The eyes flashed red and the jaw gnashed when a switch was activated. "I knew you wouldn't wear a mask so I bought that for your lapel, and you *will* wear it."

"I will—thank you. But you can't wear that all day, Mauve."

She pushed the squeaky mask up to the top of her head on its elastic band. "Well, I won't take it off any more than this. I hope a lot of people wear them. I'm sure they will; I keep seeing people buy them. I saw people buying better ones, too—full head masks. Some folks are really into it."

"More for the thrill, than for Hughes' message about the Oracle tragedy," Monty opined, getting out of bed. "Did you take it off when you showered?"

"Well…yeah. Don't tell anybody, huh?"

Monty went to take his own shower. He didn't like the mask on her. Too creepy.

Giddry would be following Cangue again today; nothing with him, yet, though he'd been seeing old friends and Giddry was busy photographing them and establishing their identities. Giddry wasn't needed at Cugok, since Captain Nedland himself was supervising the investigation there due to the great media attention. Monty and Beak intended to return today to poke around further and to sit in on the police interrogations, held there in a meeting room.

When Monty emerged from the bathroom to dress, Mauve (in a black blouse and tight black skirt, skull mask atop her head) seized his hand and drew him to the window. "It's already starting!" she gushed.

It was like volcanic ash sifting down thinly. Black flakes lazily floating, already accumulating on surfaces like soot. Passing vehicles swept the loose dust after them in swirls. It was a dirty-looking, ugly sight. Industrial waste or nuclear fallout. And

Monty had a terrible thought, which he voiced.

"I guess it would be too late now, but what if Eric Hughes turned out to really be Toll Loveland? And this—" he nodded at the black snow "—was his latest project?"

Mauve chewed on that one for a moment. "Wow…"

There was a distant muffled thud from the sky and the window rattled. Monty had heard two while showering but had taken them for sounds in the building. Now he realized it was the cannons at the air factory firing, bringing about this miracle—Eric Hughes' vision.

"I'm sure it's only snow," Mauve dismissed, but a little nervously.

"I know," Monty said, and went to dress.

Black shirt buttoned to the top button, black trousers, black shoes, his turquoise jacket with the skull pin on his lapel, placed there by Mauve. The vidphone rang— probably Beak, anxious to get to Cugok. Monty went to it.

The face of Vern Woodmere appeared, a little more like the ravaged Vern he knew and less like the suave gangster from the *Bone Club*.

"Who's with you, man?" Vern hissed in a whisper.

"With me? My girlfriend, is all—why?"

"Is your phone clean?"

"I would hope so. It doesn't have any special blockers, though. What's wrong?"

"I, ah, I've got a tip for ya."

"A tip?"

"I think. I think it's a tip."

"A tip about what?"

Mauve came in from the kitchen but Monty waved her away impatiently. A bit irritated, she hung back in the kitchen threshold but listened.

"I want in on it, if it is," Vern said. "I'll be blowing my thing with the Teebs but if it's what I think it is then it's worth it, man, and I want you to count me in. This is my thing, too, even if I'm not an agent anymore—right?"

"What…"

"The *Loveland* thing, man."

"Tell me."

"Let me work with you and Beak?"

"As much as I can. Tell me."

Vern straightened up, glanced over his shoulder. "I heard something from my friend Blud Fulcrum. He's big at Teeb and he hears a lot, like I told you. He told me this thing because he knows I know the person, but he obviously doesn't see the significance in it I saw…"

"What person?" Monty didn't care for Vern's dramatic build-up.

"Helga Greenberg. She contacted the Teeb Family about having someone cloned.

But it had to be done at her house, she specified. So they're gonna send over two top technicians this afternoon. Now the kicker."

"Yeah?"

"The cloning is already half finished, she told them, but there was a problem and she needs them to take over. She has all the equipment needed in her *home*. All she wants is their knowledge."

"*Fuck*," hissed Monty. "Fuck *me...*"

"Do you see it?"

"I see it. God love you, Vern. I fuckin' see it, man."

"For one thing, someone sent Cangue to Teeb for his memory wipe. Because Dwork is dead and he couldn't do it..."

"And now Helga Greenberg needs Teeb to have a cloning completed," Monty said. "Because Dwork is dead and couldn't do it."

"She owned Greenberg Products, where Loveland did *Pandora's Box*. She sold it to Cugok, who doesn't exist...but where Westy Dwork just happened to work."

"And her husband died of Garland Syndrome a little after the chem spill that ruined Greenberg. How do we know that she didn't arrange that with Loveland? Loveland must have been her lover..."

"Yeah—right. And now the person she's cloning. It's got to be him."

"Right." Monty thought of the painting *Matter of Life and Death*. Baby emerging from a skeleton. "I thought he was already alive and around, but he wasn't. He must have been waiting to reemerge when the *Big Frown* thing happened, but it never did. Dwork had started on the clone to have him ready to return on the scene. But we nailed Dwork, and little Helga had to go to your buddies to have Cangue's memory erased and Loveland finished developing."

"We could be off, but I doubt it," said Vern. "If it was just Cangue or just her coming to Teeb for help I might not have thought she was involved—but both, and so close together? And why the fuck does she have a cloning set-up in her house?"

"It's her," Monty said, without any doubts. It all made sense. And there they had been inside her house, Vern and he, a whole year ago, without knowing that the seed of Toll Loveland was hidden there, buried, waiting to bloom again into life, dramatically timed to coincide with *The Big Frown*.

"Let's go cuff her, Monty," Vern said.

"Vern, you can't come...Nedland would have my balls."

"Hey, I told you man, this is my thing, too! I lost my job because of that fuck! You can't deny me my right to participate in this, man. You, me and Beak—look what he did to us. You, me and Beak have to be the ones to take him and his fuckin' girlfriend."

"This is big—I should report it before I move..."

"You know you don't mean that, man—Christ! Think of *Opal!*"

"You think I've forgotten about her?" Monty snapped. "All right, I don't have to report my every move to Nedland…but if you go with me, it will come out after and he'll blow his top. Can't you see that? You did your part, Vern, you did it just now. Let me and Beak sweep up the rest of it…"

Monty saw the fury rippling beneath the shadow-bruised face of the Red War veteran. That he was a Red War veteran returned to the front of Monty's mind, to see this mounting rage replace the previous furtiveness. Vern no longer whispered. "You haven't denied Beak his due and you won't deny mine. I'm going down there, Monty…*now*. You can meet me there if you're fast enough, but I won't wait long so you'd better call Beak…"

"Don't do this, Vern, I mean it!"

"I won't wait long. I'm on my way."

"Vern, don't! I'll stop you when I get there, I swear it! I'll cuff you, Vern—don't make me do it. I won't have you fuck this up!"

"So go call Nedland on me, you fucking traitor!" Vern stepped back from the screen, half turned to take something from a desk drawer. "*Try* to stop me." He lifted a heavy pistol at the screen and Monty almost instinctively jumped back, dove for cover.

Muzzle flash. The picture went black.

"Fuck!" Monty roared, and punched out Beak's number. In his haste he messed up and had to punch it out again. Now Mauve came to stand behind him.

"He's crazy," she said. "Are you going to call your boss?"

"No."

"No?"

"No. Me and Beak will go down there." Shit—Beak wasn't answering. If he were already on his way to Cugok, Monty decided, then he would go on to Helga Greenberg's place alone.

"Monty, you saw him—he's dangerous! If you try to stop him from going in there he might kill you!"

"He won't…" His ringing still unanswered.

"Monty…"

"He *won't!*" Monty snarled at her.

Beak came on, towel over his shoulders, his fur sleek like an otter's from a shower. "I'm almost ready, Monty."

"You're ready now. Helga Greenberg is in with Loveland—Vern found out from his people. He's going down there to arrest her…maybe to kill her. He may or may not wait for us. You know where she lives to meet me there?"

"I know the park, but not the exact house."

"It's a ten story, light greenish apartment building with her place on top, and that's made of dark green and peach-colored tiles covered in ivy. Look, just meet me instead. There's a white arched bridge in the park, pretty close…well, shit, there's a couple of those…"

"I'll find it. Go. I'll be there. I'll find the apartment building. Just go stop him… don't wait for me."

"Don't tell Nedland."

"I won't." Beak punched off.

Monty whirled, and Mauve was there.

"Look…" she said.

"I'll be all right." Monty took her upper arms and kissed her forehead. Her mask fell off to the floor behind her. "This is it," he told her. She didn't like the strange look in his eyes, and his funny tense smile. Or that, as he plunged toward the door, he flipped the switch to make his skull pin's jaw work and eyes glow red, even though she had bought the crazy thing for him.

It was a full-force blizzard now, and made for slowed progress. Despite his anxiousness, Monty could at last acknowledge the beauty of the storm. Where a half-hour ago it had looked like soot or ash, thinly spread on surfaces, now as it began to stick together and pile up—coat and cloak objects—it became a stranger sight with less to be compared to. It was an increasingly awesome visual, and the beauty of it was full of mystery; disquieting, even disorienting. Parked cars looked as if they'd been draped with black blankets. Blackness clung to moving pedestrians. The air was thick with it, dark with it. Monty had to have his headlights on.

At a stoplight he checked the clip in his pink semi-automatic, felt inside his coat for his extra magazines of solid shells and plasma capsules. Christ, he thought, it might've been quicker to take the train. Some children on the sidewalk to his right caught his eye. Full head rubber skull masks on two of them, another with a cheap plastic mask like Mauve's. A man and woman using the crosswalk wore skull faces. Monty looked in his rear-view monitor. There was a grinning cousin to Death behind the dash of the vehicle in back of him.

"It's beginning to look a lot like Doomsday," Monty sang quietly to himself as traffic moved forward again.

At one point, not far from the park, Monty had to drive between two gangs of kids hurling black snowballs across the street at each other. One exploded against his side window and he hissed a curse. A huge robot snow melter was ahead of him, also. "Come on, come on, come on," he chanted. He was tempted to beep Beak and check on his progress, but the robot turned to the left and he was instantly free to zip forward.

The park stretched before him, the greatest unbroken field of black yet. Like some volcanic desert, sparkling obsidian sand. Kids tramped in it (school had been called off, half because of the snow's impediment and half as a kind of holiday). Monty saw a black snowman, then another one, and a black snow fort rising up.

Then he saw the mint green apartment house looming beyond the veils of snow. The jade and peach-tiled house atop it, tangled in vines forever as lush and green as in summer. As he drew nearer he watched for Vern outside the guard station, waiting for him. He wasn't there.

He ran from his car into the station, stamped his feet on a mat as he produced his badge, black crystal flakes sparkling in his hair. "Health agent—I need to get into Helga Greenberg's apartment to make an arrest. If you make any attempts to contact her you'll be arrested as an accomplice to her crimes. How can I get in there on my own?"

A uniformed woman behind the counter sputtered, "We don't have access to her apartment…we have no emergency code breaker for her."

"Not even the super has one," growled a burly uniformed man, giving Monty a plasma-hot glare.

"Has a man come through here, graying slicked-back hair, intense-looking, in a red and gold-striped jacket?"

"Yeah," said the burly guard. "He's a health agent, too. About five minutes ago."

"He's not a health agent," Monty hissed. "Don't call the forcers; I've got this under control. My partner is on the way—he's an Enisku named Beak. Tell him I went up, and to come on after me." And with that, Monty bolted into the apartment building toward the elevator.

The lift deposited him on the open roof of the mint green structure. The wind up here was bitterly cold, the whipping snow stinging Monty's face as if the crystals were tiny shards of volcanic glass.

It took only a moment to see that the lock on the front door to Helga Greenberg's parasitic house was melted through. Monty remembered the gun he had seen in Vern's hand for a moment before the screen went blank. It looked like an old-fashioned toy locomotive engine, a heavy black thing covered in details and tiny jewels of light. A real heavy-duty zapper…thanks to the Teeb Family's resources. Had an alarm gone off when Vern found his way inside?

He drew his semi-auto, poised to one side of the door and pushed it open with his shoe. His heart was hammering as he swung into the building; a foyer. Jade and peach tiles covering walls, ceiling and floor, huge potted plants, a large oil painting of the park below. Monty didn't recall it from last time, but remembered the oil portrait he'd seen of Mrs. Greenberg, painted by her late husband—a patron of the arts.

He stole into a corridor, wide and plant-lined. Softly spotlighted antiques on display, pools of glinting fish. Sculptures, and some ancient bas-reliefs also spotlighted on the walls. One, positioned above the door at the end of the hall, portraying some tentacled sphinx-like monster, caught Monty's eye and gave him an odd chill.

Patron of the arts. Patron of...

Jesus, Monty thought. Could that be it?

He entered a side doorway. He couldn't exactly remember which way they'd taken before, but who was to say she would be in the same room, if she were in the building at all?

This was a sitting room, in violet and darker purple tiles, dominated by a huge purple stone fireplace with rounded edges and a stripe of chrome trim. The round-edged purple velour furniture also had silvery trim. Quite a room. A pterodactyl-like creature with an oil-slick iridescence to its skin and wing membranes was mounted above the fireplace. Inside the base of the clear plastic coffee table was a large, pale blue arachnid or crustacean moving slowly across a bed of violet crystals.

Monty cut across the room to another door, nudged it gingerly open.

A bright kitchen, yellow and white tiles. Monty slid inside.

A few steps in and he saw the blood pooling thick on the floor. A few more steps and there were legs. Woman's legs...

He swung around a counter, aiming his gun down at the body.

It was the voluptuous, coppery-haired maid who had admitted them that time, the one Vern had been so enamored of. Linda, Monty recollected. Well, Linda was as sexy as ever from the neck down: black uniform, black stockings and heels, cleavage looking as powdery soft as a baby bottom. And a face like a huge ragged mouth framed in frizzy red hair soaked in blood. Vern. Not so enamored now.

She had a small pistol in her hand, Monty was a little relieved to note. Hopefully it had been self-defense.

Monty stepped over her to a swinging door, cracked it open a sliver.

A dining room. Monty stole into it, his eyes snapping furtively from here to there to there with a bird's darting paranoia. The long table and the wood of the chairs was a pale polished green, like a fungus varnished over. A realistic oil painting of three women making love, at the end of the room. Their long braided hair was knotted around each other's ankles and wrists. Patron of the arts. A fine, realistic painter, the late Mr. Greenberg.

A long, very narrow hallway was beyond this; murky, low-ceilinged, like a tunnel. Black glossy tiles. A few potted plants with vivid red fern leaves.

Monty floated through an arched doorway. Steps. He took them upwards. Stairwell and stairs were glossy obsidian black, dimly lit.

There was another narrow hall. A closed door near to hand. Monty turned the knob.

It was a bedroom. But an odd one. The decor was black, with furniture made of strange black metal pieces fused weirdly together. On a table against a wall was a red crystal statue of that monster from the bas-relief.

Monty knew what kind of furniture design this was, and recognized the idol at last. One of the mysterious gods of the Bedbugs. This was a guest room suited to their tastes and needs.

The Bedbugs, or at least a renegade band of them—most likely the gang called the Dimensionals—had helped Loveland construct his teleporter. He had become cozier with the beings than Monty had guessed.

The next bedroom along the hall seemed to have been Linda's. Yes, Monty determined, finding a photograph of a red-haired child with two adults, no doubt her parents. Monty continued down to the end of the hall.

More stairs. He ascended stealthily, pistol's nose tilted up as if to warily sniff.

Another claustrophobic hallway. Monty moved into the first room.

Had to be the master bedroom. Helga's mesmerizing smell was here. A vast bed, canopied, the canopy and bedcovers a heavy black velour. The furnishings were black, the fireplace was black marble with red swirling cloud patterns. The wall tiles were glossy red, like the tiles in Red Station but without the trapped faces.

A soft clicking sound; Monty whirled.

The Bedbug lunged through the doorway.

One man was an Earth human, the other a Choom, both nattily attired. The Choom gave a rambling suave grin. "Hello…could you please buzz Helga Greenberg and let her know we're here to repair her climate control? She's expecting us."

"Ahh," said the woman guard, looking toward her partner, "that could be a problem."

"She's busy today—come back tomorrow," said the burly guard.

The Choom reversed his grin. "She's expecting us, sir…could you please call her? She'd be extremely disappointed if we couldn't come."

"There's been an emergency; she's not available. I can't let you go up, sir, so you'll kindly have to leave."

"Can't you just *call* her, for God's sake?" said the human.

"No—sorry."

"Come on, Chaz," said the Choom, "my phone's in the car. We'll call her ourselves and tell her to have these morons let us up."

"Who are you calling a moron, ass-lick?" snarled the male guard.

"Bite me, pudge."

Chaz took the Choom by the elbow. "Easy, Pulf…let's go to the car."

"Yeah—get the hell out of here before I call the force on you."

"What'sa matter, pudge, can't deal with us yourself?" sneered Pulf.

The guard came out from behind his counter, hand on his holstered gun. "*Out!*" he boomed. "*Now!*"

"What's going on?" asked a newcomer, stepping into the guard shack, snow blowing in with him. He was a black-beaked, tall and thin Enisku with a purple ski hat on.

"Nothing," said the guard. "Go on in, man, your partner's waiting for you up there."

"Partner?" said Chaz. "Is there some kind of problem in Helga Greenberg's apartment?"

"You might say that," Beak said. "Who are you?"

"Climate control repairmen. We can come back."

Beak took in the men's sporty dress. "Where are your tools?"

"In the trunk. If there's a problem we'll give her a call tomorrow." Chaz reached for the door.

Beak didn't like it. He moved his hand to his gun. "Hold it a minute…"

Pulf's gun slipped out first. A blue ray bolt tore through the empty top of Beak's hat, pulling it off his head.

Beak fumbled his gun. Dropped it. There was another shot.

The Choom crumpled, a sleep dart in his temple. The burly guard turned his gun on Chaz, the human.

Chaz held up empty hands. He was a technician, not a soldier. "Don't shoot!"

Beak scooped up his pistol and slammed Chaz backwards into a wall. The human blurted, "Who are you, fucker?"

"Who the fuck are *you*?" Beak kneed him in the crotch.

"*Ah!* Shit! Don't!" the man sobbed.

Beak pressed his gun muzzle hard into the ear of his doubled-over prisoner. "I don't have time for games, slime! Talk!"

"Teeb," the man whimpered. Definitely not a soldier.

"What are you here for?"

"To help Helga…Helga Greenberg."

"Do what?"

"Clone somebody."

"Clone *who*?"

"I don't *know*!"

"Okay, cry-baby." Beak handcuffed the man's wrists behind his back. He addressed the security guards. "Cuff sleeping beauty and stash him someplace. Don't call the police yet."

"I know, I know," the burly guard grumbled, holstering his dart gun.

Though only as tall as a child, the Bedbug drove Monty back into the bedroom, onto the bed. It clambered on top of him.

There were six whip-like tentacles. Two had his right wrist and his gun firmly coiled. One had encircled his left wrist. Another slipped around his throat and two went into his mouth.

Monty gagged. He bit down hard and pushed his feet off the floor, doing a backwards shoulder-roll off the bed.

They fell to the floor on the opposite side of the bed, Monty on top now. Whipping his head from side to side, he kept the tentacles out of his mouth but they slashed his face and the one around his neck tightened.

Black ameba-like things swam on his eyeballs. Multiplying.

Monty pressed his knee down hard on the being's underside, and it was chattering wildly now, but it was so armored he knew it was crying out in fury rather than pain. If only he could angle his gun a little bit, or switch it to his left hand suddenly, but as if anticipating this strategy the extra-dimensional coiled a second tentacle around his left wrist.

The black amebas were fusing together. No; snow. That's what it was. Black snow. Deepening…burying him. Suffocating…

Monty saw metallic gold slippers through the snow.

The Bedbug's chittering reached a higher pitch just before there was a flash and a violet-blue ray beam struck it in the head. Viscous green blood bubbled free. The tendrils released Monty and he rolled onto his side, almost losing consciousness.

He heard chattering beside him; madly thrashing tentacles slapped him and he squinted, covered his face with one arm. Around the shielding arm he saw another lightning flash. No more chattering or thrashing tentacles. Slowly Monty lowered his arm.

Vern Woodmere loomed over him, his bulky black pistol loosely pointed down at him.

"See, man? If I wasn't here that fuck would've killed you. Now are we together on this or what?"

"All right," Monty rasped, rubbing his throat. He was shaking.

Vern offered a hand, hoisted Monty to his feet.

The insect-like being was cracked open as if stomped by a giant foot, oozing green sap. Vern kicked at a tentacle. "Good thing it didn't have a weapon. So were you really gonna cuff me or what, boy?"

"I don't know. Come on—she may have heard us and be trying to escape."

They entered the hallway together. "I haven't seen her yet but I wasted that redhead bitch."

"I noticed."

"She had a blaster, man. So where's Beak?"

"Still on his way, I guess." Monty felt steadier now, though still shaken up. "Thanks," he told Vern as they moved down the hall.

"Forget it, partner."

They came to another room, looked in, and Vern saw a blur duck behind a billiards table. "Hey!" He leapt into the room in a wide stance and opened fire with his jumped-up blaster.

Beams ripped through the billiards table with its paisley-patterned baize, and a Bedbug popped up into view with a green spatter. "Die, you fuck!" Vern snarled, eyes blazing as if it were they shooting the ray beams. Bolt after bolt drove the Bedbug backwards into a massive fireplace. It almost succeeded in scrambling up the flue despite its great blasted wounds, but it dropped and did a mad dance in the fireplace's maw as Vern's short ray lances hammered it to pieces. At last it was still, a shattered black egg in a puddle of green yolk.

"Come on," Vern snapped, setting off down the hall again.

"Take it easy," Monty urged, skipping to catch up with him. "We want her alive!"

"They didn't want us alive, did they? Opal? Beak's wife? You and me?"

"I mean it, Vern."

"Agency boy, is that what you are, Black? After all you've been through? You Nedland's little doggie all of a sudden?" They had come to a door at the end of the hall. Vern aimed his gun at the knob without even trying it first to see if it were unlocked.

Violet flash. There was a blasted hole in the door, and the impact sent it swinging open.

The Stem was there, and it lifted its tubular black weapon and discharged it into Vern's face from only three steps away.

Vern spun, bounced off the wall, screaming, both hands up to his face. Black crystal spears burst between his fingers. A large one plunged out of his mouth, stretching it until the corners tore back to the ears, out of which more were stabbing. A huge spear thrust up through the top of Vern's skull as he slid down the wall and his spasming hands fell away. A black crystal chunk now instead of a head; and that toppled away from the shoulders, rolling a little bit. No blood came from the headless body.

This all in seconds, and Monty didn't watch. As soon as Vern fell out of his way he opened up with his pistol, shot after shot. He wasn't really shocked. It was as if he'd expected it to happen.

A solid bullet caromed off the Stem's gun, perhaps the easiest target to hit. The black tube flipped away through the air. Emitting an ear-skewering whistle, the red stick-creature surged forward at him.

It had on a belt-like thing from which it had pulled its weapon; Monty ducked under its swinging arms (he heard them cleave the air with a *whump*) and tucked a full magazine of plasma bullets there. Then he somersaulted in a tight ball between its tripod legs.

The Stem whirled to face him. Monty came up in a crouch.

He fired. At his plasma clip.

An explosion of plasma. Monty dove into a somersault again, scrambled on hands and knees across the room. A safe distance away, he looked back over his shoulder.

The stick-creature had split in half through the middle. The three legs kicked in mindless nerve spasms. The upper half dragged itself across the floor a few feet toward him, whistling. Monty jumped to his feet and backed against the wall.

It stopped. Still sizzling, melting. The hook jerking up at his heart loosened and gave him some slack. Glancing around the room, he slapped a fresh clip of solid bullets into the semi-auto, then went back into the hallway.

Vern. "My God," he breathed, shaking again. "My God…"

He tore his eyes away from the crystal chunk that had been his friend's head moments before. His eyes lighted on the dropped blaster. He knelt and picked it up in his left hand.

Monty slowly turned back into the room he had killed the Stem in…

It was an art studio.

It had more windows than any of the other rooms he'd seen, though two were fully obscured by green vines. Black snow falling out there. There were realistic oils hanging on the walls.

One was of Ferule Cangue. The dwarf was unmistakable.

The paint stains on the palettes were dry, there was no work in progress on the easel. But this room had been used long after the death of the artistic Mr. Greenberg by the hideous Garland Syndrome.

A door beyond. Monty went to it. He leveled Vern's blaster at the lock.

Flash. The door flew open. Monty stepped through.

Helga Greenberg extended her gun in both hands and fired.

Monty crouched and fired the blaster. His skull pin's eyes blinked redly.

The bolt burned into the wall near a clear plastic globe. There was a greenish liquid burbling inside. The baby in the bubble looked like an embryo in a bottle of formaldehyde, one of those freak babies one might see in a carnival. Only it was a very normal, attractive-looking baby. And although its eyes were shut, it was alive.

"Drop your gun or I'll kill him!" Monty yelled.

Helga Greenberg straightened up slowly, hesitated.

"*Drop it!*"

"Don't! Don't!" She tossed the pistol onto a divan. Holding up empty palms, she slowly came out from behind the single white marble pillar in the center of the circular, white-tiled room. "Don't shoot him."

Monty straightened up also, but didn't lower his gun from aiming at the blissfully floating baby. Monty smirked, his face flushed red.

"I'm feeling a little better than the last time I saw you, Helga. That was over a year ago—remember? I had M-670 then. Remember?"

"I remember."

"You were sympathetic about the death of my partner. You also hinted that you'd like to get together with me some time…if I ever recovered…remember? You wanted me to hold on so I could. Well, I did. So I guess this is it. Our date."

Her beauty was nearly as hypnotic as then. The wide-spaced, eerily too-pale blue eyes, sultry and mysterious under fleshy, somewhat Asian folds. Button nose and full sullen lips. She wore a black dress (in keeping with the unusual holiday, perhaps), cut low to a shallow chest and baring her shoulders, her waist-length tangle of dark blond hair parted on the side to half-cover one side of her face. *Nearly* as hypnotic. Most of her effect, her natural beauty aside, hinged on her confident composure, and that was faltering though she clung to it bravely. She looked more like a child, despite her sexier attire, than the last time he'd seen her.

And though he acknowledged her beauty, he didn't ache to fuck her this time. He wasn't that pathetic. Besides, he was strangely more afraid of her than he had been facing the Stem back there.

"Sit down in that chair. Keep your hands on the rests."

She complied, lowered herself into a white round-edged chair with chrome trim. She crossed one bare leg demurely, but she was barefoot, her feet delicate and cute. Monty glanced away, around the room, his pink semi-automatic pointing toward her and the blaster at the baby in the softly gurgling fish bowl.

It was a lab. Adjacent to the art studio. *Part* of the art studio, actually—wasn't it? There were shelves filled with old machine components, labeled boxes. Semi-circular work counters along the walls, covered with machines…some stacked atop each other, some hooked up to computer monitors. A low humming. Constellations of lights, some flashing rhythmically. Near the baby's globe there was a concentration of equipment, tubes running in and out of the green liquid, lazily snaking wires affixed to the baby like multiple umbilical cords.

"Your husband, Mrs. Greenberg?" Monty jerked his gun at the globe.

"You'd better just arrest me, Agent Black, and let me call my lawyer. I won't talk to you." She was trying to sound composed but her voice trembled under the surface, and he saw how her fingers clenched the armrests.

"You'll talk or I'll put a ray bolt through your husband's head."

"He isn't my husband."

"Don't *fuck* with me!" Monty bellowed, and let off a bolt from his gun. It missed the container by a foot; blackened white tiles clattered to the floor and shattered.

"No, don't!" Helga cried out, almost rising. Nails digging.

"I'll do it."

"You can't touch anything until I call my lawyer!"

"Fuck you, lady—I'm a health agent. I'll tear this fucking room apart and get a medal for it. I want you to tell me your story, and if you do I'll leave things intact until you call your lawyer. Fuck with me and I'll give your husband a well-deserved abortion."

Helga turned her head in profile, pouting like a model. Monty saw the water filming her eye glisten, but still she held her dignity. Haughty as a teenage princess.

"He is my husband," she muttered.

"He cloned a double and gave it Garland Syndrome to fake his death, just like he cloned himself and gave his double M-670 to fake his death again. So he could come back later as a new person."

"Yes," she sneered.

"He arranged the chem spill at Greenberg so you could supposedly sell your plant to Cugok."

"Yes."

"Is Greenberg his real name, or does it go back beyond that?"

"Greenberg. Emmanuel Greenberg."

"Emmanuel. Manuel. Manuel Hung," Monty said to himself. "And you. Is your condition natural or did he do something to keep you this young?"

Helga smirked at him, gorgeously contemptuous. "No, but it's what initially attracted him to me."

"Cugok. Who is he really, and where?"

"An actor. He's gone now, far away. He was only an actor."

"*Who?*"

"Clem Zazone. He went to school with Manny at P.U.."

Manny, thought Monty with disgust. "Why the companies? Did he have a taste for money, too?"

"Doesn't everyone, Mr. Black? Manny likes his comforts. Money is power and power is intoxicating, yes…but it gave him the resources to fulfill his *vision*. He's an artist. The companies were mine, primarily—I inherited money."

"Him—an artist?" Monty barked a laugh, jittery with energy. He stole a glance at the baby with its fungoid greenish flesh. "A psychopath. A mass murderer, maybe. He's no fucking artist. Artists don't kill their audience…they entertain them."

"No—they manipulate them. The old Earth film director Alfred Hitchcock said actors are cattle. Manny says that's not so. It's the *audience* who are cattle."

"Yeah, see what I mean? He doesn't care about his audience, or want to move or inform them…he just wants them to know how supposedly better he is than they are. It's as much an ego and power trip as money obsession. As *rape* is. He just wanted to see how many people he could overpower and rape at once. He's just a self-fascinated sociopath who likes to see his face in the papers, like any serial killer."

"You're a limited man, Mr. Black," Helga said, pale eyes blazing, their liquid sheen gone. She looked scary again. Feline. "Manny is unlimited."

"An artist *cares*. He doesn't hate his audience…"

"You're naive. Manny is aware."

"An artist reflects the human condition."

Helga smiled frighteningly. "Manny does."

Monty fell silent a moment, chilled. His extended guns were getting heavy.

He went back to gathering information, filling the gaps. "He had himself cloned only up to his twenties and had his face changed from Greenberg to his Loveland incarnation."

"Naturally."

"Dwork died and couldn't complete the last clone. Now you need Teeb."

"Westy. He had become quite troublesome…"

"How is that?"

"He was supposed to have finished the cloning so that Manny would be here already just before *The Big Frown* opened…Manny's latest piece."

"I'm familiar with it."

"Manny would come back and open *The Big Frown* himself that very day. But Westy had become rather enamored of me. In fact, he wanted me for himself. He threatened not to revive Manny unless I agreed to leave Manny for him. I told him that was impossible. He wanted me, then, to at least go to bed with him. I wouldn't. I wouldn't do that—he was my husband's best friend."

"How honorable of you." Monty suddenly grew concerned. "His memory is there in the computer, isn't it? Dwork didn't hide it…"

"It's there. But I'm not mechanically inclined, Mr. Black. I needed Westy to finish the clone and restore its memory. He would have done it—I knew he couldn't bring himself to shut Manny down. He knew he was being irrational. He knew if he didn't give in soon I'd have him killed and find someone else…"

The door opened behind Monty.

He spun, the blaster aiming first. He saw a gun pointed at him already…

"Hey, easy!" Beak said.

"Christ. Learn to knock, huh?"

Beak glanced at Helga, tensed in her chair to flee. She lowered herself fully down again. "Hello, little girl…what's your name? Helga?"

"Go to hell, chicken-face."

"Sweet." Beak looked to Monty. "Seen Vern?"

"You didn't?"

"No…" Beak's expression became wary, full of dread.

"He's dead, pal," Monty told him. "The other Stem. I nailed it. I'm sorry, man."

Beak switched his bright rage-filled eyes to the forty-three-year-old twelve-year-old. "I should kill you now, you fucking piece of *shit*!"

"Easy, man—come on. We got her. It's over."

"And that…that's him?" Beak gestured at the baby.

"That's our man. Cute, huh?"

"Blast him, Monty."

"No!" snapped Helga.

"Shut up!"

"No, Beak."

"Why not? It's an illegal clone! We're health agents; we can shut this shit down!"

"Wait until Neptune Teeb's boys get here. Vern said two are on their way to complete the clone."

"They're here. One's drugged in the guard shack, and I locked the other one in the bathroom downstairs when I saw that dead girl in the kitchen."

"Good. Go get him up here."

"Why?"

"Go get him."

Beak shot a glare at Helga and departed.

"What are you going to do?" Helga hissed.

"Quiet."

"You promised you wouldn't hurt him!"

"So I did."

"Oh—I see. You won't hurt him, but the Teeb man will!"

"I keep my promises. I won't hurt him or let him be hurt."

They waited tensely for Beak to return. Soft gurgling sound. Helga watched the eyes on Monty's skull pin flash rhythmically, the grinning teeth gnash.

Beak reappeared, pushing the ashen-faced technician Chaz ahead of him. "Want me to uncuff him? He's a noodle…nothing to worry about."

"Go ahead." Monty moved closer to the baby in the bubble.

"What do you want me to do?" Chaz stuttered, rubbing his wrists. His testicles still ached and he was very, very frightened. There was also the anger of Neptune Teeb to consider, now that he had been caught and confessed his mission here.

"Take that clone's memory chip out of the computer and give it to me," Monty said.

"*No!*" Helga shrieked—a child's horrified scream—and dove from her chair onto the nearby divan.

Beak shoved the Teeb technician to the floor. "Don't!" he roared, leveling his pistol.

Half-sprawled on the divan, Helga lifted the handgun she had tossed there, pointing it at Monty…

Manny…floating behind him in the bubble. She couldn't shoot…

Rising to one knee, she shifted the gun to point at Beak.

"Don't!" Beak shouted again, crouching to fire.

The bullet from the pink semi-automatic, a solid chunk of metal, ripped into her long slender neck. Out the other side. Tile cracked. Helga flipped over the back of the divan…out of view…

Beak looked over at his partner. Chaz looked up from the floor.

Monty still held the semi-auto extended. His expression was blank.

Beak glanced back at the divan. He heard her bare heels drumming the floor and saw an arterial jet of blood squirt the tiled wall above the divan.

A pool of blood already began to emerge from under the divan, vivid against all the whiteness.

Beak went stealthily toward it, weapon ready. He pointed his gun down at what he saw—then lowered it. He knelt, came up with Helga Greenberg's pistol. Monty could still hear the thumping, but winding down…like a heart.

Then nothing. Beak still stood over her, maybe transfixed by her long, blood-soaked, dark blond hair. Maybe her eerie blue eyes stared open, gorgeous and terrifying. Maybe in death she looked like a child and nothing wiser, nothing more evil. Monty was glad he couldn't see her.

But he could still see her long bare legs flashing as his bullet tossed her over the back of the divan. He swivelled to stare at the baby suspended placidly in its aquarium.

In a quiet voice, he told Chaz what to do.

Monty watched his urine, a twinkling glassy rope, cascade into the handsome black toilet off Helga Greenberg's master bedroom. He still felt numb.

Opal. The rest. Over a year of his life. Over…

He watched his urine trickle away and stop.

He reached his hand into the pocket of his turquoise jacket.

The chip was tiny—less than a poker chip. As featureless as one, however. A blank white disc. Monty held it up in front of him.

"I wish I could have seen you face to face, my man," he said to the chip softly. He fantasized about going back with it…instructing Chaz to complete the clone, imbue it with the memory program. He would then face Emmanuel Greenberg as a man. And shoot him.

But even still, this was better, wasn't it? More…artistic.

"My statement," Monty said, but then changed his mind, remembering the critic Yancy Mays. "No. This is my *critique*, Toll…"

He dropped the memory disk into the toilet with his urine. All that Emmanuel Greenberg—Toll Loveland—was. His identity. His essence. Turning over and over in slow motion in the urine-yellowed water.

Montgomery Black flushed the toilet, zipped his fly, and washed his hands.

Captain Nedland came. The forcers came. Ambulances for the bodies. In his call, Beak had told Nedland about the fate of Vern Woodmere.

"*Fuck*," Nedland had hissed in genuine anger and sorrow into the vidphone.

Nedland clapped Beak on the arm when he saw him. "Damn good work, Beak… damn good work. Commendation for certain."

"Thanks, sir. But I just wanna go home to my kids."

"Fill out your reports tomorrow and you got two paid weeks. Where's Monty?"

"In the bedroom down that hall, there."

Nedland noticed the hole burned through Beak's recovered ski hat. "Christ. Buy a new hat on your vacation, will ya?" No longer—at least for the moment—his usual funereal self, Captain Nedland bounced as he strode down the corridor.

"Monty?" He peeked in. He saw Monty sitting on the edge of a vast canopied bed.

Monty looked up. "Captain."

"What the Christ?"

The health agent held a newborn baby in his arms and lap, cozily bundled into a thick white bath towel. It was squinting and sneering, a little disgruntled to be out of the womb, as babies tend to be, but was pink and healthy looking. Monty held a tiny hand between thumb and forefinger.

"Cute, huh, Captain? Innocent. Make somebody a nice adopted son, wouldn't you say?"

Nedland realized the truth. Fucking bizarre…

"Not you, I hope," he said.

"No," Monty said, smiling a little. "Good Christ, no. Not me."

TWENTY

One day they spent browsing around the Canberra Mall, and another at Quidd's Market and its surrounding stores, Christmas shopping, but Monty stayed in their apartment for the bulk of his two-week vacation. Much of his time was filled by the new vidgame channel he had subscribed to.

He would sit on the very end of the couch, leaning so far forward that only the barest necessary amount of his rear was still on the cushion, playing with an intensity that amused and amazed Mauve. At first. His favorite game was an extremely elaborate and difficult sword and sorcery quest, the many monsters so real and vicious that they often startled Mauve. Thank God it wasn't a hologram game with the things swarming throughout the apartment!

He would often swear out loud in frustration, and told Mauve his heart thumped heavily whenever he engaged in a challenging battle over a particularly important bit of treasure. In his enthusiasm (if she could call it that—were his exhausting struggles *fun*?) he tried to encourage her to play, but they got in a fight one time after she continued to bungle her way to an early death while he hovered at her shoulder coaching her tensely, sometimes snapping at her bad choice of strategy.

The longest single period of play she witnessed was ten hours straight. Usually it was only half that…but even that was something. When he wasn't playing he was taking two- or three-hour hot bubble baths with a thick paperback collection of short horror stories.

At last, toward the end of the vacation, he had come up against the vidgame's primary villain. Mauve noticed how Monty shut the game off when she neared, so she couldn't see what it looked like; he said he wanted her to be surprised, should she decide to keep trying the game.

Her curiosity about the villain's appearance overcame her. While Monty slept one morning (having stayed up all night, well past dawn) she accessed the game and punched up his recorded information, cut into the latest level he had achieved. In order to see what was going on from that point, all she knew how to do was go into the game itself, and did so with Monty's character—who looked exactly like him, reproduced from a holographic picture fed into it, though dressed in chain mail and a white smock with a Crusader's red cross on it.

She was killed in under half a minute, though she fought furiously. Her effort was admirable, considering her shock. The leader of the forces of mythical evil looked exactly like Toll Loveland. Monty had fed a photo of him to the computer. To see Loveland moving, talking (laughing sadistically), and killing the Monty character (until he could return in the next round) was profoundly unsettling. In fact, she was left scared by the experience, shut down the game.

While brooding over a cup of tea, she seriously considered erasing the villain. Substituting another nemesis, something from a horror movie or from the game files, in Loveland's place. But she didn't dare, knowing Monty's love of the game, or at least its hold on him…picturing his intense face in her mind.

Should she even bring it up at all?

She decided against it. For now. He needed a little more time. He still had to come down all the way. Work it out of his system. And, she realized, he needed to battle and kill Toll Loveland face to face at last…if only in the arena of his mind.

The day after Monty plunged his magic sword through Loveland's throat (blood burst from his mouth like vomit, his eyes bulging in very satisfying terror and pain), he waited until Mauve went out to do a little grocery shopping, and then—after pacing the apartment for half an hour—at last went to the vidphone…

Her mother was home, thank God. She looked more surprised than hateful to see him again. She even spoke with him for a few moments.

"You killed him, huh?" she said. She'd seen it on VT.

"Yeah, I guess I did." He told her what he wanted. She nodded and punched the message up for him, once again, from the beginning…

"Monty. There's a few things…I want to tell you…

"Please listen to me…"

He lowered his eyes. Didn't want to catch a glimpse of her again when she leaned forward out of the shadows. This time he let the recording play to its very end…

"I…it's wrong for me to be mad at you…I know. I'm scared.

"I know you didn't do this to me on purpose. I know it isn't your fault. I'm mad at you because…I'm so scared…

"I was looking for him for a while. I thought maybe…I don't know…

"I traced him back to his various identities, but I never got far with any of them. But I found out something weird…that happened when he was…when he was…at school. Paxton Polytech. When he was Manuel Hung. I went down there and spoke to people…they told me a funny story. During his stay at school some animals disappeared from the labs. They pinned it on him, but I guess…charges were never brought. He paid for their replacement…

"I never could trace his identity back to his childhood. HAP and the police can't trace him. Who knows where he came from. I'm too...I can't do anything any more. I'm dying.

"I got it real good, huh?

"If you find him before it gets you too, kill him for me. But try to hang on. A cure is just around the corner—right?

"I've got to go...

"My poor mother...

"Best of luck to you, Monty. God bless you. It wouldn't hurt you to look for just a little faith...even if it's just a painkiller...

"I'm sorry—I was selfish not to see you in person while I still could. This is the best I could do. I had to be mad at somebody. Please understand...I wanted to say goodbye but this is the best I could do.

"Monty...

"I guess I really did love you, after all. Too bad I didn't give it a chance...huh? I'm sorry. I'm sorry...

"Okay. That's enough. That's all I can say.

"Goodbye, partner. I miss you...

"And I forgive you. Okay? I forgive you..."

Monty put his head down on the table edge and cried—and laughed a little—for a good long time.

And when Mauve came home he asked her to go outside with him for a walk in the brisk city streets, where the last vestiges of Eric Hughes' black snow were finally fading away.

About the Author

Jeffrey Thomas has set a series of books in the milieu of *Health Agent*, such as the novels *Deadstock, Blue War, Monstrocity* and *Everybody Scream!* (the latter from Raw Dog Screaming Press), and the collections *Punktown, Punktown: Shades of Grey* and *Punktown: Third Eye*. Those books of his not set within the Punktown universe include *Letters From Hades, Voices From Hades, Ugly Heaven Beautiful Hell, Boneland, Thirteen Specimens* and *Doomsdays*. Thomas lives with his wife Hong in Massachusetts.

Other Novels from Raw Dog Screaming Press

Blankety Blank, D. Harlan Wilson
hc 978-1-933293-50-9, $14.95, 188p
tpb 978-1-933293-57-8, $29.95, 188p

Rutger Van Trout has problems but the worst is not that his son might be a werewolf. It's not his obsession with transforming his house into a three-ring barnyard or his wife's haunted skeleton. The complication has invaded his community in the form of a new breed of serial killer, who stalks from house to house leaving a bloodbath that would make Jack the Ripper himself blush.

Isabel Burning, Donna Lynch
hc 978-1-933293-49-3, $29.95, 236p
tpb 978-1-933293-56-1, $15.95, 236p

Isabel's new job as housekeeper at Grace mansion allows her to observe the habits of the enigmatic Dr. Edward Grace. Captivated by his tales of travel to Africa, she is inexorably drawn into a tumultuous relationship which eventually reveals the Grace family's dark heritage and lays bare every secret, even the ones she keeps from herself.

Sin Conductor, John Edward Lawson

tpb 978-1-933293-65-3

Willis Lowery is just your average occupational hazards estimator until one day, while inspecting a factory, he happens across a chemical burn victim. Her name is Dusyanna, and the passion she ignites in him threatens to melt away every fiber of his morals. As he soon learns, there is no escape from her circle of degenerates, so he vows to become the devil to beat the devil.

Jesus Coyote Harold Jaffe
hc 978-1-933293-55-4, $24.95, 148p
tpb 978-1-933293-63-9, $13.95, 148p

This docufictional novel based on the Manson murders proves that, like his coyote totem, the myths around Manson hold irrevocable power. In one swooping panoramic arc, with the bloody killings at its center, Jaffe captures the perspectives of Manson, his devotees, the prosecutors, and the victims while firing a shot against the hypocrisy of institutionalized morality.